A LIAM H

TRACK SHIFT

NEW YORK TIMES #1 BESTSELLER TONY LEE WRITING AS

JACK GATLAND

Hooded Man Media

Published by Hooded Man Media.

Cover design by L1graphics

First Edition: November 2025

PRAISE FOR JACK GATLAND

'This is one of those books that will keep you up past your bedtime, as each chapter lures you into reading just one more.'

'This book was excellent! A great plot which kept you guessing until the end.'

'Couldn't put it down, fast paced with twists and turns.'

'The story was captivating, good plot, twists you never saw and really likeable characters. Can't wait for the next one!'

'I got sucked into this book from the very first page, thoroughly enjoyed it, can't wait for the next one.'

'Totally addictive. Thoroughly recommend.'

'Moves at a fast pace and carries you along with it.'

'Just couldn't put this book down, from the first page to the last one it kept you wondering what would happen next.'

LIQUIDATE THE PROFITS

FOLDED HANDS

Declan Walsh. Ellie Reckless. Tom Marlowe. Liam Harper. Carlyle & Silver. Danny Charming. Ryder Waites. Damian Lucas.

Discover the worlds of Jack Gatland and Tony Lee in their VIP Reader's Club!! And gain two EXCLUSIVE PREQUELS, completely free to anyone who joins!

Join at http://bit.ly/jackgatlandVIP

Also by Jack Gatland

DI DECLAN WALSH BOOKS

LETTER FROM THE DEAD

MURDER OF ANGELS

HUNTER HUNTED

WHISPER FOR THE REAPER

TO HUNT A MAGPIE

A RITUAL FOR THE DYING

KILLING THE MUSIC

A DINNER TO DIE FOR

BEHIND THE WIRE

HEAVY IS THE CROWN

STALKING THE RIPPER

A QUIVER OF SORROWS

MURDER BY MISTLETOE

BENEATH THE BODIES

KILL YOUR DARLINGS

KISSING A KILLER

PRETEND TO BE DEAD

HARVEST FOR THE REAPER

CROOKED WAS HIS CANE

A POCKET FULL OF POSIES

CHEATING MY DESTINY

STAND AND DELIVER

WE PLAY WITH DEATH

HIS DEAD MAN'S HAND

DIGGING YOUR GRAVE

TOM MARLOWE BOOKS

SLEEPING SOLDIERS

TARGET LOCKED

COVERT ACTION

COUNTER ATTACK

STEALTH STRIKE

BROAD SWORD

ROGUE SIGNAL

SNIPER ALLEY

SHADOW THREAT

SENTRY POINT

BURNING LEDGERS

ELLIE RECKLESS BOOKS

PAINT THE DEAD

STEAL THE GOLD

HUNT THE PREY

FIND THE LADY

BURN THE DEBT

TAKE THE KING

LIAM HARPER BOOKS

FINAL STRIKE

BLOOD RIDGE

TRACK SHIFT

CROSS ROADS

CARLYLE & SILVER BOOKS

SILVER AND THE SUNDAY CYPHER

SILVER AND THE CHRISTMAS CAPER

DAMIAN LUCAS BOOKS

THE LIONHEART CURSE

THE EXCALIBUR QUEST

STANDALONE BOOKS

THE BOARDROOM

As Tony Lee

STANDALONE

TWELVE TASKS

THE PLAYING CARD WAR

KNAVE OF SPADES

QUEEN OF BLADES

CHARMING

LAST PRINCE STANDING

HAPPILY NEVER AFTER

For Mum, who inspired me to write.

For Tracy, who inspires me to write.

CONTENTS

1

SCENIC ROUTE

THE COFFEE SHOP IN GALENA LOOKED LIKE SOMEONE HAD GIVEN a Victorian mansion a hipster makeover – exposed brick walls with pieces of deliberately missed plaster, Edison bulb chandeliers, and enough reclaimed wood to build a bloody ark. Harper sat near the window, sketching the old riverboat moored at the dock while his flat white turned lukewarm. The afternoon sun made the place uncomfortably warm, but at least it meant fewer customers to notice him.

Tourism suited him well enough. Three weeks of being nobody special, just another traveller with a camera and questionable fashion sense. He'd perfected the art as he travelled – consulting maps with mild confusion, photographing historical plaques like they contained the secrets of the universe, sketching with the unhurried pace of someone whose biggest decision was where to eat lunch.

Three weeks since Blüdridge. Since Mike's funeral and everything that followed.

The Bonneville had carried him through Wisconsin cheese country and Iowa corn fields, never staying anywhere long enough to become memorable. Small towns with names like *Prairie Dog Creek* and *Sunset Hope*, places where the most exciting thing to happen all year was probably the high school football team making it to regionals.

It had worked brilliantly.

Until this afternoon.

The barista – *Courtney*, according to her name tag – approached for the fourth time in an hour. She had elaborate sleeve tattoos and the earnest enthusiasm of someone who genuinely believed coffee was a spiritual experience.

'You sure I can't get you a new one?' she asked, nodding at Harper's barely touched flat white.

'I'm good, thanks.' Harper added a detail to the riverboat's paddle wheel. 'Excellent oat milk, by the way.'

'We source it locally. The farm's only about ten miles from here.' Courtney lingered, adjusting pottery that didn't need adjusting. The afternoon lull meant Harper was one of only four customers – an elderly couple sharing what looked like the world's most expensive slice of cake, and a woman with a laptop who'd apparently decided to write her memoirs in their establishment.

'You're an artist?' Courtney asked, looking down at the paper, because apparently baristas were required by law to make conversation.

'Hobby,' Harper replied without looking up. 'I collect old things. History.'

'That's amazing. You should totally check out the Grant house if you haven't. It's like, pure Victorian excess. Perfect for sketching.'

Harper made an appropriately interested noise while his attention shifted to the street outside. A dark-blue Mercedes had cruised past the coffee shop three times in the last hour –

now it was parked across the street, engine running, with two shapes visible through the windscreen.

Professional surveillance was supposed to be invisible. These clowns might as well have hung a sign reading *"Definitely not watching anyone. Go on with your day."*

'Where are you headed next?' Courtney asked, apparently settling in for a proper chat.

Harper paused his sketching. The Mercedes' passenger door opened, and a tall man stepped out. Jeans, polo shirt, light jacket – an aggressively casual outfit that screamed *"I'm definitely not working right now, just hanging about in my off-duty clothes."*

'Haven't decided yet,' Harper said, closing his sketchbook. 'Depends on the weather.'

Courtney followed his gaze to the street, where Tall and Casual was checking traffic that didn't exist before crossing. His movements had the deliberate quality of someone following a script.

'Friend of yours?' she asked.

'Doubt it.' Harper reached for his wallet. The driver had stayed put, hands visible on the steering wheel. It felt unnervingly like the standard formations he'd used in the UK Special Forces – one mobile, one ready for extraction. They'd done this before, just not very well.

'Seven-fifty for the flat white and biscotti,' Courtney said. Harper hadn't ordered biscotti, but he appreciated her trying to justify his table-hogging.

Harper left a twenty.

'Cheers.'

The door chimed – an actual brass bell, because of course it was – as Tall and Casual entered. He paused just inside, letting his eyes adjust while scanning the room.

When his gaze found Harper, there was no surprise, no searching.

He'd found exactly who he was looking for.

Harper stayed seated. *Let them make the first move,* his father had always said. *Control comes from patience, not aggression.*

Of course, Harper had been ten when he'd been taught that, in one of the sporadic appearances his father made before ghosting him forever. Why his father had thought such a lesson was relevant for a child was never explained.

'Liam Harper,' Tall and Casual said, claiming the chair across from him.

Statement, not question.

'Depends who's asking,' Harper replied.

Tall and Casual produced a phone with the careful movements of someone trying not to seem threatening, turning it on. The screen showed a photo of Harper that was recent enough to include his current scruff of beard. Clear image, proper surveillance kit. These weren't amateurs, just obvious ones.

'Mason Carrick sends his regards,' the man said. 'He'd also like a word.'

Mason bloody Carrick. Harper's father's business partner, co-founder of *Aegis Security,* which these morons were likely part of, and the man Harper blamed for getting the old bastard killed in Myanmar. They'd met a few times when Harper was a child, and only more recently in a mayor's mansion in Nevada – a tense encounter where Carrick had tried to recruit him, offering money and threats in equal measure. Harper had walked away from that meeting knowing exactly what kind of man Carrick was.

Charming, dangerous, and utterly without conscience.

Harper studied the photo without touching the phone. They'd been tracking him since Blüdridge, probably. Maybe caught his trail a week after he'd left that charming town behind. Still didn't explain how they'd found him in the arse-end of Illinois, as he thought he'd lost them a few days ago.

Looks like Aegis were better than he gave credit for.

'Uncle Mason,' Harper said, using Carrick's familial nickname deliberately. 'What's he want to chat about?'

He noticed a slight tightening around the eyes. This one knew the history between Harper and his father's business partner.

Briefed properly, then. Not just hired muscle.

'That's between you and him,' Tall and Casual replied. 'He's flexible on location. Neutral ground.'

'How thoughtful.' Harper could see Courtney hovering near the coffee machine, trying not to stare. The elderly couple had stopped pretending to eat their cake. Even Laptop Woman had paused her typing. Small-town excitement was rare enough to draw attention.

'And if I'm not in a chatty mood?' Harper asked.

'He hopes you'll reconsider.'

Polite threats. Harper almost admired the restraint. Street muscle would have started with intimidation. This felt like negotiation, which made it infinitely more dangerous.

'Tell Mason I'm touched,' Harper said, standing slowly. 'But I'll pass.'

Tall and Casual's posture shifted – weight forward, hands repositioning. *Preparation.*

'He was quite insistent, Mister Harper.'

'I'm sure he was.' Harper slipped his sketchbook into his jacket. 'Give him my best.'

He walked to the counter where Courtney was rearranging coffee beans with the concentration of someone performing surgery.

'Thanks for everything,' he said with a smile. 'Sorry about the newer clientele.'

'Thanks!' Her smile was genuine, but her eyes kept flicking to the man at Harper's table. 'Come back anytime. We're open till eight.'

Harper headed for the exit, aware of multiple stares following him. The bell chimed again as he stepped outside into air that felt like breathing soup.

Instead of going to the street, Harper turned left towards the alley behind the shops. If these pricks wanted privacy for their conversation, he'd accommodate them. *Better to choose the battlefield than let them pick it.*

The alley was narrow, lined with industrial bins and service doors that probably hadn't opened since winter. Harper walked to where he'd stashed the Bonneville earlier, tucked between a skip and a loading bay where passing traffic wouldn't spot it. He'd learned to be careful about parking – the bike was distinctive enough to make tracking easier.

He unlocked his helmet but left it on the seat – no point rushing into protective gear when you were about to have a friendly chat.

The wait wasn't long.

Tall and Casual followed him from the entrance and down the alley, moving like he had all the time in the world. His partner – Broad Shoulders from the Mercedes – emerged from the opposite end, completing their little pincer movement.

'Last chance, Harper,' Tall and Casual called out. 'Mister Carrick really does want that conversation.'

'And I really don't want to have it,' Harper replied, positioning himself to keep both men in sight. 'Nothing personal. Just not feeling sociable.'

Broad Shoulders moved first.

Big mistake.

He came charging in like a prop forward, all momentum and bad intentions. Harper could see the bulge under his jacket shift as he reached for whatever party favour he'd brought to the discussion. Harper stepped inside the man's reach, caught his wrist before the weapon cleared its holster. The bloke was strong – military build, and what looked like proper training – but Harper had timing on his side. He twisted the wrist until joints popped, then drove his knee up into the man's breadbasket.

The impact folded him like a deck chair. Harper grabbed the back of his head and introduced his face to the brick wall – the sound was wet and final. Broad Shoulders dropped like he'd been unplugged.

Tall and Casual, deciding a simple hand-to-hand wasn't going to cut this, had produced a telescoping baton that snicked open like an angry snake. He approached more carefully than his friend, holding the weapon properly.

'That was unnecessary,' he said, circling left.

'Your mate reaching for his pistol was unnecessary,' Harper replied, tracking the baton's tip. 'I just responded appropriately.'

The man feinted high then swept low, trying for Harper's knee. It was quick, textbook, the sort of move that would put most people on the ground clutching their patellas.

Harper wasn't most people.

He stepped back from the sweep, caught the extended wrist on the follow-through, and used the man's own grip against him. The leverage was beautiful – physics and anatomy combining to make his arm bend in ways God never intended.

Something snapped in his elbow with a sound like kindling breaking, and the baton hit the asphalt as Tall and Casual let out a shriek that probably scared every pigeon in a three-block radius.

Harper didn't let go of the wrist. Instead, he spun the man around and drove his elbow into the base of his skull.

Tall and Casual joined his partner on the ground, conscious but not going anywhere quickly as Harper checked them both for additional hardware. Broad Shoulders had been going for a Glock 19, while Tall and Casual carried nothing more dangerous than a wallet and breath mints.

'When you can speak again,' Harper said to neither man in particular, 'tell Mason I appreciate the invitation. But I prefer my social calls voluntary, and this felt a little... forced.'

He pulled on his helmet, fired up the Bonneville, and rode out of the alley without a backward glance. In his mirrors, he could see Tall and Casual trying to help his partner sit up, both moving like they'd been hit by a freight train.

HARPER MADE IT EXACTLY THREE BLOCKS BEFORE THE NEXT interruption.

The traffic light at Main and Bench caught him behind a delivery truck, boxed in by cars on both sides. That's when the second team made its appearance – two different men stepping out from behind parked vehicles with the synchronised timing of a bad action film.

Fresh operatives. These looked more switched-on than

their predecessors, moving like they'd actually read the manual on urban surveillance.

Harper didn't wait for introductions.

He gunned the Bonneville straight through the red light, threading between cross traffic while horns blared like air raid sirens. A pickup truck locked its brakes to avoid him, the driver leaning on his horn and contributing some colourful commentary about Harper's ancestry.

The two men reached the intersection just as Harper cleared it, one making a grab for his jacket that came up with nothing but air. In his mirrors, Harper watched them sprint back towards yet another blue car.

Bloody hell. How many teams had Carrick sent?

Harper took random turns through residential streets lined with white picket fences and the sort of lawns that probably required more maintenance than most people's relationships. American dream suburbia, where the most exciting thing to happen was probably the weekly bin collection.

After ten minutes of tactical touring, he found Highway 20 again. There didn't seem to be any pursuit visible, but that meant nothing. They'd found him once despite his precautions. They could find him again.

Harper settled the Bonneville into a steady cruise, farmland rolling past on both sides like a green carpet stretching to the horizon. *Four operatives minimum. Multiple teams, proper coordination, serious kit. Carrick wasn't playing games.*

Which meant Harper was definitely asking the right questions.

The timeline bothered him. He'd been careful about his route, avoiding motorways and major cities, paying cash for everything. But the Bonneville was memorable, and Harper had fallen into patterns without realising it. Tourist traps, historic sites, diners and coffee shops with overpriced pastries.

Amateur hour, really. His SRR instructors would have been ashamed.

The question was why now? What had changed to make Harper worth hunting across three states?

He wasn't sure, but he wondered whether the answer waited in Chicago. He'd found a cryptic entry from his father's journal that had been nagging at him for weeks now.

Carrick. South Yards. Track 17. Slate. Paid to keep it quiet.

His father's handwriting in his father's private notebook, the one Dominic Kane had left with explicit instructions not to involve authorities, not to trust official channels. A dead man's insurance policy, full of secrets that had gotten him killed in Myanmar, and a location, a debt owed, and surprisingly, his partner's name.

Harper knew Carrick wouldn't be meeting to explain this – by now he probably worked out Harper's movements, saw he was driving past various points of his father's life. He knew Harper had gained Dominic's personal items… he just didn't know what these were, and how they affected him.

A chat for a later time, then.

Harper had been drifting towards Chicago slowly, taking the scenic route, putting off whatever confrontation waited there. But Carrick's sudden interest suggested urgency. Whatever connected his father to the South Yards was worth mobilising teams of operatives to keep buried.

Time to stop being a tourist and start being a hunter.

The inherited property would be watched – his father's

apartment overlooking the lake, part of the estate Harper had been liquidating for charity. Walking into that building would be like volunteering for surgery without anaesthetic. But Chicago was enormous, full of anonymous places where a man could disappear if he knew what he was doing. Harper would need somewhere close enough to watch the apartment, cheap enough to pay cash without paperwork, unremarkable enough to blend into the urban landscape. A base of operations while he figured out what *Track 17* meant, what a *Slate* was and why his father's business partner was willing to commit multiple felonies to possibly keep it secret.

Harper pushed the Bonneville harder, the speedometer climbing as afternoon shadows lengthened across the highway. Somewhere ahead lay answers about Mason Carrick's current game, about whatever toxic secret his father had been paid to bury.

Harper had inherited his father's wealth, his father's guilt, and his father's enemies.

But he hadn't inherited his father's silence.

Time to find out what was buried in Chicago – and who was willing to die to keep it there.

2

WINDY CITY

CHICAGO IN THE LATE AFTERNOON LOOKED LIKE GOD HAD spilled paint across the sky and couldn't be arsed to clean it up. Harper rode the Bonneville through traffic that crawled with the enthusiasm of a Sunday morning funeral procession, weaving between cars whose drivers had apparently learned to drive by correspondence course.

The city stretched around him like an urban fever dream – glass towers trying to out-penis each other while neighbourhoods below got on with the business of actually existing. Every few blocks announced a new personality disorder – here, money flashed its teeth; there, desperation kept its head down; and everywhere the two shook hands in back alleys.

He'd taken the slower route in, avoiding motorways in favour of streets where he could stop at the shops he needed. He'd made three stops: *Best Buy* for tiny wireless cameras that cost more than his first motorcycle, *Radio Shack* for the bits and pieces to make them work properly, and a hardware store where the clerk looked old enough to have sold nails to Noah.

Everything required to play Big Brother from a distance.

His destination sat in Streeterville, which sounded like somewhere children played hopscotch but was actually where rich people went to feel better about being rich. The apartment his father had apparently owned was in a building that rose thirty floors, standing like a middle finger to anyone earning less than six figures, all glass and chrome with a doorman at reception, watching passersby like a hawk.

Harper parked the Bonneville in a visitor's spot and studied the building from across the street. No obvious watchers, but then if Mason Carrick's people were any good, they wouldn't be obvious.

Could be inside, could be in any of the dozen vehicles that looked like they belonged.

Could be the woman walking her dog or the bloke pretending to read his phone.

Paranoia was just pattern recognition with anxiety issues.

Harper crossed the street and walked into the lobby like he owned it, which technically he supposed he did, and the doorman looked up from a newspaper. The man had a moustache that belonged in an eighties police procedural and wore a name tag reading *Frank*. Sixty-something, broad shoulders gone soft, the look of someone who'd done actual work before ending up in a uniform that was mostly for show.

'Help you?' Frank asked, not unfriendly but clearly running his mental database of faces.

'I'm here about one of the apartments,' Harper said, keeping it vague. 'Twenty-eighth floor. The Kane place.'

Frank's posture changed instantly – he became straighter, more alert.

'You a lawyer? Another one from the estate?'

'Something like that.' Harper watched Frank's reaction carefully. The man seemed interested rather than defensive, which was promising. 'I take it you knew Mister Kane?'

'Knew him? Dammit, I've been the Super here for fifteen years. Dom was one of the good ones.' Frank's expression went soft with what looked like genuine grief. 'Always asked about the wife, remembered my grandson's birthday. Not like some of the assholes in this building who treat me like furniture.'

The familiarity – calling him “Dom” – suggested an actual relationship rather than professional courtesy, although Harper couldn't help feeling a pang of jealousy when he heard his father had asked about Frank's family, while ignoring his own son. But, that said, he decided to risk more information.

'I'm trying to sort out some of his personal effects,' Harper explained. 'Family matters.'

'Family?' Frank studied Harper's face with the intensity of someone doing a puzzle, and then recognition hit like a light-bulb switching on.

'Christ on a bike. You look just like him! Same eyes, same way of standing like you're ready for trouble.' Frank stood up, extending his hand. 'You're the son, aren't you? The one who was in the military?'

Harper shook the offered hand, surprised by the grip and the recognition.

'He mentioned me?'

'Course he did. Proud as a new father, even if he worried

himself sick about you. Always checking news from wherever you were deployed, though he never said exactly where that was.' Frank's handshake was firm, honest, belonging to someone who'd earned his calluses. 'Frank Styles. I was sorry as hell to hear what happened.'

Harper felt something unexpected – warmth, maybe, or just surprise that his father had talked about him to anyone.

'Thanks. I appreciate that. Liam Harper. My friends call me Harper.'

'Come on, then.' Frank gestured towards the elevators. 'Been keeping an eye on the place since we heard. Nobody's been up except the lawyer bloke who came by months ago. Decent fellow, very respectful. Said you'd be coming eventually.'

THEY RODE THE CARRIAGE IN COMFORTABLE QUIET. FRANK went to unlock apartment 28C with a master key, but Harper paused him, pulling out the keys he'd inherited along with everything else that came with being Dominic Kane's only living relative.

'I'm not sure which is which,' he said sheepishly as he checked the keys.

'That's easy to sort out,' Frank said, stepping aside. 'This one's the mailbox, storage locker downstairs, that's the key to the parking space – though I see you prefer two wheels.'

Harper smiled. *Frank really was observant.*

The apartment was exactly what Harper had expected and everything he'd dreaded. Expensive furniture arranged by someone who confused cost with taste, windows showing off a lake view that probably added more to the rent than most people earned in a year, art on the walls that screamed "I have money" in several languages.

His father's idea of what success looked like. All surface, no substance.

'He didn't spend much time here towards the end,' Frank said, following Harper inside. 'Always off somewhere – Kosovo, Colombia, places that sounded dangerous on the news. But when he was around, he was good company. Knew everyone's names, asked about their kids. Made you feel like you mattered.'

Harper walked to the windows, looking out at Lake Michigan stretching to the horizon like a particularly ambitious puddle. A few boats moved across the water like bath toys – pleasure craft and the occasional Great Lakes freighter hauling grain or ore between cities Harper had never cared to visit.

The apartment felt like a museum exhibit; everything perfectly arranged, nothing that suggested the occupant had ever relaxed or felt at home.

'Frank,' Harper said, still staring at the water. 'You knew my father for fifteen years. I'm trying to understand some of his business dealings. He ever mention the South Yards? Maybe Track 17?'

Frank moved to the kitchen island, considering the question while he checked appliances.

'South Yards? Yeah, he mentioned that area now and then. Said he had some business down there years back. Something to do with that security company he set up.'

'What kind of business?'

'Never said exactly. Your dad was careful about work talk – corporate security types always are, aren't they? But I got the impression it was some kind of contract work. Back when his business was just getting started.' Frank opened the fridge; found it empty as expected. 'He said something once about environmental assessments, making sure certain areas stayed secure. Corporate crap, basically.'

Harper turned from the window.

'Environmental assessments?'

'Something along those lines. Making sure nothing nasty was left lying about, I think. Your dad mentioned once that Aegis – it is Aegis, right? Anyway, they did cleanup work in the early days – industrial sites, old military places, that sort of thing.' Frank checked the freezer as well, clearly following some routine. 'Said Chicago had plenty of spots where people had buried problems instead of solving them.'

Damn right.

Harper walked through the apartment, cataloguing details. The desk drawers were empty – lawyers had probably hoovered up anything useful. The bedroom contained suits that cost more than cars, all in colours that suggested their owner had the fashion sense of an undertaker. The bathroom had toiletries that probably required a small loan to purchase – shaving cream from places Harper couldn't pronounce, cologne that claimed to contain rare herbs, moisturiser that probably cost more per ounce than decent whisky.

In the study, bookshelves held volumes on military strategy, corporate management, and international security. A few novels tucked between the textbooks – *le Carré, Forsyth, Tom Clancy.* His father's light reading apparently ran towards professional development, even when it was fictional.

But what struck Harper was what *wasn't* there. No photographs, no personal items, nothing suggesting the bloke who lived here had ever been married or had a son.

The apartment was a performance; a stage set designed to impress and intimidate in equal measure.

'Frank, I need to ask you something,' Harper said, returning to the main room. 'I can't stay here. Too many people know about this place. But I need somewhere nearby where I can keep an eye on things. Any suggestions?'

Frank studied Harper's face with the careful attention of someone who'd learned to read people over decades of building management.

'What sort of place you after?'

'Anonymous, takes cash without asking awkward questions.'

'Ah.' Frank nodded like Harper had just confirmed something he'd suspected. 'You're thinking like someone who doesn't want to be found. Fair enough. Your dad mentioned he had some complicated business relationships. Said there were people who might come looking someday.'

Frank pulled a business card from his wallet and scribbled on the back.

'There's a place couple blocks west. The Riverside Hotel. It's not winning any awards, but it's clean, and Eddie – the manager – doesn't ask questions long as you pay upfront. Tell him Frank sent you, and that you're Dominic's boy. He'll see you right.'

'Cheers.' Harper pocketed the card. 'One more thing. The South Yards area – what's it like now?'

'Complete transformation from when your dad was working down there. Used to be all freight trains and industrial buildings, abandoned lots where nobody asked what might be buried underneath.' Frank shook his head like he'd seen it all before. 'Now it's development projects and luxury flats. Some woman with a posh company buying up everything, promising jobs and prosperity.'

'Any particular developer?'

'Slate something, I think. Always on the news in her hard hat and expensive suits, banging on about urban renewal and transformation.' Frank's tone suggested he'd heard similar promises before and knew how they usually ended. 'Your dad mentioned her once, actually. Said she was either very brave or very stupid, building where she was building.'

Slate. Interesting. Harper filed that away.

'Mind if I take a few minutes alone?'

'Course. I'll be downstairs if you need anything. Take your time.'

Frank left, and Harper got to work.

He pulled the small cameras from his bag – the first camera went behind a book on the shelf, angled to cover the main entrance. Proper spy movie stuff, though considerably less glamorous when you were the one crawling about on expensive carpet trying to get the angle right.

The second camera he positioned in the bedroom, hidden behind a picture frame showing some landscape, with a clear view of both the bed and door, motion-activated, with battery life measured in weeks.

The third was a motion detection camera, placed in the corner of the hall outside, showing anyone who walked to the door, the fourth was in the window, looking out at the street.

Harper synced them with his phone, testing the feeds. Clear images, decent sound quality, connected to a personal Wi-Fi network. If anyone came poking about the apartment, he'd know about it before they'd finished wiping their feet.

Harper stood at the window again, watching traffic crawl along Lake Shore Drive like ants with driving licences. His father had likely stood in this exact spot, probably planning operations that got people killed, making decisions Harper was still dealing with months later.

The apartment felt like everything Harper hated about his inheritance – the money, the isolation, the careful distance from anything that might require actual human connection. But it also felt like a warning. His father had lived here like a man expecting trouble, keeping secrets from everyone including his own son.

Time to bugger off before someone noticed he was here.

Harper locked up and rode the elevator down to find Frank back at his newspaper, probably reading the same stories for the third time.

'All sorted?' Frank asked.

'Yeah. Thanks for everything.' Harper paused at the desk. 'Frank, if anyone comes asking about me being here...'

'Never saw you,' Frank said without looking up from his paper. 'Your dad asked the same favour a few times. Some habits are worth keeping.'

THE RIVERSIDE HOTEL TURNED OUT TO BE EXACTLY WHAT Harper had expected – a place that had seen better decades and wasn't holding its breath for them to return. Four storeys of brown brick and faded ambition, squeezed between a laundromat and a restaurant advertising "Authentic Chicago Pizza" in letters that suggested *authentic* was a flexible concept.

Eddie, the manager, looked like he'd been born exhausted and had spent fifty years perfecting the art. After hearing he'd been sent by Frank, he accepted Harper's cash for a week without asking for ID and handed over a key without ceremony.

'Room 312,' Eddie said unenthusiastically. 'Ice machine's broken, vending machine works when it feels like it. You want something from me, knock on the office door. You don't want something from me; we'll get along brilliantly.'

Harper liked him instantly.

Room 312 had a view of an alley and furniture that belonged in a display dedicated to questionable decorating choices from the seventies. But it was clean, the lock worked, and Harper could see his father's building in the distance if he craned his neck and used his imagination.

Harper unpacked his kit and tested the camera feeds. All working perfectly, showing empty rooms that looked exactly as he'd left them. Anyone searching the apartment would trigger the motion sensors, giving Harper advance warning and entertainment value.

He pulled out his father's notebook and found the entry that had dragged him across three states.

Carrick. South Yards. Track 17. Slate. Paid to keep it quiet.

Frank's information had provided context – his father had done security work in the rail yards for Aegis, possibly environmental assessments. Now this Slate woman was developing the area. The question was what his father had been paid to keep quiet about, and whether it was still buried down there waiting to cause problems.

Problems just waiting to be revealed by Harper.

Rather than using his laptop and potentially traceable Wi-Fi that probably moved slower than continental drift, Harper decided on old-fashioned research. A walk through the local area had revealed a Chicago Public Library branch six blocks south. There, he knew he'd find public terminals, anonymous access, and librarians who'd seen everything and judged nothing.

The library sat like a fortress of knowledge in an urban landscape that seemed allergic to the concept. Red brick and arched windows, suggesting permanence in a neighbourhood where everything else looked temporary.

The reference desk was staffed by a woman in her fifties with silver hair and the patient expression of someone who'd helped researchers find everything from forgotten ancestors to lost puppies over the years. Her name tag read "Margaret".

'Can I help you?' she asked, looking up from returned books that probably hadn't been missed.

'Hope so. I'm working on a book about Chicago's industrial history,' Harper gave his most winning smile. 'Specifically, the South Yards area. Looking for historical records, development plans, anything about the rail infrastructure there.'

Margaret's expression shifted – not suspicious exactly, but more cautious; like someone who'd heard this request before and hadn't liked how it ended.

'The South Yards? That's an interesting area to research. Few people ask about it any more.'

'Why's that?'

'Most of the records were transferred to private archives when the city sold the land for development. Public access became... let's say complicated.' She stood up, gesturing towards computer terminals that looked older than Harper's military service. 'I can show you what we have, but you might find the information has more holes than a Swiss cheese convention.'

Harper followed her to a terminal tucked in the corner, away from other researchers.

'Here's what I can access publicly,' Margaret said, logging him in with a guest account. 'Basic zoning records, some historical photos, newspaper archives. But the detailed infrastructure records, environmental assessments – those were sealed when Veronica Slate and Slate Urban Development took over the project.'

'Sealed how?'

Margaret glanced around the library, then leaned closer like she was sharing state secrets.

'Look, I don't know what kind of book you're writing, but I've had other people ask about the South Yards,' she explained. 'Journalists, mostly. None of them seemed particularly chuffed with what they found.'

'What did they find?'

'Gaps. Missing records, restricted access, official documents that had been reclassified for various creative reasons.' Margaret's voice dropped to barely above a whisper. 'One reporter told me she'd been warned off the story by her editor. Said it wasn't worth the legal hassle.'

Harper felt that familiar tingle that meant he was on to something properly interesting.

'What kind of legal hassle?'

'The kind that comes from very expensive lawyers and corporate security firms with more resources than patience,' Margaret said. 'Listen, I'll give you what access I can but be careful who you share your research with. The South Yards project has some powerful people who'd prefer it stayed successful.'

She pulled up database searches, showing Harper how to navigate the system. Historical photos of the rail yards from decades past, zoning changes over the years, newspaper articles about development proposals that had come and gone like London weather.

But Margaret was right – there were gaps big enough to drive freight trains through. Entire years missing from environmental monitoring reports. Zoning hearings held in closed sessions. Corporate filings that mentioned Track 17 but provided no details about what had been located there or why anyone should care.

Harper spent two hours digging through what was available, building a timeline of the South Yards transformation from active rail hub to abandoned industrial wasteland to current development goldmine. Veronica Slate's company had acquired the land through a maze of purchases, often buying parcels through shell companies before revealing the larger plan.

What caught Harper's attention was the timing. Slate's interest in the South Yards had intensified dramatically over the past two years – roughly when his father had been working his last operations for Aegis.

Margaret returned as Harper was printing a map of the rail yard from 1985, showing the original track layout including Track 17.

'Find what you needed?' she asked.

'Some of it. Thanks for the help.' Harper folded the map carefully. 'One last question – any suggestions for finding people who worked in the yards back in the day? Someone who might remember Track 17 specifically?'

Margaret considered this.

'You might try the area itself. There are still some old-timers in the area who remember when the yards were active. But I'd be careful about asking too many questions. Like I said, this project has made some people very nervous.'

HARPER LEFT THE LIBRARY WITH MORE QUESTIONS THAN answers, but at least now he had direction. The South Yards held secrets that powerful people wanted to keep buried. His father had been paid to help bury them. And now Veronica Slate was building over the whole area, potentially destroying evidence of whatever had happened there.

The map from 1985 showed Track 17 running through what was now the heart of Slate's development project. According to the old zoning records, that particular section had been designated for hazardous materials storage – chemical containers, industrial waste, cargo that required special handling, but which Slate's company had agreed, at considerable expense, to remove.

Time to take a closer look at Track 17 itself.

Harper walked back towards his hotel as the sun began setting over Chicago. Somewhere in this urban maze lay answers about his father's past, about Mason Carrick's current games, about whatever toxic secret connected them to the South Yards.

His phone buzzed with a motion alert from the apartment cameras; Harper checked the feed and saw nothing – just shadows moving as the building's automated lights went through their evening routine. For now, the apartment remained undisturbed. But Harper had the feeling that wouldn't last.

Mason Carrick knew he was heading to Chicago by now. It was only a matter of time before the game proper began. He'd come to Chicago looking for answers about his father's past, but now he was beginning to suspect those answers were going to come looking for him... whether he wanted them to or not.

3

INTERVENTION

THE SOUTH YARDS AFTER DARK LOOKED LIKE SOMEONE HAD given up on it halfway through and decided to let entropy finish the job. Harper walked the perimeter fence, using his phone's torch sparingly while his eyes adjusted to the orange glow bleeding through Chicago's perpetual urban haze.

Charming place for a stroll. Nothing said 'luxury development' quite like abandoned rail infrastructure and the lingering scent of industrial neglect.

The 1985 map from the library showed Track 17 running roughly east-west through what would soon be Slate's pride and joy. According to the old zoning records, that particular section had been designated for general freight storage – nothing that would raise eyebrows or suggest why it might need to stay buried decades later, but then at some point it'd been changed to enable toxic items to be dumped here – toxic items that apparently were now being removed before development started.

Harper found where Track 17 would have been. The rails were long gone, but the raised bed remained visible – a gentle ridge running through scrubland that estate agents would soon transform into "Heritage Court" or "Railway Gardens" or some other bit of marketing bollocks designed to make people forget they were living on top of God knew what if Slate was lying.

He'd parked the Bonneville a couple of streets away, taking a wandering route through neighbourhoods where gentrification fought a running battle with reality. Here, the battle was nearly finished, and construction fencing surrounded most of the site, decorated with signs promising

A Better Tomorrow for Chicago
Courtesy of Slate Urban Development

Lovely. Nothing like corporate optimism to warm the cockles of one's heart.

What Harper saw wasn't the promises, though – it was the activity.

Work lights blazed in three separate areas despite the hour being well past nine. Heavy machinery sat ready for immediate use and security patrols moved through the site with the methodical precision of people ticking boxes rather than having a casual wander.

Someone was definitely in a hurry.

Harper used the shadows cast by abandoned rail infrastructure to move closer. Years of skulking about in places he wasn't supposed to be had taught him that patience beat enthusiasm every time. The raised sections provided decent cover while the construction noise masked any unfortunate crunching sounds his boots might make on loose gravel.

Two articulated lorries sat near what would have been

Track 17's midpoint. Their drivers waited beside the cabs while security personnel with clipboards supervised the loading. But what caught Harper's attention wasn't the careful handling – it was that one of the security supervisors was smoking what looked like an expensive cigar, the sweet scent cutting through the industrial night air. Even from his position, Harper could see the distinctive yellow and black band.

Expensive habits for site security. Either these people were paid very well, or they had access to things most people couldn't obtain as that looked Cuban.

The cigar smoker's radio buzzed, and listening to whatever was being said he nodded to the drivers and walked off, passing the clipboard to another security operative – Harper couldn't make out details from his position, but the careful handling suggested something more valuable than standard demolition debris.

Or considerably more dangerous.

Harper spent a couple of minutes more watching the drivers, checking if anything else could be seen there, but a shout from near the fence line turned him. Not work-related – this carried the sharp edge of violence about to happen.

Harper moved towards the sound, using construction equipment for cover. What he found made his evening considerably more complicated.

Three men had cornered someone near a gap in the perimeter fencing. The trapped man was shorter, maybe forty, with the build of someone who worked with his hands rather than keyboards. His face was already bloodied, one eye swelling shut, and his shirt was torn where someone had grabbed him.

Two of the men doing the grabbing looked like they'd

stepped out of a corporate security brochure. Dark suits, earpieces, and that particular brand of controlled menace that came with legal immunity and expense accounts. The third had recently arrived, like Harper, cigar still in his mouth as he spoke.

Bloody marvellous. Corporate muscle having a chat with the locals.

'—told you what happens when you start getting ideas,' the largest was saying, his accent placing him somewhere between Boston and Belfast. 'Slate's been very patient with your concerns, but patience has expiry dates.'

'I signed the paperwork for her,' the bloodied man replied, his voice carrying a Hispanic accent and barely controlled terror. 'I did what you asked.'

'You signed it,' the second enforcer agreed, this one built like a marathon runner who'd discovered protein shakes. 'But your heart wasn't in it, was it? Been asking questions, talking to people who don't need to hear your life story.'

Harper didn't need to hear more to know this was classic intimidation choreography. One physical threat, one psychological manipulator, one observer to ensure nobody forgot their lines. Harper had seen this performance in Belfast, Kabul, Tripoli, and half a dozen other places where reasonable conversation had gone to die.

The bloodied man shook his head desperately.

'I haven't talked to anyone. I swear on my mother's grave, I haven't said anything about the reports.'

'Your problem,' the third enforcer said quietly, 'is that you think too much. We didn't pay you to think. We paid you to sign papers and keep your mouth shut.'

Paid. Past tense. A bribe, perhaps? Who was this scared, beaten man?

'But the contamination levels—'

'Are none of your bloody concern beyond what the paperwork says they are.' The cigar smoking enforcer stepped closer. 'You're a safety inspector. You inspect. You find everything tickety-boo. You file reports saying so. That's the alpha and omega of your job description.'

Harper had heard enough. He stepped out from behind a concrete mixer, hands visible but ready.

'Evening, lads,' he said conversationally. 'Lovely night for a discussion but seems like your friend here might prefer to head home to his dinner.'

The three enforcers turned as one, their positioning shifting automatically to contain both Harper and their original target; muscle memory from whoever had trained them, definitely ex-military or law enforcement.

'This is a private conversation,' the lean one said. 'I'd suggest you keep walking and mind your own business.'

'I might,' Harper replied, 'if it looked like a conversation. But from where I'm standing, it looks more like three grown men picking on someone half their size. That's not really cricket, is it?'

The big enforcer smiled without warmth.

'You want to make this your problem?'

'I'm hoping I don't have to.' Harper kept his voice reasonable, non-threatening. 'Seems like whatever business you have could be sorted without anyone getting their kit dirty. Why don't we all take a step back, let temperatures drop a few degrees?'

'Walk away,' the third enforcer said flatly. 'Final offer.'

Harper glanced at the bloodied man, who was watching with the desperate hope of someone who'd been drowning and suddenly spotted a lifeguard. Blood trickled from his nose, and his left hand was cradled against his ribs like one or two might be broken.

'Can't do that,' Harper said, rolling his shoulders slightly. 'My conscience wouldn't let me sleep.'

The big enforcer tossed away the remnants of his expensive cigar and reached inside his jacket.

Nobody did that unless they intended to bring something bigger out.

Harper moved while the motion was incomplete.

What happened next was over a decade of making violence look effortless compressed into three seconds of controlled brutality. Harper closed the distance before the enforcer's hand cleared fabric, driving the knuckles of his off hand into the man's throat, while trapping the gun hand with his strong side. The enforcer folded around the impact like a closing book, and Harper used his momentum to send him careening into his colleague.

The lean enforcer was quicker, producing a telescoping baton from his belt with the fluid motion of someone who'd done this dance before. He swung for Harper's head in an arc that would have made most people permanently horizontal.

But not someone from the UKSF.

Harper ducked the swing, caught the extended arm, and introduced the enforcer's elbow to some basic principles of physics. Joints weren't designed to bend that way, and the resulting crack echoed off the construction equipment like a starter's pistol, followed by a high-pitched scream.

The third enforcer had produced a gun by now, but the bloodied man – showing considerably more backbone than Harper had expected – threw himself at the gunman's legs. Both men went down in a tangle of limbs and creative profanity.

Harper stepped on the dropped weapon, then helped the injured man to his feet while the three enforcers reconsidered their career choices.

'Name's Tomás,' the man said quietly as they moved towards the fence gap. 'Tomás Alvarez. Thank you.'

'Harper,' he replied, keeping himself between Tomás and the enforcers. 'Let's go, yeah?'

Behind them, the big enforcer was speaking urgently into his radio, telling his supervisors what had happened, and Harper heard his name mentioned. Obviously he hadn't said it softly enough.

Wonderful. Now he was on their bloody Christmas card list.

'Like I said,' Harper called back over his shoulder, 'lovely evening for a chat. Perhaps next time try flowers and dinner first.'

Time to leave before the reinforcements arrived.

TOMÁS LIVED IN A NEIGHBOURHOOD THAT WALKED THE tightrope between working class pride and economic reality. Narrow streets lined with two-storey houses that had seen better decades, where residents fought entropy with fresh paint and small front gardens, despite everything else falling apart around them, and four-or-five-storey red-brick apartment blocks that looked as if the better days they once had were nothing more than a distant fever dream.

Harper had offered to take Tomás to a hospital, but the man had refused with the sort of panic that suggested involving official authorities would create more problems than it solved. Instead, he'd directed Harper through increasingly narrow streets to an apartment block with yellow siding and a garden out front, no bigger than a skateboard, where someone had attempted to grow roses with varying degrees of success.

'Rosa's going to kill me,' Tomás muttered as they climbed the stairs and approached the front door of his third-floor apartment. 'She told me this would happen.'

'Your wife?'

'My sister.' Tomás touched his swollen eye gingerly. 'She's been worried about me for weeks. Said I was acting strange, spending money we don't have, meeting people who don't belong in our neighbourhood.'

'Smart woman.'

'Too smart for her own good sometimes.' Tomás fumbled for his keys with hands that shook from adrenaline and fear. 'But she's right. This whole thing... I never should have gotten involved.'

The front door opened before Tomás could fish out his keys. A woman in her mid-thirties stood in the doorway, dark hair pulled back in a ponytail, wearing scrubs that suggested she worked in healthcare. Her expression shifted from relief to alarm as she took in her brother's condition.

'Jesus, Tomás, what happened to your face?'

'Rosa, this is Harper,' Tomás said, gesturing weakly. 'He found me having a disagreement with some people. Thought I might need a hand getting home.'

Rosa's eyes moved between Harper and her brother, cataloguing the bloodied shirt, the swollen eye, the way Tomás favoured his left hand.

'Inside,' she said decisively. 'Both of you. Tomás, sit down before you fall down.'

The living room was small but immaculate, decorated with family photos and furniture chosen for durability rather than fashion. Rosa guided her brother to a chair while Harper remained standing, feeling like he'd gate-crashed a family crisis.

Which, to be fair, he rather had.

'I need to clean those cuts,' Rosa said, studying Tomás's face. 'Some of them look deep.'

'I can help,' Harper offered. 'Did some field medicine training.'

Rosa studied him more carefully.

'Military?'

'Yes, ma'am.'

She seemed to reach a decision.

'Kitchen's through there. First aid kit's in the cupboard above the sink. There's a sewing kit in the drawer beside it if we need stitches.'

Harper found the supplies while Rosa continued her assessment. The kitchen was as neat as the living room, everything in its place, the refrigerator covered with children's drawings and medical appointment cards.

'You have kids?' he asked when he returned.

'Tomás does,' Rosa replied, accepting the first aid kit. 'My nephew and niece. They're staying with their aunt tonight, thank God.'

She began cleaning the worst of the blood from her brother's face, her movements gentle but efficient.

'This needs stitches,' she said, looking at a gash above Tomás's left eyebrow. 'Three, maybe four.'

'I can do it,' Harper said. 'Not my first rodeo. You deal with the ribs as I think that's the bigger issue right now.'

Rosa hesitated, then handed him the needle and thread.

'You've done this before.'

'More times than I'd care to remember.'

Harper cleaned the needle with antiseptic, then began working on the gash. His hands moved automatically, muscle memory from too many field dressings in too many unpleasant places. Tomás sat still, staring at the wall while Harper worked.

'So,' Rosa said quietly, wrapping the ribs with gauze, 'who were these people who disagreed with my brother?'

Tomás flinched, and not from the needle.

'Rosa—'

'Don't "Rosa" me,' she said firmly. 'For three weeks you've been acting like someone's hunting you. You've got more money than you've ever had, but you jump every time the phone rings. Now this.'

Harper finished the stitches and stepped back to check his work. Clean, even, should heal with little scarring.

'There,' he said. 'That should hold.'

'Thank you,' Rosa said, then turned back to her brother. 'Now talk, or I get your new friend to use the needle again to practise acupuncture on you.'

Tomás looked between his sister and Harper, clearly wrestling with how much to reveal.

'I can leave if this is private,' Harper offered.

'No,' Tomás said quickly. 'You saved my life tonight. You deserve to know what you walked into.'

He took a shaky breath.

'I'm a union safety inspector for construction sites,' he explained. 'Three months ago, I was assigned to the South Yards development project.' He touched the fresh stitches gingerly. 'I found contamination. Chemical residue, levels way above what's safe for residential construction. The kind of thing that would shut down the project permanently.'

'I thought they'd removed all this contamination?' Harper asked. 'As part of the agreement to build there?'

'They agreed, yes,' Tomás nodded. 'But it isn't exactly what they did.'

Harper leaned against the wall, the pieces falling into place.

'But it didn't go into your report,' Harper said.

'Someone from Slate Urban Development approached me. Offered fifty thousand cash for filing a clean report, saying they'd done their due diligence, and cleaned up the land.' Tomás met his sister's eyes. 'Rosa, Miguel needed that surgery. You know we couldn't afford it otherwise.'

Rosa sat down heavily.

'So, what changed? Why were they beating you up tonight?'

'Because I've been having second thoughts. I keep thinking about all the families who'll live in those apartments. The contamination levels... they'll cause cancer, birth defects.'

'What kind of contamination?' Harper asked.

'Industrial chemicals, heavy metals, some compounds I couldn't identify. The whole area should be a Superfund site, not luxury housing.'

Harper went to reply but stopped as Rosa crossed her arms, studying him with the sharp assessment of someone who'd spent years reading people in crisis.

'Hold on a minute. Let's back up, Mister Harper.' Her voice carried the authority of someone used to getting straight answers. 'Thanks for saving my brother and all that, but could you explain what the hell *you* were doing wandering around the South Yards at that time of night? That's not exactly tourist territory.'

'Rosa, he saved my life—'

'Doesn't give him a free pass, Tomás,' Rosa shook her head. 'For all we know he could be part of this.'

Harper met her gaze. It was a fair question, and she deserved an honest answer.

'I'm looking into some business dealings connected to that area. Old contracts, environmental work that was done there years ago.' He kept it vague but truthful. 'Someone I used to know was involved in the original development.'

'What kind of someone?' Tomás asked.

'My father. He did security work there back when the area was being assessed for redevelopment, and probably when the agreement was made to clean it up. I'm trying to understand what he was involved in.'

Rosa wasn't satisfied.

'And you just happened to be there at the exact moment my brother was getting beaten up?'

'Actually, yes. I was scouting the area, trying to understand the layout. Wrong place, right time.' Harper shrugged. 'Or right place, right time, depending on your perspective.'

Tomás looked between them.

'The man from Slate Urban Development who approached me – he said the offer was from Veronica Slate. She runs the entire operation.'

'She's the one behind all this?'

'You know her?' Rosa asked, suspicion still evident.

'I know of her.' Harper leaned forward, deciding not to mention the only knowledge he had was from a doorman and a cryptic note in a journal. 'Maybe if you could provide evidence of what she's covering up – the actual test results, documentation of the bribes?'

'And why would he do that?' Rosa asked.

'Because people are apparently going to get sick,' Harper still wasn't sure of the complete story, but he felt this was important. ' If so, it might be possible to expose this whole thing before that happens.'

After all, that's probably why Dad sent me here. To expose this, to solve another of his problems.

'And then what?' Tomás asked. 'If I spoke out, I'd go to prison.'

'Maybe. But probably not if you're cooperating to expose a larger conspiracy. Whistleblower protections exist for a reason.'

Tomás was quiet for a long moment.

'I need time to think. To figure out how to protect my family.'

Harper nodded and moved towards the door.

'Take the time you need. But don't take too long. Those people tonight were serious.'

Tomás nodded, staring down at the floor. Harper knew he wouldn't get anything more here.

Rosa followed him out of the apartment building.

'Thank you,' she said. 'For helping him tonight, for not walking away.'

'Your brother's in an impossible situation,' Harper replied. 'But he doesn't seem to be a bad man. He's just someone who made a difficult choice for the right reasons.'

'Those are often the most dangerous people to be.'

Harper looked at her more carefully. There was intelligence in her eyes, and strength that suggested she'd been holding her family together through sheer bloody-mindedness for some time.

'Where's his wife?'

'Passed away two years back. Cancer. He's had a tough time of it. I moved in about six months back.'

'You work in healthcare?' Harper nodded at the scrubs.

'Trauma nurse at Northwestern Memorial. I've seen what happens when people get caught between powerful interests and their own conscience.' She glanced back towards the building. 'It usually doesn't end well.'

'This time might be different.'

'Why? Because you're involved?'

Harper thought about the question. For the last few months he'd been drifting across the American Midwest, following cryptic clues from his father's journal and avoiding Mason Carrick's pursuit teams. Now he was standing outside a building in Chicago, promising to help a family he'd known for less than an hour expose a conspiracy that could destroy them.

His father would have recognised the pattern. Dominic Kane had apparently always been drawn to lost causes and impossible situations, always convinced that the right person in the right place could make a difference.

Whether that had worked out particularly well for him was another question entirely, as by the end he'd apparently decided that his way was the right way and damn the consequences.

'Because someone needs to make it different,' Harper said finally.

Rosa studied his face in the porch light.

'You're not really investigating a business dealing, are you? This is personal for you.'

'Most things are, eventually.'

She nodded, seeming to understand something in his answer that he hadn't quite articulated himself.

'Be careful, Harper. People like Slate don't just threaten – they follow through. And they have more resources than you might expect.'

'I'll keep that in mind.'

HARPER WALKED BACK TOWARDS WHERE HE'D LEFT THE Bonneville, thinking about contaminated soil and frightened families, about corporate corruption and impossible choices. Somewhere in the South Yards lay answers about his father's past and Mason Carrick's present. But now those answers were tangled up with Tomás Alvarez's crisis of conscience and his sister's determination to protect her family.

Bloody brilliant. He'd come to Chicago to hide from one problem and stumbled arse-first into another.

His phone buzzed with a motion alert from the apartment cameras. Harper checked the feed and saw someone had walked past the door in the hallway, trying it before continuing on. The game was accelerating, and Harper found himself caught between his father's secrets and a family's survival. Tomorrow, he'd need to decide which took priority.

Tonight, though, he'd settle for making it back to his hotel without collecting any more of Slate's attention than he already had.

Fat chance of that, really.

4

RESERVES

HARPER WOKE TO RAIN HAMMERING HIS HOTEL WINDOW LIKE IT had a personal grievance. Chicago's idea of a morning greeting was about as charming as you'd expect. He checked his phone – three motion alerts from the apartment cameras overnight.

Mason Carrick's people were definitely taking an interest.

He rolled out of bed and padded to the window, keeping to one side while he peered down at the street, looking down towards his father's – no, *his* – apartment building. In the distance were two cars he could identify, probably more he couldn't. They weren't being particularly subtle about it, which suggested either overconfidence or deliberate intimidation.

Probably a bit of both, knowing Mason. But the fact they were still focused a couple of blocks away meant they hadn't worked out he was here.

Harper made coffee with the room's kettle – instant, naturally, because apparently suffering built character – and settled at the small table to review his father's journal. He'd been through it dozens of times since receiving it, but something from last night's conversation with Frank had been nagging at him.

Environmental assessments. Corporate cleanup work. Making sure nothing nasty was left lying about.

His father's handwriting stared back at him from the pages – neat, controlled, full of operational details and cryptic references that were probably meaningless to anyone except Dominic Kane. Harper had been focusing on the obvious entries, the ones that mentioned South Yards and Track 17 directly, which were few and far between.

But there, tucked between notes about a job in Kosovo and expense receipts from Ethiopia, was something he'd dismissed as unimportant:

F told about Loops Reserves. Hopefully still operational. Old banking habits die hard.

Harper pulled his river stone from his pocket, rolling it between his fingers while he thought.

Frank. Reserves. Banking habits.

Frank had mentioned knowing his father for fifteen years, talked about him like they'd been mates rather than just building doorman and tenant. And Frank struck Harper as the sort of man who noticed things, remembered details.

Worth a conversation, anyway.

Also, the Loops was an area of Chicago, which meant this could be more relevant that he'd previously thought.

Harper checked the apartment surveillance feed one more time. The watchers were still there, patient as vultures. Which meant visiting Frank was going to be complicated.

He gathered his kit, made sure nothing important was left in the room, and headed for the door.

Time to find out what Reserves meant, and why his father thought Frank would know about it.

GETTING TO THE BUILDING WITHOUT BEING FOLLOWED required more than just walking two blocks, as there was every chance Aegis was watching him after all. Harper took the L two stops north, then doubled back on a different line, used the underground pedway system to move between buildings, and finally emerged from a department store a couple of blocks from his destination. It was old-fashioned counter-surveillance, the sort of thing his SRR instructors had drilled into him until it became second nature. The SRR weren't the sort who kicked in doors or announced themselves with flashbangs – that was someone else's job entirely. Harper's people melted into crowds, became part of the furniture in coffee shops and hotel lobbies; the bloke reading a newspaper on the park bench who'd been there so long you stopped noticing him, ghosts with military training and the patience to sit motionless for hours while targets convinced themselves they were safe.

The headlines always went to the SAS or SBS – the dramatic raids, the last-minute rescues, the sort of operations that made good television. But it was the Special Reconnaissance Regiment who'd spent weeks beforehand, watching, cataloguing, building the intelligence picture one careful observation at a time. They made sure the right bastard was in the crosshairs when the shooting started, that the raid teams hit the correct building, that the bomb disposal lads knew exactly where to look.

Their weapon wasn't superior firepower or tactical brilliance. It was patience, persistence, and the professional skill of becoming invisible until the moment they chose to be seen.

Most people couldn't be arsed to follow someone through that much tedium, and if they found Harper at any point of his travelling, they wouldn't know he'd started so close to them. Which was kind of the point.

Unfortunately, Carrick's people weren't most people.

Harper spotted the first tail at the department store – a woman in a tracksuit who browsed shop windows with the studied casualness of someone being paid to look uninterested. The second was on the street outside the building, reading a newspaper while leaning against a lamppost like he was auditioning for a spy film from the 1970s.

Subtle as a brick through a window though, these people.

Harper used a service alley to approach the building from the rear, found the delivery entrance, and spent ten minutes watching the patterns of foot traffic before making his move. The loading dock was busy enough to provide cover, and Harper's jacket and jeans let him blend with the maintenance workers coming and going.

Frank was in the building's basement office, going through maintenance requests when Harper arrived.

'Harper!' Frank looked up from his paperwork, genuine pleasure on his face. 'Didn't expect to see you back so soon. Is everything all right with the apartment? Or the room Eddie sorted you?'

'Fine, thanks. Actually, I wanted to ask you something else.' Harper glanced around the office – cramped but organised, walls covered with building schematics and maintenance schedules. 'My father left some notes that mention something called Reserves. Banking habits. Said it could be connected to the Loops? Ring any bells?'

Frank's expression shifted subtly – not suspicious, exactly, but more cautious.

'Reserves?' He set down his pen, giving Harper his full attention. 'That's an interesting question.'

'Interesting how?'

Frank was quiet for a moment, studying Harper's face like he was solving a puzzle.

'Your dad ever tell you about his drinking habits?'

'Not particularly. We weren't that close.'

'Dom liked his whisky, but he was particular about where he drank it. Most of the rich bastards in this building, they go to those fancy cocktail lounges where the drinks cost more than I make in a day.' Frank leaned back in his chair. 'But your dad? He preferred the high-class drinks, sure, but he only went to places with character. History.'

Harper waited.

'There's a place called *Reserves*,' Frank continued. 'In the old Continental Bank building down in the Loop, not "The Loops". It's where the business district is. The bank went bust in the eighties, but someone bought it in the millennium and eventually turned it into a private club. Well, more a bar that you pay to join, to keep the scumbags out. Still has the original vault in the basement – that's where they keep the good stuff.'

'Just for drinks?'

Frank's smile was knowing.

'Among other things. *Reserves* caters to a particular type of drinker – you know, one who values discretion, who need secure storage for items they'd rather not keep in traditional banking facilities. The old safe deposit boxes aren't just for show.'

Harper felt that familiar tingle that meant he was on to something important.

'You think my father kept something there?'

'Wouldn't surprise me. Dom was careful about keeping certain business separated from his legitimate affairs.' Frank wrote an address on a Post-it. 'Look for Mickey. Tell them Frank from the Kane building sent you. They'll know what that means.'

Harper pocketed the card.

'Thanks, Frank. I appreciate it.'

'Just be careful,' Frank said, his expression serious. 'Your dad's business attracted some dangerous attention. Some of those people are still around, still interested in what he might have left behind.'

Harper nodded, understanding the warning. *Frank had noticed the watchers too.*

'I'll keep that in mind.'

LEAVING THE BUILDING WAS WHERE THINGS GOT COMPLICATED.

Harper emerged from the service entrance to find the woman in the tracksuit positioned with a clear view of the alley. She was talking on a phone, describing something to whoever was listening.

Probably describing *him.*

Harper ducked back into the alley, pulled out his own phone, and called a taxi. When it arrived, he had the driver drop him at Union Station – the perfect place to disappear into crowds and multiple exits.

That's when the *real* pursuit began.

They were good; he had to give them that. Three-person team, rotating positions, using earpieces to coordinate. Harper spotted them as he moved through the station concourse, trying to look like a tourist while actually mapping escape routes.

The first mistake they made was staying too close. The second was underestimating how well Harper knew the city from his research.

Harper bought a ticket for the Blue Line, went through the turnstiles, then immediately doubled back through an emergency exit that set off alarms but got him clear of the platforms. By the time security responded, he was already moving through the underground pedestrian tunnels that connected Union Station to the surrounding buildings.

Construction work provided perfect cover – hard hats and safety vests scattered around equipment that Harper borrowed just long enough to blend with the workers. He emerged three blocks away, looking like he belonged there, while the pursuit team was probably still searching the train platforms.

Harper kept moving, using reflective surfaces to check for new tails while making his way towards the Loop district, using more construction sites, more crowds, and more opportunities to change his appearance and direction as he did so. By the time he reached the address Frank had given him, Harper was confident he'd lost them.

For now.

Reserves occupied what had once been the Continental Bank building – all limestone and carved stonework, the sort of structure that announced its importance to anyone walking past. The discreet brass plaque was the only sign of its current purpose, tucked beside the original bank entrance that still looked like it could withstand a siege.

Harper climbed the stairs to what had once been the main floor; the original banking hall was still there – high ceilings, marble columns, mahogany fixtures that spoke of an era when banks looked like temples to commerce.

Now it was a private club, with all leather chairs, booths and quiet conversations. The sort of place where people conducted business without worrying about eavesdroppers.

Harper paused, taking in the atmosphere. Frank had made it sound down to earth, but this was exactly a place his father would have loved – all understated elegance and old money respectability. Typical Dominic Kane, really.

Should have known the old man would have expensive tastes even in his hiding spots.

The bartender was polishing glasses when Harper approached – in her mid-sixties, shortish silver hair, the sort of no-nonsense bearing that suggested decades of managing people who thought money made them important.

'Help you?' she asked, looking up from her work.

'Frank from the Kane building sent me,' Harper said, keeping his voice low. 'Said someone here might be able to help with some family business. Called Mickey.'

'Well, you found her,' she smiled at Harper's obvious surprise. 'Mickie O'Brien. And you are?'

'Harper. Liam Harper.'

Mickie's expression didn't change, but Harper caught the

subtle shift in her posture – recognition, perhaps, or at least acknowledgement that the name meant something.

'ID,' she said simply.

Harper showed her his passport. Mickie compared the photo to his face, then looked at the name.

'Kane's boy,' she said finally. 'You've got his way of moving, like you're always ready for something to go wrong.' She handed back the passport. 'Your daddy mentioned you a couple of times. I was sorry to hear he passed.'

'Thank you,' Harper looked around. 'I was told this was a private club – I don't suppose I qualify for membership?'

'Your daddy's been a member here since his Army days. We're flexible about legacy memberships for family.' Mickie gestured around the club. 'Technically we're private, but it's more about keeping the wrong sort of people out than being exclusive.'

'I heard there was a chance my father left something here?'

'Safe deposit box in the vault downstairs. Paid up for five years in advance.' Mickie moved to a cabinet behind the bar, produced a key ring with several small keys. 'He said if anything happened to him, one of his sons would come collecting. That would be you, I'm guessing—'

'Wait,' Harper grabbed her arm. '*Sons*? I don't—'

He stopped as she chuckled.

'Don't you worry, boy, I'm just screwing with you,' Mickie led him to a side door that opened onto a spiral metal staircase that descended to the original bank vault. Once down it, Harper saw that the massive circular vault door was still there – chrome-plated, impressive – now permanently open to reveal a secure storage area lined with the original safe deposit boxes.

She inserted her key into box 47, then handed Harper a second key.

'Both keys needed to open it,' she explained. 'Bank security from the old days. Your dad was particular about following proper procedures.'

Harper inserted his key, turned it as she did, and heard the satisfying click of the mechanism opening. Inside was a manila envelope, thick with documents, and a small digital recorder.

'I'll leave you to it,' Mickie said. 'Maker's Mark's on the house when you're finished. Your daddy's favourite.'

Harper opened the envelope carefully. Inside were photographs – high-resolution images of construction work in what looked like the South Yards area. Heavy machinery, unmarked trucks, men in hazmat suits handling containers that Harper couldn't quite identify.

The documentation was more circumspect than he'd expected. Environmental assessment reports dated eighteen years ago, but they were incomplete – pages missing, conclusions redacted. What remained suggested contamination issues that required "specialised containment protocols" rather than standard remediation.

His father had been careful not to document the full extent of whatever they'd covered up.

Harper picked up the digital recorder, and pressed play. His father's voice filled the small space – older than Harper remembered, tired, but unmistakably Dominic Kane.

'If you're hearing this, it means I'm dead and you've figured out where to look. The South Yards project has complications, Liam. Carrick and I were brought in to assess and contain a contamination issue years ago. We followed protocol, suggested ways to

remove the contamination as per the city's rulings, but the client wanted solutions that weren't exactly by the book.'

Harper leaned back against the wall, processing what he was hearing.

'If I expose this myself, the fallout would destroy everything – Aegis, the legitimate operations, and everyone connected to it. Including you, son. By staying quiet, I'm keeping you safe. But if something happens to me, you'll have choices I never had.'

The recording continued.

'The current development is being built over that containment. Veronica Slate thinks she's buying clean land with manageable issues – or maybe she knows and doesn't care. I'm not sure. Either way, the contamination was supposed to be gone when they broke ground, and last I heard, that definitely hadn't happened. But if the containment fails, or if someone starts digging too deep...' his father paused. *'Well, let's say the consequences would be significant. Mason's working for Slate now, trying to manage the situation. But Mason's always thinking three moves ahead, always positioning himself to come out on top when things go sideways. And they will go sideways, son. They always do. The evidence in this envelope will give you leverage but be careful how you use it. There are people who'll kill to keep this buried, and others who'll kill to use it for their own purposes. Sometimes the right thing and the smart thing aren't the same thing. You'll have to decide which matters more.'*

The recording ended.

Harper sat in the vault, staring at the evidence spread before him. Years ago, his father and Mason Carrick had covered up a contamination issue that was now threatening to resurface, rather than actually cleaning it. Slate was building on top of it, possibly unaware – although what he'd seen the previous night countered that idea – and Mason was helping her manage the risks.

No wonder they were so keen to find Harper and whatever he might know.

Harper was preparing to return the documents to the safe deposit box when he heard voices from the adjacent viewing room. Someone else was accessing their box, their conversation carrying clearly through the thin partition.

'—timeline's been accelerated,' a man was saying, his voice carrying the authority of someone used to being obeyed. 'Slate wants the South Yards groundbreaking moved up to next week. Something about new investors who want to see immediate progress. She's gonna announce everything in a couple of days.'

'What about the safety concerns?' another voice asked.

'Handled. The inspector's been brought into line, and any remaining issues will be resolved through appropriate channels.'

'So, it's clean?'

'He's *saying* it's clean, and that's enough.'

Harper moved closer to the partition, trying to hear more clearly.

'And the interference from last night?' a third voice asked.

'Being addressed. Our people are tracking the individual responsible. He won't be a problem much longer.'

Shit. They were talking about him. Harper eased back, mind racing. Whoever these people were, they were clearly connected to Slate's operation. And they knew about his intervention at the South Yards.

Which meant they probably knew he was investigating the whole thing.

Harper quickly returned the documents to the safe

deposit box, then climbed the stairs to find Mickie behind the bar, and three men in expensive suits settling into a corner booth, thanking her politely while completely ignoring Harper's presence.

'Maker's Mark?' Mickie asked as Harper approached the bar.

'Please.' Harper took a seat where he could watch the booth without being obvious about it. The three men looked like corporate success stories – expensive suits, confident body language, the sort of calm authority that came from never having their credit cards declined. But something underneath didn't quite match the boardroom polish. The way they sat, the way their eyes moved – more like soldiers playing dress-up than actual executives.

Mickie set the whiskey in front of him.

'Maker's Mark Private Selection. Your dad always ordered the same thing,' she said quietly. 'Used to sit right there, actually.' She nodded towards a stool at the far end of the bar. 'Never said much about his work, but he talked about you constantly.'

Harper felt that familiar twist in his chest. Frank had said the same thing.

'We weren't exactly close.'

'Maybe not in miles, but you were never far from his thoughts.' Mickie polished another glass. 'Always worried about keeping you safe from his world. Said it was dangerous enough without dragging family into it.'

'What brought him here originally? The vault?'

'Actually, no. He started coming here when he was still Army, back in the early noughties. We're close to the UK Consulate, so we get a lot of military personnel through here, and we'd just opened. Your dad liked the atmosphere;

said it reminded him of the membership clubs he'd never been allowed in back home,' Mickie smiled. 'The vault came later, when he needed somewhere secure for certain items.'

'Still get military people?'

'Oh yes. Especially when there are events. There's a big Veterans' Fundraiser at Palmer House in a couple of days – we'll be packed with old soldiers reliving their glory days.' She gestured towards the window. 'Just across the square there. I seem to recall your daddy saying you were a soldier. You should get a ticket, go along.'

Harper nodded, filing away the information.

'Cheers,' Harper said quietly, raising the glass. The bourbon was good – smooth, expensive, the sort his father would have appreciated.

That's when he saw him. Walking past the front windows, visible for just a moment before disappearing from view – a face Harper recognised instantly. Shorter than Harper remembered, leaner, with the sort of careful movement that suggested constant awareness of his surroundings.

Alfie Reeves. Sergeant Alfred Reeves, formerly of the 22nd Special Air Service Regiment, attached to Harper's SRR unit for a joint operation in Syria in 2019.

The same Alfie Reeves who'd died in a vehicle explosion outside Aleppo six months later.

Except he was very much alive and walking the streets of Chicago.

Harper set down his glass, mind reeling. Unconsciously, he pulled his river stone from his pocket. It was a smooth grey stone from the River Wye, worn to the size of a fifty pence coin from years of handling, and he rolled it between his fingers while he processed what he was seeing; the familiar weight helped ground him, a habit he'd developed during his first SRR deployment and never quite shaken.

Alfie had been facing a court martial when he'd supposedly died – Harper had never learned the specifics, but it was something from when Alfie was operating in the Syrian conflict zone.

Alfie Reeves, alive and apparently thriving in Chicago. The same Alfie who'd been decent enough in the field but had always pushed boundaries, always seemed to know where to find things that weren't supposed to exist. Harper had wondered about some of the gear that had appeared in their kit, the sort of modifications that didn't come through official channels.

And now he was here. Or was he? Had Harper seen a man, a ghost or a memory?

Harper left money on the bar and moved towards the exit, catching Mickie's questioning look.

'Family business,' he said by way of explanation. 'I'll be back, if I'm allowed?'

'You're a member,' Mickie waved the money. 'I said this one was free.'

'Is information free too?' Harper leaned closer. 'The three men in the booth. Are they Aegis?'

'Your daddy's team? Hell no,' Mickie grinned, keeping her own voice low. 'They wish they were. Meridian men. More a subcontractor for the bigger guys.'

Harper nodded, tipping an imaginary hat.

So, it wasn't just Aegis looking for him. Meridian were too.

But who the hell were Meridian?

HARPER EMERGED ONTO THE STREET, SCANNING FOR ALFIE'S distinctive walk.

There – half a block ahead, moving with the sort of careful awareness Harper remembered from their time together, Harper saw Alfie reach a panel van, speak briefly with the driver, then accept what looked like a package. There was nothing unusual about it, except for the small matter that Alfie Reeves was supposed to be six feet under in a military cemetery outside Birmingham, West Midlands.

Harper pulled out his phone, took several photos from a distance, noting the logo on the side of the van – a bold capital M, stylised with subtle horizontal cuts like those on a rifle sight or tactical reticle, then watched as Alfie disappeared into the crowd again.

Time to make a phone call.

Harper found a quiet side street and dialled a number he hadn't used in months. It rang twice before a familiar voice answered.

'Well, well. Captain Harper. Thought you'd disappeared off the face of the earth.'

'Colonel Crowe,' Harper said. 'Good to hear your voice, sir.'

'I've not been Colonel for a couple of years now, Liam. What can I do for you?'

Harper hesitated, then decided on the direct approach.

'I think I just saw Alfie Reeves.'

Silence on the other end of the line. When Crowe spoke again, his voice had changed.

'That's not possible, Harper. You know that.'

'I know what I saw, sir. Here in Chicago. Very much alive and collecting packages from delivery vans.'

'Jesus Christ.' Crowe was quiet for a moment. 'You're certain?'

'Certain enough to call you about it.'

'Well, this is interesting timing,' Crowe said slowly. 'I'm actually in Chicago myself. Veterans' thing in a couple of days at the Palmer House hotel. I'm one of the UK military liaisons for it. If you're in town, we should probably have that conversation in person.'

Harper felt that familiar chill that meant coincidences were piling up in dangerous ways.

'Tonight?' Harper suggested.

'I'm staying at the Hilton, so meet me in the hotel bar, *Kitty O'Sheas*, six o'clock. And Harper? Watch yourself. If Alfie really is alive, there are implications we need to discuss.'

Ending the call, Harper pocketed his phone and started walking away from the Loop District. Now he had two mysteries – his father's buried secrets and a supposedly buried colleague walking the streets of Chicago.

Both were connected to his past. Both were dangerous.

And Harper had the uncomfortable feeling that both were about to get considerably more complicated.

5

HIDDEN GROUND

THE MIDDAY SUN CAST SHARP SHADOWS ACROSS CHICAGO'S industrial landscape as Harper knocked on the Alvarez apartment door. Three sharp raps, then a pause - standard protocol when you weren't sure what reception awaited.

Harper's hands were still steady despite everything he'd learned at *Reserves*.

His father's voice echoed in his head, warning about people who'd kill to keep secrets buried. The conversation he'd overheard confirmed they knew about him now. Coming back here was definitely masochistic stupidity.

But sometimes stupidity was the only option that felt right.

Tomás answered, looking like someone who had spent the night wrestling with demons and losing badly. The bruising around his eye had ripened into an impressive palette of purples and yellows that would have made a sunset jealous.

'Christ, didn't expect to see you back here.'

'Rosa at work?'

'Double shift at the hospital.' Tomás glanced past Harper towards the corridor, checking for watchers. *Smart man.* 'Thought you'd have left town by now. Most sensible people would have.'

'Sensible's never been my strong suit,' Harper said. 'Mind if I come in?'

Tomás stepped aside, still processing Harper's return.

The living room looked the same as the night before – family photos on the mantelpiece, children's drawings stuck to the fridge with magnets, the comfortable clutter of people who actually lived in their space rather than just occupying it.

'Coffee?' Tomás asked, moving towards the kitchen on autopilot.

'Thanks.'

Harper watched him work, noting the careful movements around his wrapped ribs. The man was in pain but functioning, which said something about his determination. Or his stupidity. Often the same thing, in Harper's experience.

The kitchen was a monument to making do with countertops that showed their age, but everything clean and organised. A list on the refrigerator showed medication schedules in Rosa's handwriting, and bills had been stacked neatly on the counter, some marked with payment dates in different coloured pens. It was the sort of careful financial management that spoke of people who couldn't afford mistakes.

'So,' Tomás said, spooning instant coffee into mugs with the resignation of someone who'd given up on life's finer pleasures. 'What changed? Last night you said to take time to think. Now you're back before lunch.'

'Had an interesting morning. Turns out my father left me more than just questions.' Harper accepted the coffee, noting that Tomás had made it strong enough to wake the dead. 'He left me evidence.'

'Evidence of what?'

'That Veronica Slate isn't the only one with dirty hands in this mess.'

Harper took a sip of the coffee and immediately regretted it; the damn thing tasted like someone had dissolved charcoal in battery acid. Definitely an acquired taste, but he'd made worse out on operations, sometimes stuck out for days, making do with reusing grounds or turning to substitutes like chicory or roasted grains, even grinding scavenged coffee beans with the butt of his rifle when needed.

Compared to that, this was barista level.

'I think my father and his business partner covered up the original contamination, and lack of cleaning up years ago,' he explained. 'Now they're all scrambling to manage the fallout.'

Tomás sat down heavily, wincing as his ribs protested. The kitchen chair creaked under his weight – everything in this apartment had been used hard and maintained carefully.

'So, that's why you were really there last night? Not as some kind of avenging angel?'

'Let's just say the timing was fortuitous.'

'Go on then, how much fallout are we talking about?'

'The kind that kills people.' Harper set down the coffee mug. 'The kind that's already started killing people, if the health records are accurate.'

Harper paused, watching Tomás.

'But you knew that already, didn't you?' he continued. 'After all, you took a bribe to look the other way, change the reports you'd created.'

Tomás looked away, ashamed.

'I was given the reports, told to put them in, but I saw the originals,' he admitted. 'They claimed the originals were old, before they started removing the soil.'

'So, they are removing it?'

Tomás nodded.

'There's rumours, saying they attempted to clean it, but it didn't work. Rosa's been working emergency for six years, and she's seen patterns over the last couple. Cancer clusters, birth defects, respiratory problems. All concentrated in neighbourhoods where there's stories that Slate Urban used that contaminated soil as fill.'

Harper stared at Tomás, horrified.

'And you knew about this?'

'Everyone does!' Tomás snapped back. 'It's one of the worst-kept secrets here. But nobody can prove it. And nobody in power wants to. What do you think happens to the councillors and mayors who signed off on this? I was paid to look the other way so they don't need to worry.'

'Your sister knows about this?'

'She's suspected. But proving it...' Tomás shrugged. 'That's a different problem entirely. Hospital administration doesn't want to hear theories about environmental causes. Bad for business relationships with development companies.'

Harper pulled out his phone, scrolled to the photos he'd taken at *Reserves*. His father's evidence, digitised for convenience and uploaded to secure cloud storage.

'Well, now we can prove it.'

Tomás leaned forward, studying the images on Harper's phone. His expression shifted from curiosity to horror as he processed what he was seeing. Documents, photographs, measurements that painted a picture of systematic deception stretching back decades.

'Jesus Christ. They've been planning this for years.'

'Decades, from what I can tell. You didn't know this?'

Tomás shook his head.

'The documents I saw...'

'Were likely doctored years earlier, but still showed the rot underneath,' Harper placed the phone away. 'The question is whether you're still interested in stopping this.'

'After seeing this? You're damn right I am.' Tomás stood up, moving to the coat closet. 'But that? Even with the originals, unless your father wants to take the stand—'

'My father's dead,' Harper replied. 'It's kinda why I'm here.'

'Well, if he's gone? Then these images, folders? Someone like Slate, she can claim it's all fabricated. It'll be tossed out of court,' Tomas muttered. 'If we're going to do this properly, there has to be no more sneaking around in the dark like amateurs.'

'What do you have in mind?'

'We go back to the South Yards. Daylight hours, official business.' Tomás pulled on his jacket, clipping on his union ID. 'I'm a safety inspector, so it won't be out of the ordinary to be seen. However, you're...'

'Law enforcement,' Harper interjected with a smile. 'From out of state, following up on related violations.'

Tomás considered this.

'That'll work. Question is, do you have any credentials, or are we relying on charm and good looks?'

Harper patted his jacket pocket where Sheriff Eric Coble's badge rested; another inheritance from his recent adventures, though Tomás didn't need to know the details of how Harper had gained it.

'Let's just say I've got what's needed.'

Tomás looked at him more carefully.

'I'm not going to ask.'

'Probably better if you don't,' Harper smiled. 'So, are you up for this now?'

'No,' Tomás replied honestly. 'But if I don't step up, who will? Besides, I need to cleanse my soul. This'll help.'

THEY ARRANGED TO MEET TWO BLOCKS FROM THE SOUTH Yards main entrance. Tomás would take the bus – less conspicuous than trying to fit two grown men on Harper's motorcycle, and it wouldn't raise questions about why a visiting law enforcement officer was riding around on a British bike.

Harper spent the ride practising his accent, letting the American inflections strengthen while burying the British undertones that marked him as foreign. For the next couple of hours he was Sheriff Eric Coble from Nevada, following up on interstate environmental violations. It was a routine bureaucratic cooperation between jurisdictions – and if anyone asked, they could check Prosperity, where Coble came from, and see they'd had a massive environmental issue a couple of months earlier. It was the mundane sort of official business that made people's eyes glaze over and their cooperation automatic.

Of course, if they *did* check carefully, they'd also see Coble had been stripped of rank and arrested, so this wasn't going to be a long-term identity.

He parked the Bonneville close enough for a quick exit but far enough to avoid awkward questions, and the walk gave him time to shift mental gears, transforming from infiltrator to authority figure; different posture, different bearing, different way of moving through space.

The neighbourhood between his bike and the meeting point told its own story. Houses that had been working-class respectable twenty years ago were now showing the strain of economic reality. Some had been gentrified – fresh paint, new windows, small gardens that spoke of disposable income. Others were hanging on by their fingernails, elderly residents who couldn't afford to move and couldn't afford to stay. Progress, Chicago-style. When whatever Slate was building took shape, these houses would be next to go – and the inhabitants already knew it. Why spend money on property that'd be pulled down in years, maybe months?

Tomás was waiting at the agreed corner, looking nervous but determined.

'Ready for this?' Harper asked, his voice now carrying the flat vowels of the American West.

'No. But let's do it anyway.'

The South Yards sprawled before them like a vision of urban optimism made concrete. Cranes reached towards the sky, their shadows cutting geometric patterns across the development site. Workers moved between building phases with the organised chaos of a billion-dollar enterprise. In the daylight, it was a different world from the abandoned wasteland Harper had explored in the dark. Progress had a way of making everything look cleaner, more legitimate. *Money could buy a lot of respectability, given enough time and the right marketing.*

'Soil remediation,' Tomás muttered as they approached the main gate, pointing towards the eastern section where trucks moved with mechanical efficiency. 'That's what they're calling the cover-up.'

Harper could see the operation clearly now. Systematic excavation, soil removal, and transportation to unknown destinations. It was the sort of industrial-scale operation that required planning, resources, and official cooperation at multiple levels.

'How many people know what's really happening here?' Harper asked.

'More than you'd think. Less than you'd hope.' Tomás adjusted his tie nervously. 'City planning, environmental oversight, construction permits – they all require sign-offs. Question is how many people are getting paid to look the other way, and how many just don't want to know.'

The security guard at the main gate was young, eager, the type who'd been told to be helpful to law enforcement while maintaining proper protocols, which was an impossible balance that usually resulted in people choosing cooperation over conflict.

Harper approached with the confidence of someone whose authority had never been seriously questioned. He'd learned the bearing from watching actual cops – the way they moved through space like they owned it, the assumption that people would cooperate because that's how the world worked.

'Afternoon,' he said, producing Coble's badge with the casual ease of someone who'd done it a thousand times. 'Sheriff Eric Coble. Following up on some environmental violations in Nevada that might connect to your operation here.'

The guard studied the badge with the intensity of someone trying to spot a forgery but having no idea what one would look like. Harper waited patiently, projecting the mild boredom of someone dealing with routine bureaucracy.

'I wasn't told about any law enforcement visits.'

'Interstate cooperation. Routine follow-up.' Harper gestured towards Tomás. 'Mister Alvarez from the union is helping us understand the site layout. Environmental violations have a way of crossing jurisdictional boundaries if they're not handled properly.'

The guard's uncertainty was visible, caught between security protocols and the general principle of not pissing off cops. Harper could practically see the mental calculations – weighing potential trouble for letting them in against certain trouble for obstructing law enforcement.

'Maybe I should call my supervisor—'

'Course. Though if you could point us towards Track 17 first, save us some time while you sort the paperwork? We're just doing a preliminary assessment, nothing that requires disturbing your operations.'

Magic words. People wanted to be helpful, especially when it meant avoiding bureaucratic complications that might reflect poorly on their job performance.

'Over there, where they're doing the soil work. Follow the access road, can't miss it.'

Harper thanked him and grabbed two hard hats before heading towards the indicated area, Tomás falling into step beside him. Workers paid them no attention – just another pair of officials ticking boxes in the endless bureaucratic dance that surrounded large construction projects.

The access road was well-maintained, designed for heavy truck traffic. Harper noted the positioning of security cameras, the natural choke points that could be used to control access, automatic after years of moving through potentially hostile territory.

'That was almost too easy,' Tomás said quietly.

'Best cons usually are. People want to believe you belong, especially if you're wearing the right uniform and carrying the right credentials.'

'Is that what this is? A con?'

Harper considered the question.

'Depends on your perspective. We're law enforcement investigating environmental crimes. That one of us isn't technically law enforcement, and the other is technically a criminal is just details.'

'You have a flexible relationship with the truth,' Tomás visibly winced at the "criminal" line, but Harper was correct. Even if he was redeeming himself, he *had* taken money to look the other way.

'Occupational hazard,' Harper smiled.

They crested a small rise offering a clear view of the Track 17 area; heavy machinery worked hard, removing soil from a grid pattern and loading it into unmarked trucks. He hadn't been this far the previous night and the operation was larger than Harper had realised from his reconnaissance – an industrial-scale enterprise.

'Bloody hell,' Harper said, forgetting his accent momentarily.

'Two decades of contamination,' Tomás replied, watching another truck rumble past loaded with what should have been treated as hazardous waste. 'They're not treating it, just spreading it around the city. Diluting the problem instead of solving it.'

Harper pulled out his phone, documenting the operation while pretending to check messages. The trucks bore no company markings – definitely a professional job designed to avoid the sort of attention that came from concerned citizens with cameras.

'Where's all this poison ending up?'

'Rumours are they turn up at night at south-side construction projects. Mixed with clean soil, used as fill. Won't show up in standard testing, but it doesn't eliminate the contamination. Just makes it someone else's problem.'

'Plausible deniability,' Harper nodded. 'If anyone gets sick in ten years, there's no way to prove it came from here.'

'Exactly. And by then, the people responsible will have moved on to other projects, other cities, other opportunities to get rich while poisoning people.'

Movement caught Harper's attention. Three expensive SUVs were now approaching with purpose, heading directly towards them. The vehicles moved in formation – lead car, two flankers, the sort of coordination that suggested professional security rather than casual transportation.

'Company,' Harper said, shifting back into character.

The convoy stopped fifty yards away, positioning to block potential escape routes while maintaining clear fields of fire. Harper noted the tactical deployment automatically – *these people had military training.*

Six people emerged from the vehicles – four security types moving with the sort of coordinated dance that suggested recent military service, plus two executives who carried themselves like people accustomed to being obeyed without question. One was a woman in her forties, managing to look elegant even in construction gear. Dark hair pulled back in a severe bun, features that belonged on someone who'd never heard the word 'no' and didn't plan to start learning. She hadn't bothered with a hard hat and moved towards them with the confidence of someone accustomed to owning whatever space she occupied.

Veronica Slate. Had to be.

Harper had met the type before – corporate predators who'd learned to disguise ruthlessness as business acumen. Dangerous in ways that straightforward thugs weren't, because they operated within systems of law and respectability that made them effectively untouchable.

'Sheriff Coble?' she called out, voice carrying over the construction noise. 'I'm Veronica Slate. I understand you have questions about our operation.'

Harper adopted the bearing of a small-town sheriff dealing with big-city authority. Respectful but not intimidated, professional but slightly out of his depth.

'Ma'am. Appreciate you taking time out of your schedule. Following up on some environmental violations from Nevada that might connect to your operation here.'

Slate approached, eyes assessing every detail. Harper felt like a specimen being catalogued – height, weight, potential threat level, probable weaknesses. She was evaluating him with the cold calculation of someone who'd built an empire by accurately assessing risks and eliminating them.

'What sort of violations?'

'Improper disposal of industrial waste, contamination of groundwater supplies. Things that tend to cross state lines if not handled properly.' Harper repeated the lie as he gestured towards the soil operation. 'We've been tracking some contractors and disposal methods that showed up in your operation here.'

'And you think our development is connected how?'

Harper gestured towards the soil operation, noting how Slate's security personnel had positioned themselves to cut off escape routes while maintaining the appearance of casual positioning.

'Same contractors, same methods, same materials. We

had a company called *Aegis* involved in Nevada, hear they've been attached to this project. Interstate environmental crimes have a way of following patterns.' He nodded towards Tomás. 'Mister Alvarez here's been helping us understand how these operations typically work.'

Slate's attention shifted to Tomás, and Harper saw recognition flicker in her eyes. She knew exactly who he was, which meant she'd been briefed on the previous night's incident.

'Mister Alvarez. I don't believe we've been formally introduced.'

Tomás maintained composure despite the obvious threat in her tone. Whatever internal steel had allowed him to overcome his fear and return here was holding up under pressure.

'Union safety inspector, ma'am. Just doing my job.'

'Of course you are.' Slate's smile could have cut steel. 'Well, Sheriff, I'm sure you understand that Slate Urban Development operates strictly within all environmental regulations. Our soil remediation work here is being conducted under proper supervision, with all necessary permits and oversight.'

'I'm sure it is,' Harper replied, projecting the sort of mild scepticism that came naturally to law enforcement officers. 'Mind if we take a look at your documentation? Just for our records, interstate cooperation and all that.'

The request was perfectly reasonable – exactly what any legitimate law enforcement officer would ask when investigating potential violations. Which made Slate's refusal both expected and telling.

'I'm afraid that would require proper warrants and jurisdictional coordination,' Slate said smoothly, her tone suggesting polite regret while her body language radiated barely controlled impatience. 'Interstate environmental investigations involve rather complex legal procedures. I'm sure you understand the bureaucratic requirements involved.'

Harper nodded, projecting small-town disappointment at big-city bureaucracy.

'Fair enough. We'll go through proper channels, file the appropriate requests.' He touched his hard hat in a gesture of respectful acknowledgement. 'Appreciate your time, Ms Slate.'

'Always happy to cooperate with law enforcement, Sheriff, no matter how painful the results are.'

Polite words hiding unmistakable threat. Veronica Slate hadn't said it would be painful for her, instead she'd just told him, in language that was diplomatically correct but practically unambiguous, that his inquiry was unwelcome and pursuing it further would be inadvisable.

'Oh, one other thing?' Slate added. 'This "Aegis"? We stopped working with them years ago. They were, shall we say, a little too keen to smudge the lines of law.'

'Oh, that's good news,' Harper smiled. 'They're not the sort of people a professional like you should have, believe me. Who do you use now?'

'Applying for a job?'

'Professional curiosity.' Harper thought back to the Reserves. 'Hear good things about Meridian, if you're looking.'

Slate didn't reply, but the micro expressions at the name gave everything away.

So, Meridian were working with Slate. Was the line about Aegis true, though?

The conversation obviously over, and deciding not to

push it, Harper and Tomás headed back towards the gate, maintaining the unhurried pace of officials concluding routine business. Harper could feel Slate's attention like a physical weight, every step measured and assessed, while his professional paranoia suggested she was already planning how to deal with the problem they represented.

'Think she bought it?' Tomás asked quietly.

'Definitely not. But she's too smart to leave it there. She'll be checking my credentials within the hour.'

'What happens when she finds out Sheriff Coble is either dead or fictional?'

'Then things get considerably more complicated. But one thing's for sure. I might have lied about myself, but I'd bet everything in my pockets she was lying through her teeth when she said Aegis wasn't involved. They might not be on the books any more, but they're around.'

They cleared the gate without incident, the guard obviously relieved to avoid complications that might require explanations to his supervisors.

'What's the verdict?' Tomás asked once they were walking back towards where Harper had parked his bike.

'Your sister was right. Veronica Slate is exactly as dangerous as she looks.' Harper allowed himself to breathe normally again, the tension of maintaining character finally easing. 'And I just painted a target on my back the size of a billboard.'

'What's our next move?'

'Short term? We get the hell away from here before Slate's people finish checking our story.' Harper pulled out his keys, calculating routes and timing. 'Long term? You carry on as if nothing happened, like you were just doing your job, and I was the problem that pulled you to the side. Hopefully they'll ignore you now, as I'm something new. Meanwhile, I figure out how to stop them before they bury the evidence so deep it'll never surface.'

'Any ideas?'

'Few. None of them particularly safe.' Harper looked back towards the site, where machinery continued its systematic destruction of evidence. 'But then, safe's never been my strong suit either.'

SLATE WATCHED THE TWO MEN DISAPPEAR BEYOND THE GATE, her expression thoughtful. Something about the sheriff bothered her – not the credentials, which seemed legitimate enough, but something underneath. The way he moved, maybe. Or how his questions cut straight to relevant details without the usual bureaucratic meandering.

And his mention of Aegis.

She turned to a man walking up beside her, a sling supporting his left arm.

'Is that him?' she asked.

The injured enforcer nodded, his expression troubled.

'Yeah, that's the guy from last night. But last night he sounded British, called himself Harper. Just now, completely American accent.'

Slate's eyes narrowed as she processed this information. British man using American law enforcement credentials, switching accents like clothing. Professional deception, which meant professional training. And professional training meant he was considerably more dangerous than he'd appeared.

'Find out everything about Sheriff Eric Coble from Nevada,' she hissed. 'Background, current status, recent activities. And find out how someone named Harper got hold of his identity.'

'What about the union inspector?'

Slate's smile held winter's promise.

'Mister Alvarez has been very helpful to our operation. It would be unfortunate if he forgot where his loyalties lie.'

'You don't think we can trust him?'

'Possibly,' Slate mused. 'But why worry about it when we can just force the issue permanently, with some kind of unfortunate attack?'

The man smiled.

'Bad neighbourhood he lives in,' he said carefully. 'Bad elements.'

'Make friends with those bad elements,' Slate smiled. 'And make sure none of this comes back on me.'

6

TRAUMA WARD

HARPER SPENT THE AFTERNOON SECOND-GUESSING EVERY decision he'd made since arriving in Chicago. The Track 17 visit had gone too smoothly, Slate too controlled, too calm. In Harper's experience, when dangerous people appeared reasonable, it usually meant they were planning something unreasonable.

He pulled his river stone from his pocket, rolling it between his fingers as he walked towards Northwestern Memorial. The familiar weight helped him think, helped him focus on what he could control rather than the dozen variables spiralling beyond his influence.

Northwestern Memorial rose from Chicago's medical district like a cathedral dedicated to human resilience. Glass and steel reaching towards the sky, emergency vehicles cycling through the ambulance bay with the sort of organised chaos that suggested life-and-death decisions were routine here. Harper had spent enough time in military hospitals to recognise the atmosphere – the particular tension that came from people fighting losing battles against time, physics, and human fragility. He knew the smell would hit him the moment he walked through those doors: antiseptic trying to mask blood, fear, and the sort of hope that came with nowhere else to turn.

Finding Rosa Alvarez in a hospital the size of Northwestern should have been impossible, but Harper had learned that healthcare workers operated on their own communication networks. A mention of her name to the information desk, a casual reference to being connected to family, and within ten minutes he was being directed towards the trauma ward, which occupied most of the seventh floor, its corridors humming with the sort of quiet urgency that suggested people were dying with efficiency. Harper approached the nurses' station, where a woman in her forties was reviewing charts with the focus of someone whose decisions affected whether people went home or went to the morgue.

'Excuse me,' Harper said. 'I'm looking for Rosa Alvarez? I understand she's working a double shift today.'

The nurse looked up, automatically assessing whether Harper represented a problem that needed security or just another worried relative.

'Family?' she asked.

'Friend of her brother's,' Harper replied, which was technically true even if it omitted several relevant details. 'Tomás asked me to check on her. He had a bit of an accident last night, ended up in hospital himself. Nothing serious, but Rosa was worried about missing work.'

The nurse's expression softened slightly. Healthcare workers understood family crises.

'She's in trauma two, helping with a multi-vehicle accident from this morning. Might be another hour before she can take a break.'

'Mind if I wait? I can grab coffee, won't get in anyone's way.'

'Cafeteria's on the second floor, or there are chairs down that corridor,' she pointed towards a waiting area with the sort of institutional furniture designed to be uncomfortable enough to discourage lingering while remaining functional enough to avoid lawsuits.

Harper chose the waiting area, positioning himself where he could see the trauma ward entrance while keeping his back to a wall – old habits from too many years in places where relaxing meant dying. The corridor provided an excellent vantage point for watching the controlled chaos of emergency medicine; doctors and nurses moved between rooms with an efficiency that suggested lives hung in the balance and Harper found himself cataloguing details automatically – who looked stressed, who looked competent, who looked like they might crack under pressure.

Through the half-open door, Harper saw a doctor emerge from trauma room two into the washroom that worked as a kind of airlock between corridor and surgical area, scrubs stained with what Harper recognised as arterial blood. She moved towards the nurses' station with a particular exhaustion that came from fighting death and losing. Behind her, Harper glimpsed Rosa Alvarez cleaning equipment, her movements suggesting someone processing stress through routine. A few minutes later, Rosa emerged from the trauma room, pulling off gloves and moving towards a sink to wash her hands. She looked exactly like someone who'd spent the last several hours trying to keep people alive, so Harper waited until she'd finished at the sink before approaching, knocking on the door.

'Rosa?'

She turned, surprise flickering across her face before settling into wariness.

'Harper. What are you doing here?'

'Wanted to check on you. And ask you some questions, if you've got a few minutes.'

Rosa glanced towards a clock on the wall, calculating time and responsibilities.

'I can take fifteen minutes,' she said.

THE HOSPITAL CAFETERIA OCCUPIED A LARGE SPACE ON THE second floor, filled with the sort of furniture and fluorescent lighting that made everything look slightly unreal. Rosa led them to a corner table away from other staff, accepting a cup of coffee that looked strong enough to revive the dead.

'You go visit Tomás?' she asked, settling into her chair with the careful movement of someone who'd been on her feet for twelve hours.

'Briefly.'

'How is he?'

'Healing. Stubborn about following medical advice, but that probably runs in the family.'

'It does,' Rosa smiled slightly. 'So, what questions do you have for me?'

Harper leaned forward, keeping his voice low enough to avoid drawing attention from neighbouring tables.

'In your work here, have you noticed any patterns?

Specific types of injuries or illnesses that seem concentrated in particular neighbourhoods?'

Rosa's expression shifted from tired friendliness to professional wariness.

'You're not really investigating a business dealing, are you? This is something bigger.'

Harper met her gaze, noting the intelligence behind the exhaustion. Rosa Alvarez was clearly someone who'd learned to read people accurately – a skill that probably kept her alive in emergency medicine.

'It's personal,' Harper said finally. 'As I said last night, my father was involved in whatever happened at the South Yards years ago. I'm trying to understand what he was part of, and whether it's still affecting people.'

'And you think it might be connected to what Tomás lied about?'

'I think your brother stumbled into something that powerful people want to keep buried. And I think those same people have been burying evidence for decades.'

Rosa sipped her coffee, considering.

'Hypothetically,' she said slowly, 'if someone wanted to track environmental health impacts, they'd look for specific patterns. Respiratory issues in select age groups. Neurological symptoms without clear causation. Cancer clusters that don't match regional averages.'

'And hypothetically, have you seen anything like that?'

Rosa was quiet for a long moment, staring into her coffee cup.

'About six months ago, I started noticing an increase in respiratory complaints from the South Side. Nothing dramatic, but enough to catch my attention. Patients complaining of persistent coughs, breathing difficulties, fatigue. Mostly in the twenty-five to forty-five age range.'

'Construction workers?'

'Some. But also residents of the neighbourhoods around the South Yards. People who shouldn't have occupational exposure to industrial chemicals.'

'Did you report it?'

'I mentioned it to my supervisor. She said it was probably seasonal allergies, maybe some kind of environmental irritant. Nothing that required official documentation.'

'But you didn't agree?'

Rosa's smile held no warmth.

'I've been working emergency medicine for years, Harper. I know the difference between seasonal allergies and chemical exposure. These patients were showing symptoms consistent with industrial contamination.'

'What kind of contamination?'

'Based on the symptom patterns? Probably volatile organic compounds, maybe some heavy metal exposure. The sort of thing you'd probably see from improper disposal of industrial waste. But I couldn't work out how two separate areas had the same issues, especially when one area was supposed to have been cleansed, and the other was unconnected.'

Harper leaned back, pieces falling into place. Tomás had shown him the trucks spreading the contaminated soil to other locations, including the South Side. Rosa was seeing the health effects in emergency patients from that area. His father's note and evidence suggested the problem had been covered up for decades.

'How many patients are we talking about?'

'Fifteen to twenty over the last six months. Not enough to

trigger official investigation protocols, but enough to suggest a pattern.'

'And your supervisor wasn't interested in pursuing it?'

Rosa's expression darkened.

'My supervisor's Doctor Josephine Fleming. Big name in Chicago, been here for twenty years, very concerned about the hospital's relationship with community leaders and corporate donors. The sort of person who prefers not to see problems that might create uncomfortable questions.'

'Corporate donors like Slate Urban Development?'

'Among others. The hospital depends on community support, Harper. Creating public health scares isn't good for fundraising.'

Harper absorbed this, understanding another layer of the cover-up. It wasn't just about bribing inspectors and manipulating environmental reports. It was about controlling every institution that might detect or report them.

'These patients,' Harper said. 'Do you still have their contact information?'

Rosa hesitated.

'That would be a HIPAA violation. I can't share patient information without legal justification.'

'What if there was legal justification? What if someone was building a case against the people responsible for their exposure?'

'Then that someone would need to go through proper channels. Subpoenas, official investigations, legitimate law enforcement involvement.'

Harper nodded, understanding her position. Rosa was a healthcare professional with ethical obligations and legal constraints. She couldn't just hand over patient information to someone claiming to investigate environmental crimes.

But she could point him in the right direction.

'If someone wanted to document environmental health impacts in that area,' Harper said carefully, 'where would they start?'

Rosa finished her coffee, clearly reaching the end of her break.

'They might start by talking to community health workers in the affected neighbourhoods. People who know the residents, understand the local patterns. The South Side Community Health Centre, for example. Doctor Michael Santos runs their environmental health programme.'

'Santos?'

'Good doctor, dedicated to his community. The sort of person who might have noticed patterns that larger institutions prefer to ignore. Works the graveyard shift, so you'll find him there after seven.'

Rosa stood, checking her watch.

'I need to get back. But Harper? Be careful who you trust with this information. If there really is a cover-up, then the people involved have resources you probably can't imagine.'

'Your brother said something similar.'

'Tomás is right. And he's also in danger, whether he admits it or not.' Rosa's expression hardened. 'These people already tried to silence him once. They won't hesitate to try again.'

HARPER'S PHONE BUZZED AS HE EXITED THE HOSPITAL LOBBY; A text message from an unknown number.

Your friend Tomás needs to be more careful about the company he keeps. So do you.

Harper deleted the message and quickened his pace towards the parking garage. The game was accelerating, and subtlety was apparently over. Slate's people weren't just investigating him any more – they were making threats.

Which meant it was time to stop being reactive and start being proactive.

The afternoon sun cast long shadows across Chicago's urban landscape as Harper retrieved the Bonneville, thinking about Doctor Santos and the South Side Community Health Centre. If Rosa was right, Santos might have documented patterns that could provide the evidence needed to expose the cover-up. But first, Harper needed to understand exactly how much danger Tomás was in, and whether they had time for careful investigation or needed to move immediately to prevent more violence.

His phone buzzed again. This time it was a number he recognised – Colonel Crowe.

Remember – 6pm tonight.

Harper checked his watch – it was just past five in the afternoon, but it seemed Crowe was eager for this conversation about Alfie Reeves, and whatever the hell had happened in Syria that had left a supposedly dead SRR sergeant wandering the streets of Chicago.

THE RIDE BACK TOWARDS DOWNTOWN TOOK HIM THROUGH neighbourhoods that told Chicago's story in real time. Gleaming towers giving way to working-class residential areas, then to blocks where "urban renewal" meant displacing poor people to make room for expensive developments. Slate's South Yards project was just the latest chapter in an old story – economic progress for some built on environmental costs for others.

Harper had grown up just privileged enough to avoid these costs, especially while living with his grandfather, but his father's journal suggested Dominic Kane had spent years helping to impose them on people who couldn't fight back. Whether that had been deliberate or just the inevitable result of corporate security work was a question Harper was beginning to think might not matter.

The Chicago Hilton and Towers occupied prime real estate on South Michigan Avenue, and Harper left the Bonneville with valet parking. *Kitty O'Sheas* occupied the hotel's ground floor, styled as an authentic Irish pub complete with dark wood panelling and Guinness taps. The prices suggested only tourists with healthy expense accounts could afford to drink here regularly, which probably suited everyone perfectly.

Colonel Crowe sat at a corner table, looking older than Harper remembered. Grey threading through what had been dark brown hair, civilian clothes that were probably bespoke since he left the army a couple of years earlier, but the bearing was still unmistakably military.

'Harper,' Crowe stood as he approached. 'Drink?'

'Just a Coke, please.' Harper settled across from him, noting how Crowe had positioned himself with clear views of both entrances.

Old habits.

The barman brought a glass without being asked twice – clearly Crowe had been here long enough to establish expectations.

'So,' Crowe said once they were alone, 'Alfie Reeves. You're certain it was him?'

'Unless he's got a twin brother with the same walk and the same scar on his left hand.' Harper sipped his Coke. 'That said, you don't seem surprised at the news. What happened in Syria, sir?'

Crowe was quiet for a long moment, staring into his whisky.

'Alfie was selling weapons,' he said finally. 'Not to insurgents – to Syrian opposition groups we were officially supporting. Problem was, he was modifying them first, and some of those modifications made their way to people who shouldn't have had them.'

'How bad?'

'Three SAS operatives died in an ambush. The weapons used against them had Alfie's modifications.' Crowe met Harper's eyes. 'He wasn't selling to the enemy directly, but his greed got our people killed.'

Harper absorbed this.

'Was he there?'

'Of course not.'

'But the official reports said there was a vehicle explosion after the attack, and he was killed in it.'

'The body they found wasn't Alfie.' Crowe sipped at his drink. 'It was another soldier, one who was "off books".'

'You mean a spook.'

'Whatever, but the fact of the matter was that nobody should have died. I staged the whole thing. The plan was to pull him out before the convoy was hit, make sure the explosion looked convincing, then exfiltrate him through unofficial channels.'

'You say "the plan" in a way that suggests it didn't work.'

'We couldn't get to him in time. The ambush was two streets earlier than expected. By the time we got there, the SAS soldiers were dead, and the vehicle was nothing more than charred wreckage, the spook nothing but barbecue. Rather than explain why an unknown civilian was in their vehicle, with Alfie missing, believed either blown from the truck or vaporised, we simply matched the records to give him a "body" to be buried.'

Crowe sighed.

'The plan was to prevent a scandal that would have destroyed regimental cooperation between British and American forces. The weapons trade he was involved in implicated people on both sides of the Atlantic.' Crowe downed the rest of the glass. 'Problem is, Alfie doesn't know that. He thinks we left him for dead in that convoy. He's spent five years believing his own unit abandoned him, rather than he screwed up his own *get-out* clause.'

'And now he's in Chicago.'

'Most likely working security for the Veterans' Gala in a couple of days. Perfect cover to get close to me.' Crowe signalled for another whisky. 'He wouldn't have tried while I was serving, he's too much of a soldier for that, but I've been corporate for two years now. He wants me dead, Harper, and he's got the skills to make it happen.'

Harper leaned back, whistling.

'Why tell me? Why not just skip the event?'

'Because if I run, he'll follow. And eventually he'll

succeed.' Crowe's voice carried old regrets. 'At least this way, it's controlled. Predictable.'

'You want to let him kill you?'

'Honestly, if he's in town? I want you to talk him out of it. He might listen to someone from the unit, someone who knew him before everything went wrong.'

Harper considered this. Alfie had been decent enough in the field, but always pushing boundaries.

'Where's he been for five years?'

'Officially? Dead. Unofficially? All over the place. He's ex-SRR, Liam. He would have had an untraceable new identity, clean records, spending cash within hours. Hell, half of us had that while we were serving. I heard a year back he was out there, working private security. I was out too by then, so I sent feelers out, saying that I was sorry for what happened and wanted to start over.' Crowe's expression darkened. 'Apparently that wasn't enough.'

'Maybe he doesn't want to start over. Maybe he wants justice.'

'Maybe. But killing me won't bring back the men who died – both from his weapons and from the explosion, and it won't expose the people actually responsible for the weapons trade.'

Harper sipped his drink, now understanding why Crowe had wanted this chat.

'The people actually responsible – they still out there?'

'Very much so. Still profiting from arms sales, still using official channels to facilitate unofficial business.' Crowe looked directly at Harper now. 'Your father's old company, for instance.'

The words hit like cold water.

'Aegis?'

'Aegis facilitated the transport and documentation for Alfie's weapons modifications. They provided the legitimate cover that made his illegal sales possible.' Crowe leaned forward. 'Dominic Kane was the Aegis representative who signed off on the paperwork.'

Harper felt his world shift slightly. *His father hadn't just known about the weapons trade – he'd enabled it.*

'You're saying my father got those SAS operatives killed?'

'I'm saying your father was part of a system that prioritised profit over proper oversight. Whether he knew the full implications...' Crowe shrugged. 'That was between him and his conscience.'

'Why the hell were you dealing with him?'

'Because I needed to keep a lid on things!' Crowe snapped. 'Your father kept in touch a lot, believe it or not. He wanted to make sure you were okay. I realised he was an off-books option I could use, and when he realised this was a problem he'd started – or, at least his company had – he offered to help. I just didn't realise how permanent that was.'

Harper's phone buzzed, which gave him a moment to look away, still reeling from the ramifications of what Crowe had said.

His father had been keeping tabs on him, after all.

It was another text from the unknown number.

> Still in Chicago? Your father's friends are getting impatient. Time to leave.

Harper showed the screen to Crowe.

'You know anything about this?'

Crowe studied the message.

'Your father didn't have many friends, so this must be

Mason Carrick's people, I'd guess. They've been tracking you since you arrived.'

'How did they get my number?'

'How would *you* get a number?' Crowe shrugged. 'They're not idiots, Liam.'

'I only picked this number up a week back.' Harper leaned back on the booth. 'That's impressive, especially as it's a burner phone.'

Crowe shrugged.

'Then I have no idea. But there's something else. If he's here and on a mission, Alfie isn't just planning to kill *me* at the gala.'

'What do you mean? Who else does he want?'

'Mason Carrick.'

Harper forced his expression to stay neutral as he took this in.

Suddenly Chicago was becoming significantly more complicated.

'Carrick will be at the gala?'

'Carrick's one of the event sponsors. Major donor, gets a table near the stage.' Crowe finished his second whisky. 'Alfie blames him as much as he blames me. Carrick ran Aegis operations; I ran military coordination. He might have been the greedy screw up, but as far as he's concerned, between us, we destroyed his life.'

'And now he wants revenge on both of you.'

'Justice, from his perspective. Which might be the same thing.'

Harper considered his options. Slate's people had identified him, Carrick's people were hunting him, and now he was caught between a colonel who might deserve to die and a soldier who definitely didn't deserve to live as a dead man.

'What do you need from me?'

'Talk to him. Make him understand that killing Carrick and me won't fix what's broken.' Crowe stood, leaving money on the table. 'And Harper? Watch yourself. Alfie's not the broken soldier he used to be. From what I've heard, five years of believing everyone betrayed him has turned him into something else.'

Crowe walked away, leaving Harper alone with his half-finished Coke and the growing realisation that the Veterans' Gala was going to be a bloodbath unless he could stop it.

At least now he understood why everyone wanted him gone. Chicago wasn't just hiding environmental crimes – it was hiding military secrets that connected to international arms dealing, staged deaths, and the sort of shadow operations that governments preferred to deny existed.

Bloody brilliant. Just another typical weekday in the life of Liam Harper.

Time to stop reacting and start hunting.

7

HOUSE HUNTING

THE SOUTH SIDE COMMUNITY HEALTH CENTRE LOOKED LIKE someone had taken a warehouse and given it a medical degree – all good intentions and making do with whatever funding could be scraped together from guilty consciences and government programmes. Harper parked the Bonneville three blocks away this time, because paranoia was just pattern recognition with anxiety issues, and his pattern recognition was working overtime these days.

The health centre itself was a testament to optimism over funding. Fresh paint couldn't quite hide the old brick underneath, solar panels looked like they'd been donated by someone's guilty conscience, and the car park held vehicles that suggested patients who scheduled medical appointments around work shifts they couldn't afford to miss.

Harper spent ten minutes watching who came and went; elderly folks moving like every step cost money, young mothers juggling children and worry, working-age adults grabbing healthcare between everything else. The sort of people who'd be canaries in Slate's coal mine.

Doctor Michael Santos emerged from his car at exactly seven p.m., which made him either very punctual or very tired. Probably both. Younger than Harper had expected – maybe forty – but carrying himself like someone who'd spent years fighting bureaucracy armed only with medical ethics. Harper had seen his photo on a Google search, but the man here looked way more tired than he did six months earlier, it seemed.

'Doctor Santos?'

Santos turned, automatically shifting into the polite wariness that healthcare workers developed when strangers approached them in car parks after dark.

'Yes?'

'My name's Harper. Rosa Alvarez suggested we talk about environmental health issues round here.'

Recognition flickered across Santos's face.

'Ah. Rosa dropped me a message, said you might turn up. You're investigating the South Yards mess?'

'Among other things. Fancy a chat somewhere that doesn't involve standing in a car park like we're conducting a drug deal?'

Santos actually smiled at that, checking his watch.

'I've still got half an hour before I start, and there's a diner two blocks over,' he was already walking. 'Come on then, let me give you the horror story.'

THE DINER WAS EXACTLY WHAT HARPER EXPECTED – VINYL booths that had witnessed decades of questionable life choices, fluorescent lighting that made everyone look like they were dying of something terminal, and coffee that had been sitting on the burner since the Clinton administration. Santos chose a corner booth away from other customers, sitting where he could watch the entrance.

Smart man. Harper was starting to like him.

'So,' Santos said once they'd ordered coffee, 'Rosa says you're looking into contamination round the South Yards. What's your angle?'

Harper kept it simple.

Mostly.

'Family connection to the original development. Trying to understand what got buried and who's still paying for it.'

Santos studied him. Harper had the feeling he was being assessed for trustworthiness, competence, or possibly mental stability.

'You're not a journalist?'

'Christ, no.'

'Law enforcement?'

'Not in any official capacity.'

Santos seemed to reach a decision.

'Right. Because what I'm about to tell you probably violates half a dozen professional guidelines, and I really don't need official complications on top of everything else.'

Harper leaned forward, unconsciously rolling his river stone between his fingers.

'I'm listening.'

Santos pulled out his phone, scrolling through notes.

'Over the last eighteen months, I've documented forty-three cases of respiratory complaints, neurological symptoms, and skin conditions that don't match regional patterns. All from residents within a two-mile radius of the South Yards development.'

'Forty-three confirmed cases?'

'That's just what I've personally treated. There are probably twice that many who haven't sought medical attention because they can't afford it, don't trust doctors, or assume feeling like shit is just part of living where they live.'

Harper absorbed this. Forty-three people sick enough to seek medical help, probably eighty more suffering in silence.

'This is from people nearby? Not living on?'

'Nobody lives there yet,' Santos shook his head. 'Being honest? I think this was a sleeping dog issue.'

'You mean as in "let sleeping dogs lie"?' Harper frowned.

'Twenty years they've had toxic waste buried there,' Santos explained. 'All done legitimately, professionally. Two years back, Slate takes over the site, started to "clean it" as per the deal she made when she bought it. I'm guessing you've seen how she does this?'

'Scoops up dirt and dumps it elsewhere,' Harper nodded. 'Let me guess. By doing this she's exposed the bad ground two years ago, and now it's just left exposed while they carry on?'

'Pretty much.'

'What sort of symptoms are we talking about?'

'Persistent coughs that don't respond to treatment. Breathing difficulties in people with no history of respiratory problems. Chronic fatigue, skin rashes, headaches, memory issues. Three cases of childhood asthma in families with absolutely no genetic predisposition.' Santos stared into his coffee for a moment, then continued. 'There's this eight-year-old girl, Maria. Brought in by her grandmother because she couldn't stop coughing. Healthy kid, no allergies, no family history of respiratory issues. But her lungs sound like she's been smoking for thirty years.'

His voice carried the weight of too many similar cases.

'Grandmother keeps asking me what's wrong with her granddaughter, why she can't breathe properly. What am I supposed to tell her? That someone's poisoned the ground where they live?'

Harper felt the anger building in his chest.

An eight-year-old girl.

'Then there's Carlos Batista, forty-two, construction worker on the South Yards. Comes in with skin lesions that won't heal, neurological symptoms that make his hands shake so badly he can't work. Man's got three kids and a mortgage, but now he can barely hold a cup of coffee.' Santos's jaw tightened. 'His supervisor sent him to three different doctors trying to find one who'd say it was a pre-existing condition, something not work-related.'

'Did they find one?'

'Company doctor said it was probably hereditary. Carlos's family has lived in that neighbourhood for two generations – his parents, his siblings, none of them ever had anything like this. But corporate doctors don't care about family medical history when there's liability to avoid. And his company doctor works for...'

'Slate,' Harper connected the dots together. 'You've reported this?'

Santos's smile could have curdled milk.

'Filed reports with the city health department, state environmental agency, the CDC. Want to guess what response I received?'

'Let me think... bureaucratic bollocks?'

'Worse. Two months ago, someone from Slate Urban Development paid us a visit. Very polite, very professional, very generous. Offered substantial funding for our community outreach programmes.'

Harper felt that familiar tingle that meant he was on to something properly nasty.

'In exchange for what?'

'They didn't say directly. But they made it abundantly clear that continued reporting of environmental health concerns might affect our eligibility for their community investment initiative.' Santos's expression darkened. 'Corporate speak for "shut up or we'll cut off your funding".'

'You told them to sod off?'

'I did. My board of directors was considerably less enthusiastic about that decision. Apparently, medical ethics are negotiable when the electricity bill isn't.'

Santos pulled out a manila folder from his briefcase, glancing round the diner before sliding it across.

'I put this together when Rosa texted. Anonymised case summaries. Names and addresses removed, but symptom patterns, onset dates, geographic distribution intact. Not enough for a formal epidemiological study, but enough to see what's happening.'

Harper accepted the folder, noting the weight of forty-three lives reduced to medical shorthand.

'Why risk this?'

'Because forty-three people trusted me with their health, and I can't help them by pretending their problems don't exist.' Santos finished his coffee like it was medicine. 'And because whoever's responsible for this contamination is about to build luxury housing on top of it. Hundreds more families poisoned so someone can turn a profit.'

Harper flipped through the case summaries. Geographic clustering round the South Yards, symptom progression that painted a picture of systematic environmental poisoning.

'These match what Rosa's seeing at Northwestern Memorial?'

'Rosa sees the acute cases – people sick enough to need emergency intervention. I see the chronic low-level exposure effects. Together, it's a textbook example of environmental health disaster that's being systematically ignored.'

'Any idea what specific nasties we're dealing with?'

Santos hesitated, then seemed to decide Harper was worth the full truth.

'I managed to get soil samples analysed independently. Cost me personally – had to send them to a lab in Wisconsin to avoid local political complications.'

'And?'

'Heavy metals, volatile organic compounds, industrial chemicals I couldn't even identify. Concentration levels that should have triggered immediate area evacuation and federal environmental emergency protocols.'

Harper closed the folder, understanding another piece of the puzzle.

'Instead of which, it's being buried under expensive flats.'

'Literally and figuratively.' Santos stood, dropping money on the table. 'Harper, whoever you really are, be bloody careful who you share this with. My car's been broken into twice this month – nothing stolen, just everything searched. Office was burgled last week – again, nothing taken, but every file rifled through.'

'Looking for evidence?'

'Looking for anything that could compromise their operation. Medical records, test results, correspondence with regulatory agencies.' Santos met Harper's eyes. 'These people don't just make threats. They follow through. Keep the envelope, I can always make more copies.'

HARPER WALKED BACK TOWARDS THE BONNEVILLE, THINKING about poisoned children and corporate intimidation, about medical ethics and systematic cover-ups. Santos's folder felt like documentation of ongoing atrocity, but without official backing, it was just a paper trail of suffering that powerful people preferred to ignore.

His phone buzzed. Text from an unknown number.

Still in Chicago? Unfortunate.

Harper deleted it and quickened his pace. Whoever this was thought they were scaring him, but in actuality they were just pissing him off, especially as he still didn't know how they got his number. Subtlety was apparently over, though. Time to check whether his digs were still secure.

Another buzz. Different number.

Last chance to leave voluntarily.

This time Harper tried calling back. But it went straight to an automated system claiming the number was no longer in service. Professional intimidation but executed like amateurs. Either Slate's people were getting sloppy, or they wanted Harper to know he was being hunted.

Probably both.

Harper was still a block from his father's building when he spotted the surveillance. Two blokes in business suits having a chat near the entrance, positioned to observe everyone coming and going. Professional setup, but too obvious for serious operational security.

They *wanted* to be seen.

Harper continued on and parked four blocks away before approaching on foot, using shop windows and building reflections to watch the watchers. The original two were still there, but now Harper could spot others – the same woman from that morning, now reading a newspaper in a coffee shop across the street, and a man checking his phone at a bus stop, while glancing his way.

After spending time watching, he saw at least six people conducting surveillance. This was either serious overkill for intimidation, or preparation for something more aggressive.

Harper pulled out his phone and checked the motion alert history from his father's apartment cameras. Nothing unusual – the apartment remained secure, cameras showing empty rooms exactly as he'd left them.

But that didn't mean his *hotel* room was.

Harper continued past the building without breaking stride. In his peripheral vision, one of the watchers spoke into their radio. They'd spotted him but weren't moving to intercept, still just watching.

Which suggested they'd already found what they were looking for elsewhere.

Bloody brilliant. Time to check whether the Riverside Hotel was still viable.

Harper used the same department store he'd used before, one with multiple exits for basic surveillance detection – ten minutes moving through different floors, using escalators, changing direction randomly. By the time he emerged through the loading dock, he was confident he'd lost any pursuit.

But if they knew where he was going, then all of this was for nothing.

THE RIVERSIDE HOTEL LOOKED EXACTLY AS TIRED AS WHEN he'd first seen it. Same faded signage, same brick frontage that had given up caring years earlier. But Harper had developed an eye for details most people missed, and something felt wrong.

He approached through the back alley, using the service entrance. The lock on his door looked normal, but Harper had learned paranoia was a survival skill and had left a tiny piece of tape along the door frame – invisible unless you knew where to look, displaced if the door opened.

The tape was displaced. Someone had opened the door.

Harper stood in the corridor, considering options. Whoever had searched his room might still be inside, or they'd left surveillance equipment. Or they'd just had a poke about and departed, leaving him with compromised accommodation and nowhere secure to kip.

Probably should have kept a camera for here. Oh well, only one way to find out.

Harper unlocked the door and stepped inside.

Everything looked exactly as he'd left it. *Too* exactly. The glass of water on the bedside table hadn't moved, clothes over the chair were precisely positioned, even his battered paperback remained open to the same page.

It had been a professional search. Someone had been through every inch, then replaced everything with military precision. They'd been looking for something specific and had probably found it.

Or had they? Was he just being paranoid now? Had they pulled the tape just to screw with him?

Harper checked his kit systematically and immediately knew he'd been correct. The laptop was powered down, but the hard drive was warm – they'd accessed it, but Harper wasn't stupid enough to leave sensitive files on an unencrypted machine. His sketchbook sat exactly where he'd left it, but the pages showed stress marks from being flattened and photographed. Even his wash kit had been gone through, his toothbrush moved, toiletries replaced in positions that matched his habits but didn't align exactly.

They'd been thorough, but they'd found mostly bread-crumbs. The actual evidence – his father's notebook was constantly in his satchel right now, as well as the photographs he'd grabbed from the Vault, and now Santos's medical files. It wasn't a brilliant plan, as if they'd taken him off the street they'd have it all, but he'd only just picked up some of this, and it was still fresh.

Still, they'd have learned enough. His browsing history, his research patterns... they'd probably even traced his movements through Chicago, which meant they now knew he was asking the right questions, even if they hadn't found all the answers.

His burner had been connected as a hotspot to his laptop the previous day. Was this how they got the number?

They knew he'd been to the South Yards; knew he'd posed as Sheriff Coble.

Probably worked out he was connected to Tomás and Rosa.

Harper felt a cold anger building in his chest. This wasn't just surveillance – it was violation. Someone had touched his belongings, invaded his space, rifled through his life like he was a filing cabinet. The game had changed completely. He wasn't investigating any more – he was in open warfare with people who had resources, connections, and absolutely no scruples about using both.

Wonderful. Time to relocate before watching became something more aggressive.

His father's building offered better security than the Riverside, but more than that – if Slate's people were going to hunt him anyway, might as well stop hiding. They knew he was in Chicago, knew what he was investigating. Playing the invisible game was over – time to use the advantages his inheritance actually provided. Proper security, discreet staff, and Frank, who'd already demonstrated he understood operational discretion. Plus access to resources Harper might need if things got more complicated.

He packed quickly, leaving behind anything non-essential. The room was blown, which meant the entire hotel was probably under surveillance.

He didn't even check for cameras or bugs. Hopefully, when they went back, the fact he hadn't might confuse them even more.

FRANK WAS READING HIS NEWSPAPER WHEN HARPER SLIPPED IN through the side entrance.

'Thought you might be back,' Frank said without looking up. 'Had visitors earlier. Very polite, very professional. Asked lots of questions about your father's apartment.'

'What sort of questions?'

'The sort that suggested they weren't actually from any estate lawyer's office.' Frank folded his paper. 'Told them what I tell everyone – building management doesn't discuss tenant information without proper legal documentation.'

'They buy that?'

'They did when I mentioned our security system records everyone entering the premises, and those recordings get automatically forwarded to our legal department.' Frank's smile suggested he was enjoying himself. 'Amazing how quickly people remember urgent appointments when you mention lawyers and camera footage.'

Harper almost smiled. Frank was clearly more than just a doorman.

'Frank, hypothetically speaking, if someone needed to stay in the building without being noticed by people watching from outside, how would they manage it?'

Frank studied Harper's face.

'Hypothetically?'

'Hypothetically.'

'Freight elevator to the apartment goes straight to the parking garage. North side entrance, street view blocked by loading dock. Your motorbike would fit in the elevator if someone wanted to keep transport close.'

'You've considered this before.'

'Your father asked similar questions. Some habits are worth keeping.' Frank returned to his newspaper. 'I think he even bought the place based on the proximity to the elevator.'

There wasn't any point using the freight elevator this time, so Harper simply travelled up to his father's – no, *his* – apartment, and once inside called in some takeout under Frank's name, deciding to at least wait comfortably while planning his next moves. As he waited for his burger and fries, Harper set up his laptop and reviewed Santos's evidence alongside his father's photographs.

There was a knock at the door – checking, Harper saw a paper bag on his doorstep, and Frank walking off. Opening the door and bringing it inside, Harper pulled out the food and wolfed it down ravenously.

Forty-three documented cases of environmental poisoning. Geographic patterns linking directly to South Yards contamination. Combined with decades of cover-up evidence, it painted a picture of ongoing public health disaster being buried under corporate development.

But evidence was only useful if you could present it to people with power to act. So far, everyone with that power seemed compromised or intimidated into silence.

Time to shout a little louder then, it seemed.

8

GHOSTS

HARPER WOKE AT FIVE-THIRTY, HIS BODY CLOCK STILL SET TO AN almost subconscious military time despite the comfortable bed in his father's apartment. Outside, Chicago was having one of those mornings where the sky couldn't decide between rain and just *threatening* to rain, settling on the sort of persistent drizzle that made everything look like a damp postcard nobody wanted to send home.

Yesterday's chat with Crowe had added another complication to an already messy situation. Alfie Reeves – alive, bitter, and planning to turn tomorrow night's Veterans' Gala into his personal revenge fantasy. Problem was, Harper already had his hands full with Slate's environmental cover-up, the escalating threats against the Alvarez family, and Mason Carrick's teams hunting him across Chicago.

Now he had to worry about a dead soldier planning to commit very public murder at the same event where Harper needed to expose decades of contamination?

Great.

The threats against Tomás and Rosa were escalating. Santos's medical evidence showed children getting sicker. Slate's people had searched his room and were clearly preparing for something more aggressive than surveillance.

Again, great.

Harper made coffee – this time using a coffee machine rather than the instant he'd had the previous morning – and considered his options, considering what he'd heard the previous day at the Reserves.

'Slate wants the South Yards groundbreaking moved up to next week. Something about new investors who want to see immediate progress. She's gonna announce everything in a couple of days.'

Did they mean the Veterans' Gala? If so, it might be his best chance. Slate would probably be there networking, cementing political connections. Media would be present. If Harper could expose the contamination publicly, in front of cameras and politicians, it would be harder to bury.

Except now Alfie was planning to turn the event into a bloodbath, so Harper had a new puzzle – tracking down a supposedly dead soldier who was wandering around Chicago like some sort of military ghost with employment issues.

His phone buzzed. Another unknown number, because apparently his contact details were being passed around like a particularly unpopular party invitation.

Final warning. Leave Chicago today.

Harper deleted the message. Whoever was sending these had clearly never met him properly. Threats just made him stubborn, and he was already naturally bloody-minded enough to annoy a saint.

He pulled out his river stone, rolling the smooth grey surface between his fingers while he planned his approach. Finding someone who didn't want to be found was like playing hide-and-seek with someone who'd read the rulebook, but everyone left traces. Even dead people.

Alfie had been collecting something from a van outside the Vault. Regular contact, by the look of it, and a professional handover. But people were creatures of habit, and habits could be exploited if you knew what to look for.

Harper opened his father's notebook, searching for anything connected to private security firms in Chicago. His father had been thorough about documenting business contacts, probably because he'd learned early that today's ally could be tomorrow's person trying to kill you.

There, halfway through a list of Chicago security companies with his father's neat handwriting providing commentary, was a familiar name.

Meridian Protective Services – Executive level, discreet, cash flexible. Ask no questions, good for off-books personnel.

Off-books personnel. The sort of people who existed in the gaps between official records.

Like dead soldiers, for instance.

A quick google, and Harper found the company's website, complete with company logo; a logo he'd seen on a van's side yesterday.

A bold capital M stylised with subtle horizontal cuts like those on a rifle sight or tactical reticle.

However, as Harper studied the list, something else caught his attention. Several of these security firms had notes about South Yards contracts, environmental assessments, and what his father had euphemistically called *site preparation services.* Aegis had subcontracted work to local firms, including cleanup operations that were probably less about cleaning up and more about covering up. Aegis had subcontracted to Meridian. Was that what Slate had meant when she said Aegis wasn't working with her any more? They were simply under another name?

Whatever; this meant tomorrow night's gala wasn't just where Alfie would make his move, it was where all the people responsible for the South Yards contamination would likely be gathered in one place, celebrating their success while children got sick from poisoned soil.

Harper checked his watch. He needed to coordinate with Tomás and Rosa, make sure they were safe, and figure out how to use tomorrow night's chaos to expose the contamination. Then he could track down Alfie and decide whether to stop his revenge plot or use it as a distraction.

THE RIDE ACROSS TOWN TOOK HIM THROUGH CHICAGO'S morning rush hour, which moved about as quickly as an arthritic tortoise, even on a motorcycle. Everyone was heading to jobs that probably didn't involve hunting ghosts or investigating environmental cover-ups, lucky bastards, but it didn't help his travel speed.

Arriving back in the Loop District, he found a coffee shop near the Reserves with windows facing the right direction and settled in with a "flat white" that felt more like a quickly made Americano and tasted like it had been filtered through someone's gym socks.

At least it was hot.

He waited forty-seven minutes, during which he learned that the woman at the next table was having relationship problems with someone called Ryan who apparently couldn't remember to put the toilet seat down.

Fascinating stuff.

Really.

Then Alfie walked past Reserves.

Harper left money on the table and followed, staying back far enough to avoid detection while close enough to keep visual contact. Alfie moved through the Loop like someone with places to be, stopping twice – once at a newsstand where he bought a paper and had a brief chat with the vendor, once outside an electronics shop where he checked his phone like someone running counter-surveillance.

Old habits. The sort that kept you alive in unfriendly places but also created patterns for people who knew what to look for.

Alfie's destination was a three-storey brick building that had probably been a factory before someone decided factories weren't trendy enough for modern Chicago. Now it housed the sort of businesses that didn't advertise much: legal services, accounting firms, and other outfits that preferred discretion over flashy marketing.

Harper positioned himself across the street behind a parked van, feeling slightly ridiculous but knowing that surveillance was ninety per cent patience and ten per cent not looking like you were conducting surveillance.

At eight-thirty-seven, Alfie emerged again, carrying a package and what looked like paperwork.

Work pickup, then. Regular contractor collecting assignments.

Harper used his phone to zoom in on the building directory. Twelve different companies, most with names that could mean anything. But one matched his father's notebook and the van.

Meridian Protective Services – Executive Security Solutions.

Right. Time to see where dead soldiers went after collecting their assignments.

Harper followed Alfie for the next hour, mapping his route and timing his stops. Three different coffee shops, a deli where he bought a sandwich, and enough window-shopping to suggest he expected to be followed. Which he was, but Harper had been trained by instructors who'd taught him that the best surveillance looked like a complete accident.

Eventually, Alfie's wanderings brought him to Lincoln Park Zoo, where he sat on a bench near the Great Ape House and watched families enjoying their morning out. Seemed appropriate, really – a dead soldier watching normal life from a safe distance.

Harper found a spot behind an information board about prairie wolves and studied Alfie's face. Five years hadn't been kind. He looked older, more careful, with the sort of stillness that came from constantly expecting trouble.

Time for the direct approach.

Harper walked over, timing it casually, and when he was ten feet away, Alfie spoke without turning round.

''Bout bloody time. Spotted you an hour back. Couldn't work out if you wanted to kiss me or kill me.'

'Alfie.' Harper sat on the far end of the bench, leaving space between them because approaching dead soldiers required certain diplomatic protocols. 'You're looking well for someone who's supposed to be fertilising a grave in Birmingham.'

Alfie turned, and Harper saw what five years of being officially non-existent had done to features he remembered as younger and considerably more optimistic. The scar on Alfie's left hand was still there – souvenir from a training exercise that had gone spectacularly wrong in Herefordshire, but there were new ones on his cheek, old, maybe three, four years at best.

'Captain Harper.' Familiar warmth underneath the hard edges. 'Should have known you'd turn up eventually. Heard you were in town.'

'Oh?' Harper was actually surprised at this. 'How's that work, then? You keeping tabs on ex-SRR personnel, or just the ones stupid enough to come to Chicago?'

Alfie almost smiled.

'Word gets around. Ex-SRR captain with connections to Aegis, poking about in places that make people nervous. Chicago's not that big if you know where to listen.'

'And you've been listening.'

'Part of the job. Corporate security means knowing who might cause problems for your clients.' Alfie checked his watch. 'Problem is, I've been working this city for three years, and your name never came up until this week.'

Harper leaned back, trying to look relaxed while staying ready to move quickly if things went sideways.

'What changed?'

'Mason Carrick started making inquiries, putting word out that he was looking for someone matching your description. Right down to that bloody motorcycle you insist on riding everywhere.'

So, Carrick was definitely hunting. Harper filed that information under "Things That Complicate My Life".

'What's Carrick's interest in me?'

'That's what makes it interesting.' Alfie pulled out cigarettes, then remembered where he was and put them away. 'Man like Carrick doesn't mobilise teams and offer bounties for personal grudges. Whatever you've got on him, it's making him very nervous. Probably something to do with your dad. I don't know much, but I know you shot him on a boat or something.'

'I didn't shoot him.'

'You didn't? That's a shame. I thought you'd finally grown a pair,' Alfie sighed. 'So, what, you're now the heir apparent for Aegis, right?'

'Wrong,' Harper replied coldly. 'I never wanted anything to do with my father's life.'

'Yet you've definitely prospered from his death, though, ain't you?'

Harper felt the conversation turning into a fight and took a breath.

'What do you mean by bounties?'

'Nothing official, obviously. But word's out that finding Liam Harper comes with financial incentives. Problem was, nobody knew who Liam Harper was until Crowe started making calls about former SRR personnel and Carrick mentioned his old partner's kid.'

Harper felt that familiar chill when operational security went to pieces.

'Crowe's been talking about me?'

'Retired Colonel bloody Crowe, asking questions about ex-SRR in Chicago, specifically mentioning your name.' Alfie's expression darkened. 'Made me very curious why my supposedly dead arse might be of interest to my former commanding officer.'

'So you know Crowe's in Chicago.'

'I know Crowe's been here a week, preparing for tomorrow night's gala. I know he's staying at the Hilton, and I know he's been having meetings with people who don't officially exist.' Alfie turned to face Harper properly. 'What I don't get yet is why you're *not* investigating the same bastards who destroyed my life.'

Harper studied Alfie's face, looking for tells. Anger, definitely, but controlled.

'Tell me about Syria. Your version.'

Alfie's laugh held about as much humour as a funeral programme.

'My version? Christ, Harper, you want the whole bloody story or just the highlights?'

'Start with the weapons modifications.'

'Right. Syrian opposition forces we were officially supporting needed better kit to fight Assad's troops. Standard British equipment wasn't cutting it against Russian hardware, so I started making modifications. Better sights, improved firing mechanisms, more reliable ammunition feeds.'

'Unauthorised modifications.'

'Unauthorised by whom?' There was an edge of old frustration in Alfie's voice. 'The official mission was helping Syrian opposition forces become more effective. My modifications did exactly that.'

'Until three SAS operatives died.'

'Three good soldiers, Harper. Men I'd worked with, shared bloody awful ration packs with.' Alfie stared at his hands. 'They died in an ambush, killed by weapons I'd modified. But here's the thing – those weapons weren't supposed to be there. My modifications were distinctive, traceable. Someone had deliberately moved them to that location.'

Harper processed this.

'Someone used your modifications to set up the ambush.'

'Someone used my modifications to make sure I'd take the blame when it went wrong.' Alfie stood, checking the surroundings automatically. 'I'd been threatened with a court martial a day or so before that, and I knew they were looking to make an example of me. Didn't expect how far they'd go, though. Question is whether it was Crowe covering his reputation, or someone else entirely.'

A family walked past, parents trying to manage two boys who wanted to run ahead and see the lions. Normal people doing normal things, completely unaware they were passing two ex-soldiers discussing weapons trafficking and military betrayals.

'What about Carrick?'

'Back then, Aegis was providing security for weapons shipments. Did a lot of stuff for suits at the time. Officially protecting humanitarian supplies, but...' Alfie shrugged. 'Let's just say Mason Carrick was profiting from keeping the war going longer than necessary.'

'And my father?'

'Not so much,' Alfie admitted. 'I think he was trying to keep a low profile, what with you being the chosen one and all that.'

'You have proof?' Harper ignored the insult.

'I have suspicions. Different thing entirely.' Alfie's expression was grim. 'But I know for certain that the night before that ambush, Carrick had a private meeting with Syrian government representatives. Next day, three SAS operatives walk into a trap using weapons I'd modified.'

Harper pulled out his river stone, rolling it between his fingers while he thought. More complexity than Crowe's sanitised version had suggested. And something about the timing felt wrong.

'And you?' he asked. 'I was told you were in the attack. How did you survive?'

'I was supposed to be,' Alfie nodded slowly. 'But the night before, I came down with something. A couple of minutes before the attack, I needed to puke up whatever was causing me the shits, so I was leaning against a building when the ambush hit. I was caught in the blast when they took out the transport, but not at ground zero. I was injured and taken into a medical facility, but nobody knew who I was.'

'Didn't they check your ID? Dog tags?'

'I thought this was a hit on me,' Alfie shrugged. 'I tossed them before the medics arrived. And as I'd taken off my jacket and equipment so I didn't get puke on it, they didn't even know if I was a soldier. When they asked, I claimed I was a contractor, using a backup legend I'd created earlier.'

Harper considered this, comparing to what Crowe said. It was similar but had definite glaring issues.

'They thought the other man was you.'

Alfie nodded.

'Some MI6 spod. Poor bastard was just cadging a lift.'

'And for five years you just hid?'

'Kind of,' Alfie shook his head. 'I genuinely thought it was your dad, Colonel Crowe and Carrick – you know, who wanted me dead – so dead I stayed. And that continued up until a few months back when your dad died, and Carrick took over the whole thing.'

'Why?'

Alfie paused, staring at Harper as if he were stupid.

'You don't get it, do you?' he said softly, realisation creeping in. 'Carrick and your dad? They *were* Aegis. But Carrick had plans. Ones that couldn't be enforced as a democracy.'

Harper leaned back at this – strangely this was making more sense than he'd expected. The Mason Carrick in Prosperity had been different from the one he knew as a child.

Like he'd been let off a leash.

'So, tomorrow night at the gala, you're planning what exactly?'

Alfie's smile could have frozen Lake Michigan.

'Justice, Harper. For three dead soldiers, a dead spook and five years of my life.'

'And you think killing Crowe and Carrick brings them back?'

'No. But it stops them from destroying anyone else.' Harper could sense pain underneath the anger now. 'Five years, Harper. Five years of being officially dead, working cash jobs under false names, no family contact, no future. Because someone decided I was expendable.'

Harper studied Alfie's expression, looking for the man he'd known during joint training exercises. Still there, underneath the bitterness, but harder now, damaged in ways that went deeper than visible scars.

'Will Slate be at the gala tomorrow night as well?' Harper chanced.

'Veronica Slate? Course she will be. Major donor, political connections. Half the city's power structure will be there.' Alfie's expression sharpened. 'Why?'

'Because she's been covering up environmental contamination that's poisoning children. South Yards development is built on contaminated soil, and she's been burying the evidence for decades.'

'And you think exposing that matters more than stopping Crowe and Carrick?'

'I think forty-three documented cases of environmental poisoning matter more than settling old scores.' Harper's voice carried edge now. 'There are families, Alfie. Kids getting sick because someone decided profits mattered more than public health.'

Alfie was quiet for a moment, processing this.

'You're working the contamination case.'

'I'm working everything. Slate, Carrick, the South Yards cover-up, and now you planning to turn tomorrow night into a shooting gallery.' Harper leaned forward. 'Question is whether we can coordinate, or whether you're going to destroy my chance to save innocent people for the sake of revenge, and you're working security for the gala to get close to the same people I want to take down.'

'I'm working security because Meridian pays well and doesn't ask awkward questions about employment history that doesn't officially exist,' Alfie snapped back, before another glance at his watch. 'But yes, tomorrow night provides opportunities.'

Meridian pays well. Harper filed the piece away.

'How many innocents get hurt when you take your opportunities?' he asked.

'Fewer than if I let them continue operating.' This was followed by a grim smile. 'These people don't just destroy soldiers' lives, Harper. They profit from conflict, prolong wars, sell weapons to anyone with cash. How many innocents die so they can get rich?'

Harper stood, keeping his movements casual while staying ready for trouble.

'There might be another way.'

'Such as?'

'Help me expose what they're really doing. Environmental crimes, weapons trafficking, corporate corruption. Take them down properly instead of just personally.'

Alfie considered this, expression unreadable.

'You think evidence matters to people like them? They own judges, buy politicians, control media coverage.'

'Maybe. But I've got something that's making them nervous, otherwise they wouldn't be hunting me across three states.'

'What sort of something?'

Harper hesitated. *How much could he trust Alfie?* The man had legitimate grievances, but five years of believing everyone had betrayed him might have pushed his judgement beyond rational limits.

'My father left records. Operations, financial transactions, personnel files. Enough to cause serious problems if it reaches the right people.'

'Your father was part of the system that destroyed my life, Harper. Whatever records he left, they're insurance policies, not evidence of wrongdoing.'

'You don't know that.'

'I know enough.' Alfie checked his surroundings again, then seemed to reach a decision. 'Three weeks ago, someone broke into my apartment. Professional job, nothing stolen, everything put back exactly where it belonged.'

Harper felt a familiar cold settling in his stomach.

'Same thing happened to me yesterday.'

'Right. Except they left something behind – a photograph of my parents, taken the previous week.'

'Any idea who?'

'Could be Carrick's people, could be someone else entirely. Point is, they wanted to let me know I'm not untouchable, and they're just waiting for the right moment. Either when I step out of line, or when I'm of no use. Basically, we're both being hunted by people with serious resources.' Alfie stood, having a final watch check. 'Difference is, I know exactly who I want dead. Question is whether you're prepared to do what's necessary.'

Children's laughter carried across the park as families enjoyed their morning out. Normal life continuing while ex-soldiers negotiated the price of revenge.

'I've got work to do,' Alfie said finally. 'Security briefing in an hour, then reconnaissance work. Professional obligations and all that.'

'This won't bring back what you've lost.'

'No. But it might prevent them from taking it from someone else.'

'Why Crowe?'

Alfie stopped.

'What?'

'You said my father, Crowe and Mason Carrick,' Harper continued. 'You think Carrick and my father tried to kill you, so why go after Crowe?'

Alfie chuckled.

'Because Crowe's just as guilty as they are, and the day you understand why, you'll finally get why they all have to die.'

He disappeared into the crowd before Harper could respond.

Harper remained standing beside the bench, rolling his river stone between his fingers while processing the conversation. The worn surface was warm from handling, a familiar weight that helped him think clearly when everything else was chaos.

Alfie believed his version of events, but five years of isolation and resentment could twist anyone's perspective. Still, his account had details Crowe's story had glossed over. And the timing of that meeting between Carrick and Syrian government representatives was bloody convenient.

Harper started walking towards his motorcycle. He needed to check on Tomás and Rosa, then make sure Slate's escalating threats hadn't turned into direct action. Then he needed to figure out how to get the environmental evidence to the right people tomorrow night.

The Alfie situation was now both opportunity and complication. His revenge plot would create chaos, but chaos could provide cover for Harper's own operations. The trick was making sure innocent people didn't get caught in the crossfire.

A day and a half until the Veterans' Gala. Time enough to gather more intelligence, prepare contingencies, and decide whether Alfie Reeves was seeking justice or just very elaborate revenge.

Harper wasn't entirely sure the distinction mattered any more. But tomorrow night at Palmer House, three different stories were going to collide – his investigation into environmental cover-ups, Mason Carrick's hunt for him, and Alfie's plan for very personal justice.

His job was making sure the right people survived the impact while the environmental evidence reached the right hands. The children getting sick from contaminated soil couldn't wait for Harper to sort out military grievances.

Assuming he could figure out how to juggle multiple crises without dropping all of them, that was.

There was drizzle in the air, as if Chicago's sky still looked like it couldn't be bothered to make proper weather. Harper rode back towards the city centre, thinking about dead soldiers and buried secrets, about fathers who left dangerous inheritances and the price of keeping quiet when keeping quiet meant other people got hurt.

Tomorrow was going to be bloody interesting. In the sort of way that usually ended with people in hospital.

Or worse.

9

CONVERGENCE

VERONICA SLATE'S OFFICE OCCUPIED THE TOP FLOOR OF A STEEL and glass tower in downtown Chicago. Minimalist décor, expensive everything, windows overlooking the city like a corporate throne room – everything you'd expect from a developer who prided herself on being the future.

She was sitting at her chrome and glass desk, reading though the Veterans' Gala brochure for the following night when her assistant knocked hesitantly on the door.

'Mrs Slate? Your two o'clock is here.'

'I didn't know I had a two o'clock—' Slate started, but paused as Mason Carrick, current CEO of *Aegis Security Services* entered without ceremony. Mid-sixties, silver-haired, radiating the quiet authority of someone accustomed to being obeyed, his suit was immaculate, his manner cordial, his eyes absolutely cold.

'Mason.' Slate stood, extending her hand. 'Please excuse me. I hadn't been made aware you were coming.'

'Veronica.' His handshake was firm. 'I didn't book a meeting, decided not to call ahead. Only just arrived, you know how it is.'

He looked around the office – not with a casual stare, more with an evaluation. It was a look she'd seen many times before.

'I understand, however, we have mutual interests.'

Slate's assistant entered with some well-timed refreshment, and once they were settled with coffee, Slate dispensed with pleasantries.

'Actually, I was just thinking about you,' she said as she picked up the Veterans' Gala brochure. 'A few of us are attending this shindig tomorrow night, and I saw your company's name in the marketing. I was curious as to your role at the gala.'

'Aegis sponsors the event annually,' Mason explained. 'I attend as co-founder, maintain military relationships, pursue new contracts.'

He set down his cup.

'Routine business, and one you've not given a shit about for years, Why the sudden interest now?'

'Because someone's been investigating South Yards development,' Slate stared out of the window as she spoke. 'Environmental questions, soil contamination, regulatory compliance. Tomorrow night represents years of planning and millions in investment, Mason. We intend to use it as a kick-off point, announce the groundbreaking, but we can't risk the negative exposure if... well...'

She didn't need to continue. Mason Carrick had been there since the start – he knew the secrets that could fall out of the closet.

'Local investigators?'

'Initially, yes. However, recently we've had a new face,

someone posing as law enforcement from Nevada, accompanied by a union inspector. They gained site access before security intervened.'

Mason's expression sharpened.

'Nevada law enforcement?'

'Sheriff Eric Coble, according to his credentials. Problem is, we looked into the town he came from, Prosperity, and we learned that the real Eric Coble is currently in federal custody on corruption charges.'

Everything about Mason's demeanour shifted. His posture straightened, hands stilled, the corporate mask slipping.

'Describe this fake sheriff.'

'Early thirties, about six feet tall, dark hair, slight scar over his eyebrow. Moved like military, spoke American but something felt off about it.' Slate studied his reaction. 'You know him?'

'Unfortunately, yes. And weirdly, this is where I think we have mutual issues. I'm here looking for Liam Harper – Dominic Kane's son – and you just described him perfectly. Also, the last time I faced him was in Prosperity.'

Slate processed this. Dominic Kane had been her primary Aegis contact for years and had been involved in countless environmental assessments throughout the South Yards planning stages. They'd worked together until his death in Myanmar six months ago.

'Your former partner's son is investigating my operation?'

'Among other things. Harper's been off the radar since inheriting his father's secrets.' Mason moved to the windows, something shifting in his expression. 'I thought he was just grieving, lying low after Prosperity. But now…'

'Now what?'

'Now I'm realising I've been an idiot.' Mason's voice carried a note of grudging respect mixed with concern. ‘He got little from the will, doesn’t really have a say in the company. Not that he seems to want it, as he’s selling off most of his father’s assets and sending the money to a variety of charities or causes.’

‘Like what?’

Mason winced.

‘Well, to start with we thought he was just being philanthropic, but now we’re realising every dollar of funding has been aimed at organisations that are either against us, or in our way. We think also he gained a last, secret gift from his daddy – documentation of Aegis contracts, financial records, personnel files. Everything Dominic compiled as insurance against people like us.'

'He knows about the contamination cover-up.'

'Christ, he probably knows about everything. Myanmar operations, weapons trafficking, environmental crimes spanning decades. His father was thorough about documenting our activities, it seems.’ Mason turned back to face her. 'I got a report a few weeks ago from an associate in Maryland. Said Harper had been asking questions about old business there, stirring up trouble with local operations. I travelled there and had a meeting with the last guy who crossed him, a guy named Victor Daggett.’

‘Am I supposed to know the name?’

‘No, and I didn’t either. But what Daggett said to me was very interesting. Seems young Liam is “travelling across America with a notebook of his father’s sins, fixing them before he could finish”, according to Daggett.’

'And now he's in Chicago,’ Slate’s voice had darkened on this news.

'And now he's in Chicago, investigating your operation, using stolen law enforcement credentials.' Mason was quiet for a moment, pieces clicking together. 'Veronica, I think I've been underestimating young Harper. He's working systematically through his father's notebook, fixing what Dominic's told him to make right from beyond the grave.'

'You think this is coordinated?'

'I think this is revenge. Or justice, depending on your perspective.' Mason's expression was grim. 'He's not just investigating – he's resolving, one operation at a time.'

'How many operations did his father document?'

'Too bloody many.' Mason stared out of the window. 'If Harper's working through them chronologically, or by priority, Chicago won't be his last stop. But it might be ours if we don't handle this correctly.'

'What do you know about Harper's capabilities?'

'Military background, Special Reconnaissance Regiment. His father had him well-trained before he even enlisted. Resourceful, stubborn, completely reckless when he thinks innocent people are being hurt – my team saw the wreckage he left in Maryland.' Mason leaned forward. 'And he has a particular talent for turning our own people against us.'

'Meaning?'

'Meaning everywhere Harper goes, our local assets start asking uncomfortable questions, developing inconvenient consciences, deciding they want out of arrangements that used to be profitable.' Mason's voice carried old frustration. 'The boy has a gift for making people remember they used to have moral boundaries.'

Slate nodded at this.

'The union inspector who accompanied him. Tomás Alvarez, construction safety for the city. Harper's recruited him, probably convinced him he's saving children's lives by exposing contamination.'

She pulled up Alvarez's file on her computer. Employment history, family details, photographs.

'Widowed, two children, sister works at Northwestern Memorial Hospital.' She looked up. 'He took fifty grand from us to look away and then gained a conscience. Your man Harper saved him from a beating – I'd assumed this was coincidence, but maybe not.'

'Harper responds badly to threats against civilians. Makes him more dangerous, not less. We need different tactics if we're to remove him from the board.' Mason paced at the window. 'Isolation. Remove his allies, force him to operate alone. Desperate people make mistakes.'

'You're talking about taking hostages.'

'I'm talking about protective custody. The Alvarez family disappears into secure accommodation while we resolve the Harper situation. Clean, professional, minimal violence. Unless you've gone full scorched earth?'

Slate considered this. The approach made tactical sense, but kidnapping children was escalation she'd prefer to avoid. Too many variables, too much potential for media attention if things went wrong.

'I may have targeted the father.'

'Of course you have,' Mason didn't seem surprised in the least. 'Well, he made his own bed. But what about containment instead of elimination?'

'Or we offer Harper something he wants?' Slate suggested.

'Such as?'

'Partnership. Bring him inside, convince him we're reforming operations, cleaning up past mistakes. Make him part of the solution instead of fighting him as the problem.'

Mason's laugh was harsh.

'Veronica, I've known this little shit since he was a kid. Harper isn't interested in reform or partnership. He's interested in justice, which in his mind means destroying everything his father helped build. You can't negotiate with someone whose goal is your complete destruction.'

'Then you eliminate him.'

'*I* eliminate him?'

'As you said, he's your problem. It's just he's decided to take a shit in *my* backyard.'

Mason Carrick considered the option.

'I won't kill him, but I do want to speak to him,' he said slowly. 'Carefully, quietly, away from tomorrow night's media attention.'

'What about the extraction? Your people can handle that?'

'Conflict of interest,' Mason returned to his chair. 'Aegis maintains federal contracts – and thanks to the crap Harper pulled in Nevada, we can't risk domestic operation exposure right now. Officially? We no longer work with you. Unofficially? Our subcontractors are your muscle. If you want this union guy and his kids removed, then your security team handles family pickup.'

Slate nodded, picking up her phone and speed-dialling from memory.

'It's me. Team deployment, immediate action. Family extraction, professional standard. Two adults, two children.' Brief pause. 'Coordinates to follow.'

She ended the call and sent a message to her assistant, informing them of what needed to be completed, before she turned back to Mason Carrick.

'The Alvarez family will be secured within six hours, once

the information is passed across. So, I've covered my side of this bargain, Mason. What about Harper himself?'

'Harper's staying at his father's building downtown. Expensive address, decent security, but nothing I can't handle.' Mason moved towards the door. 'I'll deal with him personally after the family's contained. Clean resolution, no complications.'

'And if he escapes? If this goes public?'

'He won't escape. Not this time.'

Slate considered this.

'Why didn't his father destroy the evidence? Why leave it for Harper to find?'

'Insurance policy. Dominic always said if anything happened to him, the truth should come out. I thought it was just paranoid rambling.' Mason shook his head. 'Turns out he meant every word.'

'So, it wasn't a man having a "road to Damascus" moment?' Slate raised an eyebrow. 'It was a man knowing his partner was about to screw him over, and leaving a burn list for his son?'

'Stay safe, Veronica,' Mason didn't answer the question, placing the now empty coffee cup down and leaving the office.

After he left, Slate turned to the windows overlooking Chicago. Tomorrow night represented the culmination of years of planning, millions in development costs, and political relationships cultivated over decades. But if Mason Carrick was right, Harper's crusade extended far beyond environmental contamination.

Her phone buzzed.

Package secured. Beginning delivery.

She shuddered. This was outside her wheelhouse. In the past, it'd been Kane, Carrick and Aegis that had sorted this.

And that, it seemed, was a problem that claimed vengeance even after death.

HARPER PULLED UP OUTSIDE NORTHWESTERN MEMORIAL Hospital, the Bonneville's engine ticking as it cooled. The morning's conversation with Alfie had raised more questions than answers, plus the growing certainty that tomorrow night's gala would be an absolute bloody disaster regardless of what he did to prevent it.

First priority remained the Alvarez family. Check they were safe, coordinate next moves, figure out how to expose the contamination during tomorrow night's chaos without getting innocent people killed in the crossfire.

Simple plan, really. What could possibly go wrong?

The hospital lobby buzzed with the controlled chaos of a major medical facility. This time, rather than wandering around, he'd called ahead – meet in the staff car park, neutral ground with good escape routes for when things inevitably went sideways.

Harper positioned himself near the staff entrance, watching movement patterns, noting security cameras and potential exits – paranoid habits, but useful for civilian surveillance detection in hostile urban environments.

Rosa emerged twenty-five minutes later, looking exhausted. Emergency medicine drained anyone, but she moved purposefully, probably managing multiple crises simultaneously.

'Harper.' She approached cautiously. 'You look like hell. Have you even slept?'

'Had better days. I wanted to check in on you. How are things here?'

'Surviving, as ever. Did Santos help?' Rosa asked. 'I called; told him you were coming.'

'He did indeed,' Harper gave a smile. 'If things move the way I hope, we could be getting something out there tomorrow night. There's a veterans' gala in town, and I know—'

'Harper.'

A calm, forceful voice spoke from behind, carrying an edge that made his combat instincts flare like a struck match. Harper turned slowly, hands staying visible while mentally cataloguing escape routes and potential weapons.

Three men in dark suits were approaching confidently. Definitely corporate security operatives. Not street muscle – instead, these were professionals who carried expensive weapons and knew how to use them without creating media spectacles or leaving witnesses. One of them looked familiar – and after a moment Harper realised he'd been one of the men who'd been attacking Tomás that first night – the large, possibly Irish cigar-smoking man.

He'd faced Harper. Which meant he wasn't going to underestimate Harper this time.

Which meant he'd be *prepared.*

'Liam Harper,' the familiar one continued, 'we need you to step aside, and Miss Alvarez to come with us. Official business.'

Rosa stepped closer to Harper, protective instincts over-riding caution.

'What kind of official business?'

'Environmental safety investigation. We need to verify medical assessments, cross-reference with current contamination case files.' The man's smile was professionally reassuring and completely empty. 'Routine procedure, ma'am. Looking to help, nothing more. Your brother sent us.'

Harper assessed the tactical situation rapidly. Three operatives positioned to block obvious escape routes. Rosa stood between him and them, a civilian with no combat training. Hospital security possibly compromised or simply uninformed about the threat.

'I doubt that, considering the last time you saw him, you were trying to beat the crap out of him,' he replied.

The big enforcer – for that's what Harper had named him that first night – blinked, not expecting a refusal phrased like that.

'Rosa,' Harper said quietly, voice carrying command authority, 'start walking towards the hospital entrance. Now.'

'I'm afraid that's not possible,' the big enforcer said, his hand moving inside his jacket towards a concealed weapon. 'She needs to come with us immediately—'

Military training bypassed conscious thought, muscle memory taking over as Harper grabbed Rosa's arm, pulling her behind a parked ambulance while the big, familiar enforcer was still reaching for his weapon. Harper's position behind the ambulance's engine block gave him protection against anything short of armour-piercing rounds – they'd prepared for intimidation and quiet extraction, not urban combat.

'This doesn't have to escalate, Harper,' one of them said. 'Just cooperate and nobody gets hurt.'

Harper spotted a maintenance cart twenty feet away – emergency repair tools including a heavy wrench that would serve adequately as an improvised weapon. He'd need to close distance, neutralise threats quickly before hospital security responded to gunfire.

For a second he regretted not keeping the Springfield Armory Hellcat 9mm semi-automatic, taken from a man named Doyle in Maryland, on him, but that was in his father's apartment with his laptop. Harper preferred not to use guns when not needed, however, the small red "Mac-Gyver" pocket knife he had wasn't really an adequate alternative.

The standoff lasted perhaps twenty seconds but felt like twenty minutes. Three professionals calculating angles and odds against one unarmed man with better position and absolutely nothing to lose.

Harper broke the stalemate.

He sprinted towards the maintenance cart, using parked vehicles for concealment while the operatives adjusted their positions. The nearest one tried flanking left – Harper reached the cart, grabbed the heaviest wrench available, and kept moving.

'Go!' he shouted to Rosa. 'Hospital entrance, now!'

She ran while Harper engaged the closest operative. The man was professional, well-trained, but Harper had learned close-quarters combat in places where tactical mistakes meant death rather than just embarrassment. He got inside the operative's guard before the man could draw his weapon, delivering a strike that broke the man's wrist with a wrench to the gun hand that sent the weapon clattering across concrete.

Close-quarters combat. Harper's speciality.

The second operative had a clear shot, but Harper was already moving, using his disarmed opponent as a human shield while closing distance rapidly. Another precise wrench strike to the side of the knee toppled his opponent, eliminating him as an immediate threat.

The third operative was smarter, having met Harper before, and was repositioning towards the hospital entrance to cut off Rosa's escape route.

Harper couldn't allow that.

He snatched the first dropped weapon – a Sig Sauer P320, professional quality hardware – and put a round into the big enforcer's thigh. Non-fatal but completely incapacitating.

Three down, Rosa safe, situation contained.

Harper quickly collected their remaining weapons and spare magazines, smashed their phones, and secured them with zip-tie restraints from his kit. Professional habit – always carry restraints when expecting trouble, because trouble always found him, eventually.

As Harper did this, something caught his attention near where the cigar-smoking enforcer had fallen. A silver cigar case, high-quality metal with Cuban customs stamps still visible, and likely fallen from the man's jacket during the fight. Harper picked it up, noting the weight and craftsmanship. Inside, three *Cohiba Esplendidos* nestled in individual slots – Cuban cigars sometimes worth more than most people made in a day.

'Professional hazard pay?' Harper asked the wounded operative.

The man's reaction was telling – more concerned about the cigars than his bullet wound. Like they represented status rather than just tobacco.

Harper resisted the urge to take the cigars out and snap them one by one, and instead simply tossed the case to the ground.

'Rosa!' he called towards the hospital entrance. 'All clear!'

She emerged cautiously, medical staff peering out nervously behind her.

'You hurt?' Harper asked, conducting a rapid visual assessment.

'Terrified but not injured.' Rosa looked at the three incapacitated operatives. 'Who the hell are they?'

'Slate's people. Which means she knows exactly who I am, knows about our investigation, and is escalating from surveillance to direct action.'

Harper felt cold certainty settling in his chest.

'Routine procedure, ma'am. Looking to help, nothing more. Your brother sent us.'

'Rosa, where's Tomás right now?'

'At the apartment, I think. Why are you asking?'

Rosa pulled out her phone before Harper answered and speed-dialled Tomás's number. Straight to voicemail after four rings. She tried again immediately, but gained the same result – voicemail pickup, no answer.

'We need to get to your brother's place immediately,' Harper said. 'You rode on a bike before?'

THE ROUTE TO TOMÁS'S APARTMENT TOOK THEM THROUGH Chicago neighbourhoods where gentrification was fighting urban decay for control of every street corner.

'Harper,' Rosa shouted into his ear as they navigated traffic, 'those men knew exactly who you were.'

Harper manoeuvred around a double-parked delivery truck, considering how much additional information to reveal.

'There's a man named Mason Carrick in Chicago. He's

been coordinating with Slate, probably since I used false Sheriff credentials at South Yards. They've identified me as the primary threat to their operations.'

'And now they might have Tomás.'

'Now they *probably* have Tomás, which means they're escalating beyond intimidation to direct action. Taking hostages, forcing confrontation on their terms.' Harper's voice carried the old anger that came from seeing innocent people hurt by his enemies. 'They've made this personal.'

'What does that mean for my brother's safety?'

'It means we get him back before they can move him to a more secure location or eliminate him as a potential liability,' Harper replied curtly while negotiating a turn. 'Rosa, I need you to understand something important. These people don't make empty threats or issue warnings they don't intend to follow through on. If we don't stop this situation now, Tomás dies and the contamination evidence stays buried forever.'

‘How do you know this Mason?’

‘He’s kind of an uncle,’ Harper said, and Rosa was wise enough not to continue.

THEY REACHED TOMÁS'S FAMILIAR APARTMENT BUILDING, AND Harper parked across the street, immediately noting the unnatural quiet that hung over the area like fog.

Too quiet for this time of day. Wrong kind of quiet.

'Wait here,' Harper told Rosa firmly. 'Keep the engine running, be ready to move fast if things go bad.'

'I can’t ride a bike—’

'Rosa.' Command authority, the tone he'd used with subordinates in hostile territory. 'If this situation goes badly, someone needs to survive to tell people what happened here. That responsibility falls to you. If you can't use the bike, steal a car but get the hell away.'

With Rosa reluctantly agreeing, he approached the building using available cover, noting details that felt wrong. The front door propped open, when building security protocols required it to be locked. Lobby completely empty when families would be passing through. Unnatural silence where there should be normal urban background noise.

Tomás's apartment was on the third floor. Harper took the stairs two at a time, acquired weapon ready but concealed beneath his jacket. The hallway was empty, fluorescent lights flickering mechanically.

Door slightly ajar when it should be securely locked.

Harper pushed the door open with his foot, staying clear of the doorframe while scanning the interior systematically.

Completely ransacked. Furniture overturned, drawers pulled out and emptied, papers scattered across the floor like confetti after a particularly grim celebration. Someone had conducted a thorough professional search, looking for specific documentation.

There was no sign of Tomás anywhere.

Harper moved through the apartment methodically, checking every room for clues about what had happened. The bedroom showed clear signs of a physical struggle – broken lamp, shattered picture frames, bedding twisted and pulled as if someone had fought against being forcibly removed.

In the kitchen, Harper found Tomás's mobile phone on the floor, screen cracked but still functional. Recent call history showed multiple attempts from Rosa's number, which explained why the calls had gone straight to voicemail.

But they'd left the phone behind, which meant they hadn't taken Tomás willingly or quietly.

Harper returned to Rosa, who was sitting on the Bonneville.

'Gone,' he reported. 'Place is completely trashed, clear signs of violent struggle.'

She closed her eyes, gripping the handles of the bike hard enough to turn her knuckles white.

'Where would they take him?'

'Unknown at this point. Could be anywhere within the city, or they might have transported him outside Chicago entirely.' Harper studied her face, watching hope transform into desperation. 'But the fact that they took him alive means they need him for something, which gives us operational time.'

'Time for what exactly?'

'Time to get him back.'

Rosa turned to stare at him with disbelief and desperate hope.

'You actually think we can rescue him? These people have unlimited resources, political connections, professional military operatives—'

'These people made a critical, tactical mistake,' Harper's voice carried experience born from years of combat experience. 'They took someone who was under my personal protection. Now this situation has become personal rather than just professional. Rosa, I need you to do exactly what I tell you over the next few hours. Your brother's life depends on following my instructions precisely.'

'What do you need from me?'

'Trust, mainly.'

Rosa nodded at this, but then her face fell.

‘If they have him, then they might be going for the kids. They’ll be at our cousin’s – she babysits them.’

She pulled out her phone, speed-dialling with hands that shook slightly. After the third ring, it answered.

‘Hey, is Carmen there? It's Rosa... Yeah, I’m okay. Listen, you need to take the children and leave the house right now... I can't explain over the phone... No, not a drill... Take Miguel and Ana, go to your mother's place, don't tell anyone where you're going... Yes, right now.'

She ended the call, immediately dialling another number.

'Maria? I need that favour we talked about... The big one... Yes, tonight... I'll be there within the hour... Gracias.'

She disconnected the call, looking back at Harper.

'Tomás's kids will be safe outside of town, and these people don't know about the connection to our cousin.’ Rosa's voice carried the sort of determination Harper recognised from combat zones. ‘Also, Maria’s an old schoolfriend, lives in Pilsen. Two jobs, minds her own business, doesn't ask questions about why people need places to stay.'

'Good choices. Take a taxi from here, pay cash, change cabs once if you think you're being followed.' Harper pulled out two hundred dollars from his wallet. 'Emergency funds.'

Rosa studied his face in the street lighting.

'What about you? How are you going to find Tomás?'

Harper's smile held no warmth whatsoever, only cold, tactical calculation.

'I politely ask the people who took him. And if politeness doesn't work, we get considerably less polite.'

10

HUNTING SEASON

HARPER USED THE SERVICE ENTRANCE TO HIS FATHER'S building, taking the private lift that Frank had shown him – direct route from the parking garage to the apartment he still didn't class as his, without bothering the lobby's security.

His father's paranoia paying dividends again. The old bastard had been many things, but stupid wasn't one of them.

Harper retrieved the Hellcat from the apartment, checking the action as he also gathered his kit: tactical light, zip-ties, first aid supplies, everything needed for having unpleasant conversations with unpleasant people in unpleasant places. Checked and loaded, the Hellcat's familiar weight settled beneath his jacket like an old friend saying hello. That said, the thought of still carrying a killer's gun as his own felt wrong, and Harper decided that once this was over he'd toss the weapon deep into the river and pick up a replacement – perhaps a Hellcat Pro Comp, with the new 17 round mags. After all, he might not like guns, but if he needed to use one, he'd prefer one he could trust. Before he left, however, he placed some items into the bedroom's safe – the notes from Santos, and his father's journal.

If he was caught or killed, the last thing he wanted was to leave them that on his body.

He needed a lead first. Maybe it was time to find out what had happened to those hospital operatives, especially the cigar-smoking one he shot.

Harper started with Chicago police scanners – a bit of kit every sensible person kept handy in cities where gunfire was just part of the urban soundtrack – and found one, a *5-0 Radio Pro* in his father's bedside drawer after five minutes of searching. Twenty minutes of monitoring radio chatter about domestic disputes and traffic accidents, then comments about the *Northwestern Memorial gunfight* an hour earlier.

Right, so the operatives had been found. Question was whether Chicago's finest had bothered arresting them or just processed them through the equivalent of the UK's National Health Service.

Harper rode towards the Twentieth District police station, as it was the closest, and he was running short on time. The building looked like someone had tried to make a warehouse look friendly and given up halfway through the project. He approached on foot, walking into the lobby like he belonged there, which was half the trick with authority figures – act like you had every right to be somewhere, and most people assumed you did.

'Sheriff Coble, Nevada,' Harper told the desk sergeant, presenting Coble's identification with the sort of bored authority that suggested this was routine paperwork. 'Following up on suspects detained late this afternoon at Northwestern Memorial Hospital. Interstate environmental crimes investigation.'

The sergeant perked up at "interstate". Federal involvement usually meant someone else's problem, which was every local copper's favourite kind.

'Environmental crimes, Sheriff?'

'Corporate fraud, illegal waste disposal, bit of conspiracy thrown in for flavour.' Harper let his accent drift towards American while keeping his expression professionally bland. 'Your men detained three suspects all zipped, I believe; I need to confirm their status for the federal prosecutors.'

The sergeant nodded and then proceeded to spend several minutes typing and frowning at computer screens that probably hadn't been updated since the Clinton administration.

'I'm not showing any response to Northwestern Memorial today, Sheriff. Routine welfare check this morning, there was a hoax called in later in the afternoon, but nothing about armed suspects.'

Interesting. Harper kept his expression neutral while his mind processed the implications.

'You sure? Three armed men, assault charges, hospital security called it in?'

'Sorry, Sheriff, but there's no record of any detention operation at that location.'

Of course there wasn't. The operatives hadn't been arrested – they'd been collected by colleagues before Chicago's boys in blue could complicate matters. Which meant Meridian Security had either excellent intelligence on emergency service radio traffic, or friends in useful places.

'My mistake,' Harper said, maintaining his official tone. 'Wrong details passed on. You know how federal coordination works.'

The sergeant's knowing nod suggested he did indeed

know how federal coordination worked, and thought it was bollocks.

However, even though he didn't yet have a name or a location, Harper left the station with considerably more information than he'd arrived with. Slate's people weren't just corporate muscle – they were operating with the sort of cover that came from political connections or federal contracts.

Time to have a conversation with someone who might know where they'd taken Tomás.

HARPER RETURNED TO THE MERIDIAN OFFICE HE'D SEEN ALFIE enter earlier that day, in a converted factory building that had probably been churning out widgets when his grandfather was still changing nappies. Third floor, wedged between a law firm and an accountancy practice that both looked like they preferred clients who paid in cash.

Harper took the stairs; elevators were for people who enjoyed being trapped in small boxes while unfriendly types waited outside with unpleasant intentions.

The corridor was empty, lit by fluorescent strips that had clearly given up trying to provide adequate illumination years ago. Most offices had closed for the evening, but light still leaked from under Meridian's door along with the sound of voices discussing "asset relocation" and "timeline acceleration".

They weren't big, it seemed. That said, Harper had already learned that the bigger companies liked to look small. Aegis, for example, had used a Portakabin in Prosperity.

Harper positioned himself beside the entrance, eavesdropping like a nosy neighbour. Two men talking shop – corporate security types didn't work late unless circumstances had gone thoroughly sideways.

Fifteen minutes later, chairs scraped and papers shuffled. Harper found an alcove near the fire exit where he could observe without looking like a stalker as the door opened, revealing two men in suits that screamed "expense account".

'Site Seven locked down?' the first out, a man in his early sixties, stocky with a grey buzz cut asked as they secured the office.

'Tight as a drum, Pascoe. Subject's going nowhere, and the client wants final resolution by midnight.' The younger bloke checked his watch like punctuality mattered in kidnapping. 'Six hours to tidy up loose ends.'

They moved towards the elevator, still discussing "Harper situations" and "federal complications" and "permanent solutions". The sort of conversation that confirmed Harper's suspicions about Tomás's life expectancy.

Once the doors closed, Harper returned to Meridian's office. It was a standard commercial lock – clearly they'd spent their security budget on more interesting kit than door hardware, and likely elsewhere. The six other sites, perhaps.

Two minutes later, Harper was inside what looked like a military command centre that had been dressed up as a respectable business. Maps covered entire walls, surrounded by communications equipment that belonged in embassies, and computer terminals that likely cost the same as small countries' defence budgets.

This wasn't a security consultancy. This was a full-spectrum intelligence operation with corporate letterhead, and an office tricked out with toys that cost more than the rent.

Harper started with the filing system, looking for operational schedules and client contracts. The cabinets were organised by company rather than chronology, each folder representing months or years of ongoing nastiness.

Slate Urban Development Corporation – Environmental Compliance Support.

Harper opened the folder and immediately wished he hadn't. Operational summaries dating back three years, personnel assignments, facility locations, and what the documents euphemistically described as "community relations management". Which was corporate speak for "intimidating potential witnesses and eliminating opposition to development projects".

Looks like Aegis wasn't doing this for Slate after all.

Harper photographed everything, noting patterns that painted a picture of systematic corruption. Meridian hadn't just provided muscle for Slate – they'd conducted comprehensive intelligence operations against environmental groups, municipal officials, and federal inspectors. The thorough, methodical approach that his father would have recognised and probably admired.

One document made Harper's blood run cold: a personnel file on Rosa Alvarez, complete with work schedules, home address, daily routines, and what they called "vulnerability assessments". They'd been watching her for weeks, probably since Tomás first agreed to look the other way.

Charming bunch, really. Made the Stasi look like amateur hour.

But it was the next filing cabinet that revealed the true scope of Meridian's business model. Client files stretching back five years, contracts with development corporations, mining companies, pharmaceutical firms – all requiring what they called “discreet problem resolution services”.

Harper found references to other “environmental compliance” operations in Detroit, Cleveland, and Milwaukee. Same pattern every time: local opposition to corporate development projects, followed by Meridian contracts for “community consultation”, ending with suddenly withdrawn complaints and abandoned legal challenges.

The methodology was consistent and thoroughly unpleasant. Identify key opponents, conduct comprehensive surveillance, apply graduated pressure through intimidation, property damage, and if necessary, “protective custody” arrangements for family members. Clean, efficient, highly effective.

Interestingly, they’d also been at Prosperity, although possibly not when Harper had been there. One name appeared repeatedly in the client communications, though; *Mason Carrick,* listed as “strategic consultant”. Aegis apparently still maintained ongoing contracts with Meridian, subcontracting work that Carrick's company couldn't handle directly due to federal oversight restrictions.

So, Uncle Mason was outsourcing the nastier bits of the family business. How very modern of him.

Harper continued taking photos, building a comprehensive picture of the conspiracy he'd stumbled arse-first into, while also locating the address of Meridian sites, including one named “Site Seven”. However, a sound in the corridor interrupted Harper's amateur documentary work – footsteps approaching, keys jingling, voices discussing something about “forgotten paperwork” and “client deadlines”.

Bugger. They were coming back.

Harper quickly closed the filing cabinet, moving towards

the window while assessing escape routes. The voices were getting closer, and he could distinguish Pascoe's authoritative tone directing someone to "grab the operational summaries from the secure cabinet".

Harper reached the window, testing the latch. Old building, original hardware – the window opened onto a fire escape that connected to the building's rear alley. Perfect for making dramatic exits when things went sideways.

The office door opened as Harper swung his leg over the windowsill.

'Can I help you?' Pascoe's voice carried the sort of dangerous authority that came from years of telling people to do things they didn't want to do.

'Private investigator,' Harper replied, keeping his hands visible while positioning himself onto the windowsill. *No point starting fights when escape routes were available.* 'Insurance fraud case, checking backgrounds on potential suspects.'

Pascoe's expression suggested he wasn't buying Harper's cover story. Clearly a man of discernment.

'Insurance investigators don't usually conduct after-hours surveillance operations.' His hand moved inside his jacket towards what Harper assumed was a concealed weapon. 'Especially ones involving breaking and entering.'

'Desperate times call for desperate measures.' Harper noted Pascoe's positioning while calculating tactical options. 'Divorce case, husband disappeared with assets, wife needs documentation for court proceedings.'

'Fascinating story.' Pascoe pulled out his phone, holding it up. 'Want to tell it to the police?'

'Not particularly.' Harper swung his other leg over the windowsill and quickly descended the fire escape while Pascoe dialled a number and called in what would probably be described as a security breach requiring immediate response.

Harper had gained himself time – he now knew where "Site Seven" was. All he had to do was rescue Tomás before someone moved him.

THE WAREHOUSE OCCUPIED A CONVERTED TEXTILE FACILITY IN an industrial district. Brick frontage lined with loading docks and security cameras, surrounded by the sort of neighbourhood where people minded their own business and asked no questions about unusual noises after dark.

Harper approached from the south, using abandoned railway infrastructure for cover while conducting what his SRR instructors would have called tactical reconnaissance but was really just having a careful look around before doing something stupid.

There were two vehicles in the car park: a black Range Rover Evoque and a grey BMW 3 Series saloon. Corporate transport positioned for rapid departure if things went sideways, which in Harper's experience they usually did.

Light leaked through tinted windows, suggesting the facility was occupied. No visible guards, which meant either overconfident security or people who knew how to remain unobtrusive while still being dangerous.

Harper reached the service door, testing the handle. Locked, but standard commercial hardware rather than proper security measures. A minute or so with his pocketknife and his lock-picking tools, and he was inside.

The warehouse had been converted into office spaces and what looked to be detention areas, with the main storage section retained for operational use. Harper moved carefully through administrative areas, following voices towards what sounded like a briefing room.

Through a partially open door, Harper could see three men in basic tactical gear, as one spoke into a phone.

'—subject remains secured, no complications. Client wants situation resolved by midnight—'

'What's the definition of resolved?' another voice asked, someone outside of Harper's view.

'Permanent solutions. Alvarez knows too much about historical contamination, and the Harper problem requires direct action before federal interest develops.'

Right. They weren't just holding Tomás – they were planning to eliminate him within the next few hours, along with anyone else who might complicate Slate's development timeline.

Harper moved towards the makeshift detention area while avoiding the briefing room. He worked quickly, and it didn't take long before he found Tomás in a converted office space, secured to a metal chair with zip-ties and looking like someone who'd had a thoroughly unpleasant few hours.

'Tomás,' Harper whispered, approaching.

Tomás looked up, his expression shifting from resignation to desperate hope with a speed that was almost painful to watch.

'Harper? How did you—'

'Later,' Harper said, cutting the restraints while scanning for additional threats. 'We need to move quickly. Are you injured?'

'Bruised, scared, but nothing permanently damaged.' Tomás stood carefully, testing his balance after hours of restraint. 'Harper, there's something you need to know—'

'Tell me when we're clear of this place,' Harper interrupted, leading Tomás towards the rear exit. 'Right now we focus on getting out before they discover you're missing.'

But, as they reached the corridor, Harper heard the sound that meant everything had just become considerably more complicated – multiple voices calling orders, footsteps moving rapidly through the warehouse, radio communications coordinating response to what was obviously a security breach at Meridian's offices.

'This way,' Harper whispered, guiding Tomás towards an alternative exit. The loading dock was compromised, but warehouses always had multiple access points for precisely this reason.

They reached a side door that opened onto an alley, but Harper could see vehicle lights manoeuvring to block escape routes. Standard tactical response – contain the threat while maintaining operational security.

'Harper.' The amplified voice echoed through the warehouse complex like the voice of doom, and it sounded familiar, but Harper couldn't work out how. 'I believe you've found what you came for.'

Harper positioned Tomás behind a concrete support pillar while assessing their tactical situation. Three armed operatives, probably more outside, defensive positions, and limited escape routes. Not impossible odds, but not particularly encouraging ones either.

His phone buzzed with an incoming call from an unknown number.

'Answer it,' Tomás urged. 'They want to negotiate.'

Harper accepted the call, though his definition of negotiation might differ from theirs. It didn't even occur to ask Tomás how he knew.

'Mister Harper, this is Veronica Slate. We need to have a civilised discussion about terms.'

'I'm listening.'

'You're trespassing in a private facility, surrounded by security personnel with authority to detain intruders.' Slate's voice carried the sort of cold amusement that came from holding all the good cards. 'Surrender now, and we can resolve this situation like reasonable adults.'

Harper looked at Tomás, who was staring at the floor with an expression Harper couldn't quite read. Something between guilt and desperation, with a healthy dose of fear thrown in for flavour.

'What kind of resolution?'

'You leave Chicago permanently. Tonight. Tomás returns to his normal life with corrected understanding about environmental safety protocols. Everyone moves forward without further complications or misunderstandings.'

'And if I refuse?'

'Chicago Police respond to reports of armed trespass in an industrial facility, arrest a mentally unstable veteran who couldn't adjust to civilian life, and discover evidence of a harassment campaign against innocent city employees.'

Harper recognised the setup for what it was. Slate had prepared multiple contingencies, including law enforcement coordination that would frame him for the crimes his opponents were committing.

His father would have approved of her operational planning, even if he'd have deplored her methods.

But there was something in Tomás's expression that suggested another layer to this particular situation.

'Tomás,' Harper said quietly. 'What aren't you telling me?'

Tomás finally met his eyes.

'Harper, I'm sorry. I really am.' Tomás's voice carried the weight of impossible choices. 'But they've been following the children. They showed me photographs – Miguel walking to school, Ana playing in the garden. Current photographs, taken this afternoon.'

Understanding hit Harper like a bucket of cold water. Slate hadn't just taken Tomás – she'd leveraged his entire family, forcing him to choose between exposing contamination and protecting the people he loved most.

'They made me an offer,' Tomás continued, his voice breaking slightly. 'Complete cooperation, including testimony that you've been harassing me for days, forcing me to falsify environmental reports, threatening my family when I refused to comply with your demands.'

He looked away, unable to maintain eye contact.

'In exchange, Rosa and the children remain safe and unharmed.'

'And you believed them?'

'What choice did I have? You're asking me to choose between exposing contamination that might save future families and protecting my own family right now.' Tomás's hands shook as he spoke. 'What would you choose in my position?'

Harper knew the answer, and it wasn't one that would help either of them.

Through the warehouse doors, Harper could hear vehicles arriving – multiple engines, police sirens that suggested law enforcement response, and the sound of both car doors slamming and equipment being distributed.

'Tomás,' Slate's voice carried through the warehouse like a theatrical announcement, no longer happy to talk through a phone. 'Time to make your statement to the officers.'

Harper looked at Tomás, reading the genuine anguish in the older man's expression.

'You're going to do it,' he said. It wasn't a question.

'I have to. I can't let my kids pay for my mistakes.' Tomás stared at the lights shining through the windows. 'They're all I have left.'

The warehouse doors opened, revealing tactical officers with weapons drawn.

'Liam Harper,' one of them called. 'Drop your weapon and place your hands where we can see them.'

Harper looked at the Hellcat in his hand, then at Tomás, who was already moving towards the officers with his hands raised and his story prepared.

He could have fought. Three tactical officers in a confined space, the element of surprise, urban combat training that had kept him alive in considerably more hostile environments than a Chicago warehouse. But fighting meant killing police officers, which would confirm every aspect of Slate's narrative while doing nothing to protect Tomás's family or expose the contamination that was making children sick across the South Side.

Harper placed the Hellcat on the concrete floor, straightening slowly with his hands raised.

The arrest was efficient: hands secured behind his back with steel restraints, rights read with bureaucratic precision, property confiscated for evidence processing. Through it all, Tomás provided detailed statements about Harper's harassment campaign, his demands for false environmental reports, his threats against innocent family members.

An Academy Award performance, really. Complete with genuine emotion and convincing detail born from actual fear for his family's safety.

As they loaded Harper into the police car, he caught sight of Veronica Slate observing from a black Mercedes S-Class saloon parked across the street. She nodded once – acknowledgement of a game played and decisively won.

The car doors slammed shut, cutting off Harper's view of the warehouse and the people who'd outmanoeuvred him completely through the simple expedient of threatening innocent children, and then Chicago's lights streamed past the windows as they drove towards the city lockup, where Harper would await federal prosecutors building cases for kidnapping, extortion, environmental fraud, and whatever other charges Slate's lawyers could construct from the evening's events.

The game was over.

Harper had lost.

But, as the police car navigated through evening traffic towards his temporary future behind bars, Harper was already considering how games could be restarted, rules could be changed, and losses could be transformed into entirely different sorts of victories.

Prison bars held bodies. They didn't hold ideas, connections, or the sort of stubborn determination that had kept Harper operational through years of military service in places considerably more hostile than Chicago.

Slate had won this round by playing better chess and threatening the right people at the right time.

Time to see what happened when Harper stopped playing chess entirely and started playing by rules that Veronica Slate had probably never encountered before.

11

FAMILY DEBTS

Chicago's city lockup had the same institutional charm as every other holding facility Harper had experienced during his travels – lights that flickered like dying stars, green paint that had given up pretending to be cheerful sometime during the last twenty years, and the particular aroma of industrial disinfectant losing a decades-long war against human misery.

Harper had been trying to catch some sleep for the better part of four hours, his internal clock keeping precise time while his mind processed just how thoroughly Veronica Slate had outplayed him. The woman was sharp as a scalpel and twice as dangerous, using Tomás's family as leverage while maintaining perfect legal cover through federal contracts and bought politicians. Harper had walked straight into a trap.

The familiar nightmare had jolted him awake twice – that bloody mask coming away in his hands, his father's dying words echoing in the Myanmar heat. But dwelling on past failures was a luxury Harper couldn't afford when current problems demanded immediate attention. Besides, self-pity had never been his style.

He was mentally sketching escape routes when footsteps echoed down the corridor. Multiple sets, moving with the sort of purpose that suggested this wasn't routine patrol work.

Someone important was coming to chat.

The cell door's lock disengaged with an expensive-sounding clunk, and Mason Carrick stepped through the doorway like he owned the building, which he probably did through some labyrinthine network of shell companies and federal kickbacks. He wore a charcoal suit, his silver hair perfectly styled despite the late hour. Two men in cheaper suits flanked him, their positioning screaming "private security" to anyone with eyes.

Harper took a moment to study the man who'd been around as Harper grew up, then systematically corrupted everything his father had built – although this was taken from his father's side of the story, and Harper knew there were never just two sides.

Mason looked older than Harper remembered from Nevada – closer to seventy than sixty – but he carried it well. Still had that sharp intelligence that missed nothing, still moved like someone who expected the world to rearrange itself for his convenience.

'My God,' Mason said softly, genuine warmth creeping into his voice. 'It bloody well is you. Little Liam Harper.'

'Hello, Uncle Mason,' Harper replied, but the sarcasm was already bleeding through the childhood nickname.

Mason's smile flickered, recognising the shift from affection to weapon.

'Did I ever tell you about the time little Liam here got into the server room at Langley?' Mason turned slightly, as if addressing his security team, but his eyes never left Harper. 'Must have been twelve years old. Your father was still in the military then, meeting with the director, and you slipped away from his secretary.'

Harper remembered the incident – the panic when they'd found him, his father's fury, Mason being the one to calm everyone down.

'Found you an hour later, sound asleep under a desk, surrounded by about two million dollars' worth of computer equipment,' Mason continued, chuckling at the memory. 'Jet lag, you said.'

'Still say that.'

'And that fundraiser at the Plaza in New York,' Mason pressed on, warming to his theme. 'You convinced the senator's daughter to help you raid the kitchen. Came back covered in chocolate sauce. Your father had to cancel three meetings to take you shopping for a new suit.'

The memory hit harder than Harper expected. He'd been maybe ten, bored out of his skull at another corporate function, and she'd been equally bored. They'd snuck into the kitchen and discovered an industrial vat of chocolate sauce meant for dessert. By the time security found them, they'd painted themselves head to toe.

'Your mother nearly burst a blood vessel when she heard about it,' Mason said, his voice softening. 'Called your father for an hour, ranting about his lack of supervision.'

The mention of his mother caught Harper off guard, which was exactly what Mason intended. Emotional manipulation wrapped in nostalgia.

No. These were the exact same two stories he'd told the last time they'd met, in Bickford's mansion. Almost word for bloody word, as if learned, like a speech. Were these the only two stories Mason Carrick remembered? Or perhaps bothered to learn in case he needed to fake empathy with Harper down the line?

'You've got her eyes, you know,' Mason continued. 'That same way of watching everything, cataloguing details.'

He gestured towards Harper's eyebrow scar.

'Thought that would have healed better.'

'Scars are permanent, Uncle Mason.' Harper's voice turned cold. 'Only time he hit me, but it left a message.'

'He regretted that.' Mason's tone carried what might have been genuine remorse. 'Called me afterwards, drunk as hell, crying about what he'd done. Said you were too much like him as a kid – too stubborn, too curious for your own good.'

Harper felt something twist in his chest. His father had never apologised, never even acknowledged what had happened. But apparently he'd shared his guilt with Mason.

No. Again, this was the same thing said in Prosperity.

Christ, his playbook only had three pages.

'Funny how he never told me that himself.'

Mason was quiet for a moment, studying Harper's face.

'When you went into the SRR,' he said finally. 'Your father called me when you passed selection. Proudest I'd ever heard him.'

'Did he?' Harper kept his voice level – again, the familiar conversation. 'We hardly talked in those days.'

'I know.' Mason's voice carried acknowledgement of that failure. 'He was always better at protecting people than connecting with them.'

Interesting. For the first time, Mason Carrick had given something new.

'Is that what this is?' Harper gestured around the cell. 'Protection?'

Mason's corporate mask slipped back into place.

'This is business, Liam. Which brings me to why I'm here.' His voice turned professional, efficient. 'I want Dominic's notebook.'

Harper tilted his head, affecting puzzlement.

'What notebook? Dad wasn't much of a writer. More of a doer, you know?'

Mason's laugh was about as warm as a Glasgow winter.

'The “analogue database”. Unhackable, as he used to say. Names, operations, financial arrangements – everything your father thought worth documenting about our business.' Mason stepped closer, his voice dropping. 'Stop playing games. I know about the London arms dealer, safe deposit box, daddy's birthday as the combination. Touching, really.'

Bollocks. Mason knew about Deacon Brodie, the key, probably everything since Harper had left Nevada. *But how much was confirmed intelligence versus educated guesswork?*

'You've been working through his little list of sins,' Mason continued, frustration creeping into his tone. 'Riding that pathetic motorcycle across America, trying to fix things that were never broken.'

'Still don't know what you're talking about,' Harper replied with practised innocence.

'A tourist who impersonated a sheriff, infiltrated private facilities, coordinated with union officials, took down an entire garage criminal scheme – but I don't exactly get why you bothered with that, as it wasn't part of your father's make-a-wish list.' Mason's voice hardened. 'We have witnesses, documentation, recordings.'

'Sounds fascinating. Sure it wasn't someone else?'

'Don't piss with me, boy! I was there!'

Mason took a breath after his outburst and studied

Harper for several long moments, recognising the stubborn determination that had characterised their relationship since Harper was twelve.

Harper smiled.

Gotcha.

'Tell me something, Liam,' Mason said, his voice carrying old affection mixed with new menace. 'Do you remember what your father said the last time you spoke?'

Harper's jaw tightened involuntarily. The memory was burned into his consciousness – three identical conversations, three times being pushed aside for more important business.

"I can't speak now, Liam, I'm busy. Call back later," Mason mocked Dominic Kane's voice. 'And he *was* busy. The Myanmar operation was becoming a nightmare, with pirates threatening commercial shipping, your father personally commanding security teams because the situation was too sensitive for remote management.'

Harper kept quiet while processing this information. Mason was revealing operational details he'd never shared before.

'He was trying to protect you by keeping distance,' Mason continued. 'Aegis work was getting dangerous, drawing attention from people who eliminated problems permanently. Your father thought if he kept you away from the business, you'd be safe.'

'Safe?' Harper's voice turned bitter. 'Safe from what? Having a father who gave a damn?'

'Safe from ending up like him – dead on a container ship, bleeding out while enemies closed in from all sides.' Mason's voice carried genuine emotion now. 'He loved you more than you knew, Little Liam. But love and protection aren't always the same thing.'

There was a moment of uncomfortable silence, and then Mason Carrick sighed.

'One last favour owed to Dominic,' Mason said finally, his tone shifting from threat to negotiation. 'I get you out of here, you give me the book, walk away from Chicago permanently, leave Aegis alone and we call it even. Clean slate. No more family obligations.'

Harper raised an eyebrow.

'And if I don't?'

'Next time you come for me, I won't arrange your release.' Mason's voice carried the sort of arrogance that came from years of making problems disappear. 'I'll arrange your funeral.'

The cell fell silent except for distant institutional sounds – radio chatter, metal doors, the ordinary bureaucracy of containing society's problems. Mason was offering freedom with limitations. No more investigation, no more pursuit of his father's last mission. Just walk away, disappear into civilian life, pretend the notebook didn't exist.

But Harper had learned something about himself during months of travelling America with his father's sins documented in leather-bound pages. He wasn't capable of walking away from fights that needed finishing, particularly when innocent people were getting hurt by the sort of systematic corruption Mason had perfected.

'Generous offer,' Harper said finally. 'But I'm not sure I trust your definition of calling it even.'

'You shouldn't trust me at all,' Mason replied with brutal honesty. 'But you should understand this is the best deal you're going to receive. Veronica Slate has federal prosecutors preparing cases that will put you in maximum security for the next decade. I'm offering you a way out.'

Before Harper could reply, however, they both heard footsteps echoing in the corridor outside, accompanied by raised voices and what sounded like a bureaucratic argument. Harper recognised the rhythm of institutional confrontation – someone challenging established procedures.

One of Mason's security team appeared in the doorway.

'Mister Carrick? There's a Sheriff from Nevada here about the prisoner.'

Mason's expression shifted to confidence mixed with mild amusement. He'd obviously anticipated this development as part of Harper's eventual exposure for identity theft.

'The Sheriff from Nevada is right here,' Mason said, gesturing towards Harper with dismissive authority. 'Mister "Coble" and I are having a lovely chat.'

The security operative looked confused, consulting notes or credentials outside Harper's view.

'No sir, this one's got proper credentials. Federal database confirms active status. Says her name's Cortez.'

Harper felt genuine surprise mixed with something that might have been relief. Cortez had tracked him to Chicago, which meant she'd connected his use of Coble's identification to legitimate law enforcement databases. Whether she was here to arrest him or help him remained unclear, but this wasn't part of Mason Carrick's plan, and anything that derailed him, even a little, was good.

Mason's expression shifted from confidence to calculation as he processed this unexpected complication.

'Lisa Cortez,' he repeated, his tone carrying recognition. 'Interesting.'

Harper could see the man's mind working through implications – another player entering a game he'd thought he controlled completely.

'Your little sheriff friend seems to have developed an unfortunate habit of involving herself in family business,' Mason said, his corporate mask slipping slightly.

The security operative waited for instructions while Mason weighed options Harper couldn't fully calculate.

'Show her in,' Mason said finally. 'I'd like to renew our acquaintance.'

The operative disappeared, presumably to escort Cortez through whatever bureaucratic maze was required to access holding facilities, and after a moment Lisa Cortez entered the cell carrying herself like someone who'd spent years dealing with difficult people in difficult situations. She wore civilian clothes – dark jeans, leather jacket, boots designed for function rather than fashion – but her bearing screamed law enforcement in every line. Her dark hair was pulled back practically, and her expression suggested she'd driven through the night to reach Chicago.

She glanced at Harper briefly, her face unreadable, before focusing on Mason.

'Mister Carrick,' she said with a nod that acknowledged their previous encounter without suggesting warmth. 'Fancy meeting you here.'

'Deputy Cortez.' Mason's corporate smile returned, but Harper could see tension around his eyes.

'Sheriff now.'

'Sorry, force of habit,' Mason grinned humourlessly. 'I heard about your promotion. Congratulations. Though I'm curious what brings you to Chicago.'

'Identity theft investigation,' Cortez replied efficiently. 'Someone's been using ex-Sheriff Eric Coble's credentials for interstate law enforcement activities. Since Coble's currently in federal custody in Nevada, my office takes that sort of impersonation seriously.'

Harper appreciated Cortez's tactical approach. She was doing her best to establish legitimate authority while creating jurisdictional complications that would make his detention more complex.

'Of course,' Mason said smoothly. 'Though I believe Chicago police have already arrested the individual responsible.'

He gestured towards Harper.

'Mister Harper here has been quite busy.'

Cortez turned to study Harper as if seeing him for the first time.

'Mister Harper,' she said formally. 'I'll need to interview you about your use of Sheriff Coble's identification.'

'Of course, sheriff,' Harper replied carefully.

'Interstate identity theft creates federal jurisdiction,' Cortez now added, looking back at Mason. 'I'll need to coordinate with my office before any local charges proceed.'

Mason's expression shifted slightly, recognising the bureaucratic complications Cortez was introducing. Multiple jurisdictions meant multiple agencies, extended timelines, opportunities for information to leak beyond his control.

'I'm sure Chicago authorities will be cooperative,' he said carefully.

'They'd better be,' Cortez replied with steel beneath professional courtesy. 'The Governor takes identity theft seriously.'

Harper watched the verbal chess match between Mason and Cortez, recognising that both were manoeuvring for advantage while maintaining facades of official cooperation.

'Well,' Mason said finally, 'I'm sure you have procedures to follow, but as I said to your friend here, Ms Slate is considering dropping charges if he agrees to leave the city limits.'

He turned back to Harper, his expression hardening.

'Think about what we discussed, Little Liam. Offers like this don't remain available indefinitely.'

He moved towards the cell door, pausing to study Cortez.

'Sheriff Cortez,' he said with what felt like a large portion of insincere corporate courtesy. 'I do hope your investigation proceeds smoothly. Chicago can be a complicated city for outsiders to navigate safely.'

The threat wasn't subtle. Cortez met his gaze steadily.

'I adapt quickly, Mister Carrick.'

Mason was quiet for several moments, and Harper watched him process the implications. This wasn't just about containing one problematic ex-soldier any more. Cortez represented legitimate law enforcement with federal backing, someone who'd already cost Aegis a major operation in Nevada and had the authority to make Mason's life considerably more complicated.

Mason's laugh was harsh.

'We'll see about that.'

He left the cell, his security team falling into formation behind him, but as he reached the door, Harper rose from the bed.

'Carrick.'

For the first time, he hadn't stated Mason's name. The word was cold, emotionless. And it gained Mason's attention as he turned around.

'You're wrong when you said you knew my father's last words,' Harper replied. 'There were two more times after that. One where he lay in my arms bleeding out, and another in a video message, left after his death. And you'll *never* get to know what was said in either conversation.'

Mason Carrick stared at Harper as if suddenly unsure of his footing and then motioned to his security to follow him out. Their footsteps echoed down the corridor until silence returned to the holding area.

Harper let out a breath. Mason had offered freedom as one last favour to Dominic, but Cortez's arrival had changed the game completely. Now Mason had two problems instead of one, and Harper suspected the man's solutions would involve permanent elimination rather than negotiated resolution.

Which right now? Was absolutely fine with him.

12

AFTER HOURS

It had taken another hour but mysteriously the charges against Harper had been dropped. Slate and Tomás no longer felt like pressing charges and, seeing that Cortez had hung around after Harper picked up his items, noting the Hellcat had definitely been examined in his absence, the two of them left the station, looking for somewhere to talk. They found it at the Olympia Diner, two blocks down, and the sort of place that survived on insomniacs and shift workers. Red vinyl booths with duct-tape patches lined the windowed walls next to chrome fixtures that had lost their shine decades ago, but it was open twenty-four hours, served coffee, and most importantly, nobody gave a damn what you talked about as long as you kept buying it.

Harper slid into the booth across from Cortez.

'Coffee?' the waitress asked, materialising with a pot that looked older than Harper's motorcycle.

'Please,' Cortez said.

'Same,' Harper added, pushing aside a laminated menu that had probably been wiping tables for years.

The waitress filled their mugs and vanished, leaving them alone. Outside, Chicago did its late-night thing – traffic lights changing colours for empty streets, the distant rattle of the L, the usual urban symphony that provided perfect cover for conversations you didn't want overheard.

'So,' Cortez said, wrapping her hands around the coffee mug like it might be the only warm thing she'd touch all night. 'Want to tell me what the hell that was about back there?'

'Mason Carrick settling old family debts,' Harper replied, tasting the coffee. Christ, it was strong enough to wake the dead and bitter enough to strip paint. Exactly what he needed. 'One last favour owed to my father, then we're square.'

'Square?' Cortez raised an eyebrow. 'That didn't sound particularly square to me. Sounded like he was planning your funeral.'

Harper almost smiled. Trust Cortez to cut straight through corporate bollocks to the actual threat.

'Next time I come for him, he arranges my funeral instead of my release,' Harper confirmed. 'So, yeah, I'd call that a fairly direct threat.'

Cortez studied him over her coffee mug. She looked tired – likely a bone-deep exhaustion from driving through the night to reach Chicago – but her eyes were sharp. Still processing, still calculating. Still being a Sheriff, even when she was technically outside her jurisdiction.

'How did you know?' Harper asked.

'Know what?'

'That I was using Coble's identification. That I was in Chicago.'

Cortez leaned back in the booth, her expression shifting to something between amusement and professional pride.

'Slate had it checked when you used it at her development site. She did it off books, a subtle call to Prosperity to check on Coble's whereabouts...' she paused, letting that sink in. 'Since I'm sheriff of Prosperity now, and Coble was arrested there, that call came straight to me. The moment they started describing "Coble" I knew it was you, and that you were probably in deep shit.'

Harper pulled out his river stone, rolling it between his fingers. He'd known using Coble's ID was risky, but he'd assumed it would take longer for anyone to notice. Apparently Slate was more thorough than he'd given her credit for.

'You've been tracking me,' he said.

'I've been following reports,' Cortez corrected, noting the stone, and knowing what it meant. 'Did you know there was some trouble in Maryland recently? Small-town corruption, sheriff taking bribes, federal charges, Garage mechanic killed. Stranger coming in and the whole town going into some bullshit lockdown... word gets around law enforcement circles when someone's stirring up that kind of mess.'

Harper kept his expression neutral. *Trust Cortez to connect dots across multiple jurisdictions. She'd always been too bloody clever for her own good.*

'Sounds fascinating,' he said.

'Fascinating enough that when Eric Coble's ID popped up in Chicago, I thought I'd come see what you've gotten into here.'

'You think I'm some kind of vigilante?' Harper asked.

'I think you're someone who doesn't trust the system to handle things properly,' Cortez replied. 'Someone who's seen too much corruption, too many cover-ups, too many innocent people getting hurt while powerful people walk away clean.'

She wasn't wrong. Harper had lost faith in official channels after learning his father's legitimate security company had transformed into whatever shadow operation Aegis had become. Sometimes the system worked, but too often it protected the wrong people while the right people got buried.

'So,' Harper said, deciding to change the subject, 'how's Prosperity these days?'

'Better than it was,' Cortez replied. 'Environmental teams are still working on containment protocols for whatever the hell was processing up in those mines. Tom Bickford's in federal custody, awaiting trial for conspiracy, fraud, and about half a dozen other charges I've lost count of. Coble too. Turns out shooting at deputies while threatening civilians doesn't play well with prosecutors.'

Cortez's smile was grim.

'Reynolds took over as interim sheriff, but the state appointed me after the dust settled. Apparently I had the best credentials for dealing with unusual situations.'

Harper could understand that. Cortez had proven she could handle corporate manipulation, federal agencies, and armed confrontations while maintaining her integrity. The sort of experience that looked bloody impressive on a resume for cleaning up corrupted jurisdictions.

'Mason Carrick disappeared before we could arrest him, and then lawyers – real expensive ones – turned up and proved without a doubt Aegis were simply contractors, and had no idea what Bickford was doing,' she continued. 'Figured he'd surface eventually, but I wasn't expecting Chicago.'

'He's here coordinating with an industrialist named

Veronica Slate,' Harper said. 'Development company that's been covering up contamination, probably for years. Different operation than Prosperity, but same corporate corruption playbook.'

Cortez absorbed this information, her expression hardening as she recognised the pattern. Harper could see her mind working, connecting this to what she'd seen in Nevada, understanding that Mason's operations stretched far beyond one small mining town.

'And you're here to stop them.'

It wasn't a question. Cortez had connected the dots.

'Something like that,' Harper confirmed.

'Something like that?' Cortez's tone carried amusement mixed with exasperation. 'Harper, you broke into a dozen different buildings, had a gunfight outside a hospital, impersonated a sheriff, and now you're sitting in a diner at midnight with someone who should probably arrest you. "Something like that" doesn't quite cover it.'

Harper almost laughed. When she put it that way, it did sound a bit mental.

'Fair point,' he said. 'Yes, I'm here to stop them. Among other things.'

Before Cortez could respond, Harper's phone buzzed – a text message. He glanced at the screen, then showed it to Cortez.

'Rosa Alvarez. Tomás's sister.'

'Who?' Cortez frowned. 'Wait – the person who had you arrested for stalking him?'

'It's a little more complicated than that,' Harper said as he read the message.

Any news about Tomás?

Harper dialled the number while Cortez watched. Rosa answered on the first ring, her voice tight with worry.

'Harper? Thank God. Have you found him? Is Tomás alive?'

Harper felt Cortez's eyes on him, studying his reaction. He could see her processing – *another woman connected to whatever Harper was really doing in Chicago.* But this conversation was going to be more difficult than explaining contamination and corporate corruption.

'Tomás is alive,' Harper said carefully. 'But the situation is... complicated.'

'Complicated how? Where is he? Are you getting him out?'

Harper glanced at Cortez, who was listening with growing confusion. She didn't know about the kidnapping, didn't understand that from Rosa's perspective, her brother had been abducted by corporate thugs.

'He's not being held any more,' Harper said. 'But Rosa, he's made some difficult choices about how to handle the situation.'

'What do you mean he's not being held? Did you rescue him? Is he coming home?'

There was desperate hope in Rosa's voice, the sort of raw emotion that came from someone who'd been imagining the worst for hours.

'He's safe, but he's not coming home yet,' Harper kept his voice gentle. 'The people who took him... they offered him a deal. Protection for his family in exchange for cooperation.'

There was silence on the other end of the line. Rosa was processing this, probably understanding what "cooperation" meant in this context.

'He gave them what they wanted,' she said finally. It wasn't a question.

'Yes.'

'To protect me and the children.'

'Yes.'

Another long pause. When Rosa spoke again, her voice carried the weight of someone who'd seen too much corruption, too many good people forced into impossible choices.

'Is he really safe?'

'For now,' Harper said honestly. 'As long as he keeps his end of whatever deal they made.'

'And the contamination?'

Harper glanced at Cortez, who was listening to his side of the conversation, her expression unreadable.

'Still being addressed,' he said. 'Through different channels.'

Rosa was quiet for several moments, probably weighing her response. Harper could hear voices in the background – maybe her friend Maria asking questions she couldn't answer, people worried about Tomás who didn't understand the forces he was up against.

'Thank you for being honest with me,' she said finally. The call ended – after all, what else could she say, now her brother had seemingly switched sides – leaving Harper and Cortez in the sort of silence that followed hard truths.

'Another one?' Cortez asked, her tone carrying what might have been amusement.

'Another what?'

'Another attractive woman caught up in whatever you're really doing here,' Cortez's smile was sardonic. 'You seem to collect them. Rosa, that widow in Maryland – what was her name? Sarah something? The one whose husband got murdered?'

Harper almost laughed despite the circumstances. Trust Cortez to find humour in the situation while people's lives hung in the balance. And trust her to have done enough research to know about Sarah Colton from Maryland.

'It's not intentional,' he said.

'No? What would you call it then?'

Harper touched his river stone again, considering how much to reveal. Cortez had proven trustworthy during the Prosperity situation, but Chicago represented federal jurisdiction and complications that could affect her career. On the other hand, she'd driven all night to Chicago to check on him. That suggested she was already committed to whatever this was becoming.

'Finishing what my father started,' he said finally.

Cortez nodded, apparently unsurprised by the personal motivation.

'And what did your father start?'

Harper was quiet for several moments, weighing his options. This was new territory – Cortez knew he was Dominic Kane's son from their time in Prosperity, but she didn't know about the notebook, didn't understand the full scope of what his father had documented.

'Documentation on Aegis operations,' he said carefully. 'Records of contracts, financial arrangements, personnel files. You remember what Ashfield said back in the mine – about my father owning half the company?'

'He was gaining evidence.'

'Insurance, originally. But yes, evidence now.'

Cortez absorbed this, her expression shifting to something more professional. As a sheriff, she understood the value of documented evidence, the challenges of building cases against well-connected defendants. She also understood how dangerous that evidence could be to the people who possessed it.

'Federal jurisdiction?'

'Almost certainly. Environmental crimes, conspiracy, probably RICO if you dig deep enough,' Harper paused. 'But also the sort of evidence that gets people killed if they're not careful about how they use it.'

'Which is why you're working outside official channels.'

'Which is why I'm trying to stay alive long enough to see justice done, one issue at a time.' Harper drained his coffee mug, grimacing at the bitter dregs. The conversation was getting into territory that could make Cortez complicit in whatever he was doing, could compromise her position as sheriff. But she'd chosen to come to Chicago, chosen to track him down, chosen to sit in this diner at midnight discussing federal crimes. She was already complicit, whether she admitted it or not.

'Question is,' he said, 'what happens now?'

Cortez studied him for several long moments, clearly weighing options.

'Now we figure out how to expose this conspiracy without getting killed,' she said finally. 'Because whatever Mason Carrick's protection was worth, I don't think it extends much beyond tonight.'

Harper felt something that might have been relief. Cortez was committing, choosing sides, deciding that some fights were worth the risk.

'We?' he asked.

'We,' Cortez confirmed. 'You've got evidence, I've got federal law enforcement authority. Together we might actually accomplish something. Separately, we'll probably just get ourselves killed. And I do kinda owe you for fixing my town.

So, what's the plan?'

'Find somewhere safe to regroup, figure out next moves.' Harper checked his watch. After midnight. 'My father's apartment has a spare room if you don't mind corporate minimalism.'

'Your father's apartment?' Cortez raised an eyebrow. 'Mister Harper, are you inviting me back to "your place"?'

'Inherited property. One of the few I haven't sold yet,' Harper explained, ignoring the jibe. 'Secure, private, and Mason Carrick arranging my release suggests he might still have some boundaries he won't cross.'

'What kind of boundaries?'

'Family obligations ended tonight,' Harper stood, leaving money on the table. 'Mason made it clear – one last favour to Dominic, but after this we're even. The question is whether Slate's already convinced him I'm too much trouble to keep breathing.'

THEY LEFT THE DINER TOGETHER, WALKING THROUGH Chicago's empty streets towards where Harper had left his Bonneville before being arrested. The conversation had established ground rules – Cortez understood the stakes, recognised the federal implications, and accepted that Harper was operating outside normal channels for legitimate reasons. But Harper could sense she was still deciding exactly how much official support she could provide without compromising her position as sheriff.

'Tell me about the notebook,' she said as they walked.

Harper glanced at her, noting how she'd shifted from general questions to specific intelligence gathering. Professional mode, building the case she'd need to justify whatever actions came next.

'He called it his analogue database,' he said. 'Names, operations, financial records. Everything my father documented as insurance against people who might betray him. Which, given what happened in Myanmar, turned out to be bloody prescient. It's a list of things he needs to make right. I don't know if he intended to do them himself, or whether I was always the plan, but either way, I have it now.'

Harper touched his river stone, considering how much to reveal.

'After he died, I got a video message. One of those "if you're watching this, I'm dead" things soldiers make. Funnily enough, I later found out the disc was sent by Ashfield on his behalf.'

'Ashfield?' Cortez asked, and Harper knew she remembered the man. 'I wondered what happened to him.'

'He played the corporate game better than the others,' Harper smiled. 'Anyway, the video disc? Told me to take down Aegis, make it what it was supposed to be instead of what Mason had turned it into.'

'And the notebook?'

'That came later. Took some digging – London arms dealer called Deacon Brodie had been holding a box for my father. Opened with a birth date; contained a key to a safe deposit box. Inside was this leather-bound book, handwritten entries going back years. Every dirty deal, every cover-up, every time Aegis crossed lines they shouldn't have crossed.'

Cortez absorbed this information.

'How much does it contain?'

'Enough to destroy the company completely. Enough to

expose federal black operations, international arms deals, environmental cover-ups spanning decades.' Harper's voice hardened. 'It's a roadmap to everything corrupt about modern corporate security work.'

'Why not go to the authorities, or the press?'

Harper shrugged.

'You saw a small part of them in Prosperity,' he replied. 'Do you honestly think they'd allow it? That the people they control could do anything?'

Cortez nodded, understanding.

'And Mason Carrick wants it back.'

'Mason Carrick wants to control it. Destroy it, probably, after finding anything he can use in it, along with anyone who's seen it.'

'Which includes you.'

'Which includes me.'

The streets were quieter now, the late-night energy fading as Chicago settled into the small hours. Occasional cars passed, their headlights sweeping across empty sidewalks. A police patrol car cruised by, its occupants paying no attention to two people walking through their city. Just another night in a city full of people with their own problems.

Harper found himself thinking about Tomás, probably sitting in his apartment right now, trying to find ways to explain why he couldn't talk about his decision. Trying to justify choices he'd never wanted to make, protecting people he loved by betraying principles he'd believed in. The sort of impossible situation that powerful people used to control good people, turning their strengths into weaknesses.

'You're thinking too loud,' Cortez said.

'Occupational hazard,' Harper replied. 'Too many people are getting hurt by things they can't control.'

'Like Tomás?'

'Like everyone. Tomás, Rosa, and an eight-year-old girl Santos told me about who can't stop coughing because someone buried poison where her family lives.' Harper reached into his pocket, and touched his river stone again, grounding himself. 'Even people like Mason, probably. He started out trying to do good work, protect people, make the world safer. Somewhere along the way, it became about money and power and control.'

'You sound like you feel sorry for him.'

'I feel sorry for what he used to be,' Harper said. 'What he is now? That's a different matter entirely.'

They reached the warehouse, picked up the motorbike and rode back to Harper's father's building – or at least the building Harper's father had an apartment in – in silence, its pre-war architecture standing like a monument to old money and older secrets. Parking in the car park underneath, they came up the back steps, into a lobby that was empty except for a security guard who barely glanced up from his newspaper as they emerged from the side entrance.

Frank's night-time replacement, probably, someone who got paid to notice nothing and remember less.

The elevator ride to the apartment was silent, both of them processing the implications of what they were doing. By morning, Cortez would be officially involved in whatever Harper was planning. By morning, they'd either be building a case against some of the most powerful people in America or they'd be running for their lives.

By evening, there was a gala to attend.

'This is it,' Harper said, opening the apartment door and switching on lights.

The apartment looked exactly as he'd left it – expensive

furniture, corporate art, the impersonal luxury that came from having money but no time to develop taste. Cortez took in the space, probably noting the same things Harper had when he'd first seen it; security cameras, reinforced locks, the paranoid preparations of someone who'd made dangerous enemies.

'Nice place,' she said diplomatically.

'My father wasn't much for personal touches,' Harper replied, moving to the kitchen and starting coffee. Old habits – *make coffee, assess situation, plan next moves.* The sort of routine that kept you functional when everything else was falling apart. 'But it's secure, private, and the guest room has clean sheets.'

'I appreciate the hospitality.'

Harper could hear the exhaustion in her voice now that they were somewhere safe.

'Get some sleep,' he said. 'Tomorrow we figure out how to expose this without getting killed.'

'What about you?'

'I'll be fine, caught some naps in the police station. Too wired to sleep anyway.'

Harper wasn't lying. His mind was racing, processing everything that had happened, trying to anticipate what Slate and Mason would do next. They'd lost the advantage of surprise, lost the protection Mason's family connection had provided. From now on, they were operating in hostile territory with resources that didn't match their opponents'.

Cortez was about to respond when a sharp crack echoed through the apartment – glass breaking somewhere near the windows. Harper's tactical awareness kicked in immediately, recognising the sound he'd heard too many times in too many places.

Suppressed sniper rifle. Professional shooting. Multiple positions. The sort of precise operation that took time to plan and expensive resources to execute.

'Down!' he shouted, tackling Cortez to the floor as more glass exploded around them.

It looked like Mason Carrick's protection had just expired, and Veronica Slate was cleaning up loose ends with extreme prejudice.

The war had officially begun.

13

SHOOTING DUCKS

THE KITCHEN WINDOW EXPLODED INWARD IN A CASCADE OF tempered glass, fragments spinning through the air like deadly confetti. Harper rolled left, pulling Cortez behind the marble kitchen island as another crack split the night air.

A bullet punched through the probably expensive leather sofa where they'd been standing moments before, sending Italian leather and high-end stuffing across the hardwood floor. The projectile embedded itself in the far wall with a solid thunk that spoke of serious stopping power.

'Multiple shooters,' Harper assessed, his tactical mind automatically cataloguing threats while glass crunched under his elbows. 'At least three positions, probably more. High-rise buildings across the street giving them overlapping fields of fire.'

Cortez drew her sidearm while pressed against the floor, wincing as she moved; a vicious-looking shard had caught her left shoulder deep, blood soaking through her shirt where the fabric had torn.

'You hit bad?' Harper asked, noting how she held her arm.

'Hurts like hell, but I can still shoot.' Her jaw was tight with pain, but her voice remained steady. 'What the hell are they waiting for?'

As if on cue, the living room's floor-to-ceiling windows began exploding systematically. One after another, precise shots destroyed tempered glass while creating maximum psychological impact. This wasn't random violence – it was calculated intimidation designed to herd them like cattle towards a predetermined killing ground.

'Goddamned set-up,' Harper continued, his mind cataloguing tactical details while debris rained around them. 'They've been watching this place, waiting for us to arrive. We walked straight into Slate's trap.'

As he said the name, the realisation hit him like a physical blow. Slate had *wanted* them here. She'd orchestrated Harper's release from custody, not as a favour to Mason, but knowing he'd bring Cortez to the one place in Chicago he considered safe. His father's apartment wasn't a refuge – it was a kill box with panoramic views for multiple sniper teams.

'Clever bitch,' Harper muttered. 'She played us perfectly.'

Another window shattered, this one in the bedroom. The systematic destruction was almost artistic in its precision.

Harper's phone buzzed against his chest. Text message from an unknown number. The screen, however, didn't show a message – instead, it showed a photograph that made Harper's blood freeze. His father's notebook, spread open on what looked like a corporate conference table. Names, dates, operations – everything Harper had been using to work against Aegis, laid out for examination like evidence at a trial.

The notebook he'd left in the bedroom safe.

'They took it,' he breathed, showing Cortez the image

while staying low behind the marble counter. 'During the arrest. Slate's people searched the apartment while we were at the station. Shit, if they got that, they got Santos's notes, too.'

'Thorough bastards,' Cortez observed, wincing as she shifted position to get a better view of the screen.

Another message arrived before Harper could respond. This image made his stomach drop completely.

Tomás Alvarez.

Dumped in what looked like an alley behind industrial buildings.

Very obviously dead, with a single bullet wound to the forehead, execution style. His body was crumpled against a dumpster like discarded rubbish, arms at unnatural angles, blood pooling beneath his head.

Harper stared at the image, feeling rage and guilt building in his chest like molten metal. Tomás had died because Harper had involved him, had given him hope that fighting corruption was possible, had convinced him to take risks that got him killed by people who treated human life like a balance sheet entry.

Another innocent person destroyed in Harper's investigation. Another name for the list of people he'd failed to protect.

'Jesus Christ,' Cortez whispered, seeing the image over his shoulder. 'They executed him like a dog.'

Harper's phone began ringing; Rosa Alvarez's number showing. Harper stared at the screen for several rings, dreading what he was about to hear but knowing he had to answer. The woman deserved that much, at least.

'Harper!' Rosa's voice was raw with grief and fury, barely controlled emotion crackling through the phone speaker. 'I just had a photo arrive – one of my brother! Is it real?'

Harper closed his eyes, the image on his phone seared into his memory.

'Rosa, I'm so sorry—'

Crack. Another window shot out. The snipers were just pissing around now.

'Sorry?' Her voice cracked with anguish. 'You got him killed! You came to our neighbourhood, filled his head with ideas about fighting back, convinced him he could make a difference, and now he's dead!'

'Rosa, please, let me explain—'

'Explain what? That you convinced him to be a hero? That you made him think standing up to these people was worth it?' She was sobbing now, the words barely coherent through her grief. 'They left him in an alley like garbage! His children will grow up without a father because of you!'

Another window exploded as a sniper's bullet punched through the apartment, glass showering across the floor. Harper had to raise his voice over the sound of systematic destruction.

'I know you blame me,' Harper said, his own voice thick with guilt. 'And you're right to. But, Rosa, they'll come for you next if they think you know anything—'

'Don't you dare!' Rosa screamed through the phone. 'Don't you dare make this about protecting me! You've done enough damage! *Stay away from my family!*'

The line went dead, leaving Harper staring at the phone while bullets continued methodically destroying his father's apartment.

'She's right,' Harper said quietly, pocketing the phone. 'Tomás died because I got him involved. Because I thought I could fix things without understanding the cost.'

'Sounds like this Tomás died because he tried to do the

right thing in a world run by criminals,' Cortez replied firmly, checking her ammunition despite her bleeding shoulder. 'And when I arrived, it was his testimony against you that was keeping you in cuffs. That's not your fault, Harper. That's theirs.'

'Isn't it?' Harper touched his river stone, the familiar weight providing no comfort this time. 'I could have walked away after the first meeting. *Should* have walked away. Instead, I dragged good people into something that got them killed.'

A new sound reached their ears – boots on the stairwell outside the apartment. Heavy tactical movement, multiple personnel, what sounded to Harper's trained ears as a coordinated assault team moving with professional precision.

The snipers were to soften them. The assault team was to end them.

They had maybe thirty seconds before Slate's people reached this floor.

'We have to go,' Cortez said urgently, hearing the same boots.

Harper looked around the destroyed apartment – his inheritance, his father's last gift, now turned into an execution chamber with broken glass and bullet holes decorating every surface.

'All the evidence,' Harper said, his voice hollow with the realisation. 'The notebook, Santos's paperwork, everything we needed to expose Slate – it's gone. She has it all now.'

'Then we find another way. But first we survive this.'

'Stay low – I've got an idea,' Harper said, moving fast while staying grounded to avoid the continuing sniper fire. 'Gas line under the stove.'

He yanked the flexible gas line free from the stove

connection, hearing the sharp hiss as natural gas began flooding the apartment. The smell was immediate and dangerous – one spark would turn the entire space into a bomb that would take out half the floor.

Cortez understood immediately, positioning herself by the hallway entrance with her weapon ready despite her wounded shoulder.

'This is completely insane, Harper.'

'Better than being executed in a fancy flat like sitting ducks.' Harper grabbed his satchel, stuffing his laptop and his close-by items into it, throwing it over his shoulder before grabbing a dish towel from the kitchen counter and, pulling a vodka bottle from the bar, liberally soaked it in the bottle's contents while gas continued pouring into the air. 'When I say move, we go for the stairwell. Fast and low, through whatever's left of them.'

'And if this doesn't work?'

'Then at least we die fighting instead of cowering behind furniture like victims.'

Breaching charges blew the apartment doors inward, the blast echoing through the hallway like thunder. Four men in black tactical gear poured through the doorway, assault rifles raised. It was definitely a professional execution squad, probably ex-military, definitely expensive.

Harper didn't give them time to establish firing positions or coordinate their assault.

He dropped his lighter onto the soaked towel and hurled it towards the gas-flooded kitchen in one smooth motion, diving behind the marble island as the world exploded.

The blast was tremendous. It blew out what remained of the windows, sent the assault team diving for cover behind overturned furniture, and filled the apartment with smoke, flame, and superheated debris. The explosion rattled the entire building, set expensive drapes ablaze, and knocked paintings off the walls while the sprinkler system activated in response to the inferno.

Harper grabbed Cortez, pulling her towards the chaos rather than away from it – the last thing the assault team would expect from targets who were supposed to be cowering in terror.

'Move!'

They sprinted through the smoke and fire, Harper putting two rounds into the head and neck of the first assault team member who tried to recover from the explosion. The man went down instantly, his rifle skittering across the burning hardwood floor.

Cortez took the second man with a shot to the chest as they reached the hallway, her law enforcement training showing despite her injured shoulder. Years of tactical exercises had prepared her for exactly this sort of close-quarters combat, and Harper was glad for it, as he reached down and checked the groaning team member Cortez had shot. The man's rifle was attached to his tactical vest by a combat sling, and Harper knew he only had seconds, so he grabbed two flash bang grenades off the vest and carried on.

The remaining two assault team members were shouting into their tactical radios, calling for backup, trying to coordinate through the chaos Harper had created while smoke detectors shrieked throughout the building.

'Stairwell!' Harper kicked open the fire door, checking quickly for ambush positions. The concrete stairway appeared clear, but that wouldn't last long.

They pounded down the stairs, Harper's ears ringing from the explosion, Cortez favouring her injured shoulder but keeping pace despite the pain. Behind them, Harper could hear the surviving assault team members regrouping, coordinating pursuit with other teams positioned throughout the building.

Over twenty floors. Move fast.

'How many more do you think?' Cortez asked between breaths as they eventually reached the third-floor landing.

'At least a dozen, probably more. Vehicle teams, perimeter security, command coordination.' Harper calculated tactical odds while they descended. 'They've planned for everything except our being willing to burn the place down.'

'Remind me never to invite you to a dinner party,' Cortez winced as pain shot through her shoulder. 'Now I'm wondering if it *wasn't* you who set light to half of Prosperity, given this apparent love of blowing shit up.'

They reached the parking garage level, Harper pressing against the access door to listen carefully. Voices echoed in the concrete space – at least three men, positioned to cover all exits with enfilading fire. Professional ambush, exactly what Harper had expected.

'They're waiting for us,' Cortez observed, checking her remaining ammunition while blood seeped through her shirt.

'Slate's people know their business.' Harper assessed their tactical situation through the small window in the door. 'But they made one mistake.'

Before Cortez could ask what that was, a door burst open behind them—

'Hello, Liam.'

Harper spun, weapon raised, to find Mason Carrick stepping through the stairwell entrance. He was flanked by four

Aegis operatives in full tactical gear, assault rifles trained on Harper and Cortez.

Unlike his previous corporate appearance, Mason was dressed for war this time – body armour, communications headset, sidearm visible in a tactical holster. This wasn't Uncle Mason from Harper's childhood memories. This was Mason Carrick, the man who'd built an empire on violence and corruption.

'Mason,' Harper replied, not lowering his weapon despite the impossible odds. 'Lovely family reunion. Did you bring cake?'

'Always with the jokes.' Mason's voice carried the cold amusement Harper remembered from childhood. 'Your father had the same sense of humour. Right until it got him killed.'

'You got him killed,' Harper corrected. 'Myanmar, remember? Your operation, your screw-up, his blood.'

Mason's expression didn't change, but Harper caught the slight tightening around his eyes. *Direct hit.*

'This your work?' Harper pointed up the stairs, the implication obvious.

'No,' Mason shook his head. 'I'm covering the exits down here as a favour. Whatever happened upstairs was Meridian.'

'Well, Meridian just declared open season on me,' Harper snapped back. 'So, your favour had better be paying off a bloody large debt.'

There was a moment of silence, and Harper could see Mason working through the situation.

'Your protection just expired permanently,' Mason eventually replied, signalling his men to maintain their firing positions. 'No more family obligations, no more favours owed to

Dominic. From now on, you're just another target who knows too much.'

'Touching,' Harper said, keeping his voice steady despite the tactical impossibility of their situation. Four assault rifles against two handguns, no cover, no escape routes. 'What happened to that offer you made in the cell? Walk away, forget everything, pretend to be a good little civilian?'

'You should have taken that deal.' Mason checked his watch like a businessman late for a meeting. 'Veronica Slate has been very patient, but patience has limits, and we're quits.'

'I don't think so,' Harper replied calmly. 'You didn't get me out. She did – purely to kill me in my father's apartment. Therefore, you still owe me a get out of jail free card. Was it your men who killed Tomás Alvarez?'

'Mister Alvarez chose poorly. Accepted our generous offer, then developed a conscience at an inconvenient time.' Mason's tone suggested discussing a personnel issue rather than murder. 'These things happen in business. People make bad decisions, refuse reasonable compromises, force unpleasant solutions.'

'You mean murder.'

'I mean problem-solving.'

'You're all bastards,' Harper said quietly.

'We didn't do it,' Mason replied. 'That was Slate. I just want the journal...'

He trailed off as Harper started to chuckle.

'What?'

'I thought you had it,' Harper replied. 'But it seems while you had a little chat with me in jail, Meridian came to the apartment and picked the journal up. Slate has it, Mason. Not me.'

Mason's corporate mask slipped back into place, the brief moment of vulnerability disappearing like it had never existed.

'One last offer,' Mason said, his tone shifting back to business. 'You're right. I still owe you. Walk away from Chicago tonight. Disappear permanently. Forget about Slate, forget about the South Yards, forget about your father's crusade for justice. Clean slate, no more family obligations.'

'And if I refuse?'

'Then we finish this here.' Mason's voice carried a coldness. 'Slate wants to conclude this matter personally, but I'm flexible on methods.'

Harper glanced at Cortez, who was listening to this exchange while keeping her weapon trained on the Aegis operatives. Her face showed the same calculation Harper was making – four professionals with automatic weapons versus two targets, one wounded, with handguns.

The parking garage's sprinkler system chose that moment to activate as the building above went into full safety mode. If he was being honest, Harper had expected it to activate earlier, but he wasn't going to complain about this well-timed distraction as water cascaded down like an industrial waterfall, creating steam and confusion as the Aegis operatives tried to maintain target acquisition through the chaos.

'Now!' Harper shouted, tackling Cortez behind a concrete support pillar as automatic-weapons fire erupted.

Muzzle flashes strobed in the artificial rain while Mason shouted orders to cease firing. But the water was reducing visibility to near zero, and Harper knew this garage better than they did, if only from a couple more visits than they'd had.

He spotted his Bonneville across the space – thirty metres

of open ground under direct fire. Suicide run under normal circumstances, but Harper had prepared for this.

Pulling one of his two stolen flash bangs from his jacket, pulled the pin and tossed it towards the Aegis operators. He leaned into Cortez's ear and yelled over the noise.

'Open your mouth wide, close your eyes and turn away – then give me covering fire after the detonation!'

Cortez, wide-eyed, nodded and seconds later, an immense, blinding flash of bright white light accompanied by a deafening 170 decibel boom seared through the garage.

Unprepared for the blast, the Aegis personnel were blinded, deafened and disoriented while Cortez, impacted but fairing far better than their opponents, laid down suppressing fire as Harper sprinted for his bike, water and smoke swirling around him, bullets sparking off concrete and punching through car windows.

One round passed close enough to his head that he heard the supersonic whipcrack as the bullet passed his ear, but he reached the Bonneville and kick-started it with one smooth motion.

The engine roared to life as Harper spun towards Cortez's position, sliding the bike sideways to provide mobile cover. He alerted Cortez, then tossed the second flash bang at the Aegis group. The explosion caught their opponents just as they were starting to recover from the first blast and sent them even further into pain and disorientation.

She leaped onto the back as he gunned it towards the garage exit, wild, unaimed automatic weapons fire chasing them up the ramp.

'Hold on!' Harper warned, taking the bike up the ramp at a dangerous speed while Cortez pressed her good hand to her bleeding shoulder.

They burst onto Chicago's streets like escaping convicts, Harper immediately weaving through late-night traffic to break any target locks the snipers might still have. The Bonneville's engine note rose to a howl as they gained speed, putting distance between themselves and Slate's kill teams.

'That was completely mental!' Cortez shouted over the wind noise.

'Worked though!' Harper checked his mirrors, spotting black SUVs already following in coordinated pursuit. They were likely professional drivers who knew Chicago's streets, but they hadn't expected Harper to escape at all, much less on a motorcycle that could go places their vehicles couldn't follow.

Harper took a hard right onto Lake Shore Drive, accelerating into traffic that would force the pursuit vehicles to work for every gain while avoiding civilian casualties. The last thing he needed was innocent people caught in a running gun battle.

'Where are we going?' Cortez called out.

'Somewhere we can regroup and figure out how to crash a party tomorrow night!' Harper replied, taking the motorcycle up to speeds that would definitely attract police attention if there were any honest cops left in this area of Chicago.

Behind them, Mason Carrick's head had likely cleared somewhat. Undoubtedly, he'd be back coordinating the hunt for two people who'd just destroyed his best-laid plans and escaped what should have been a foolproof execution, while finding a way to blame Veronica Slate's impatience and scorched earth tactics on the apartment for the botched operation. But Harper felt a cold satisfaction building alongside his rage.

They'd lost the evidence, lost their key witness, lost any

hope of official justice. Tomás was dead, Rosa blamed him rightfully, and every authority figure in Chicago was either bought or intimidated into silence.

But they were still alive, still mobile, and still dangerous. Tomorrow night at Palmer House, everyone involved in this conspiracy would be gathered in one place for the Veterans' Gala. Slate celebrating her latest victory; Mason Carrick basking in whatever award they were giving him.

'You realise we just declared war on some very powerful people,' Cortez observed as they disappeared into Chicago's maze of side streets, leaving their pursuers behind in the urban labyrinth.

'They declared war first when they murdered Tomás,' Harper replied, his voice carrying the sort of icy determination his father would have recognised. 'We're just returning the favour.'

The city lights blurred past as they vanished into the night, two wounded survivors planning their last strike against an enemy who controlled everything except their will to keep fighting.

Tomorrow night, Chicago's elite would discover what happened when you cornered people with nothing left to lose.

And Harper knew someone else in the same position – and with a plan for the gala as well.

14

EVIDENCE AND ALLIES

HARPER GUIDED THE BONNEVILLE THROUGH CHICAGO'S BACK streets, Cortez's grip slowly getting weaker around his waist. Her shoulder was making the ride uncomfortable, but they needed distance from Mason's people before worrying about medical attention.

Brilliant tactical planning, that. Get shot at, then ride around Chicago on a motorcycle while bleeding. His father would be so proud.

He knew he could have simply gone to any hospital and dropped Cortez off – the wound wasn't a gunshot one; it was from shards of glass and there were a dozen different ways to explain it, but hospitals were public, and there was every chance they were all being watched.

Instead, Harper played a hunch and headed for the South Side Community Health Centre.

However, two blocks from the health centre, Harper spotted headlights in his mirrors that had been there too long. Black sedan – too far to make out the manufacturer and model yet, keeping distance but matching every turn. Professional surveillance, not random traffic.

'Company,' Harper said over the engine noise.

Cortez turned to look, wincing at the movement.

'How long?'

'Three minutes. Maybe four.' Harper took a sharp right down an alley, then another quick left. The headlights followed. 'They're persistent.'

Harper sped up through a series of turns that would challenge anyone not familiar with Chicago's grid system – in fairness, Harper was only mildly familiar, but what he lacked in local knowledge, he made up for as the Bonneville was narrower than a car and could slide through smaller spaces when a wrong turn became a chokepoint. And he was correct, as the strange car fell back, then disappeared entirely as Harper cut through a construction site and emerged on a parallel street.

'Lost them,' Cortez said.

'For now.' Harper's body was catching up with the adrenaline crash – hands slightly unsteady, vision occasionally blurring at the edges. He'd been running on anger and stubbornness for too long. 'But they'll be back. Probably coordinating with other teams.'

'Okay then... so where are we going?' Cortez asked.

'Doctor I met earlier. Knows about the contamination.' Harper checked his mirrors again – clear for now. 'Santos gave me evidence about sick kids. If anyone can help us understand what happened to Tomás, it's him.'

He gave a bitter smile.

'But we're mainly going to get you patched up somewhere safe.'

THE HEALTH CENTRE LOOKED BATTERED AND BROKEN UNDER the streetlights. Harper parked two streets away, in an alley behind a closed auto shop. Better to approach on foot – harder to spot, easier to run if things went sideways.

'Can you walk?' Harper asked, noting how Cortez favoured her left arm.

'I'll manage,' she said, but she was pale, probably more from shock than blood loss, and Harper could see the effort it took.

They approached the staff entrance through side streets, Harper checking doorways and windows for watchers. Chicago felt hostile now, every shadow potentially hiding Slate's people.

Through the glass doors, however, he spotted Santos at his desk, working the night shift, reviewing files.

Harper knocked carefully on the window – he didn't want everyone coming, just Santos, who looked up, wary. Then recognition hit.

'Harper?' Santos approached the door, noting Cortez's bloodied shoulder and Harper's general appearance of having recently survived a minor war. 'Christ, what happened?'

'The people poisoning your patients just tried to kill us.' Harper kept his hands visible but positioned to move quickly if needed. 'We need help.'

Santos opened the door, glancing past them into the street.

'Anyone follow you?'

'Shook them off, but they've got resources.' Harper helped

Cortez to a chair, noting how she winced at the movement. 'This escalated past anything reasonable about six hours ago.'

'How bad?' Santos was already gathering medical supplies.

'Glass fragment from sniper fire. And they murdered Tomás Alvarez tonight.' Harper felt the rage building again.

Santos went very still.

'Tomás is dead?'

'Shot in the head, dumped like rubbish.' The image was burned into Harper's memory – Tomás crumpled against that dumpster, discarded like waste. 'Sent me a photo. Also sent it to Rosa. She blames me. Can't say she's wrong.'

The guilt sat heavy. Harper had convinced Tomás that good people could make a difference, that standing up was worth the risk. Now the man was dead and his children would grow up without a father.

'Bloody hell.' Santos began cleaning Cortez's wounds. 'I knew this would escalate, but murder...'

'They won't give up,' Cortez observed, wincing as Santos worked on her shoulder. 'I've only been here for a few hours, and even I can see that.'

'Can't afford to. We know too much.' Harper resumed his restless movement around the small office. 'Slate's entire operation depends on keeping this quiet. And now they know we're wounded, on foot, with limited options.'

His phone buzzed – a new message.

Rosa Alvarez is next. Then you.

Harper felt ice in his stomach. They weren't just hunting him and Cortez – they were threatening Rosa, who'd already lost her brother because of Harper's investigation.

Who gave them the number? It was a new burner, and he'd called Crowe and Rosa, but couldn't remember anyone else. *Could they have taken it when he was arrested? If so, how did they get it before that?*

'We need to warn Rosa,' Harper said, showing them the message.

'She won't listen to you,' Cortez pointed out. 'She's stubborn. If she blames you for Tomás, then she'll ignore anything you say. Get your friend Santos to call her, get her to leave town.'

'She already has,' Harper considered this. 'Hopefully she never told Tomás where she was going. Maybe I'll get Santos to tell her to stay away from work until this is settled.'

'If she's even keeping to the plan now her brother's dead,' Cortez muttered. 'I know I wouldn't.'

Harper deleted the message, but the threat lingered. *Another person at risk because of choices he'd made.* His father would have recognised the methodology. Corporate security work taken to its logical extreme – identify threats, neutralise permanently, maintain plausible deniability.

'You said they murdered Tomás,' Santos said, focusing on extracting glass fragments. 'How do you know it wasn't random violence, and someone taking an opportunistic photo?'

'Because the photos show a professional job. Single shot to the forehead, no robbery, no struggle. Just elimination of a witness.'

'And you think Slate ordered it?' Santos paused.

'I know she did. The question is proving it.' Harper stopped pacing. 'Which is where you come in.'

'I'm a doctor, not a detective.'

'You're the only person in Chicago who knows about the contamination and isn't bought, scared, or dead.' Harper's voice carried desperate urgency. 'Official channels are compromised. Everyone with authority is either on Slate's payroll or too intimidated to act.'

'I gave you what I had.'

'I know, and I need copies again,' Harper replied. 'But I'm realising documents might not be enough here – I need a voice, and maybe a smoking gun.'

'Your last voice was apparently shot in the head *by* the smoking gun,' Santos muttered, finishing bandaging Cortez's shoulder. 'That should hold, but you need proper medical attention. Hospital, antibiotics, proper imaging to check for fragments I missed.'

'Can't risk a hospital,' Cortez said. 'Too many questions. They'll have people watching emergency rooms.'

'Then you're gambling with infection,' Santos warned. 'Sepsis kills as surely as bullets.'

Cortez tested her arm carefully.

'How long before it becomes a problem?'

'Twelve hours, maybe less if those fragments weren't clean.' Santos's expression was grim. 'You need professional treatment.'

Harper absorbed this. Another ticking clock, another factor limiting their options. Cortez wouldn't be able to function much longer without proper medical care but seeking it would expose them to Slate's people.

'Thanks,' Cortez said. Colour had returned to her face, but Harper could see the exhaustion underneath.

Santos turned to Harper.

'What exactly are you asking?'

'Help us examine Tomás's body. Find evidence proving this was murder, not a random crime.' Harper leaned against the desk. 'You mentioned you had soil samples? That would also help. And we need somewhere safe while we plan our next move.'

'You want to turn my health centre into a hideout?'

'We want to stop Slate getting away with this; to stop more children from being poisoned.' Harper thought about eight-year-old Maria, struggling to breathe because adults prioritised profit over safety. 'That girl you mentioned? She's just the beginning.'

Santos was quiet, weighing professional obligations against conscience.

'There's something else.' Harper pulled out his phone, showing Santos a photo of his father's notebook. 'My father documented Slate's operation. Environmental crimes, corporate connections, political protection.'

'Your father?'

'Dominic Kane. Co-founder of Aegis Security.' Harper touched his river stone. 'He knew what they were doing, documented it for insurance. Or revenge. By the time he developed a conscience, he was too deep to get out clean.'

'Why didn't he expose it?'

'Because he was part of it initially. Aegis provided security for Slate's operations, helped maintain the cover-up.' Harper felt the familiar weight of his father's legacy. 'So, he documented everything, left it for me to finish. Make it right. But tonight Slate got the original – all I have are my photos.'

'Which won't stand up in a court of law anyway,' Cortez was still testing the shoulder. 'You – *we* – need a new angle of approach.'

'The coroner's office,' Santos said finally. 'I know someone there. Doctor Patricia Kowalski. She's been documenting unusual patterns in autopsy results; she's working the graveyard shift as a penance.'

'Penance?'

'Kowalski's been asking questions about suspicious deaths for months. Chemical exposure signatures that don't match official records. Let's just say she asked too many questions, and a doctor at the hospital named Fleming stuck her in a box to go away.' Santos pulled out his phone. 'If Tomás was murdered professionally, she'll find evidence.'

At the name, a conversation with Rosa came back to him.

'My supervisor's Doctor Josephine Fleming. Big name in Chicago, been here for twenty years, very concerned about the hospital's relationship with community leaders and corporate donors. The sort of person who prefers not to see problems that might create uncomfortable questions.'

'Corporate donors like Slate Urban Development?'

'Among others. The hospital depends on community support, Harper. Creating public health scares isn't good for fundraising.'

'Do you mean Doctor Josephine Fleming?' he asked.

'You know her?'

'Of her,' Harper replied. 'Rosa mentioned she was a recipient of large donations from Slate.'

'Sounds like the same one.' Santos accepted the comment as he dialled a number. 'Let's see.'

The conversation was brief – medical professional to medical professional, coded language about "unusual case" and "second opinion needed". But eventually Santos disconnected the call and looked back at Harper and Cortez.

'She'll meet us at the morgue,' Santos said. 'But we need to be careful. Kowalski says there's been unusual interest in recent autopsy reports.'

'Slate's people covering tracks?'

'Most likely.' Santos checked his watch. 'We should take separate routes. You're being hunted, and I don't want to be their next target. Sorry. I'll call Rosa, give her an update, and then come.'

Harper shook his head.

'You've done enough,' he smiled. 'We can do the rest if Kowalski meets us. You need to take your own advice and go to ground too, for a day or two.'

'Why?'

'They may have gained your notes too,' Harper pursed his lips. 'They don't know you gave them to me, but they could come knocking with questions.'

'Jesus, Harper.'

'I know, I'm sorry. Get to somewhere off grid and hole up a day or so, until this is over. And Doctor? If this goes wrong – tell people about the contamination. Don't let them bury the truth with us.'

HARPER'S FIRST APPROACH TO THE COOK COUNTY MORGUE HAD to be aborted when he spotted two men in suits positioned across from the main entrance. Not obvious surveillance – they were having a conversation, smoking cigarettes – but their positioning gave them a clear view of anyone entering or leaving.

Slate's people had anticipated their move. Either that or this was pure coincidence.

Yeah, right.

Harper circled three blocks, checking for additional watchers. Found two more – one in a car, one at a bus stop that hadn't seen a bus in hours. Standard surveillance box, definitely a professional setup.

'They're covering it,' Harper told Cortez as they regrouped in an alley behind a closed restaurant. 'Four positions that I can see, probably more.'

'Okay. What's the plan?'

'Go around them.' Harper studied the morgue's layout from their concealed position. The loading dock was on the building's south side, less visible from the street. If they could get inside through service areas, they could avoid the main entrance entirely.

They moved through back alleys, staying away from the late night viewers. Harper's exhaustion was catching up – twice he nearly walked into open sight of watchers, catching himself at the last moment. His tactical awareness was degrading, mistakes creeping in.

Shit. Now was not the time.

They approached the loading dock from behind an adjacent building, using the walls as cover, keeping from the street's view.

Doctor Patricia Kowalski – or, at least that was who Harper assumed it was – met them at the staff entrance – fifties, competent, wearing the expression of someone who'd spent decades dealing with Chicago's violent realities.

'Doctor Santos says you need to examine a body,' she said without preamble. 'Tomás Alvarez, brought in three hours ago. Officially classified as gang violence.'

'Officially,' Harper repeated, entering, checking behind them. The security teams hadn't seen them enter, but that didn't mean they hadn't expected this. A glance at Cortez showed she was thinking through the same positions.

'Unofficially, it's the cleanest execution I've seen in twenty years.' Kowalski led them through corridors that smelled of disinfectant and institutional despair. 'Single shot, close range, professional positioning.'

They reached the examination room where Tomás lay covered by a sheet. Kowalski pulled it back, and Harper felt the impact like a physical blow.

Tomás looked smaller in death, reduced from environmental engineer trying to protect his community to evidence on a steel table.

'Tell me what you see,' Kowalski said, studying Harper's reaction.

Harper forced himself to examine the body clinically, pushing aside guilt. His SRR training helped a little – UKSF had made sure their soldiers had a variety of areas of expertise, and a small stint with the Military Police had made sure Harper understood basic forensics and crime scene analysis.

'Contact wound. Powder burns around entrance. Larger hole in the rear of the skull. Close-range execution.'

'Good. What else?'

Harper studied the positioning, then noticed older injuries.

'Two sets of trauma?'

'Exactly.' Kowalski pointed to barely visible zip-tie marks. 'Older bruising on torso and face – maybe six, seven hours old. Recent ligature marks on wrists. He was beaten earlier, probably during initial capture. Then held for several hours before being restrained and executed.'

Cortez, her police instincts overriding queasiness, leaned closer.

'They grabbed him, worked him over, then came back to finish the job?'

'Two-phase interrogation. Physical coercion for basic

information, then restraint and questioning before execution.' Kowalski examined the wound with a magnifying glass. 'The ammunition's interesting too.'

'How so?'

'Hollow point, high velocity. Expensive round. Trajectory suggests shooter was about five-ten, professional stance, minimal deviation.' She moved to the evidence table. 'The bullet recovered from the alley shows distinctive rifling marks. Conventional lands and grooves, tight spacing – probably from a Walther P99 with an aftermarket barrel. Original P99s use polygonal rifling, but this one's been replaced. Professional modification, expensive work.'

Harper absorbed this, building a profile.

Someone trained, probably ex-military. The sort Slate could afford when problems needed permanent solutions.

'That's remarkably specific analysis.'

'This is Chicago – I see crap like this every day. Gang hits, professional executions, turf wars with military-grade hardware. You learn ballistics on the job fast when half your caseload involves custom weapons, and I've been doing this for eight years.' Kowalski's voice carried professional pride mixed with weary experience. 'After your first hundred gunshot victims, you start recognising patterns. This wasn't some street corner special – this was professional work by someone who knows their craft.'

Five-ten, professional stance, minimal deviation. Walther P99, aftermarket barrel. Remember. Avenge.

'Military training?'

'Almost certainly. Textbook execution technique. There's something else.' Kowalski covered the body again. 'When they brought him in, I could smell it immediately.'

'Smell what?'

'Expensive tobacco. Cuban cigar smoke still clinging to his clothes and hair,' Kowalski replied. 'Sweet, distinctive scent. Takes about an hour to fade naturally, but this was fresh. Recent. Did your friend here smoke?'

'I never saw him do it, or smelled any smoke on him, but I can't be sure,' Harper admitted. 'But if he didn't, are you saying the killer smoked near the body?'

'*On* the body would be my professional assessment. The concentration was strongest around his torso and face, and we found ash on the chest, as if some had fallen onto it.' Kowalski gestured to Tomás's covered form. 'Whoever shot him stood over the corpse and smoked a premium Cuban cigar while admiring their work.'

She walked to the evidence table, returning with a small plastic bag.

'Crime scene found this cigar stub a couple of feet away. *Cohiba Esplendidos* – fifty dollars each, completely illegal to import. Yellow and black bands, guillotine cut, barely half-smoked before being extinguished.'

Harper examined the evidence bag, noting how carefully the expensive tobacco had been cut and the casual way it had been discarded, likely put out under a shoe.

He knew who smoked these.

'DNA?'

'Processing takes weeks, but there's definitely saliva evidence.' Kowalski's expression was granite-hard. 'What kind of animal celebrates murder standing over a dead body while smoking fifty-dollar tobacco like it's some sort of victory celebration? That's someone who doesn't expect to be seen during the act or get arrested after.'

Tall, broad, and with a Belfast-ish accent. When he found the bastard, Harper would make sure to ram every cigar down his throat.

'There's something else. This isn't the first suspicious death I've documented recently.' Kowalski brought him back to the present.

'Meaning?'

'Over the past six months, I've seen five similar cases. All classified as accidents or natural causes, so not as obvious as this, although this one is being claimed as a mugging gone wrong. All involving people who lived near contamination sites or had environmental knowledge that might threaten corporate interests.'

'Five murders?' Cortez's voice carried horror.

'Five convenient deaths of potential environmental witnesses, rather.' Kowalski pulled out a thick file. 'Construction worker who died in a fall after reporting unsafe soil conditions at three different sites. Environmental scientist who suffered a heart attack the day before testifying to EPA regulators – no history of cardiac problems. Community activist who overdosed on drugs she'd never used – toxicology showed injection sites, but she had a phobia of needles. Journalist investigating industrial pollution patterns – car accident on a straight road in clear weather, brake failure. Union safety inspector who drowned in Lake Michigan despite being an excellent swimmer and knowing those waters since childhood.'

'All connected to Slate's projects?' Harper asked.

'Different companies, different locations, different time frames. But consistent patterns – and personally, I reckon they're professional elimination disguised as misfortune.' Kowalski's expression was grim. 'Someone's been cleaning house across multiple environmental crime scenes for months, maybe years. I'm probably on the list too, just for asking questions.'

Harper felt cold certainty. This wasn't just covering up the South Yards contamination – it was part of a larger operation to eliminate anyone who might expose corporate environmental crimes across the entire region, possibly multiple states.

Kowalski handed Harper the file.

'I've been documenting everything but can't prove murder without more evidence.'

'But you could testify if we built a case?'

'If you can guarantee protection from people with resources to make problems disappear.'

'Sheriff Cortez has federal law enforcement authority. She could provide official backing.' Harper glanced at Cortez, who'd been listening while leaning against the table for support.

Kowalski studied Cortez's credentials.

'You're willing to take this on?' she asked.

'They just tried to kill us,' Cortez replied, though exhaustion was evident. 'Murdered a good man for trying to protect children. So, yeah, I'd say so.'

Kowalski nodded slowly.

'Then I'll help. But we need to be extremely careful.'

'What do you need?'

'A few hours to compile comprehensive forensic evidence on all five deaths. Documentation proving murder, not random misfortune.' Kowalski checked her watch. 'But you need somewhere safe to wait. This building isn't secure – too many people with official credentials asking questions tonight.'

'I can find us a safe house.' Harper was already thinking

ahead. A few hours would put them at dawn – perfect timing for tomorrow's preparation. But they'd need more than Kowalski's evidence to make their case stick. 'We'll also need to verify this connects to the South Yards contamination. Cross-reference with the remaining documentation I have, show the pattern isn't random.'

'And after that?' Cortez asked. 'What's the plan?'

Harper thought about tomorrow night's – no, *tonight's* – Veterans' Gala, where Slate would be networking while celebrating her latest victory. Where all threads would finally converge.

'The Veterans' Gala. That's where we expose everything,' he snarled. 'The contamination, the murders, the cover-up. Slate will be there with every politician and media figure in Chicago. If we present our evidence publicly, it'll be harder to bury.'

Kowalski raised an eyebrow.

'You're planning to crash a high-security event with evidence of multiple murders and hope to do a *PowerPoint* show for them?'

'Something like that.'

'That's either brave or completely mental.'

'Not much difference, really,' Harper almost smiled, touching his river stone.

As they prepared to leave, Harper took one last look at Tomás's covered form. The man had died trying to protect his family, trying to expose soil poisoning children.

His death would either be meaningless or the catalyst bringing everyone down.

Harper intended to make sure it was the latter.

Outside the morgue, Chicago's industrial district felt different – more hostile, like the city itself was working against them. Every parked car could hide watchers; every shadow might conceal threats.

'Where now?' Cortez asked as they walked towards Harper's motorcycle.

'We'll find a bolthole, then I need to find someone I thought might be a potential threat and get them to help us.'

Cortez chuckled at this.

'Liam Harper. Never changes.'

Harper looked at Cortez.

'Can you ride?' he asked.

'I have been—'

'No, I mean take the bike and ride,' Harper continued. 'We have about eighteen hours until the gala, and I need to get my head down. You, meanwhile, need to get to a medical facility a good hour's drive from here – so you don't show up on Slate's radar – and get the antibiotics for that wound.'

'Harper—'

'Don't worry, you'll be back by the time the shit hits the fan,' Harper smiled. 'But I need you at full capacity, not fevering out because someone didn't clean my father's windows for a few months.'

He showed his maps app.

'Here, aim north, go to Saint Francis Hospital of Evanston,' he said. 'Small teaching hospital, far enough to avoid their gaze. Fix up, rest up, then contact me. I'll send you meeting locations.'

Reluctantly Cortez examined the route, nodded and, throwing on Harper's helmet with a promise to call, she rode off northwards, towards Evanston.

Chicago at night had settled on the sort of persistent drizzle that made everything feel damp and miserable. Rather like Harper's current situation, really.

Tomorrow was going to be bloody interesting. In the sort of way that usually ended with people in hospital.

But tonight, Harper was going to send someone to the morgue.

He hadn't sent Cortez away purely out of concern – he needed her to be away from him for the next few hours...

Because Harper was going to hunt down and kill Tomás's cigar-smoking murderer.

15

HUNTING SEASON

CHICAGO AT THREE IN THE MORNING HAD THAT PECULIAR quality of a city pretending to sleep while staying wide awake. The drizzle had stopped but left everything damp and reflective, turning the streetlights into scattered stars on wet pavement, as Harper walked the empty streets with the focused patience of someone hunting rather than wandering.

The image from the morgue stayed with him – Kowalski's clinical description of expensive Cuban tobacco scent clinging to Tomás's corpse, the casual arrogance of smoking a fifty-dollar cigar while standing over a murdered father. Harper had connected it to the security supervisor he'd seen at South Yards, the one smoking expensive cigars while overseeing contaminated soil loading. The one who'd also tried to take Harper and Rosa outside the hospital.

Now he had someone to hunt, and all night to do it in. Harper knew exactly where to start, too. The trucking depot from South Yards – the same place where he'd first encountered his target and his colleagues beating Tomás a couple of nights earlier. If anyone would know where to find the cigar-smoking bastard, it would be the people who worked with him.

THE DEPOT LOOKED THE SAME AS IT HAD WHEN HARPER FIRST scouted it – corrugated steel and concrete in an industrial district that had given up trying to be respectable decades ago. He approached from the south, using the same abandoned railway infrastructure for cover.

Two lorries sat in the loading bays, their drivers long gone at this time in the early morning. But there was movement in the security office – a single figure visible through grimy windows, probably the night watchman making his rounds.

Harper made his approach direct but non-threatening. The security office occupied a prefabricated building connected to the main depot, accessible through a side door that looked like it hadn't been painted since the nineties. He knocked firmly but not aggressively.

The door opened after a moment's hesitation, revealing a man in his sixties with the resigned expression of someone who'd spent too many nights dealing with unexpected visitors. His uniform was clean but worn, suggesting pride in his work despite the circumstances.

'We're closed,' he said automatically, then took in Harper's appearance – leather jacket, jeans, and a deliberate casualness that suggested he wasn't here for standard business.

'Not looking for transport,' Harper replied, keeping his voice level and reasonable. 'Looking for information. About one of your security supervisors.'

The watchman's expression shifted from tired routine to careful wariness.

'What kind of information?'

Harper pulled out two twenties, holding them where they could be seen without being obvious about it.

'The sort that helps me understand who's been giving orders around here. Particularly someone who likes expensive cigars.'

Money had a way of making conversations more productive, especially during the small hours when people questioned their employment choices.

'You talking about Murphy?' The watchman glanced past Harper into the empty street. 'Belfast bloke, always smoking those fancy ones that probably cost more than I make in a day?'

'That's the one.' Harper kept his tone conversational, professional. 'Where might I find him tonight?'

'Depends what you want with him.' The watchman accepted the notes but kept them visible. 'Murphy's not the sort who appreciates unexpected visitors.'

'Just need to have a chat. Professional matter.'

'Professional matter.' The watchman's laugh held no humour. 'Right. Well, if you're looking for "professional" advice, you might try *O'Rourke's* down by the docks. Twenty-four-hour place, serves the sort of crowd that works unusual hours.'

'Appreciated.' Harper turned to leave, but the watchman grabbed his arm.

'If this causes any blowback,' he said hurriedly, 'you didn't hear it from me.'

'Who don't you like here?' Harper asked.

'What?'

'Who don't you get on with? Who pisses you off, winds you up, irritates you?'

The watchman thought about this.

'Norton. He's a prick.'

'There you go, then,' Harper flashed a smile as he turned and left the yard. 'If anyone asks, it was Norton who told me.'

HARPER HEADED TOWARDS THE WATERFRONT, WHERE THE AIR carried the smell of the lake mixed with diesel fuel and industrial chemicals, creating that distinctive urban perfume that made you grateful for countryside whenever you encountered it.

O'Rourke's looked like the sort of establishment that had survived every economic downturn since the Great Depression by the simple expedient of serving strong drinks to people who needed them. The neon sign flickered with the persistence of something too stubborn to die, and through the windows Harper could see the warm glow of a place that understood its purpose.

The interior was exactly what he'd expected – dark wood, brass fixtures that had lost their shine, and the sort of comfortable shabbiness that came from decades of honest use. A handful of patrons occupied scattered stools and booths, the sort of people who worked when others slept and found solace in consistent surroundings.

The bartender looked up as Harper entered, nodding the universal greeting of someone who'd served every type of customer at every possible hour.

'What can I get you?'

'Pint of whatever's decent,' Harper replied, settling onto a stool. 'And maybe some conversation about regulars.'

'Conversation costs extra. Our Guinness is passable.'

'I'll take one.' Harper placed a twenty on the bar alongside the cost of the drink. 'But no shamrock on the head needed.'

The bartender chuckled.

'Not a tourist, then?'

'Looking for a regular. Belfast accent, likes cigars, works security. Goes by Murphy.'

The bartender poured the pint with the measured care of someone who'd done this thousands of times, considering Harper's question while going through the familiar motions.

'You know Murphy?' he asked finally.

'We've met here and there; we have mutual business interests.'

'Right.' The bartender passed the Guinness across, and Harper took a mouthful, realising that "passable" was definitely pushing the boundaries of truth here. 'He was in earlier, maybe two hours ago. Usually comes in after finishing work, has a couple of drinks, heads home around this time.'

'Any idea where home might be?'

The bartender's expression became more guarded.

'That's the sort of information that requires better motivation than twenty bucks.'

Harper was about to add another twenty when a voice cut through the bar's low murmur.

'Hey, English boy!' A drunk at the far end of the bar had twisted around to face Harper, his words slurred but aggressive. Mid-forties, a construction worker by the look of his clothes, and clearly several pints past making good decisions. 'You hear me talking to you?'

Harper ignored him, keeping his attention on the bartender. But the drunk wasn't having it.

'My grandfather died fighting you bastards in Derry. You

got some feckin' nerve coming in here.' The drunk slid off his stool, moving towards Harper with the sort of exaggerated care that suggested he was drunker than he looked. A few other patrons glanced up with the weary expression of people who'd seen this show before.

'Mate, you've got the wrong end of the stick,' Harper said calmly, not turning from the bar. 'But I'd suggest you go back to your drink.'

'Don't tell me what to do in my own feckin' country.' The drunk reached Harper's position, putting a heavy hand on his shoulder, and Harper could smell stale beer and decades of cigarettes.

'Problem here?' the bartender asked, but without much conviction.

Harper sighed, then turned to face the drunk. The man was bigger than Harper, probably outweighed him by thirty pounds, and had the sort of aggressive stance that suggested he'd thrown punches before.

'No problem,' Harper replied pleasantly. 'Just a misunderstanding.'

'Damn right it's a misunderstanding. You misunderstood thinking you were welcome here.' The drunk took a swing – telegraphed, wild, exactly what Harper expected from someone that drunk. Harper stepped inside the arc, caught the man's wrist, and used his own momentum to guide him face-first into the bar with just enough force to make his point without causing serious damage.

The drunk bounced off the wooden surface, stumbled backwards, and sat down hard on the floor.

'Like I said, just a misunderstanding,' Harper told him, then helped the man back to his feet. 'No harm done.'

He held out a hand.

'Don't blame me for the accent, I can't help where I was brought up,' he said. 'I'm Liam, and like your grandfather, I was born in free Derry. Now, does that sound like an English name or location?'

The drunk blinked, processing what had just happened, then shook his head slowly and returned to his stool at the far end of the bar.

The bartender watched this entire exchange with growing interest.

'Well,' he said finally. 'That was... professional.'

'I try to avoid unnecessary violence,' Harper replied, settling back onto his stool.

The bartender poured the drunk a fresh pint on the house, then returned to Harper.

'Were you really born in Derry?'

'Does it matter?'

The bartender looked at the drunk, at Harper, and smiled.

'Pilsen area,' he said quietly. 'Building with the green fire escape on Ashland Avenue. Can't miss it – Murphy's got security cameras and the sort of reinforced door that suggests paranoid tendencies. Don't know the number but believe me... if you turn up with violence on your mind, he'll find you before you find him.'

THE JOURNEY TO PILSEN WOULD HAVE BEEN FAR QUICKER ON the Bonneville but was still one that could be done through empty streets.

Harper spotted the building immediately – four storeys of red brick with a distinctive green fire escape zigzagging up the side like a geometric vine. Security cameras covered the main entrance, and Harper could see the reinforced door the bartender had mentioned. The building's layout was standard warehouse conversion – large windows, high ceilings, the sort of space that appealed to people who valued privacy over conventional comfort.

From his position across the street, Harper could see into a lit window on the fourth floor. Someone was moving around inside, and occasionally Harper caught the distinctive orange glow of something being lit, perhaps a cigar glowing as the smoker took it in.

The building's main entrance required a key card, but Harper had other options. Fire escapes were rarely secured properly – they were meant for emergencies, after all.

Harper made his approach using stealth that had kept him alive in Belfast, Basra, and a dozen other places where being noticed meant being shot. The fire escape was old but well-maintained, each step carefully placed to minimise noise. Reaching the fourth floor, Harper positioned himself beside the window of what was clearly Murphy's apartment. The window was partially open – enough for Harper to see inside and hear that the flat was currently empty.

No voices, no movement, no sound except the distant hum of a refrigerator. Either Murphy had finished his smoke and left... or he was *waiting*.

Harper slipped through the window into Murphy's living space.

The apartment was exactly what he'd expected from a paranoid ex-military contractor. Sparse furniture was arranged to provide clear access to all entrances. A small kitchen that looked barely used. Electronics that were very expensive or very basic – nothing in between that might contain tracking software or unnecessary vulnerabilities.

But what caught Harper's attention was the smell – cigars, recently smoked. And something else, something chemical that reminded him of gun oil and industrial solvents. There was no Murphy however – he'd likely left the apartment, which could give Harper hours to search, or scant moments.

Hopefully, the former.

Harper moved carefully through the space, hyperaware that Murphy could return at any moment. He could even be asleep in the bedroom, awakened by Harper making any kind of loud movement.

The living room contained a desk with multiple mobile phones, all switched off, and a laptop that was password-protected and probably encrypted beyond anything Harper could crack quickly.

In the bedroom, Harper found what he was looking for – not the man himself, as he wasn't in the bed, but evidence of Murphy's work.

A small safe had been left open. Inside were photographs of various locations around Chicago, including several of the South Yards development site. But these weren't tourist shots – they were surveillance photos, taken with telephoto lenses, showing specific individuals and their daily routines.

One set of photos made Harper's blood run cold.

Tomás Alvarez.

Entering his apartment building.

Leaving for work.

Walking his usual route to the bus stop.

Meeting with Harper outside the health centre.

They'd been watching Tomás for weeks before they killed him.

Harper pocketed the most relevant photos, then continued his search. In the wardrobe, behind expensive suits that suggested Murphy's contract work paid very well, Harper found a weapons cache. Three handguns, ammunition, and something that looked like professional surveillance equipment, although without turning on a light he couldn't tell properly.

But it was the small metal humidor on the wardrobe shelf that really interested him. Cuban cigars. Cohiba Esplendidos, with their distinctive yellow and black bands. The same cigars that had left their scent on Tomás's corpse.

Harper was examining the cigar case when he heard footsteps in the hallway outside. Heavy boots moving with purpose. Coming closer.

Harper froze, listening carefully. The footsteps stopped outside Murphy's door, and Harper could hear the distinctive sound of keys being sorted through.

Shit. Murphy was back already.

Harper had maybe fifteen seconds before the door opened. The window he'd entered through was across the room – too far to reach without being seen. The bedroom offered no cover except under the bed, which was exactly where anyone with military training would look first.

The kitchen. There was a small but narrow alcove beside the refrigerator where Harper might remain unseen if Murphy didn't turn on all the lights.

Harper moved quickly but quietly, reaching the kitchen alcove just as he heard the apartment's main door open.

Murphy, or at least someone who Harper assumed was Murphy entered, and Harper could hear him moving through the living room with the careful steps of someone conducting a security check. Professional paranoia – checking that everything was exactly as he'd left it.

Had Harper left everything that way?

No. He'd taken the photos.

Idiot.

Harper pressed himself against the wall in the narrow space beside the refrigerator, controlling his breathing while listening to Murphy's movements. The man was thorough, checking the living room, then the bedroom where Harper had just been searching. Harper heard drawers being opened, the wardrobe door creaking. Murphy was looking for something specific, or perhaps just confirming that his apartment hadn't been disturbed.

Then Harper heard something that made his situation infinitely more dangerous.

A phone ringing. Murphy answering it.

'Yeah, it's me,' Murphy's Belfast accent was clear now that Harper was in the same space. 'Just got back to check on something... No, no problems here, but I want to make sure Harper hasn't been sniffing around.'

Harper felt his pulse quicken.

They were talking about him.

'Patterson's in position at the office building. If Harper shows up there, we'll have him boxed in... Yeah, I know it's risky keeping him alive this long, but Slate wants to know what he's learned before we put him down.'

The conversation continued, and Harper realised Murphy was moving towards the kitchen while talking. Harper had nowhere to go. If Murphy walked into the kitchen and turned on the light, Harper would be completely exposed.

But, as Murphy's footsteps approached the kitchen entrance, Harper heard something else – a sound from above that made him reconsider his tactical situation entirely.

Noises from the roof – the smash of something glass.

Someone was up there.

Murphy heard it too, and his phone conversation stopped mid-sentence.

'Hold on,' Murphy said into the phone. 'Someone's on the roof.'

Harper heard Murphy moving quickly through the apartment, no longer concerned about noise. A door opened – probably to a stairwell in the corridor outside the apartment's front door.

This was Harper's chance.

He slipped out of the kitchen alcove and made his way to the window that connected to the fire escape. As quietly as possible, Harper climbed out onto the metal platform and began ascending towards the roof level. Behind him, he could hear Murphy's voice echoing in the stairwell as he climbed internal stairs towards the roof access.

Harper reached the roof just as the access door opened and Murphy emerged; phone still pressed to his ear—

A tabby cat looked up from where it had been investigating something near the roof's edge, a broken bottle beside it, likely having fallen off the edge of a small table as it ran past, then bolted across the neighbouring rooftop with the dismissive arrogance that only cats could manage as Murphy screamed out an Irish obscenity at it, tossing a half brick in its general direction.

Murphy looked around the empty roof, muttering something about urban wildlife into his phone and in the process missing Harper, who was now positioned behind him with a clear tactical advantage.

The roof was flat, bounded by a low parapet wall with excellent sight lines in all directions. Someone had set up what looked like a small seating area near the building's centre – a couple of plastic chairs, a small table with a now-broken bottle beside it, the sort of setup that suggested regular use.

And there, with his back to the fire escape, watching for cats stood Murphy, murmuring into his mobile phone while lighting what was definitely an expensive cigar. The distinctive yellow and black bands of a Cohiba Esplendidos were visible even in the dim light from the city below.

'—situation's contained for now, but the Harper problem requires permanent resolution—' Murphy was saying into the phone. '—no, two of us should be sufficient. Same protocols as the Mexican—'

Harper felt his throat tighten. They were planning another execution, and Harper himself was the target.

He moved while Murphy was focused on his conversation. SRR training emphasised surprise and overwhelming force in close-quarters situations. As Murphy ended his call, Harper covered the distance between the fire escape and Murphy's position in three seconds of silent movement, getting within arm's reach before the other man sensed danger.

Murphy spun, dropping the phone and reaching for what was probably a concealed weapon, but Harper was already inside his defensive perimeter. A precise strike to the radial nerve in Murphy's gun side forearm caused instant pain coupled with hand and wrist weakness. A hard elbow strike to Murphy's temple stunned him further. Harper slid behind his opponent and clamped around his neck, compromising his air supply and preventing any shouts that might alert neighbours or bring additional security.

The struggle was brief but violent. Murphy was professional, trained, and experienced – but Harper had the advantage of surprise and twenty years of making violence look effortless. Within thirty seconds, Murphy was face down on the roof, disarmed, with Harper's knee in his back and a very sharp scalpel, borrowed from the morgue, at his throat.

'Let's have a conversation about Tomás Alvarez,' Harper said quietly, his voice carrying the sort of controlled menace that suggested negotiation wasn't really an option, the scalpel's blade catching what little light filtered up from the street below.

Murphy tried to speak through Harper's hand over his mouth, managing only muffled sounds.

'I'm going to move my hand,' Harper continued. 'If you shout, I'll cut your throat and disappear before anyone finds the body. If you cooperate, we can discuss this like civilised people. Your choice.'

Harper lifted his hand slightly.

'You don't know what you're messing with,' Murphy gasped, his Belfast accent thick with pain and anger.

'Then explain it to me.' Harper pressed the knife point slightly deeper, drawing a bead of blood. 'Starting with who ordered Tomás Alvarez's execution.'

'Go to hell.'

Harper had expected resistance. Professional killers didn't break easily, and Murphy had probably been through interrogation training at some point in his military career. But Harper had learned interrogation in places where time was limited and information was vital.

'Wrong answer,' Harper said, jabbing a knuckle into the nerve cluster just behind Murphy's ear, as the man's body went rigid with pain. 'Let me clarify the situation. I know you killed Tomás. I know you smoked expensive cigars over his corpse like it was some sort of celebration. What I want to know is who gave the order and how many others were involved.'

Murphy's breathing became laboured as Harper maintained pressure.

'There were two of us,' he gasped finally. 'But Slate's got bigger plans than just covering up some old contamination.'

'What kind of plans?'

'She's cutting ties with Aegis. Mason's people are too unreliable, too much history with your family.' Murphy's voice was strained. 'She's funding Meridian to handle the wetwork. Clean slate – no pun intended – no baggage.'

Harper processed this.

'So, you work for Meridian?'

'Slate pays well for permanent solutions to her problems,' Murphy managed a bitter smile. 'Your environmental engineer friend was just another job – the beating, the scaring, the kidnapping... all work. Nothing personal.'

'It's personal now. Who was the second man there? Was he there to make sure you got the job done? I only saw one bullet hole.'

'You saw the body—' Murphy gasped as Harper jabbed the nerve cluster again, harder.

'Answer the bloody question.'

'Okay, okay, it's someone you've already met. Someone who's been watching you since you arrived in Chicago.' Murphy's breathing was becoming more regular now Harper eased the pressure slightly. 'Former SAS, or something like that. But you won't get within a mile of him. He knows you're coming.'

'Tell me who and where he is.'

'Meridian Security building. Third floor, corner office. He goes by Patterson this week, but that won't last,' Murphy's voice carried bitter satisfaction. 'Always there before dawn. Claims it's the best time to work, as he doesn't have to speak to anyone. Works directly for—'

Murphy moved while Harper was processing the information. The bastard had been waiting for Harper's attention to waver, using the distraction and counting on Harper's tiredness while positioning himself for a counterattack.

He twisted violently, trying to break Harper's grip while his free hand went for what looked like a backup weapon concealed in his boot. Fast, professional, the sort of move that suggested extensive close-quarters combat training.

But Harper had been expecting something like this. The scalpel drew across Murphy's throat in one swift motion, opening the carotid artery with almost surgical precision – Harper had learned anatomy the hard way. Murphy's eyes widened with shock as arterial blood began pumping across the rooftop.

'That's for Tomás,' Harper said quietly, stepping back as Murphy's hands flew to his neck.

Murphy collapsed to the rooftop, blood spraying rapidly across the weathered concrete. He tried to speak but could only manage wet, gurgling sounds as his life drained away through Harper's precise incision.

Harper watched the light fade from Murphy's eyes, feeling satisfaction mixed with the cold realisation that killing this man had solved exactly nothing. Tomás was still dead, his children would still grow up without a father, and now Harper knew there was a second shooter to hunt down.

But at least one of the bastards who'd celebrated over Tomás's corpse would never smoke another expensive cigar.

Harper wiped the scalpel clean on Murphy's jacket, then once he was sure there were no fingerprints, he broke the blade from the handle and tossed it off the roof, throwing pieces in either direction, hearing them clatter down the street. With luck it'd be ignored, and even if found it couldn't be traced back to him.

Harper searched Murphy's body quickly, finding a wallet with multiple identity documents and a small notebook containing what looked like operational details. All of it would require careful examination, but not here on a rooftop with a fresh corpse.

The Meridian Security building. Third floor, corner office. Someone calling himself Patterson this week.

After returning to the apartment and retrieving the fallen phone, seeing it was filled with encrypted contacts, Harper pocketed Murphy's kit and headed for the fire escape, leaving the body where it lay. By morning, Chicago would have another unexplained death to add to its statistics, but before then Harper would hunt down the second shooter who'd helped murder Tomás Alvarez.

One down, one to go.

16

MISTER PATTERSON

THE MERIDIAN SECURITY BUILDING HEAD OFFICE SAT THREE blocks from the lake, several floors of a glass and steel construction that screamed corporate respectability while hiding whatever sins paid the rent. Unlike the industrial warehouse where Harper had first encountered their operatives, this place projected legitimate corporate success – marble lobby, brass nameplates, the sort of expensive respectability that made murder look like risk management consulting, as Harper approached on foot through Chicago's pre-dawn streets, Murphy's blood still under his fingernails.

Third floor, corner office. He goes by Patterson this week.

Without the Bonneville, Harper had relied on Chicago's night buses and his own feet to cross the city. The journey from Pilsen to the business district took forty minutes, giving him time to examine Murphy's materials under streetlights.

The Irishman's notebook was a masterclass in operational planning – Harper's daily routine over the last day – or, at least until he'd been arrested – had been mapped with uncomfortable precision. Tomás Alvarez's family patterns had also been mapped out, including work schedules, school pickup times, and shopping habits. Everything needed to pressure or eliminate anyone connected to the South Yards investigation.

And at the back, Harper found a list that made excellent bedtime reading, if he was even considering bed yet:

Active Contracts – Priority One:
Liam Harper – $50K – Permanent
Dr. Patricia Kowalski – $25K – Accident Preferred
Dr. Luis Santos – $15K – Medical Emergency

Below that, crossed out in red ink:

Tomás Alvarez – COMPLETE

Charming. They weren't just covering up the South Yards contamination – they were systematically eliminating everyone who'd asked uncomfortable questions about corporate pollution. Harper was simply the highest-value target on a kill list that stretched across Chicago's environmental community. He'd made a point of contacting both Kowalski and Santos, getting them off grid until things scaled down.

The notebook also contained operational details about that night's Veterans' Gala. There were security protocols, VIP protection assignments, even floor plans of the Palmer House ballroom, likely to ensure they were up to task on protection. Which, considering the fact that Alfie Reeves wanted to kill a list of people there, meant a problem for whoever was replacing Murphy.

But that was for later. Now Harper was meeting the mysterious Patterson.

GETTING INSIDE THE MERIDIAN BUILDING REQUIRED CREATIVITY that Harper's SRR instructors would have called "thinking outside the manual". The front entrance featured security cameras and card readers, but new glass and shiny metal welded onto older buildings created vulnerabilities that modern consultants overlooked. A short walk around the building found a lesser-used side entrance; a door featuring basic commercial hardware – the sort installed by contractors who assumed honest intentions.

Harper's lockpicks disagreed with that assumption.

Rather than travel the elevator, Harper used the stairwell for the three flights – the landings littered with industrial cleaning supplies and the lingering scent of disinfectant, likely because building maintenance used this route to avoid bothering legitimate businesses.

Perfect for Harper's purposes.

The third-floor service corridor led towards the main office area, lined with utility rooms and electrical panels. Harper followed it carefully, pausing at each junction to listen for security patrols. He was glad he had, as even at this time of the early morning he saw one overweight guard with a torch he used more for balance than illumination, checking doors with the enthusiasm of someone who'd rather be home watching television.

Predictable routine, easily avoided.

Once the guard disappeared around the corner, Harper approached Meridian's suite.

The company occupied prime real estate – two floors with corner offices that overlooked both the lake and the business district. Frosted glass doors carried discreet lettering:

Meridian Protective Services – Executive Security Solutions

Harper smiled. *Corporate language vague enough to mean anything from babysitting oligarchs to eliminating environmental activists.*

Through the frosted glass, however, Harper could see light bleeding from beneath the corner office door. Perhaps someone working late – or early, depending on perspective.

The door wasn't locked, and Harper slipped inside, moving through a reception area decorated with corporate camouflage: neutral colours, motivational quotes rotating across still-active TV screens talking about "excellence" and "results", expensive furniture masking whatever sins paid for it all.

Carefully, Harper examined the corner office door. More bloody frosted glass, but also heavy construction, the sort of privacy that suggested either legitimate executive work or activities requiring sound dampening. He could see movement inside – someone at a desk, apparently focused on paperwork.

Patterson. The second shooter.

Harper touched his river stone once for luck, more as a habit than a belief, then opened the door and stepped inside.

The man at the desk spun in his chair, hand moving automatically towards a concealed weapon, then froze when recognition hit both ways simultaneously.

'Jesus bloody Christ,' Alfie Reeves said quietly. 'Harper.'

For a moment, neither man moved. Harper's mind raced through implications while Alfie sat perfectly still in his expensive suit, looking every inch the legitimate security executive, except for the way his hand had instinctively moved towards his shoulder holster.

'Alfie.' Harper's voice was carefully neutral. 'Or should I call you *Patterson* this week?'

'Patterson's just business. Dead men need flexible identities, and I told you I was "dead" when I left the service.' Alfie gestured towards a chair across from his desk. 'Sit. We should talk.'

Harper remained standing – every instinct was screaming warnings.

'Murphy mentioned there were two of you at the Tomás execution. Said his partner was someone I'd already met, someone who'd been watching me since I arrived.' Harper's voice carried the sort of controlled menace he'd learned in places where negotiation meant survival. 'He also said this partner worked out of the third floor corner office of the Meridian building.'

'Murphy talks too much. Always did.' Alfie leaned back in his chair. 'Is he still talking?'

'He's done talking.'

'Good. The man was a bloody liability.' Alfie opened his desk drawer slowly, pulling out expensive whisky and two glasses. 'Drink? For old times' sake?'

Harper watched Alfie's movements carefully. The whisky was probably legitimate, but the gesture was tactical – establishing normalcy while buying time to assess the situation.

'Tell me about Tomás Alvarez.'

'Environmental engineer, I believe. To be honest, I only saw what they wrote down for me. Filed false safety reports for money, got cold feet, threatened to expose the contamination cover-up.' Alfie poured whisky into both glasses. 'Became a problem requiring permanent resolution.'

'And you provided that resolution,' Harper fought to keep his voice calm.

'I provided oversight for a contract that removed someone threatening legitimate businesses.' Alfie met Harper's eyes directly. 'One man's sudden conscience against an entire economic ecosystem.'

'He had children.'

'And for months before you arrived, he was perfectly happy cashing cheques and filing false reports while those children lived comfortably on blood money.' Alfie's voice carried contempt. 'Tomás Alvarez had no problem being corrupt when the price was right. He only developed moral qualms when someone promised him a different sort of heroism.'

Harper felt cold settling in his stomach – not just at Alfie's words, but at the uncomfortable truth they contained.

'His kid needed medical help.'

'Lots of kids need medical help, don't see *their* parents taking bribes.'

'You executed him.'

'Did Murphy tell you that?' Alfie leaned back. 'Yes, there were two of us assigned to the job, but I wasn't there for the actual shooting. The bullet – that was Murphy's work. I was supposed to handle cleanup and disposal afterwards.'

'Supposed to?'

'When I arrived at the scene and saw the identification Murphy had taken from the body, I realised this wasn't just some random environmental inspector.' Alfie's expression darkened. 'It was someone connected to a certain ex-SRR captain who'd been asking uncomfortable questions around the city. I realised he'd been someone you'd been working with.'

Harper processed this, watching Alfie's face for tells.

'So, you left the body to be found.'

'I decided this cleanup could wait. Let the police find him, let them investigate, see what sort of attention it brought.' Alfie sipped his whisky. 'Turned out to be the right decision, didn't it? Led you straight to me.'

Harper pulled out his river stone, rolling it between his fingers while he considered his options. Part of him wanted to kill Alfie right here – one quick strike, justice for Tomás, an end to whatever his old comrade had become.

But that wouldn't bring Tomás back. Wouldn't expose the contamination. Wouldn't save the children still breathing poisoned air.

And Harper needed what Alfie could provide.

'How?' Harper asked. 'How does someone go from SRR to corporate assassination?'

'Same way someone goes from SRR to environmental activism,' Alfie replied. 'One compromised mission at a time until you wake up somewhere you never intended to be. If it means anything, if I'd known he was a friend of yours, I wouldn't have taken it on.'

'Would you have told me?' Harper asked coldly.

'Would it have stopped you doing what you wanted?' Alfie gestured around the expensive office – leather furniture, original artwork, corporate luxury that suggested serious success in morally ambiguous enterprises. 'After Syria, after Crowe tried to kill me – and before you argue, that prick wanted me gone so I know it was him. Anyway, after that, I had choices. Live quietly in suburban exile, maybe teach self-defence to bored housewives. Or use my skills in markets that don't ask awkward questions about employment history.'

'You chose murder for money.'

'I chose survival with purpose.' Alfie's voice carried conviction. 'These people – Slate, her associates, the corporations poisoning children for profit – they're enemies, Harper.

Just like the insurgents we fought overseas. I recognise that, but I'm stuck in the system. Different uniforms, same mentality.'

Harper wanted to kill him. The urge was immediate, physical – reach across the desk, snap Alfie's neck, end this conversation permanently. But that would solve nothing except Harper's emotional satisfaction.

'It seems that being dead gave you a whole new outlook on life.'

'I tried at the start, I really did,' Alfie's smile was bitter. 'Two years of reading books and pretending civilian life was sufficient. But knowing the truth eats at you. Knowing that the people who destroyed your life are still out there... it alters you.'

'And Chicago offered better career prospects.'

'Chicago offered clients who appreciated my particular skill set. People fighting the same enemies I wanted dead.' Alfie returned his attention to his desk. 'Corporate executives who poison children for profit. Politicians who enable environmental crimes. The same sort of people who facilitated weapons trades that got good soldiers killed.'

Harper felt moral complexity settling around him. Alfie wasn't just a murderer – he was a soldier who'd been betrayed, abandoned, left to construct meaning from the wreckage of his official death.

But understanding didn't equal forgiveness. Tomás Alvarez was still dead.

'I don't see you taking them down,' Harper said carefully. 'Instead, you work with them. For them, even.'

'It's a long game,' Alfie shrugged. 'I need to work my way up, see the complete picture.'

'You could have walked away,' Harper continued. 'Used

the evidence you had to expose the truth about Syria. Instead, you became part of the same system that destroyed you.'

'If I'd spoken out about Syria, I'd be in military prison,' Alfie laughed. 'Or did you forget it was *my* modernisations that killed people?'

'So, what, hide from it? Something that destroys people every week?'

'No, I became an effective operator in a system that destroys people every day, while waiting for my moment.' Alfie's voice carried conviction. 'Slate's organisation poisons children for profit. Not like for fun or anything; she builds houses, and these are acceptable costs for what she believes she gives back. These aren't innocent civilians, Harper – they're enemy combatants in expensive suits.'

'And Tomás?'

'Tomás was a contractor who accepted payment to falsify safety reports, then developed inconvenient moral qualms when the price of conscience became too high.' Alfie's dismissal was clinical. 'He chose corruption, then chose betrayal. Natural consequences followed.'

'I want you dead,' Harper whispered. 'For what you've become. For what you've done.'

'Understandable. But not practical.' Alfie's confidence was absolute. 'You need me more than you need revenge.'

'Do I?'

'Tonight. The Veterans' Gala. Crowe and Carrick will both be there and so will Slate and her cronies.'

Harper waited.

'And you're planning something,' Alfie continued. 'The contamination exposure, probably. Publicly, in front of cameras and politicians, where it can't be buried.'

Harper went to argue this but then stopped.

'That was the plan. Problem is that all my evidence was taken by Slate's people. I need my father's notebook back.'

'Slate doesn't have it any more,' Alfie said, sipping his drink. 'She's given it to Mason Carrick as a peace offering.'

Shit. That made things complicated.

'Carrick will be at the gala. Prominent table near the stage, surrounded by security that assumes threats come from outside the building,' Alfie's smile was predatory. 'But security assumes wrong.'

'Is this assassination attempt Slate's idea? Bit coincidental that you're planning to kill her enemy at her gala,' Harper frowned. 'Or is it enemies? Is Crowe involved?'

'Crowe's nothing more than the icing on the cake,' Alfie's smile was razor-sharp. 'Slate pays Meridian for various services, but she doesn't know tonight's specifics. As far as she's concerned, I'm just another security contractor providing VIP protection. That I'm using her event to settle old scores is... let's call it *entrepreneurial initiative*.'

'So, you're playing everyone.'

'I'm using available resources to achieve objectives. Just like we both learned during joint operations. As I said, I've been playing the long game. But all games end, Captain Harper.'

Alfie turned his laptop to face Harper now, displaying architectural plans of the Palmer House ballroom.

'Meridian has the security contract, taken over from Aegis. I'll be armed, inside the perimeter, with legitimate communications access. When the shooting starts, security will assume external threats – not internal operators with official credentials. And honestly? They'll be both blaming and looking for *you*.'

The plans were detailed – exit routes, security positions, VIP protection zones. Alfie had access to information that should have been restricted to event organisers.

'How many innocents die in this justice operation?' Harper asked.

'Define innocent?' Alfie highlighted specific seating areas. 'Slate will be there, along with political associates who've enabled decades of environmental crimes. Corporate executives who've profited from poisoning communities.'

'And if I refuse to help?'

'Then you lose your only chance to recover evidence, while I proceed with my operation regardless.' Alfie closed the laptop. 'Chaos is useful – people focus on immediate survival instead of information security.'

He grinned darkly; hand near his jacket.

'Or you decide otherwise, we fight, and I get a nice juicy bonus when I kill you.'

'What makes you think you'll win?'

'How about the fact you look like shit?' Alfie laughed. 'Have you even stopped today to take a breath? You've been attacked multiple times, arrested, questioned, hunted, and even killed an enemy or two. Your adrenaline's been spiking all over the place and you're one punch away from crashing out. You seriously think you can take me?'

Harper placed his hand in his pocket and rolled his river stone between his fingers, considering options that all involved moral compromise. Work with Alfie and become complicit in assassination. Refuse and let the environmental crimes continue while children got sicker. Try to stop Alfie and probably get killed, accomplishing nothing.

His father would have recognised the calculations. *Operational effectiveness versus ethical constraints.* The sort of choices that had driven Dominic Kane to document everything while participating in systems he'd eventually despised.

‘Fine. Partnership,' Harper said finally. 'Temporary and specific.'

'Just like Syria,' Alfie confirmed. 'Except this time we know exactly who the enemy is.'

Harper moved towards the door, then paused.

'Alfie? When this is over, when the evidence is recovered and the contamination exposed – we're done. You chose your path when you helped murder Tomás. That makes you the enemy too, eventually.'

'Eventually,' Alfie acknowledged. 'But not tonight. Tonight, we're allies with converging objectives.'

After swapping numbers, Harper using a burner he hadn’t yet used, he left the office without looking back, walking through Meridian's corridors towards the freight elevator with the taste of moral compromise bitter in his mouth.

He'd just allied himself with Tomás's killer. The thought should have horrified him, but instead it felt almost inevitable – another step down a path his father had walked decades before.

Outside, Chicago's pre-dawn streets stretched empty and grey. No weather to speak of, just the urban void between night and morning when the city held its breath.

Later that same day, Chicago would discover what happened when environmental activists learned to use the same tools as corporate killers. Harper just hoped some version of his conscience would survive to judge whether the price had been worth paying.

His river stone felt heavier in his pocket as Harper walked towards the nearest L station, wondering when he’d hit the same point as Alfie Reeves, where protecting innocent people had become indistinguishable from becoming the sort of person he'd once fought against.

Hopefully, he wouldn't live long enough to find out firsthand.

17

SAFE HOUSE

Harper's father's building looked like it had been kissed by hell and left for dead. Three fire engines clustered around the entrance like mechanical vultures, their hoses snaking through the lobby's windows while smoke still curled from the upper floor. Emergency lighting threw harsh shadows across the scene, the sort of destruction that turned luxury into wreckage in a few hours.

The twenty-eighth floor was pretty much gone. Along with Harper's temporary safe house, his cameras, and any illusion that his inheritance provided security. Harper had blown up his own apartment to escape Slate's assassination team, but someone had made sure the fire spread properly, destroying evidence and sending a simple message.

Charming. Nothing said "we're serious about killing you" quite like making sure your own explosive exit became a proper inferno.

Harper approached from the east side, using construction barriers and emergency vehicles for cover while he studied the scene. Police tape cordoned off a three-block radius, uniformed officers controlling access while fire investigators documented what was left. It wasn't anywhere near the attention it would have gained the previous evening, but even now at almost six in the morning, there was too much official attention for a simple approach.

But the setup told him things.

Federal vehicles mixed with local emergency services. Investigators photographing debris patterns rather than just damage assessment. Radio chatter mentioning "potential domestic terrorism" and "coordinated targeting".

Someone had made sure this fire looked like more than Harper's improvised escape plan. Again, a narrative was being created, aiming everyone squarely at Liam Harper.

Frank would be here. Fire in a building of this size meant all hands on deck, and the morning shift manager would be coordinating with emergency services, dealing with residents, managing the crisis that had probably started after midnight when Harper was busy surviving assassination attempts.

But getting to Frank meant navigating a perimeter designed to keep people like Harper away from the scene. Federal investigators weren't Chicago beat cops – they'd run proper background checks on anyone claiming official business.

Harper needed a different approach.

He studied the emergency response pattern for ten minutes, noting communication protocols and areas of reduced surveillance. Fire scenes were organised chaos – lots of official people moving with purpose, but also contractors, building engineers, insurance assessors, utility workers, everything and anything. The trick was looking like someone who belonged without claiming authority that could be verified.

Harper spotted his opportunity when a city utilities truck arrived, likely to assess gas line damage. The driver wore standard municipal coveralls, hard hat, and carried a clipboard.

Standard tradesperson invisibility.

Harper intercepted the utility worker two blocks from the scene.

'Excuse me, sir. Emergency Services coordination,' Harper said, showing Coble's badge briefly while moving with the sort of bureaucratic authority that suggested form-filling rather than law enforcement. 'Need you to check in with building management before accessing the damage area. Federal protocol.'

The worker – a tired-looking man in his fifties who'd probably been pulled from routine calls – just nodded wearily.

'Where's management set up?'

'Command trailer across the street. But there's a queue, and they're being thorough about paperwork.' Harper gestured towards the crowded temporary structure. 'Tell you what, we need this done fast, so I'll handle the initial coordination as I'm doing the rounds anyway. You grab some coffee, come back in twenty minutes when they've processed the backlog.'

The utility worker looked grateful rather than suspicious. Chicago municipal employees understood bureaucratic delays and welcomed any excuse to avoid unnecessary waiting.

'Appreciate it. These federal investigations, they make everything take twice as long,' the man said, passing Harper the keys to the van and the clipboard. 'Everything you need's in there.'

'Exactly,' Harper agreed, watching the man walk towards a nearby deli. 'Just following protocol.'

Searching the van, Harper retrieved the utility worker's spare coveralls and hard hat from his truck, transforming into another invisible municipal employee. The coveralls were slightly too large, the hard hat slightly too small, but in the chaos of an active fire scene, most people focused on official uniform rather than perfect fit. Now Harper could approach the perimeter as someone with legitimate business rather than a suspicious observer.

'Morning,' Harper said to the officer manning the perimeter. 'City utilities, checking gas lines before we clear the building for structural assessment.'

The officer barely glanced at Harper's borrowed uniform.

'Management's in the command trailer if you need access authorisation.'

'Cheers. Just need to coordinate with building maintenance first, make sure we're not duplicating inspections.' Harper nodded his thanks and moved towards the command area, scanning for Frank amongst the crowd of emergency personnel. There – clipboard in hand, speaking earnestly with two fire investigators, Frank looked exhausted but uninjured, which was better than Harper had hoped.

Getting to Frank without drawing attention required patience Harper didn't have and timing that depended on luck. He waited until the investigators moved on to interview someone else, then approached while Frank was alone near the perimeter.

'Frank,' Harper said quietly, moving alongside him. 'Don't react. Don't look at me directly.'

Frank's shoulders stiffened slightly, but he kept his eyes on his clipboard.

'Christ, Harper. What've you done?'

'Survived. Barely.' Harper watched the investigators, ready to move if they showed interest in Frank's conversation. 'Are you hurt? Was anyone killed?'

'Building was mostly empty when it spread. Your floor took the worst of it – apartments 28A through 28E are gutted, but the others are owned by... well, let's just say people who don't reside in the US, so no casualties, thank God. However, whatever you did up there, someone made sure it kept burning.' Frank's voice carried the controlled anger of someone who'd seen his workplace destroyed. 'Professional accelerants, they're saying. Designed to spread the fire beyond whatever started it.'

'I'm sorry about the building.'

'Buildings can be repaired. People can't.' Frank turned a page on his clipboard, using the movement to glance briefly at Harper. 'You look like hell. When did you last sleep?'

Harper couldn't remember. Somewhere between the hospital attack and walking through Chicago's pre-dawn streets, time had become fluid, measured in crisis rather than hours.

'I need your help, Frank. Somewhere to rest up, get my bearings. People hunting me know about all my usual resources.'

'Figured that might be the case.' Frank made notes on his clipboard, maintaining the appearance of routine documentation. 'But this fire's made everything complicated. Police are treating it as possible terrorism – luxury building, potential foreign connections through some of the residents – especially on the twenty-eighth floor.'

'Meaning?'

'Meaning anyone asking questions about tenants or

building access is getting flagged for federal attention.' Frank's tone suggested this was a problem worth taking seriously. 'Your father's apartment specifically; they're very interested in who might have had keys, who might've wanted to send a message.'

Brilliant. Harper was already wanted for questioning about multiple incidents, and now federal investigators would add arson and potential terrorism to his list of problems.

'Frank, I need somewhere safe. Just for a few hours, until I can figure out my next moves. I intend to bring this to a head tonight, so it's hours, more than days.'

'I might have something.' Frank made more notes, then quietly tore off a sheet and palmed it to Harper. 'Building three blocks south. 1247 North State. Apartment 4B. Tenant's been in Florida for two months, emergency maintenance key's in a keylock safe in the Super's office. 8-6-3-8.'

Harper pocketed the paper without looking at it.

'Building management?'

'Same company, different property. I handle emergency calls there when their regular Super's unavailable.' Frank's smile was tired but genuine. 'Tenant left owing three months' rent, so technically it's vacant pending eviction proceedings. Super won't start until nine, so you have time to get in.'

'How long before someone notices?'

'Building's got fourteen units, half empty because of renovations. Neighbourhood's changing, lots of turnover.' Frank gestured towards his clipboard like they were discussing maintenance schedules. 'Could be days before anyone checks 4B specifically.'

Harper felt something like gratitude, a rare emotion in his current circumstances.

'Frank, why are you helping me?'

'You might not know this, but your father, he saved my grandson's life once.' Frank's voice carried old emotion carefully controlled. 'Kid got mixed up with the wrong people, owed money to dangerous men. Dom heard about it and then fixed it, quietly, no questions asked. Never wanted payment, never mentioned it again.'

Harper hadn't known. Another piece of Dominic Kane's hidden decency, buried under years of operational security and emotional distance.

'I won't forget this.'

'Just don't get caught with the key or mention my name.' Frank returned to his official business, dismissing Harper with the sort of professional courtesy that suggested their conversation was finished. 'And Harper? Whatever you're planning, be careful. This is murder, not warning off. You were aiming at the Tracks, and one of the union guys was found last night, dead.'

Harper didn't mention he'd already taken care of this and left the command trailer area using the same confident stride that had gotten him past the perimeter, his mind racing through implications.

Professional accelerant, federal investigation, systematic escalation.

Someone was making sure Harper's improvised escape became something much bigger.

1247 North State looked like architecture by committee – bland brick frontage, generic windows, the sort of building that existed in every American city without leaving any impression. Harper approached through the alley, using service entrances and loading docks to avoid street cameras.

His lock pick got him into the Super's office, and once he unlocked the key safe with Frank's provided combination, the maintenance key worked perfectly. Fourth floor, apartment 4B, empty except for basic furniture and the lingering smell of someone who'd left in a hurry. Harper conducted a quick security sweep – no obvious surveillance, no signs of recent intrusion, curtains that could block window views from outside.

Secure enough for now.

Harper set his satchel on the kitchen counter and took inventory. Murphy's materials: wallet, phone, operational notes. His father's notebook was gone, lost when Slate took it, along with most of his gathered evidence. Santos's medical files were taken with his father's notebook. All he had was Kowalski's notes on the five deaths, and the promise of Santos's duplicate notes, including soil samples – but these weren't appearing soon.

But Murphy's phone might contain intelligence about what was really planned for tonight. Professional operatives kept contacts, schedules, operational details in encrypted formats. If Harper could crack it, he might learn who was coordinating operations around the Veterans' Gala.

He tried obvious passwords first – birthdays, military service dates, anything from Murphy's identification documents. All failed. Then, he remembered something from his technical training. Most people used personal reference points for security codes, thinking they were being clever. But personal meant predictable to anyone with basic intelligence gathering skills. If they were worried about losing the passcode, especially if it was a phone and code given to them and not using any familiarity to them, they'd find a way to back it up.

The phone would have been given to Murphy.

Harper examined Murphy's wallet again, looking for clues. Credit card receipts showing recent transactions, gym membership, loyalty cards for expensive shops. And there, tucked behind the driver's licence, was a business card for a taxi company.

The card had a phone number, but it'd been scribbled out, a new one replacing it.

555-7244

To anyone looking, it was innocuous, but Harper wasn't just anyone, and he knew 555 numbers were fake – used in movies and television to avoid real phone conflicts. With nothing to lose, he tried the remaining digits as a four-digit code.

Murphy's phone unlocked, displaying recent messages, contact lists, operational schedules. Harper scrolled through quickly, looking for patterns.

Most contacts were coded – probably operational aliases rather than real names. But the message history revealed something interesting. Not a mass assassination plot, but something more subtle.

Text exchanges about "asset positioning" and "managed transitions". References to Meridian Security taking over contracts from Aegis. Something about ensuring Alfie was in position for tonight's event.

And there, in Murphy's calendar app, tonight's entry:

VET GALA – OSWALD PROTOCOL – REEVES POSITION.

Harper felt cold understanding settle in his stomach. This wasn't about mass murder. It was about creating the perfect patsy. Alfie wasn't just planning to kill Crowe and Carrick, thinking he'd cleverly infiltrated Meridian to perform his task – he was being set up as the lone gunman while Slate's people ensured the narrative stuck.

Lee Harvey Oswald.

Alfie Reeves.

The perfect assassin because he was already dead to the world, with a clear motive and no credible defenders.

Harper pulled out his river stone, rolling the worn surface between his fingers while he processed implications. Alfie thought he was getting revenge, but Slate's people were orchestrating something bigger. Use Alfie's legitimate grievances to eliminate Crowe and Carrick, then eliminate Alfie to tie up loose ends. Prove Aegis dropped the ball – after all, if they couldn't even save their founder, what use were they – and prove Alfie was connected to old Aegis issues. Sure, Meridian hired him, but there were dozens of lawyers just waiting to argue how Meridian was the victim in this case, while Slate made a clean transition from Aegis to Meridian contracts, with any inconvenient questions buried along with the shooter.

Harper was walking into a setup designed to eliminate Crowe and Carrick, destroy Alfie, and give Slate everything she wanted while making it look like a personal military vendetta gone wrong.

But that meant Alfie was as much a victim as a threat. Someone being manipulated into throwing away his life for other people's agendas.

Harper needed help – professional help from someone

with resources, intelligence, authority to coordinate counter-operations.

He needed Colonel Crowe.

Not to warn him about Alfie – though that was part of it – but to understand what Crowe's real connection was to this mess. Why was Crowe in Chicago during the same week as this operation? What was Crowe's relationship with Aegis and Meridian? Too many coincidences. Too much operational precision around what should have been a simple military charity event.

Harper checked his watch. 7:15 a.m. Just under twelve hours until the gala. Time enough to confront Crowe, understand his role, and decide whether the colonel was a potential ally or additional threat.

But first, Harper needed sleep. Four hours of unconsciousness, minimum, or he'd be useless when multiple crises converged tonight. Professional soldiers learned to grab rest anywhere, anytime, because exhaustion killed faster than bullets in extended operations. Harper set his phone alarm for eleven, positioned himself on the couch where he could see both the door and windows, and let his body shut down while his mind filed away the intelligence he'd gathered.

Slate's people were using Alfie as a weapon and a scapegoat. Mason Carrick was being systematically undermined in favour of Meridian Security. Multiple operations were converging tonight at Palmer House, but the actual target wasn't environmental activists – it was Aegis itself.

And Harper had discovered it just in time to get himself caught in the crossfire between military conspiracies and corporate warfare.

The apartment was quiet except for distant Chicago noise filtering through the windows. For the first time since arriving in the city, Harper felt temporarily safe. Not because the threats had diminished, but because he'd finally found shelter amidst the chaos. But, as sleep claimed him, Harper's subconscious continued processing the intelligence he'd gathered. Tonight would test everything his father had taught him about operational planning, everything the SRR had drilled into him about tactical thinking, everything he'd learned about survival when powerful people wanted you dead.

His father had faced similar calculations – but Harper wondered, as sleep finally took him, whether Dominic Kane had also spent sleepless hours planning operations where the real enemy wasn't who everyone thought it was.

He never got an answer.

The Chicago Hilton's lobby bustled with the usual mix of business travellers and tourists, all looking slightly overwhelmed by Chicago's organised chaos. Harper took the lift to the eighth floor, finding Crowe's room after a brief conversation with housekeeping about delivering a broken-but-now-fixed Rolex.

Crowe answered the door in civilian clothes, looking unsurprised to see Harper.

'You look like hell,' he said, stepping aside to let Harper enter.

'Been a busy night.' Harper accepted the offered chair, noting how Crowe had arranged the furniture to maintain clear access to both the door and windows. 'We need to talk about tonight.'

'I assumed we might.' Crowe poured coffee from the room's machine. 'What's changed since yesterday?'

'Everything.' Harper pulled out Murphy's phone, displaying the operational messages. 'I killed one of Slate's operatives last night. Found this on his body.'

Crowe studied the screen, his expression darkening as he read the text exchanges.

'Oswald Protocol,' he said quietly. 'Christ.'

'You know what it means?'

'I'm guessing Lee Harvey Oswald.' Crowe set the phone down carefully. 'Someone's using Alfie as a patsy.'

'That someone being Veronica Slate. She's orchestrating tonight's events, but Alfie thinks he's getting revenge.' Harper watched Crowe's reaction carefully. 'The plan is to let him kill you and Carrick, then eliminate him as the lone gunman.'

'Clean transition from Aegis to Meridian contracts, with any inconvenient questions buried along with the shooter.' Crowe moved to the window, looking out at Chicago's skyline. 'Elegant in a thoroughly evil way.'

'You don't seem surprised.'

'I've been expecting something like this since I agreed to come to Chicago.' Crowe's voice carried old exhaustion. 'The question was whether it would be personal revenge or professional elimination.'

'And now you know.'

'Now I know the boy's being used just as badly as he was in Syria.' Crowe turned back to Harper. 'What do you want from me?'

'Help. Information. Whatever you can provide to stop this without getting innocent people killed.' Harper leaned forward. 'Starting with the truth about your connection to Aegis.'

'What makes you think there's more than I've already told you?'

'Because you're here in Chicago and attending a particular event, the same day as a coordinated operation to eliminate Mason Carrick and transition Aegis contracts to Meridian Security.' Harper studied Crowe's face. 'That's no coincidence.'

Crowe was quiet for a long moment, clearly weighing how much to reveal.

'I've been consulting for Aegis since I retired two years back,' he said finally. 'Military liaison work, primarily. Helping them maintain relationships with British defence contacts. I was doing it for a year or two before, but more... well, off the books.'

'You were taking their money while still serving?'

'More building a relationship for after I left.'

'Two years before... that makes four. Were you working with Aegis when Syria happened?'

'No,' Crowe shook his head. 'Although in a way, speaking to them while cleaning up is what started all this.'

'And this was for Mason Carrick?'

'Initially, it was your father, but after he died, yes. But lately...' Crowe hesitated. 'Mason's been making decisions that concerned some of his board members. Decisions about operational security, contract terms, personnel management.'

'Such as?'

'Such as hunting down the son of his dead partner across three states instead of letting sleeping dogs lie.' Crowe looked directly at Harper as he spoke. 'Some of us thought a transition might be necessary.'

Harper felt understanding settle like a cold weight in his stomach.

'Jesus. You're part of it. The conspiracy to eliminate Carrick.'

'I'm part of an effort to prevent Aegis from becoming the sort of organisation that destroys people like Alfie Reeves.' Crowe's tone carried conviction. 'Mason's lost perspective, Harper. He's turned your father's company into something Dominic would never have recognised.'

'And you think Slate's people are better?'

'I think Meridian Security operates within established parameters rather than personal vendettas.' Crowe moved back to his chair. 'The plan was for Meridian to handle the transition professionally. Alfie was supposed to be managed, talked down, redirected, and his testimony get them out of the contract.'

'But?'

'But from what you've just shown me, Slate's people have decided a dead patsy is more convenient than a live witness.' Crowe's expression darkened. 'I was told they'd handle Alfie's grievances through proper channels. Instead, they're using him as a weapon and planning to dispose of him afterwards.'

'Then help me stop it.'

'How?'

'By staying away from the gala. Force them to change plans, expose their operational security.' Harper watched Crowe consider this. 'Or better yet, help me get Alfie out before he becomes their Oswald.'

'Alfie won't listen to reason. Not from me, not from you, probably not from anyone.' Crowe's expression was grim. 'He's been planning this for months, Harper. Professional preparation, inside access, legitimate grievances. Probably ever since I hit the private sector.'

'Then we expose the conspiracy publicly. Show him he's being used.'

'With what proof? Operational messages that could be fabricated? The word of a dead mercenary?'

Harper felt frustration building.

'So, you just let it happen?'

'I try to minimise casualties while achieving necessary objectives.' Crowe stood, moving towards the door. 'Mason Carrick has to be stopped, Harper. He's turned Aegis into something that destroys good soldiers and covers up environmental crimes. If Alfie's the weapon that accomplishes that...'

'Then you're no better than the people who destroyed him in Syria.'

The words hung in the air between them like an accusation.

'Perhaps not,' Crowe said quietly. 'But sometimes choosing between bad options is what leadership requires.'

Harper stood, pocketing Murphy's phone.

'And sometimes leadership requires refusing to sacrifice good people for convenient solutions.' He moved towards the door. 'I'm going to save Alfie, with or without your help.'

'Harper.' Crowe's voice stopped him at the threshold. 'If you're planning to attend tonight, you should know – Slate's people aren't just targeting Carrick. They consider you a loose end that needs tying up.'

'I adapt quickly.'

'This isn't a joke. They have professional operators, inside access, legitimate security credentials.' Crowe's tone carried genuine concern. 'You'll be walking into a kill box designed by people who know your capabilities.'

'Then I'd better make sure they underestimate them.' Harper opened the door. 'If you change your mind about helping, you know how to reach me. If you don't? Then stay out of my damn way.'

He stopped.

'How do you know about Meridian considering me a loose end?'

'They told me,' Crowe shrugged. 'Look, Harper, I'm not lying. I have nothing to hide.'

Harper stared at his one-time commanding officer, and a harsh realisation took effect.

'You gave them my number,' he said. 'After I called you. It was after that I started getting texts from them. I wondered how...'

'I did,' Crowe admitted. 'But only so they could begin a narrative with you, show you a way out of Aegis's shadow.'

'If you knew anything about me, Colonel, you'd know I'm not in anyone's bloody shadow!' Harper snapped as he left Crowe standing in the hotel room, looking older than his years and carrying the weight of compromises that never seemed to end.

Harper had six hours until the Veterans' Gala. Time enough to figure out how to save a man who didn't want saving, stop a conspiracy that reached into military intelligence, and survive long enough to see justice done against Veronica Slate.

Just another bloody afternoon in the life of Liam Harper.

18

DEALS WITH DEVILS

HARPER LEFT CROWE'S HOTEL ROOM WITH THE UNCOMFORTABLE certainty that his former commanding officer was part of the mess rather than the solution. Crowe had been expecting Meridian to handle Alfie professionally – talk him down, redirect his anger, provide legitimate employment. Instead, Slate had decided a dead patsy was more convenient than a managed asset. He'd also been the one to give out Harper's burner phone number. Which left Harper with a choice: face tonight's conspiracy alone or make a deal with the devil himself.

Without the Bonneville – still with Cortez still somewhere near Evanston – Harper needed transport that wouldn't draw attention. Chicago's public transport wasn't really designed for tactical mobility, but it would have to do; the L train could get him to the financial district, where Mason Carrick would be making whatever stand remained available to him.

Harper caught the Blue Line downtown, using the forty-minute journey to review Murphy's phone intelligence while watching his fellow passengers; office workers heading to late lunch meetings, tourists clutching guidebooks, the usual mix of Chicago's afternoon crowd. Normal people living normal lives, completely unaware that tonight would determine whether environmental crimes continued being buried under corporate development projects.

The "Oswald Protocol" was elegant in its simplicity: let Alfie assassinate Crowe and Carrick at the gala, then eliminate him as an unstable lone gunman. Clean corporate transition from Aegis to Meridian once the dust settled with any inconvenient questions buried alongside the shooter. Perfect narrative; believed dead veteran suffers breakdown, targets former commanding officer who destroyed his life and his current business partner before being neutralised by the plucky Meridian security teams. Media would focus on military mental health issues rather than corporate environmental crimes.

But Harper had disrupted their timeline by killing Murphy, who'd been working with Alfie, and was probably the one expected to put a bullet into Alfie's head, just like he had Tomás. Slate's people would be adapting, improvising, probably moving their schedule up. That made them dangerous in unpredictable ways.

THE TRAIN CARRIED HIM THROUGH CHICAGO'S INDUSTRIAL sections before emerging into the financial district, where glass towers competed to scrape the sky while hiding whatever sins paid for their construction. Harper had learned to read cities during his SRR years – every major urban centre had similar patterns, and he could see expensive districts built on buried problems, corporate headquarters positioned to project power while concealing actual operations.

The Aegis building squatted amongst its neighbours like an expensive tombstone of glass and steel, designed to impress while hiding whatever business required that level of security. Harper had been here twice as a child, dragged along when his father needed to conduct meetings he couldn't discuss at home, on the very rare occasions Harper had been over in the US. The place smelled of old money and fresh betrayal.

Getting past security required more creativity than borrowed coveralls and bureaucratic authority, though, so Harper positioned himself outside the building's main entrance, studying the lunch crowd for opportunities. Corporate types moved with predictable patterns – expense account lunches, client meetings, the sort of routine that created exploitable habits.

There – nervous executive type in his thirties, expensive suit but not too expensive, briefcase suggesting middle management rather than serious authority. Someone with legitimate building access but insufficient importance to cause immediate alarm if he disappeared for twenty minutes.

Harper fell into step beside him at the entrance, timing his approach as the executive reached for his keycard.

'Afternoon,' Harper said, flashing Coble's badge briefly while moving with the sort of bureaucratic confidence that suggested paperwork rather than actual law enforcement. 'Federal compliance audit. Need to speak with Mason Carrick about some regulatory irregularities.'

The executive – a man who probably spent his days managing budgets for projects he didn't understand – barely glanced at Harper's credentials before swiping his keycard.

'He's on five. Executive level. But you'll need escort authorisation for—'

'Already sorted,' Harper said confidently, following him through the security turnstiles before anyone could verify his story. 'Just need directions to the elevators.'

Corporate security worked on the assumption that if you'd gotten this far, someone else had already validated your presence. Multiple layers of responsibility meant no single person felt obligated to challenge credentials that looked official enough, and therefore Harper took the elevator to five unchallenged, emerging into corridors covered by expensive carpets, and corporate art selected by consultants who specialised in making wealth look tasteful – the sort of understated luxury that required serious money to achieve properly.

But something felt wrong. Too quiet, even for an executive floor. Harper had developed instincts for hostile territory during his military years, and this place carried the tension of people expecting trouble.

The sound of raised voices led him to Mason's office – door slightly ajar, probably because his secretary had stepped away to avoid the shouting or grab a coffee during what sounded like a crisis management session.

'—complete bloody shambles,' Mason was saying. 'Slate's contractor is dead, Alfie's gone completely rogue, and now her people want us to provide additional security for tonight's operation.'

'Sir, we could pull our teams back, reassess the situation —' Younger voice, probably operations staff trying to suggest tactical retreat.

'Pull back from what? She's got us pinned completely.' Mason's voice carried the frustration of someone whose options had been systematically eliminated. 'Either we give her what she wants, or Aegis loses Chicago. Do you know what that'd do to our reputation? It's already smarting after bloody Liam's Funtime Show in Nevada.'

At his name, Harper stepped into the doorway.

'Uncle Mason,' he said. 'You should know better than to call the Devil, lest he appear.'

Both men spun towards the door. The younger operative – late thirties, military bearing, hand drifting instinctively towards an appendix holster – positioned himself between Harper and Mason with the sort of movement that suggested recent combat experience.

'Stand down, Collins,' Mason said wearily. 'If Liam wanted me dead, we wouldn't be having this conversation.'

Collins hesitated, clearly uncomfortable with the tactical situation, but stepped aside at Mason's gesture.

'Leave us,' Mason added. 'And close the door. Whatever happens next, it's not your responsibility.'

Collins departed reluctantly, leaving Harper alone with Mason.

The office looked exactly as Harper had expected – expensive furniture arranged to project authority, corporate art selected to avoid causing offence. Floor-to-ceiling windows showed Chicago's sprawl, but Harper noted how Mason had positioned his desk to maintain clear views of both the door and potential escape routes. He wondered if Mason had other offices across the world, and whether these all looked the same.

'You've had a busy week,' Mason observed, gesturing towards a leather chair while pouring whisky from a crystal decanter.

'Killing Murphy was particularly satisfying,' Harper

replied, remaining standing. 'Though I'm curious why one of your sub-contractors was murdering environmental engineers on Chicago streets.'

'Am I supposed to know what every one of my sub-contractors does?' Mason's voice carried genuine irritation rather than defensiveness. 'Murphy worked for Meridian Security, not Aegis. Slate's been systematically poaching my best people, offering better terms while using them for operations I never authorised.'

'So why is a property developer so bothered about security companies?' Harper studied Mason Carrick's face, looking for tells developed during years of reading people whose lies could get soldiers killed. The man seemed tired rather than evasive – an interesting development.

'Because she's an ambitious one,' Mason shrugged. 'She knows property has had its boom and is now on a downturn, while people always need protecting. Or, you know, having someone taken down.'

'Admitting something?'

'No, simply pointing out I never authorised this.'

'Convenient excuse.'

'It's not an excuse, it's operational reality.' Mason sipped his whisky, noting Harper's refusal to sit. 'Veronica Slate has been planning this transition for months, possibly years. Step one: destabilise Aegis by eliminating key personnel. Step two: use our own sub-contractors for operations that compromise us legally. Step three: present herself as the stable alternative when everything falls apart.'

'And Alfie Reeves?'

'Alfie should be dead. That he's alive, working for Meridian, and planning to kill us both tonight suggests someone's been very clever about long-term operational planning.' Mason met Harper's eyes directly. 'You worked that out yet?'

'That Slate's using him as the perfect patsy? Former soldier with documented grievances against his commanding officer and the corporate mercs who screwed him over five years back?' Harper almost smiled at the elegance. 'Lee Harvey Oswald with better training and legitimate motives.'

'Exactly. Let him eliminate me and Crowe during tonight's gala, then dispose of him as an unstable lone gunman.' Mason finished his whisky, setting the glass down with deliberate control. 'Meanwhile, you disappear during the chaos – another casualty of domestic terrorism. Clean narrative, no inconvenient witnesses.'

'What are you proposing?'

'Temporary alliance.' Mason opened his desk drawer, retrieving a familiar leather-bound notebook that made Harper's pulse quicken. 'Your father's journal. Slate's people took it from your apartment and passed it to me. Probably to set up a reason for you to kill me.'

'You're returning it?'

'Gesture of good faith.' Mason slid the notebook across his desk while watching Harper's reaction carefully. 'Though I should mention I've taken scans of all the pages. Insurance policy, you understand.'

'Last time we spoke, I got the impression our next meeting would be at gunpoint,' Harper replied.

'And yet you still came,' Mason smiled.

Harper placed the notebook into his satchel while understanding the subtext completely. Partial cooperation with maintained leverage – exactly what he'd expect from someone who'd survived decades in the corporate security business.

'And your evidence against Slate?'

'Financial records, operational communications, personnel files documenting her systematic recruitment of my contractors.' Mason's smile was razor thin. 'All available, contingent on our alliance holding. Trust works both ways.'

Harper studied Mason Carrick's expression, weighing tactical necessities against personal instincts. Every warning his father had ever given him about trusting corporate operators argued against cooperation. But facing Slate's conspiracy alone while she eliminated witnesses systematically seemed like poor odds for success.

'What exactly would this alliance involve?'

'Information sharing, coordinated response, maybe a little mutual protection during tonight's operation.' Mason stood, moving to the windows overlooking Chicago. 'You want to expose the environmental crimes and get justice for people like Tomás Alvarez. I want to survive long enough to undo what Aegis has become. Our objectives align.'

Harper felt surprised at what seemed like genuine regret in Mason's voice. He'd expected corporate deflection, not anything resembling accountability.

'What about my father? Myanmar?'

Mason was quiet for a long moment, staring out at the city below where normal people conducted normal business without worrying about assassination conspiracies or environmental cover-ups.

'Your father discovered I'd been making... let's call them *operational decisions...* without proper board oversight,' Mason said finally. 'Pursuing contracts that compromised Aegis's original mission of providing legitimate security services. He was planning to force me out, restructure the company along more ethical lines.'

'You had him killed?'

'Christ no! I asked him to check in on what should have been a routine consultation in Myanmar, to get him out of the way while I fixed my shit. Low-risk maritime security work, straightforward profit-sharing arrangement with local government forces, but they wanted to see one of the organ grinders, not the monkeys.' Mason's voice carried what sounded like genuine pain. 'They thought we'd both gone and I would have, if I wasn't shredding files. The attack was unexpected, professional, and targeted specifically at eliminating both Dominic and me simultaneously, as they thought we were both on that ship. And I'll point out that you were there too, so whoever was aiming it... they were going off intel that was Government level.'

Harper's mind drifted back to Myanmar; to that briefing room at Hereford. British-flagged merchant vessels were being systematically targeted in the Bay of Bengal, and the shipping insurance industry was screaming for military help after three successful hijackings in two weeks.

The intelligence brief had been straightforward: militant groups with sophisticated equipment were hitting commercial shipping with surgical precision. Someone was providing them with route information, security protocols, crew manifests. The sort of intelligence that suggested corruption within the private security firms contracted to protect the vessels. SRR had been tasked to look into it because this wasn't just piracy – it was organised infiltration of British commercial interests. Sure, it was an SBS op but notes from above showed that there was overlap; the only people available were Harper's SRR unit.

Harper had led four operators – Cardy, Dillon, Laverick, Ashbee – onto that container ship expecting to find evidence of systematic betrayal. What he'd found instead was his father bleeding out on the deck, whispering 'Make it right' through blood-flecked lips after saving Harper's life. The irony still burned: they'd been sent to investigate security firm corruption, only to discover that Aegis – his father's own company – had been paid to step aside and let the attacks succeed.

His father had died breaking his own company's arrangement, choosing his son's life over corporate profit margins. But Harper had never learned who'd provided the intelligence that sent SRR to that specific ship at that exact time. Someone had known about the betrayal, known Harper's team would be there, known his father would be commanding the Aegis operatives personally.

Someone had orchestrated the entire operation to ensure Dominic Kane died with his hands dirty. Had they made sure Harper was there so he'd be the one to kill his father?

Mason returned to his desk.

'Think about the timing, Harper. Your father dies; I'm left running Aegis alone. Meanwhile, here in Chicago, Slate positions herself as the stable alternative while systematically undermining our operations.'

'You're asking me to believe Slate orchestrated my father's death?' Harper almost laughed. He understood the textbook plan of making an enemy an ally, but even this felt too far-fetched. Dominic Kane may have been caught up in the drama here, but it wouldn't have been so simple.

'I'm asking you to consider that we're both targets of the same long-term operation.' Mason met Harper's eyes. 'We can work together to survive it and expose the truth or die separately while she takes everything.'

Harper considered the tactical situation. Every instinct

warned against trusting Mason Carrick, but the alternative was facing tonight's conspiracy alone while Slate's people eliminated witnesses systematically.

'Temporary alliance then,' Harper said, extending his hand. 'But if you betray this, I'll put you in the ground next to your sub-contractors.'

'Fair terms.' Mason shook Harper's hand with what seemed like genuine relief. 'Now let's figure out how to survive tonight without getting everyone killed in the process.'

LEAVING THE AEGIS BUILDING, HARPER IMMEDIATELY SPOTTED surveillance – two men in business suits positioned near the entrance. *Meridian Security, almost certainly.* Watchers with recent military experience, probably armed, definitely coordinating through concealed communications equipment.

Hunters.

Harper walked normally while using shop window reflections to monitor their approach. They fell into step behind him, maintaining standard surveillance distance while speaking quietly into earpieces – their presence confirmed that Slate's people had been watching Mason Carrick's building, probably for hours.

Harper turned right into a narrow alley connecting two main streets – it was likely a service route for deliveries, mostly deserted during afternoon hours, and halfway through, he stopped and turned around to face his pursuers.

'Afternoon, lads,' he said conversationally. 'Enjoying Chicago's weather?'

The two operatives stopped, spreading apart instinctively

while keeping their hands positioned near concealed weapons. It was a standard tactical deployment for potential hostile contact, executed with the sort of discipline that confirmed ex-soldiers. Just like the bloody hospital. Just like his father's apartment.

If he was being brutally frank about it, Harper was getting pretty sick of this.

'Harper,' the taller one said politely. 'Our employer would appreciate a brief conversation with you.'

'Your employer tried to have me killed last night,' Harper replied, noting how both men had positioned themselves to prevent his escape while maintaining plausible deniability about their intentions. 'She also killed a friend.'

'Mister Alvarez made unfortunate choices regarding his contractual obligations,' the taller operative replied with a clinical detachment. 'You could learn from his example.'

'I adapt quickly,' Harper said, shifting position slightly to prevent them from flanking him completely while calculating distances and angles.

The shorter operative made the mistake of reaching for his weapon first, and the problem was that shoulder holsters, while popular, are far from the fastest draw option available. Harper was already moving, closing the distance before the man could clear leather. Elbow strike to the throat, followed by a kick to the side of the knee collapsed him as his weapon skittered away into the shadows.

The taller man was faster, weapon half-drawn when Harper fired a vicious outside shin kick at the man's sciatic nerve, smashing him into the brick wall. They fought for gun hand control while the first operative writhed from Harper's initial attack. Training against training, desperation against professionalism, SRR combat techniques against whatever corporate security had taught Meridian's contractors, or whatever army training they'd received before joining.

The handgun fired during their struggle, the round ricocheting off brick. Harper twisted the pistol violently, almost severing his opponent's finger in the trigger guard. A vicious elbow across the operator's jaw was followed by a fast back-kick to the face of the operative who was struggling, due to extensive knee damage, to draw a backup pistol from an ankle holster.

Too many variables, too much chaos in a confined space. Harper needed to end this confrontation quickly before additional Meridian personnel arrived, or Chicago police responded to gunshots in downtown alleys and arrested him again.

However, before he could plan his next move, the distinctive roar of a motorcycle engine suddenly filled the narrow space. Harper spun to see Cortez on Harper's Bonneville, accelerating directly towards the only operator still standing, who was attempting to line up a shot at Harper's back.

The man tried to evade as Cortez braked hard, sliding the bike sideways and catching him across the legs with enough force to break both legs and send him sprawling, his weapon clattering across concrete into the same shadows that had swallowed his partner's gun.

'Need a ride?' Cortez grinned, revving the engine while both Meridian operatives groaned and tried to nurse their injuries.

Harper quickly gathered the fallen weapons, tossing them into a nearby skip before climbing onto the bike behind Cortez.

'Excellent timing,' Harper said as they accelerated out of

the alley and merged with Chicago traffic. 'How did you find me?'

'Placed an Apple AirTag in your jacket before I left for Evanston,' Cortez replied over the engine noise, weaving between cars with the sort of controlled aggression that suggested police pursuit training. 'Seemed prudent, given your demonstrated talent for attracting violent attention.'

They put several blocks between themselves and the alley before Harper felt comfortable enough to check whether they were being followed. No obvious pursuit vehicles, but that meant little when dealing with professionals who had resources and patience.

'How did your medical appointment go?' Harper asked.

'Clean bill of health, proper antibiotics, shoulder wound healing nicely.' Cortez took a right turn. 'Doctor was curious about how I'd managed to get glass fragments embedded so deeply – thought it was a domestic abuse situation – but I convinced him it was a domestic accident involving a broken back door.'

'Creative.'

'So, where to?' Cortez asked. 'I'm guessing you have a place to hide, and updates for me?'

'I do indeed,' Harper said.

INSIDE THE SPARSE APARTMENT, HARPER REVIEWED HIS GAINS from the meeting while Cortez examined his father's recovered notebook.

'We have reluctant allies, partial evidence, and multiple people trying to kill us,' Cortez observed, noting the worn leather binding and his father's careful handwriting.

Harper's phone rang before he could elaborate – Santos, sounding urgent in a way that suggested immediate crisis rather than routine concern.

'Harper, Rosa's hunting Veronica Slate,' Santos said without preamble. 'She came to the clinic about an hour ago with those photographs of Tomás, but someone sent her additional intelligence – operational details about who actually ordered the killing.'

Harper felt surprise mixed with concern.

'She's not planning to come after me?'

'She knows you didn't kill her brother. Whoever manipulated her provided enough information to identify the real culprits—'

'Did she give the names?'

'Only one, Veronica Slate. They're probably hoping she'd cause chaos that could be blamed on grief-driven revenge rather than systematic witness elimination.' Santos's voice carried the sort of worry that suggested personal involvement. 'She's hunting a weapon right now, Harper. Asked me where rich corporate types hold their fancy parties in downtown Chicago. Said you'd mentioned some event tonight, and that's where his killer – Slate – would be.'

Harper looked at Cortez, recognising the nightmare that was developing around tonight's gala. Multiple armed parties converging on the same location, each with different objectives, while professional security tried to maintain order and Slate's people orchestrated whatever ultimate solution they'd planned for eliminating inconvenient witnesses.

'She's planning to crash the Veterans' Gala?'

'That would be my assessment,' Santos confirmed. 'She left here thirty minutes ago, headed downtown with revenge on her mind and once she sources it, a weapon in her purse.

Harper, I've been trying to call her since; she's not thinking clearly. She's thinking like someone who's lost everything and wants someone to pay for it.'

Harper understood that mindset completely. He'd felt the same rage after his father's death, the same conviction that official channels would fail to deliver justice, that sometimes violence was the only language powerful people understood. The difference was that Harper had military training and operational experience. Rosa had grief, anger, and probably by now a gun, or worse – a dangerous combination that usually ended with innocent people getting hurt.

'Any chance of talking her down before she does something that gets everyone killed?'

'I tried. She's convinced that direct action is the only justice she'll get, that the system protects people like Slate while abandoning people like Tomás.' Santos paused. 'And honestly? She's probably right about that, which makes her even more dangerous.'

Harper processed this while Cortez listened to his side of the conversation. Rosa Alvarez was walking into a trap designed by people who eliminated problems professionally and had months to prepare for tonight's operation. Her righteous anger wouldn't protect her from Slate's systematic approach to witness removal, and her presence would complicate any attempt to expose the conspiracy without massive collateral damage.

'We'll find her,' Harper told Santos. 'Try to intercept her before she turns tonight into a massacre.'

'Be careful,' Santos replied. 'She's grieving, but she's not stupid. And she's got nothing left to lose.'

Harper ended the call and looked at Cortez, who was already checking her weapon and gathering her equipment.

'Multiple armed parties, competing objectives, professional killers maintaining operational security,' Harper summarised. 'The Veterans' Gala is shaping up to be a proper bloodbath.'

'Standard evening entertainment in your vicinity,' Cortez replied dryly. 'I'm guessing we find the killer before she does?'

'She thinks it's Veronica Slate.'

'Sure, but I'm talking about the trigger man—'

She paused, watching Harper's impassive face.

'Christ, Harper. You already killed him, didn't you?'

'Self-defence,' Harper shrugged. 'Didn't want to burden you with it.'

'Because of my being a cop and all that?' Cortez shook her head. 'Fine. I didn't hear that. What's the plan?'

Harper checked his watch. Three and a half hours until the gala began. Time to prepare for chaos while hoping some version of justice emerged from whatever wreckage tonight would create.

'We stop a massacre while exposing decades of environmental crimes and preventing corporate takeover by people who murder witnesses,' Harper said. 'Simple evening's work, really.'

'I do enjoy working with optimists.' Cortez almost smiled but paused when a new text message from Santos arrived.

> Just heard from a nurse friend – Rosa's heading to Northwestern Memorial – said she needs "proper equipment" for tonight.

'Bollocks,' Harper muttered as he showed the message to Cortez. 'Rosa's going to get herself killed.'

'Or she's going to kill Slate first,' Cortez observed. 'Trauma nurses know exactly what drugs would cause cardiac arrest. Make it look natural. Or, what drugs can kill with a ton of pain and misery. Still, could be worse. She could have found a gun.'

Harper was already moving towards his jacket. The Veterans' Gala would have on-site medical staff – standard protocol for events with five hundred people, most likely over sixty, consuming alcohol and rich food. Rosa could get inside with legitimate credentials and bring supplies that wouldn't be looked at twice on the door but could end someone's life in minutes.

'We need to intercept her at Northwestern Memorial,' Harper said, checking his watch. 'Before she gets what she needs and heads to Palmer House.'

'And if she's already gone?'

Harper pulled out his Hellcat, checking it over, ignoring Cortez's expression at this.

'Then we follow her and try to stop her before she destroys everything,' he said. 'I mean, it's not like we weren't going there, anyway.'

19

NURSING PRACTICE

THE RIDE ACROSS CHICAGO TOOK TWENTY-FIVE MINUTES through evening traffic, the Bonneville's engine note bouncing off buildings as they weaved between cars, Cortez holding tight behind him despite her wounded shoulder, her borrowed helmet slightly oversized.

Northwestern Memorial Hospital sat like a fortress on the city's North Side, and Harper parked up opposite, noting increased security presence around the building.

'BMW 3 Series near the main entrance,' Cortez observed, pointing to two men in suits positioned to observe all approaches. 'Professional surveillance, not hospital security.'

'Slate's people, probably following what happened yesterday.' Harper studied the building's layout, noting service entrances and staff car parks. 'But Rosa knows this place better than her own house. If she wants to avoid attention, she'll know how.'

Moving away from the surveillance team, they approached through the staff parking area, using parked cars for cover while Harper scanned for Rosa's vehicle. There – a familiar ten-year-old Honda Civic, engine still ticking as it cooled, parked near the emergency department's staff entrance.

She took Santos's car, it seemed. And Santos hadn't told him. Maybe he wanted justice for Tomás more than he'd revealed?

'She's here,' Harper confirmed, noting condensation on the windscreen and warm engine block. 'Arrived recently, maybe fifteen minutes.'

'Still inside then,' Cortez said, checking her weapon despite the shoulder wound causing obvious discomfort. At Harper's expression, she shrugged.

'You might know her, but I don't,' she said. 'She's grieving, looking for blood and likely to have a weapon of some kind. She comes at me, I'll put her down.'

At the staff entrance, Cortez took the lead, producing her sheriff's credentials.

'Sheriff Cortez. Need to speak with someone about one of your trauma nurses – Rosa Alvarez.'

The security guard examined Cortez's badge and identification, then barely glanced at Harper once she'd established legitimate authority – which was lucky, as he might have recognised Harper as one of the combatants in the parking lot the previous day.

'Rosa's inside somewhere. Came in about twenty minutes ago, said she needed to grab something from her locker.'

They entered through the checkpoint, Cortez's credentials getting them immediate access without the usual visitor procedures, Harper keeping his head down. They headed up to the trauma department, which buzzed with typical early evening activity: chest pains, minor injuries, domestic incidents, the usual chaos of urban healthcare.

Harper followed Cortez to the charge nurse's station.

'We need to talk to Rosa Alvarez's supervisor,' Cortez told the charge nurse. 'And anyone who's seen her in the last hour.'

The charge nurse checked her roster.

'Rosa's not scheduled tonight. But Doctor Bellamy saw her a few minutes ago when she came through the department. He's finishing his shift now if you want to catch him.'

Doctor Bellamy was a tired-looking resident in his thirties, who looked up from his paperwork when Cortez approached with her badge visible.

'Doctor Bellamy? Sheriff Cortez. I need to ask you about Rosa Alvarez. When did you last see her and what was her behaviour?'

'Rosa was here a few minutes back,' Bellamy replied, immediately serious when faced with law enforcement questions. 'She seemed different from usual – really focused, almost angry about something. Said she needed specific medications for private medical coverage tonight.'

'What kind of medications?' Harper asked.

Bellamy glanced at Cortez, who nodded permission.

'Cardiac emergency supplies. Potassium chloride, atropine, emergency airways, defibrillation drugs. Professional-grade emergency kit, but more comprehensive than you'd normally take to a corporate event.'

Harper felt ice forming in his stomach. He wasn't a doctor, but even he could see Rosa had gathered exactly what she needed to cause something like a cardiac arrest, one that would appear completely natural unless specifically tested for.

Which was good, in a way. Rosa was still thinking about how to get away with this. Which meant this wasn't some kind of "death or glory" suicide run.

'Did you question why she needed so much?' Cortez pressed.

'I asked about the extensive kit. Rosa said the client had specific medical concerns among the attendees – elderly VIPs with known cardiac issues, requiring full emergency preparedness.' Bellamy looked increasingly concerned as he spoke. 'She had legitimate access codes, knew exactly what she was taking. I didn't think to question it further as she seemed in a real hurry to leave.'

Bellamy paused, looking at Harper, as if for the first time.

'You were with her yesterday,' he whispered. 'When everything kicked off. Before her brother was found dead. Is Rosa in some kind of trouble?'

'We're hoping to prevent trouble,' Cortez replied diplomatically, handing Bellamy her card. 'If she contacts the hospital or returns, please call this number immediately.'

They headed back towards the staff car park, but Harper's worst fears were confirmed when they reached the space where Santos's stolen Honda had been parked. It was empty now, leaving only a small oil stain on the asphalt and the lingering scent of engine exhaust.

'She left while we were inside,' Cortez said grimly. 'Got her supplies and headed straight to Palmer House.'

Harper started the Bonneville's engine, mind already calculating timelines and possibilities. 'Fifteen, maybe twenty-minute head start. She's probably already at Palmer House, checking in as medical staff, setting up her equipment.'

'Can we stop her?'

'We can bloody well try.'

The ride to Palmer House took just under fifteen minutes through downtown Chicago's evening traffic, Harper pushing the Bonneville harder than was strictly safe while Cortez held on behind him. The hotel rose from Michigan Avenue like a monument to Gilded Age excess, its frontage glittering with lights and the sort of understated luxury that cost serious money to achieve. But Harper's attention was focused entirely on the security perimeter surrounding the building.

Professional teams positioned at strategic points around the entire block, with vehicle checkpoints at both ends of the street, controlling all access. Communications equipment was visible on several operatives, coordinating movement patterns. This wasn't standard hotel security – this was military-grade event protection with enough firepower to handle serious threats.

'Count at least a dozen visible positions,' Cortez noted as they parked up, using intervening buildings to break surveillance while they observed Palmer House's security arrangements. 'Probably twice that many we can't see.'

'Slate's not just protecting herself tonight,' Harper realised. 'She's controlling everything that happens at that gala. Every angle covered, every approach monitored.'

Evening-gowned guests were arriving, stepping from expensive cars – Range Rover Evoques, BMW 7 Series saloons, Mercedes S-Class vehicles – into the hotel's grand entrance. Among them would be Veronica Slate, Colonel Crowe, Mason Carrick, Alfie Reeves, and Rosa Alvarez, all converging for whatever finale Slate had orchestrated.

'Staff entrance,' Cortez pointed to a side entrance where uniformed personnel were moving equipment trolleys and setting up emergency stations. 'That's where Rosa would have gained access. Legitimate credentials, professional appearance, equipment that belongs at a high-profile medical station.'

Harper studied the approach routes, noting camera coverage and patrol patterns. Getting inside would be challenging but not impossible. The security was professional but focused outward – protecting against external threats rather than monitoring internal movement among allowed personnel.

'Okay, so we work on the fact she's already inside,' Harper concluded. 'Setting up medical stations, identifying her target, planning her approach. Rosa's patient – she'll wait for the right moment, create a medical emergency if necessary, then administer something that looks like treatment but causes cardiac arrest. Or, she'll pick a moment and strike. Either way, we have some time.'

'How do we get inside to stop her?'

Harper scanned the area, looking for infiltration opportunities. The security was comprehensive but as ever followed predictable patterns, and high-profile events always created chaos that could be exploited by people who understood how such operations worked.

There – a catering van was approaching the service entrance, driver looking harassed and running behind schedule.

'Health department inspection,' Harper said, quickly approaching the van, flashing Coble's badge while Cortez positioned herself to show her sheriff's credentials. 'Routine pre-event inspection. Need to verify food safety protocols before service begins.'

The driver – no more than twenty, stressed, checking his watch every few seconds – barely glanced at their credentials.

'Christ, not tonight, dude. We're already behind schedule, and the kitchen coordinator's having a nervous breakdown.'

'Just a quick verification,' Cortez said with the sort of calm authority that suggested this was standard procedure. 'Make sure everything's up to health department standards. Come on, we'll go through with you.'

The checkpoint security waved them all through without detailed scrutiny – health inspectors and law enforcement were expected at high-profile events, and inside Palmer House, the service areas buzzed with controlled chaos that Harper recognised from military logistics operations. Catering staff, security personnel, event coordinators, waiting staff and small medical teams, all moving with purpose as the gala prepared to begin.

Harper had wondered whether Slate would have flagged Cortez's badge – but the chances were Mason hadn't given her the full story on this new arrival. Either that, or Slate *wanted* them inside the building.

'Medical facilities should be near the main ballroom,' Cortez said, studying the building layout posted on corridor walls. 'Emergency access for guest medical incidents, but also discreet enough to avoid disrupting the event.'

They made their way through service corridors; Harper noting security camera positions and exit routes while listening for any signs of Rosa's presence.

'Service elevator,' Harper said, noting the building's vertical layout. 'Medical facilities will be on the same level as the main ballroom, probably connected by corridors that allow medical emergencies to be handled.'

The elevator carried them to the event level, where the controlled chaos intensified. Final preparations for a gala involving several hundred distinguished guests, significant media coverage, and the sort of political networking that required absolute precision in execution. But Harper and Cortez were ignored – the belief likely being that if they were down there, they were obviously *supposed* to be down there.

'There,' Harper said, catching sight of a familiar figure in medical uniform moving through a corridor ahead of them. Rosa Alvarez, carrying a comprehensive medical bag and wearing the crisp white uniform appropriate for high-end event medical coverage rather than hospital scrubs.

They followed at a discreet distance, using the crowd for cover while Rosa made her way towards the main event areas. She entered a small medical facility next to the main ballroom – clearly the designated first-aid station for the evening's event – equipped with emergency medical equipment and positioned for rapid response to guest incidents.

Harper waited until the corridor traffic reduced, then approached the medical bay entrance.

'Rosa,' he said quietly, stepping into the medical facility.

She spun around immediately, syringe in one hand, medical bag positioned on the equipment counter. Her face showed the strain of grief and determination mixed into something dangerous, but also the focused professionalism of someone who'd spent years dealing with life-and-death emergencies.

'Harper.' Her voice carried bitter recognition rather than surprise. 'Come to stop me?'

'Come to talk to you,' Harper replied, keeping his hands visible while noting her positioning between him and the only exit. Rosa was likely holding enough medical equipment to kill someone very efficiently, and she had the knowledge to use it properly. 'Before you throw your life away for nothing.'

'Nothing?' Rosa's grip tightened on the syringe, but her

voice remained controlled. 'My brother is dead because of that bitch. Because she ordered him killed for trying to protect children from poisoned soil.'

‘Look, I get you’re hurting, but this isn’t the way.’ Cortez stepped out from behind Harper, hands up.

'Who's this?' Rosa's eyes shifted to Cortez with immediate suspicion.

'Sheriff Lisa Cortez,' Cortez said carefully, moving slowly to avoid startling Rosa. 'Harper helped me out of a serious situation a while back. I'm returning the favour.'

'Another cop,' Rosa said bitterly. 'Come to arrest me for planning to give that murdering bitch what she deserves?'

'Come to prevent you from destroying your life for revenge that won't bring Tomás back,' Harper said. 'Rosa, killing Slate won't solve anything. It'll just get you killed too, and then who'll take care of your nephew and niece?'

'Someone has to pay for what happened to Tomás.'

'Someone already did,' Harper whispered. 'Murphy, the Irishman with the expensive cigars who attacked us outside the hospital? He did it. I found out, hunted him down in the early hours of this morning. He's dead. Won't be hurting anyone else's family.'

Rosa went still, the syringe trembling slightly in her hand as she processed this information.

'You killed him?'

‘On the roof of his flat in Pilsen. Slit his throat with a scalpel. He won't be smoking cigars over any more corpses. The man who actually pulled the trigger on your brother is dead.’

For a moment, Rosa's determination wavered. The syringe lowered slightly as she absorbed the implications of Harper's revelation.

'But Slate ordered it,' she said finally, voice cracking slightly. 'She's the one who decided Tomás had to die. She's the one who's been poisoning children for profit.'

'And she'll pay for that,' Cortez said firmly. 'But through the legal system, with evidence that will stand up in court. Not through murder that makes you no better than the people who killed your brother.'

'You think the legal system works against people like Veronica Slate?' Rosa's laugh was bitter. 'You think courts convict billionaires who buy judges and politicians? People like her don't go to prison. They buy their way out, or they disappear, or they have their problems eliminated.'

She sighed.

'This was my fault. I should have argued stronger when he first appeared with the money, but I knew Miguel needed the surgery. I let this happen.'

'No, your brother—' Harper was about to respond when the medical bay door opened behind them, and three men in expensive suits entered, moving like military operatives who'd done this sort of extraction many times before.

'Ms Alvarez,' the lead man said politely, weapon visible but not directly threatening. 'Mister Harper, Ms Cortez. Veronica Slate requests your immediate presence for a conversation.'

'This is a private chat,' Harper said, not turning around but noting Rosa's reaction to the new threat.

'Not any more,' the man replied with calm authority. 'Ms Slate has been expecting all of you. Please don't make this difficult. There are several hundred civilian guests throughout this building.'

Rosa's hand moved towards the syringe, but she stopped

when she saw the weapons the men carried and realised the impossibility of their situation.

'Harper,' Cortez said quietly, 'we don't have good options here.'

Rosa seemed to reach the same conclusion. She carefully placed the syringe on the medical equipment trolley, then raised her hands with the resignation of someone who'd expected this outcome from the beginning.

'What does she want?' Rosa asked.

'To discuss your brother's death, the environmental contamination, and Mister Harper's continued interference in legitimate business operations,' the man replied as one of his partners checked Harper and Cortez, taking their guns away. 'A comprehensive conversation about how to resolve these issues without further bloodshed.'

'Bloodshed she caused in the first place,' Rosa said bitterly.

'Ms Slate prefers dialogue to violence when circumstances permit effective resolution. Shall we proceed?'

They were outgunned, outnumbered, and trapped in a building full of innocent people who would pay the price for any resistance. The professionals had planned this extraction perfectly, leaving no room for heroic gestures or tactical brilliance.

'After you,' Harper said, gesturing towards the door while memorising faces, equipment, and movement patterns for future reference. 'But this is temporary cooperation, not surrender.'

'Understood.'

THEY WERE ESCORTED THROUGH SERVICE CORRIDORS HARPER hadn't seen on the layout map, past security checkpoints and into areas clearly not intended for public access. Palmer House was significantly larger and more complex than it appeared from outside – multiple levels, hidden passages, private facilities. Harper counted turns, elevator floors, noted exit routes, and tried to maintain spatial awareness despite the deliberate disorientation of their route.

They ended up in what appeared to be a private conference room on an upper floor – expensive mahogany furniture, and floor-to-ceiling windows showing Chicago's glittering skyline.

Veronica Slate was waiting for them. She looked elegant, composed, completely in control of whatever situation she created, and tonight she wore evening dress rather than business attire.

'Ms Alvarez,' she said warmly, as if greeting invited guests rather than prisoners. 'Harper, Ms Cortez. Thank you for joining me. I trust the escort arrangements were satisfactory?'

'Didn't realise we had much choice in the matter,' Harper replied, settling into the chair his escorts showed while scanning for security cameras, weapons, and escape routes.

'There are always choices,' Slate said, moving to an expensive coffee service and pouring three cups. 'The question is whether we make intelligent ones or whether circumstances force less pleasant alternatives.'

She offered coffee to each of them, a gesture of hospitality that somehow made the situation more unsettling rather than less threatening.

Rosa remained standing, staring at Slate with undisguised hatred.

'You killed my brother.'

'Your brother made poor decisions about his contractual obligations,' Slate replied calmly, settling into her chair. 'I regret the necessity, but business sometimes requires unpleasant solutions.'

'Business?' Rosa's voice cracked with fury. 'He was trying to protect children from poisoned soil. Children who are getting sick because you buried toxic waste under their playgrounds while claiming you'd cleaned the South Yards.'

'He was interfering with legitimate development projects after accepting substantial compensation to look the other way,' Slate replied, her tone remaining pleasant as if discussing a minor personnel issue rather than murder. 'I offered Mister Alvarez several alternatives to continued interference. He chose poorly.'

Harper watched this exchange while continuing to catalogue the room's layout. *Three guards visible, probably more positioned outside the conference room. Windows that looked like they wouldn't open. One door, certainly monitored by additional security. Their guns with the stockier guard of the three who'd escorted them, now waiting by the door.*

They were comprehensively trapped.

'What do you want from us?' Cortez asked, her law enforcement training helping her maintain professional composure despite the circumstances.

'To resolve our current difficulties without further complications,' Slate replied, checking her watch. 'The Veterans' Gala begins in thirty minutes. Several hundred distinguished guests, significant media coverage, political networking opportunities. The sort of high-profile event that benefits no one if it becomes associated with violence or unfortunate incidents.'

'So, you're holding us prisoner until it's over?' Harper asked.

'I'm offering you an opportunity to reconsider your positions before circumstances force less pleasant alternatives,' Slate smiled. 'Mister Harper, your interference has been persistent but ultimately futile. The South Yards development will proceed as planned, the environmental concerns have been addressed through proper regulatory channels, and the unfortunate deaths were isolated incidents that have been resolved through appropriate means.'

'Resolved by murdering witnesses,' Harper said flatly.

'By eliminating complications that threatened legitimate business interests,' Slate replied, her voice hardening slightly for the first time. 'Your father understood these operational necessities. Dominic Kane built Aegis on the principle that some problems require permanent solutions rather than prolonged negotiations.'

Harper felt cold anger building but kept his voice level.

'And yet you intend to kill his partner tonight.'

'I'm sure I have no idea what you mean,' Slate leaned forward slightly, fixing Harper with the sort of direct stare that suggested she was accustomed to getting exactly what she wanted from these conversations. 'Which brings us to our current situation. You have information that could be misinterpreted by people who don't understand the complexities of international business and environmental regulation. I have resources that could ensure that information never becomes public, along with opportunities that could benefit all parties involved.'

'You want to buy us off,' Harper said.

'I want to offer you alternatives to the unpleasant consequences of continued interference.'

Rosa had listened to this exchange with growing fury.

'You think money fixes everything? You think you can pay for my brother's life and make this disappear?'

'I think your brother's death was regrettable but necessary for the greater good,' Slate replied calmly. 'I also think you have responsibilities that extend beyond personal revenge. Your nephew and niece depend on you, Ms Alvarez. They've already lost their father and mother. It would be tragic if they lost their aunt as well because of poor decision-making, thrown into a foster-care situation that'd likely split them apart, never to see each other again. Maybe a donation to assist your relocation to a nicer area might help?'

Rosa understood the veiled threat immediately. Her face went white with a mixture of rage and fear.

'You touch those children—'

'I have no interest in harming children,' Slate interrupted smoothly. 'Children are the future, after all. But I do have an interest in preventing further complications that could affect their wellbeing. Aunt Rosa facing murder charges, for instance, would be quite disruptive to their stable home environment.'

Slate stood, smoothing her evening dress and checking her appearance in the conference room's mirror.

'Well, this has been fun and informative, but I need to make my appearance, deliver my remarks about the South Yards project's environmental benefits, and celebrate another successful public-private partnership that will bring jobs and prosperity to Chicago. We're going to give affordable veteran housing to the city.' She moved towards the door, adjusting a piece of jewellery with the sort of theatrical gesture that suggested she enjoyed having a captive audience for her performance. 'You'll remain here as my guests until the evening concludes successfully. After that, we can discuss more permanent arrangements for resolving our various difficulties. I'm confident we can reach agreements that benefit everyone involved.'

'And if we refuse your generous offers?' Harper asked.

'Then your time here will come to a brutal end, nothing more than an endnote in the stories coming out of the event,' Slate replied, her smile disappearing entirely for the first time. 'I hope you'll use this time productively to reconsider your positions.'

The door closed behind her with a quiet click that somehow sounded final, leaving Harper, Cortez, and Rosa alone with their armed guards and the uncomfortable certainty that they'd walked directly into Slate's carefully prepared trap.

'Well,' Harper said finally. 'This is bloody brilliant.'

'What's the plan?' Cortez asked quietly.

Harper looked around the conference room. Outside the floor-to-ceiling windows, Chicago glittered in the darkness, while inside Palmer House, the Veterans' Gala was about to begin with all the key players finally in position. Alfie Reeves would kill Mason Carrick and Crowe, the three of them would be removed quietly, regardless of what Slate just said, and Veronica Slate would be seen as a victim.

She could even run for office after this.

'We wait for our opportunity,' Harper said. 'And we hope it comes before Slate decides we're too much trouble to keep breathing.'

20

HOUSING BENEFITS

THE CONFERENCE ROOM HAD THE SORT OF EXPENSIVE furniture that screamed *'we can afford to kill you quietly.'* Outside, Chicago sprawled like a circuit board, all lights and dark spaces, while twenty floors below five hundred people drank champagne and pretended environmental crime was patriotism.

Brilliant, really. Nothing like a veterans' gala to provide cover for mass murder.

'How long do you think she'll keep us here?' Rosa asked quietly. She'd been staring at her hands for the past twenty minutes, probably replaying every conversation with Tomás, every choice that had led to him bleeding out in a Chicago alley.

'Until we stop being useful,' Harper replied, studying the nearest guard. Thirties, wedding ring, clean shaven, the sort of face that suggested killing people was just another day at the office. Professional contractor who'd probably learned his trade in Iraq or Afghanistan before privatising the skill set.

'Then we become tragic footnotes in tomorrow's terrorism story.'

The guard's expression didn't change, but Harper caught the slight tightening around his eyes. *Direct hit – these bastards knew exactly what tonight's finale involved.*

Cortez shifted in her chair, testing her wounded shoulder. Whatever makeshift bandaging she'd gained from Evanston was holding, but she still looked like someone who'd lost too much blood and was running on stubbornness and caffeine; the sort of hollow-eyed determination that came from knowing you were probably going to die but refusing to make it easy.

'Meaning what, exactly?' she asked.

'Meaning Alfie finishes his work downstairs, Slate gets her standing ovation from five hundred witnesses, and we get filed under regrettable casualties of environmental terrorism.' Harper watched the lead guard's micro-expressions while palming his river stone. The smooth surface felt familiar between his fingers – centuries of the River Wye's current had shaped it into something more useful than these professionals had imagined. 'She's announcing veteran housing to five hundred of Chicago's most powerful people. Tomorrow's headlines write themselves.'

The guard's mouth twitched. Almost a smile. These weren't street thugs or corporate rent-a-cops. They were ex-military contractors who understood operational security, tactical patience, and how to make multiple murders look like unfortunate accidents when the paperwork got filed.

Rosa looked between Harper and Cortez with the sort of desperate hope that came from having nothing left to lose.

'So, we just sit here waiting to die?'

'We wait for our chance,' Harper corrected, lowering his

voice, working his river stone between his knuckles while keeping his hands casually positioned. 'Slate's trying to coordinate multiple operations tonight. Multiple operations mean multiple failure points. Something's bound to go sideways.'

The guards maintained their positions with disciplined alertness Harper recognised from joint operations in places where boredom killed as efficiently as bullets. Professional contractors who'd learned patience in Afghan valleys and Iraqi cities, now applying those skills to corporate wetwork in Chicago conference rooms. But Harper had commanded men exactly like these in places where split-second decisions meant the difference between mission success and body bags. He understood their training, their psychology, their vulnerabilities. More importantly, he understood that they'd prepared for prisoner containment, not close-quarters combat with someone who'd learned killing where mistakes meant death.

The silence stretched between them, broken only by distant party sounds filtering through the building's ventilation system and occasional radio crackle from the guards' earpieces. Harper used the quiet to memorise every detail – furniture positions that could provide cover, potential weapons within reach, camera angles that might create blind spots during whatever was about to happen.

A wall-mounted television dominated one corner, showing the live broadcast from the main ballroom twenty floors below. Professional camera work, multiple angles, the sort of media coverage that could make or break political careers with a single story. Not streamed outside, but probably using a production team to create the best version of the story to be given out to all media sources when all hell broke loose.

Harper watched Veronica Slate's performance with grudging admiration mixed with cold fury. She stood at the podium like she'd been born to command five hundred of Chicago's most powerful people, wearing her elegant evening dress and with a confident bearing that suggested absolute control over every variable in tonight's equation.

Evil as a bag of snakes, but undeniably impressive.

'Ladies and gentlemen, thank you for joining us tonight to honour our veterans and their service to our nation,' Slate said, her voice carrying through the conference room speakers with absolute conviction. 'Their sacrifices have secured the freedom and prosperity we enjoy today, and it's fitting that we celebrate their legacy while looking towards Chicago's bright future.'

Harper felt cold understanding settle in his stomach like swallowed ice. She was doing it – wrapping systematic murder in patriotic bunting, using veteran housing as cover for poisoning families, making opposition politically impossible.

'Look at her,' Rosa said bitterly, staring at the screen with hatred that could have powered half the city. 'Standing there talking about honour and service while planning to house veterans on soil that'll kill their children.'

'She's bloody brilliant,' Harper admitted, watching Slate command her audience of Chicago's elite. 'She controls every aspect of the narrative. I hate her, but I have to admire that.'

On screen, Slate continued her presentation with perfect timing and delivery. Every pause calculated for maximum emotional impact, every gesture designed to reinforce the patriotic themes that made criticism impossible.

'—which is why I'm particularly excited to announce the South Yards Veterans' Housing Development, which will provide affordable homes for our service members while bringing jobs and prosperity to our great city. Comprehensive environmental assessments have confirmed the site's suitability for residential development. Ground-breaking begins Monday morning—'

The applause from the ballroom was thunderous, exactly the sort of enthusiastic response Slate had orchestrated through months of careful preparation. Harper could see politicians nodding approval while mentally calculating how this played with veteran voting blocks, business leaders applauding while running profit projections, media representatives capturing every moment for tomorrow's feel-good stories about helping heroes. All of them completely unaware they were celebrating systematic murder dressed as charity.

'She's got them eating out of her manicured hand,' Harper observed, noting how Slate's performance had been perfected to maximise emotional manipulation. 'Tomorrow's headlines celebrate veteran housing and patriotic generosity. Anyone opposing the development looks like they hate the military.'

Rosa's hands clenched into fists.

'Tomás died trying to prevent this. Children are getting sick from contaminated soil. And she's announcing it like some goddamned charity project while five hundred people applaud.'

'That's the beauty of controlling the narrative,' Harper said. 'Truth doesn't matter when you can make lies sound like patriotism.'

Commotion erupted outside – voices, footsteps, radio chatter. The guards tensed.

'Something's happening,' Cortez said.

One guard touched his earpiece, listened, frowned.

'Moving to Phase Two ahead of schedule.'

'What's Phase Two?' Rosa asked.

'Resolution of outstanding complications,' the guard replied with a dark smile. Harper tensed at the phrase.

Corporate speak for murder.

Slate's speech continued from the television, her voice maintaining absolute confidence while painting her vision of Chicago's future. But Harper could hear subtle changes in delivery – controlled tension that suggested things weren't proceeding exactly according to her script.

'—grateful to our partners at Aegis Security for their continued support of this project. Aegis CEO Mason Carrick and head consultant Retired Colonel Oliver Crowe will join me shortly to discuss their expanded role in veteran services—'

Harper felt his pulse quicken. Mason was about to take the stage, which meant the endgame was beginning. Whatever confession or betrayal Mason had planned, it was about to unfold in a matter of moments. But Harper also knew that somewhere in that ballroom, Alfie Reeves waited with professional killing skills and personal motivation for revenge on both men.

'Mason's making his move,' Harper realised, watching the screen with growing urgency. 'Public confession in front of witnesses and cameras. Slate's positioning to contain the damage, but she can't control what Mason says once he's got the microphone. That sounds like our cue.'

Another burst of radio chatter, sharp and immediate. The guard's face changed as he received whatever update was being transmitted, professional alertness transforming into operational readiness.

'Sir,' one of the other guards called from his position by the door. 'Control confirms Phase Two initiation. Prisoner disposal authorised immediately.'

The lead guard moved his hand towards his weapon while maintaining the appearance of routine adjustment – a professional technique designed to keep targets calm until the moment of termination. His colleagues shifted position almost imperceptibly, creating overlapping fields of fire that would ensure quick, efficient kills with minimal noise or mess. Harper had perhaps three seconds before they opened fire—

He launched himself from his chair while whipping his river stone at the nearest guard's temple. The stone – shaped by centuries of the River Wye's current into the perfect projectile – caught the man precisely where skull met jaw, slicing open the skin on impact. The impact sounded like someone dropping a melon, and the guard folded sideways into the mahogany panelling with a wet thump.

The second guard was already bringing his weapon up, but Harper was inside his firing arc, using the falling body as mobile cover. He grabbed the unconscious guard's sidearm while driving his offhand fist into the second man's trachea, crushing his larynx.

The guard was good – ex-military, proper training, didn't panic when things went sideways. He pivoted with the impact, trying to create distance for a clean shot even as his breathing was compromised. Harper stayed close however, jamming the guard's weapon hand upward while driving an elbow into his solar plexus.

Air whooshed out of the man's lungs, but he brought his knee up towards Harper's ribs. Harper twisted, took the strike on his hip, used the momentum to spin the guard around and slam his gun hand into the conference table's edge.

Bones cracked, wrist or hand, and the weapon clattered across expensive wood.

Meanwhile, Cortez had moved on the third guard despite her wounded shoulder. She tackled him low, using her good arm to grab and twist his weapon hand while her injured shoulder likely screamed in protest. The guard was bigger and stronger, but Cortez had leverage and desperation. He tried to backhand her with his free hand, but she ducked the swing and drove her good side elbow into his kidney, the sort of punch that made grown men reconsider their life choices.

Harper's opponent was still fighting but losing energy fast, going for a backup weapon from an ankle holster. Harper grabbed a leather chair – solid steel frame, looked expensive – and introduced it to the guard's skull with considerable force.

The chair won.

The third guard finally went down when Rosa, of all people, smashed him over the head with an abstract art piece that looked like a twisted metal pretzel. The sculpture probably cost fifty thousand bucks. Now it was slightly dented and covered in blood.

'That felt good,' Rosa said, breathing hard.

Silence settled over the conference room. Harper checked his acquisitions while Cortez searched the unconscious guards for their confiscated weapons.

'Found them,' she said, pulling Harper's Hellcat and her own Glock from the stocky guard's tactical vest.

Harper took his Hellcat, checking the action. Familiar weight, full magazine, exactly as he'd left it.

'Much better,' he said, holstering the weapon while keeping the guard's Sig as backup. 'How's the shoulder?'

'Hurts like bloody hell, but I can still shoot,' Cortez replied, checking her weapon's action. 'What's the plan?'

'Stop Alfie before Mason's confession begins and gets everyone killed,' Harper said, moving towards the door. On the screen, Mason was seen waving to the audience from his table, likely minutes from systematically destroying Slate's carefully constructed narrative in front of five hundred witnesses. 'Public exposure only works if people survive to remember it.'

Rosa looked between them, still holding the bent sculpture.

'What about Slate?'

'She's about to learn that controlling stories gets complicated when people rewrite them,' Harper replied, checking the corridor for immediate threats. 'Let's go prevent a massacre.'

'Problem,' Cortez said, checking magazines. 'I've got maybe twelve rounds total.'

Harper did a quick count.

'Fifteen here, full clip in the Hellcat, plus whatever spare ammunition our unconscious friends were carrying.' He knelt beside the first guard, checking pockets and tactical gear. 'Bingo.'

The guard had been carrying enough firepower for a minor war – extra magazines for the Sig, a backup Glock 26, a tactical knife, zip ties, and what looked like a small brick of plastic explosive with a timer.

'Christ,' Harper muttered, examining the explosive. 'They weren't planning to leave witnesses or evidence.'

'Or the building,' Cortez observed grimly.

Rosa stared at the plastic explosive.

'They were going to blow us up?'

'Let's just say they had a creative way of removing evidence,' Harper said, pocketing the device while handing Cortez a couple of magazines, and Rosa the backup Glock. 'You know how to use this?'

'Point the dangerous end at bad people and pull the trigger?'

'Close enough.' Harper picked up his lucky river stone and checked the corridor. It was empty, but Harper could hear boots on stairs, radio chatter, the sort of coordinated movement that meant backup was coming fast. Palmer House had gone from elegant hotel to active kill zone – all likely to prevent Mason's confession.

'We've got minutes before they lock down this entire floor. Maybe two before Mason starts speaking and Alfie starts firing.'

'Which way?' Cortez asked.

'Service elevator to the kitchen level, then maintenance corridors towards the ballroom,' he decided. 'Same way they brought us in. Avoid the principal routes where they'll expect us.'

'And if we run into security teams?'

'We adapt,' Harper said, leading them towards the service areas. 'But quietly. Soon as we start shooting, every team in the building will come for us.'

They moved through corridors that felt increasingly hostile. Emergency lighting cast harsh shadows, and the building's ventilation system carried sounds of radio transmissions echoing from stairwells. Palmer House had become a hunting ground with them as the prey.

Harper led them past guest rooms, conference areas,

administrative offices. All empty now, but the emptiness felt wrong – too quiet, too convenient.

'This is too easy,' Cortez whispered, echoing his thoughts.

A service corridor branched left towards the elevators, right towards maintenance areas. Harper paused, weighing options while radio chatter grew louder behind them.

'Left puts us in a choke point,' he breathed. 'Right takes us deeper into their territory.'

'Both sound delightful,' Rosa observed.

'Maintenance areas.' Harper made the call. 'At least we'll have room to manoeuvre when things go sideways.'

They moved deeper into Palmer House's hidden infrastructure – corridors lined with pipes and electrical conduits, storage areas full of industrial equipment, the utilitarian spaces that kept elegant hotels functioning behind the scenes.

'Movement ahead,' Cortez warned, raising her weapon.

Harper held up a hand for silence. Footsteps, deliberate and professional, echoed from the next corridor junction. At least two people, possibly more, positioning themselves to cut off escape routes.

'They're boxing us in,' Cortez realised. 'Multiple teams, coordinated sweep pattern.'

'Right,' Harper said, checking his weapon. 'Time to see if our training's better than their preparation.'

The hunt was about to become significantly more interesting.

21

THE GALA

THE SOUNDS WERE GETTING CLOSER – BOOTS ON CONCRETE, radio chatter. Harper could hear teams converging on their position.

Slate's people weren't messing about.

They moved through Palmer House's service areas, past corridors that smelled of cleaning chemicals and machine oil. The building's bones were solid – nineteenth-century construction with thick walls that muffled sound, but the new designs and structures clashed a little more where the public didn't really go.

Their pursuers were adapting, though. Radio communications coordinating new search patterns, boots changing direction. Not hotel security guards stumbling about in the dark.

Through the building's speaker system, Mason Carrick's voice carried from the ballroom sound system. Formal, confident, but Harper caught something underneath – tension that suggested things weren't proceeding exactly according to plan.

'Ladies and gentlemen, before I accept this honour tonight, I want to address some concerning developments that have come to my attention regarding our partners in this evening's celebration—'

'He's started,' Rosa whispered.

Harper paused, listening. Mason's tone wasn't what he'd expected. No dramatic confession, no theatrical exposure. Instead, measured corporate damage control, the sort of performance that turned liability into opportunity.

Charming. Mason was about to throw everyone else under the bus while positioning himself as the innocent victim.

'—Aegis Security has always prided itself on working with organisations that share our commitment to serving those who've served our nations. It's therefore deeply troubling to learn that Veronica Slate and her associates may have exploited this partnership for purposes that betray the very veterans we're here to honour—'

Clever bastard. Mason wasn't confessing to conspiracy – he was repositioning the entire narrative. Aegis as an unwitting victim of environmental criminals, rather than an active participant in corporate murder.

'—we had no knowledge of environmental contamination in the South Yards development. No awareness that safety reports had been falsified, or that environmental activists and safety inspectors were being systematically intimidated. When Aegis agreed to provide security consultation for this project, we believed we were protecting a legitimate housing initiative for veterans—'

Harper almost admired the tactical brilliance. Tomorrow's headlines would focus on environmental crimes rather than security firm corruption.

They reached the service elevator; Harper pressed the call button while listening to Mason's carefully crafted narrative echoing through the building's sound system. The man had obviously spent considerable time preparing this performance.

'—it has come to my attention that Colonel Oliver Crowe, who has been serving as military liaison for this project, has been feeding operational intelligence to Meridian Security, who have recently been bought out by Slate Urban Developments. Information about our personnel, our contracts, our security protocols. Intelligence that enabled systematic infiltration of Aegis operations—'

The elevator arrived with a quiet ding that somehow sounded ominous in the context of Mason's accusation. They stepped inside as his public denunciation continued.

'—Colonel Crowe has been working for Veronica Slate's organisation while maintaining his position as our trusted military consultant. This betrayal of confidence has enabled environmental crimes, corporate murder, and the systematic exploitation of veteran housing initiatives—'

'Jesus,' Cortez said. 'Mason's exposing Crowe as Slate's spy?'

The elevator descended towards the main event level while Mason's public accusation continued, with five hundred witnesses learning that one of their evening's guests of honour was accusing a decorated British military officer of treason and murder. Again, Harper had to admire this, as it was the sort of accusation that would dominate news cycles for weeks while burying inconvenient questions about Aegis's own involvement.

But why wasn't Alfie shooting yet? Did he need them both on stage?

They reached the ballroom level as emergency alarms began wailing throughout Palmer House.

Not fire alarms – security alerts, the sort that meant controlled lockdown rather than evacuation. Someone had made the executive decision that tonight's guests weren't leaving until certain conversations had concluded, and the elevator doors opened onto chaos that made Harper's previous encounters with corporate security look like polite disagreements.

Through the ballroom's main entrance, Harper could see the stage where Mason Carrick stood at the podium, still speaking into the microphone while security personnel moved through the crowd with urgent purpose.

But their movement wasn't protective – they were positioning for containment operations, the sort Harper recognised from crowd control training.

Emergency lighting threw harsh shadows across Palmer House's architecture, transforming the charity gala into something resembling a military checkpoint. Five hundred people in evening wear, trapped while accusations of conspiracy and murder echoed through the sound system.

And there, rushing towards the stage from the VIP seating area, was Colonel Oliver Crowe in full military dress uniform, his face carrying the sort of fury that suggested Mason's accusations had hit uncomfortably close to truth.

'These accusations are completely false,' Crowe's shouted voice carried through the ballroom as he approached the podium, his military bearing clear even in civilian surroundings. 'Mason Carrick is attempting to deflect responsibility for environmental crimes by scapegoating a British military officer!'

The two men faced each other on stage while one-percenter witnesses watched their charity gala transform into something far more dangerous than anyone had expected. Political networking and corporate glad-handing had now been replaced by public accusations that would destroy careers and possibly end lives.

'You've been feeding intelligence to Meridian Security for months,' Mason continued into the microphone, maintaining control of the narrative while Crowe approached. 'Financial information, operational schedules, personnel files. Everything Slate needed to systematically undermine Aegis while positioning herself as the ethical alternative—'

'That's a bloody lie,' Crowe snapped, reaching for the microphone with the sort of aggressive movement that suggested diplomatic conversation was finished. Mason pulled back, maintaining control of the sound system while Crowe moved closer. Physical confrontation was seconds away, and Harper could see security teams throughout the ballroom preparing for whatever came next.

But he couldn't see Alfie Reeves.

'There,' Cortez pointed towards the ballroom's upper level, where technical balconies provided discreet access for lighting and sound equipment. A figure in a security uniform could be seen watching, positioned with a clear view of the main floor. The sort of over-watch position that suggested sniper capability rather than crowd control. Alfie Reeves, watching the chaos below while calculating his next move with the sort of calm focus Harper remembered from joint operations years earlier.

Mason and Crowe were now physically struggling for control of the microphone; their argument having devolved into something resembling a playground fight in front of hundreds of witnesses.

'Alfie won't wait much longer,' Harper realised, understanding the tactical opportunity developing. 'He's got both targets on stage, public chaos for cover, perfect conditions for whatever he's planned.'

They used the service stairs to reach the balcony level, moving quietly through technical areas that smelled of electrical equipment and old carpet. Harper noted emergency exit locations, crowd movement patterns, the positioning of security personnel throughout Palmer House's main ballroom, but Cortez instead was staring behind.

'Where's Rosa?' she asked suddenly.

Harper looked around. Rosa had been with them in the corridor, but now she was gone.

'Bloody hell,' he muttered. 'She's gone after Slate.'

'The syringe is still in the medical room.'

'She doesn't need the syringe,' Harper hissed while starting up a ladder. 'She has a gun now.'

'I'll find her,' Cortez said, already moving. 'Stop her from doing something stupid, while you stop your shooter from doing the same.'

Harper nodded, watching Cortez disappear back towards the service areas while he approached Alfie's position using lighting equipment for concealment. His old comrade knelt behind professional surveillance gear; rifle trained on the chaos below.

'Alfie,' Harper said quietly, moving closer. 'Don't do this.'

Alfie didn't turn, but his finger settled on the trigger.

'Too late for conversation, Harper.'

Through the ballroom below, Harper could see Mason

and Crowe locked in a physical struggle while witnesses watched, and security tried to pull them apart. Veronica Slate, obviously deciding this was pointless, was nowhere to be seen. As he looked, Harper could see Mason trying to maintain his narrative, Crowe attempting to stop the accusations by force—

Harper lunged forward, trying to spoil Alfie's shot before his old comrade could capitalise on the chaos, but the rifle cracked before he could reach Alfie, and Harper saw Mason Carrick crumple, blood spreading across his evening jacket's shirt while Crowe stumbled backwards.

The shot had come during their fight – impossible to tell from the crowd's perspective who had been the intended target, and as the audience realised what had happened, screaming erupted from the ballroom as panic took hold and people pressed towards exits that security teams were already sealing.

'Christ,' Harper breathed. 'You got him.'

'Either target works.' Alfie spun, drawing a compact pistol and training it on Harper. 'Back off.'

Harper stared down the barrel of a Walther P99, the metal worn smooth from years of handling.

Recognition hit immediately.

Five-ten, professional stance, minimal deviation. Walther P99, aftermarket barrel. Remember. Avenge.

'That's the gun that killed Tomás.'

'Same weapon I've used for every contract since Syria,' Alfie said. 'Reliable, distinctive, perfectly suited for close-range work.'

Harper felt pieces clicking into place with the sort of clarity that came from finally understanding operational parameters that had seemed random. *Murphy had been taller than Kowalski's assessment, but Alfie Reeves was just right.*

'You weren't there to watch, were you?' he asked coldly. 'You were the shooter and Murphy was the spotter, keeping oversight while you murdered Tomás.'

'Murdered? I'd prefer to say I executed him. Just like every other environmental activist, safety inspector, inconvenient journalist who threatened legitimate operations.' Alfie kept the PPK steady. 'All with equipment that traces back to British military issue. All with weapons that can be connected to Oliver Crowe.'

The implications settled around Harper. Not random corporate assassination, but a systematic framing operation designed to destroy Crowe's reputation while eliminating inconvenient witnesses.

Again, a line from Mason Carrick came back.

'The attack was unexpected, professional, targeted specifically at eliminating both Dominic and me simultaneously, as they thought we were both on that ship. And I'll point out you were there too, so whoever was aiming it... they were going off intel that was Government level.'

'Myanmar,' he hissed. 'Government level intel. Someone connected to Aegis. Crowe set it up.'

'Your father's Myanmar assignment wasn't routine maritime security consultation. It was orchestrated to eliminate Dominic Kane and clear the way for Meridian Security to gain Aegis contracts.' Alfie's voice carried the conviction of someone who'd spent years collecting evidence. 'But Crowe wanted something special. He made sure you'd be the SRR team leader assigned to that operation.'

Harper felt ice forming in his chest, understanding the true scope of what had been orchestrated.

'He wanted me there?'

'He wanted you to be the one who found your father dying. Maybe even the son who'd killed his own father, even if accidentally.' Alfie's smile was cruel, carrying years of resentment towards everyone who'd destroyed his life. 'Psychological warfare at its finest. Break you completely, make you blame yourself for his death while eliminating the last obstacle to corporate transition. Seems Colonel Crowe wasn't as much a fan of you as you were of him. Maybe your father's constant check ins finally pushed him? Maybe he knew Dominic had found out he'd been working on off-books weapon sales and assumed you'd been told? Either way, daddy and son were supposed to die.'

The revelation hit harder than physical violence. Crowe hadn't just orchestrated his father's murder – he'd engineered it so Harper would carry the guilt forever, destroying his effectiveness as a potential threat to whatever conspiracy had replaced Aegis's original mission.

'Except your father saved your life instead of following the script. Inconvenient heroism that ruined Crowe's psychological operation while creating a loose end that needed eventual elimination.'

Harper stared at Alfie, understanding the scope of Crowe's manipulation while recognising that his old comrade had become something far more dangerous than a simple corporate assassin.

'Crowe's been playing all sides for years. Military liaison for Aegis, consultant for Meridian, supplier of intelligence to whoever paid better rates.' Alfie's positioning shifted slightly, maintaining weapon discipline while preparing for whatever came next. 'Tonight was supposed to be his masterpiece. Eliminate Mason and me, blame everything on rogue military contractors, walk away clean with an enhanced reputation for crisis management as he takes over Meridian, which, with help from Veronica Slate, buys out Aegis. Of course, now that you know I killed your buddy, I think I need to remove you, too. I mean, you failed your mission.'

'What mission?' Harper calculated distances, noting Alfie's position with his back to the balcony rail, focused entirely on maintaining weapon control while ignoring his surroundings. Professional training, but also the sort of tunnel vision that came from years of working alone. Below them, the ballroom chaos continued while security teams moved through the panicking crowd with what looked like cleanup operations rather than emergency response. Systematic elimination of witnesses who might remember Mason's accusations, disguised as counter-terrorism procedures.

Alfie straightened, and for a moment Harper thought he was genuinely hurt by Harper as he spoke.

'You agreed to help me, but here you are, judging me, like you did five sodding years back!'

Harper dived sideways as he spoke, hoping to break Alfie's concentration while creating tactical opportunities.

The Walther P99 cracked as Harper rolled behind lighting equipment, the bullet sparking off metal fixtures while Alfie tracked his movement. The confined space and technical equipment provided enough cover for manoeuvring, but not enough for extended engagement against someone with Alfie's training.

Harper launched himself forward, tackling Alfie around the waist and driving both of them towards the balcony rail.

Veronica Slate moved through Palmer House's service corridors, her evening gown torn at the hem, her operation collapsing behind her like a controlled demolition gone wrong.

The Veterans' Gala was supposed to have been her triumph. Public announcement of the South Yards development, Mason Carrick's testimony about environmental safety, political networking that would establish Meridian Security as Chicago's premier contractor for sensitive operations, then Mason killed by Reeves, Reeves killed by her own men, and eventually Aegis bought by Meridian and Slate for pennies on the dollar. Instead, everything had gone sideways the moment Carrick decided to throw her under the proverbial bus.

At least the bastard was dead now.

Her phone buzzed constantly with urgent messages from security teams trying to coordinate damage control, but Slate ignored them. The operation was blown beyond salvage. Too many witnesses, too much exposure, and federal investigators already en route according to her intelligence sources. Time to activate extraction protocols before Chicago became a liability rather than an asset.

She reached the service elevator that would carry her to the parking levels, where armoured vehicles waited for exactly this sort of contingency. Behind her, she could hear screaming echoing through Palmer House's corridors as her security teams tried to salvage what remained of the evening's objectives.

Professional failure on this scale required immediate relocation to non-extradition territories until things could be ironed out and fixed. The sort of operational security that came from years of planning for worst-case scenarios.

The elevator doors opened.

Rosa Alvarez stood inside, Glock 26 raised directly at Slate, her face twisted with murderous rage.

'You killed my brother, you goddamned bitch,' she snarled. 'Now you get to eat a bullet.'

22

BLOOD AND LIES

HARPER AND ALFIE CRASHED INTO THE BALCONY RAILING WITH enough force to buckle the metal. Both men fought for control of the Walther PPK while thirty feet below, chaos consumed Palmer House's main ballroom. The weapon discharged between them, muzzle flash illuminating their faces as the bullet sparked off technical equipment.

Alfie was stronger than Harper remembered, his five years of corporate killing having honed him into something more dangerous than the soldier Harper had known – he wasn't any slouch back then, either. He drove his knee towards Harper's thigh, but Harper twisted in time for the blow to miss wide, then smashed into Alfie's torso, slamming him against the railing. The metal groaned again under their combined weight. Harper could see the drop to the ballroom floor below, where panicking guests fled in all directions while security teams moved with deadly purpose through the crowd.

Alfie loosened Harper's grip with a vicious elbow strike, then wrenched for control of the P99 again. Harper caught his wrist and twisted the point of aim away. The battle for control of the weapon continued while the balcony rail creaked ominously beneath them.

'Should have stayed away from Chicago,' Alfie snarled, trying to drive his thumb into Harper's eye.

Harper deflected the attack and delivered a vicious Glasgow kiss to Alfie's nose with a wet crack. Blood erupted, but Alfie kept fighting, years of violence having taught him to maintain battle focus through pain.

The P99 fired again as they struggled; the hollow point bullet punching through the ballroom's acoustic ceiling this time. Harper twisted Alfie's wrist until bones ground together, finally forcing him to release the weapon.

The Walther went spinning over the rail, tumbling end over end before clattering uselessly onto the ballroom floor amongst the fleeing crowd.

'Doesn't bloody matter,' Alfie panted, blood streaming from his broken nose. 'Job's done. Mason's down.'

Harper stepped back, breathing hard, and now with a moment to take stock, drew his Hellcat, aiming it at his one-time comrade. His ribs ached where Alfie had caught him, and he could taste blood from a split lip, but he was still operational.

'You murdered Tomás Alvarez,' he said, the weapon steady in his hands.

Alfie's expression shifted to cold amusement.

'And you're next,' he muttered. 'Christ, Harper, you were always so "holier than thou" in the service. Did you ever consider that you weren't universally liked?'

'Never considered it.'

'Did you ever consider that some of us looked at that scar on your eye and wished we could give you a bigger one? Or take that stupid bloody pet rock you got from the river and ram it up your—'

He lunged forward, but Harper was already pulling the trigger.

The round caught Alfie in the shoulder, spinning him backwards against the balcony rail. He clutched the wound, blood seeping between his fingers.

'You always were too soft, Harper,' Alfie gasped. 'Should have gone for the head.'

'You don't deserve a clean death,' Harper replied, keeping the Hellcat trained on him. 'You deserve to bleed out slowly, thinking about every innocent person you murdered.'

Alfie laughed bitterly.

'Innocent? Tomás took fifty thousand dollars to sign off and falsify environmental reports. Your precious whistle-blower was bought and paid for.'

A single gunshot echoed from somewhere in Palmer House's service areas. Harper's blood turned to ice – Cortez was down there somewhere. Keeping the gun trained on Alfie, he risked a glance over the balcony. Below them, Harper could see Colonel Crowe moving towards the stage where Mason Carrick lay motionless, something concealed in his hand.

'Time to choose, Harper,' Alfie said, pressing against his shoulder wound, looking down through the railings. 'Finish me or stop Crowe from putting a bullet in Mason's head.'

Harper calculated the distance to the stage. Too far to reach in time unless he moved now.

'Damn you, Alfie, this isn't finished,' he said as he grabbed a lighting cable and swung over the balcony rail.

Cortez had heard the gunshot near the service elevator that went to the parking levels and, worrying that Rosa had been shot – or worse still, had shot – ran to the elevator, seeing them closing. Hammering the butt of the Glock against the button, the service elevator doors opened again to reveal Rosa Alvarez holding a compact Glock against Veronica Slate's throat. Slate's evening gown was torn, her composure finally cracked as she faced a grieving sister with nothing left to lose.

Rosa, deciding the elevator wasn't going to work pushed Slate back out into the corridor, and Cortez kept her weapon lowered, noting how Rosa's hands trembled with rage and adrenaline.

'Where are the guards?' she asked Slate, keeping her voice calm.

'One was shot, a level up,' Slate said calmly. 'Leg wound, I think. This mad bitch—'

She winced as Rosa pressed the gun against her temple.

'The others ran,' she admitted, and Cortez could see disgust on her face; not at the situation, but that she'd hired weakness to defend her.

'Ms Alvarez,' Cortez said carefully, now turning her attention to Rosa. 'Let's discuss this.'

'Nothing to discuss,' Rosa replied without turning from Slate. 'This woman ordered my brother's murder. Time for justice.'

Slate remained perfectly still, but her eyes tracked towards Cortez with predatory calculation. Even with a gun pressed to her head, she was still looking for tactical opportunities.

'Rosa, if you kill her, you become exactly what she is,' Cortez said. 'Tomás wouldn't want that.'

'Tomás is dead because he tried to do the right thing,' Rosa's voice cracked.

'Bullshit!' Slate's smile was triumphant. 'Your brother wasn't some noble whistle-blower! He was a corrupt inspector who accepted fifty thousand dollars to falsify safety reports, then developed a guilty conscience when it was too late. He took my money, enabled the contamination to continue, then wanted to play hero when children started getting sick from his decisions. When I sent men to remind him of his obligations, he gained a false bravery when Harper appeared and then threw it away the moment we spoke to him again!'

'Spoke? You *tortured* him!' Rosa's grip on the Glock tightened. 'You forced him—'

'I offered him a choice. Money for silence, or poverty with a clear conscience. He chose money, Miss Alvarez. Just like most people do when faced with actual decisions instead of moral fantasies. How is young Miguel doing?'

'Young Miguel is doing without a father.' Rosa wasn't playing along, and her face was flashing with anger. Cortez could hear footsteps echoing from multiple directions – security teams coordinating through Palmer House's service areas, and in seconds Slate would be back in control, and both Rosa and Cortez would likely become statistics.

'Rosa, Harper has some evidence,' Cortez said carefully. 'His father's notebook, intelligence from tonight's operations. Doctor Santos has soil samples. Doctor Kowalski has reports on at least five deaths. We can still build a case.'

'Harper got my brother killed.'

'No, Your brother did that himself.'

'How do you know? You never met him!'

'No, but I met his type before,' Cortez continued. 'And

Doctor Santos spoke of him. He told us about his kids. They'll need you now. When the evidence is shown—'

'There is no goddamned evidence, bitch,' Slate interrupted with cold satisfaction. 'Harper's apartment burned, his supporting documents destroyed, and his journal was left in Mason Carrick's possession – who now sings with the angels. Or, more likely, with whoever sings in Hell. Any medical records from Doctor Santos you may have had? These soil samples? I'll get expensive lawyers to tear them apart, even if they're real. Besides, what exactly do you think a dead man's journal and some stolen phone intelligence from an employee with dubious loyalties will prove in federal court?'

Rosa's grip on the Glock loosened slightly.

'She's right. They destroyed almost everything.'

'Did your brother ever keep backup files?' Cortez asked desperately. 'Hidden records, additional evidence?'

'Nothing that would stand up legally,' Rosa said bitterly. 'Tomás trusted the system to protect him if he offered the truth.'

Slate's smile was razor-sharp.

'Poor naïve man. The system protects people like me, not people like him. Corporate lawyers, political connections, media manipulation – we've been playing this game for decades while environmental activists stumble around hoping someone in authority will care about poisoned children. A notebook full of rants and allegations from a dead man, and some data from obviously biased sources? My legal team will tear that apart in discovery proceedings.'

'You're admitting the contamination,' Cortez said quietly.

'Admitting what? That I successfully navigated regulatory frameworks to develop valuable real estate? That unfortunate accidents sometimes happen to people who interfere with legitimate commercial operations?' Slate straightened her torn evening gown, ignoring the gun to her skull. 'Prove any of it in court. Find evidence that will convince prosecutors to take on someone with unlimited legal resources and political connections.'

'You killed my brother,' Rosa said.

'Your brother breached his contractual obligations after accepting substantial compensation for environmental compliance services. When he threatened to damage ongoing development projects with his bullshit redemption claims, protective measures became necessary.' Slate's tone suggested discussing routine business procedures. 'Nothing personal, simply operational requirements.'

'You're confessing to murder.'

'I'm explaining market dynamics to people who don't understand how proper business operates!' Slate shouted angrily, before she checked her expensive watch. 'I was supposed to be the hero here! I was going to throw everything onto Mason! He knew the grounds were contaminated! He knew it was too expensive to clean the way the city wanted it! He's known ever since he took over from his dead partner, and *he* knew years ago! And guess what? Nobody gives a shit! A kid coughs a little more? Boo hoo! An elderly couple gets cancer? Everyone gets goddamned cancer these days! They can't prove it's because of the toxins we've mixed into their dirt while cleaning ours! Now, if you'll excuse me, I have extraction protocols to implement before this situation becomes more complicated.'

'You're right,' Cortez said suddenly. 'Harper's evidence won't be enough to convict you in court.'

She pulled out her mobile phone, the screen showing a red recording indicator.

'But this confession will be.'

For a moment, Slate's composure cracked completely.

'You recorded—'

'Every word.' Cortez held up the phone. 'Confessions of murder, environmental crimes, corporate conspiracy. All admissible in federal court, especially when corroborated by Rosa and my eyewitness testimony.'

'You're—'

'The goddamned sheriff of Prosperity, Nevada,' Cortez interrupted. 'And you're not the first megalomaniac scumbag with no care for people's health I've had to deal with.'

Slate's expression shifted from confidence to cold calculation.

'Delete that recording or both of you die in this corridor.'

'Too late,' Cortez smiled grimly. 'Already uploaded to cloud storage with automatic transmission to a federal prosecutor I know – and had a long conversation with when I was getting patched up in Evanston. Something I learned the last time I met Harper was to make sure there's a backup for when shit goes wrong. Kill us now, and you just confirm everything on the recording.'

That was when Veronica Slate made her move.

She twisted sideways with surprising speed for someone in an evening gown, grabbing Rosa's gun hand while driving her elbow into the younger woman's solar plexus. Rosa doubled over, gasping, as they struggled for control of the weapon.

The confined space outside the elevator, even with the doors now open, made fighting awkward, but Slate moved with vicious desperation. Cortez lunged forward, trying to separate them, but Slate caught her with a backhand that sent her stumbling against the elevator wall. The Glock wavered between all three women as they fought in the cramped space.

Rosa recovered first, driving her fist into Slate's kidney with enough force to make the older woman grunt in pain. But Slate twisted Rosa's gun hand, trying to force the weapon towards Cortez.

'You want justice?' Slate snarled. 'Here's your goddamned justice—'

The Glock discharged as all three women fought for control; the bullet punching through the elevator's metal ceiling. Cortez grabbed Slate's hair, yanking her head back while Rosa tried to regain control of her weapon. Slate responded by twisting, throwing Cortez to the floor and driving her heel into Cortez's injured shoulder, reopening the wound and sending fresh blood soaking through her shirt.

The pain made Cortez's grip loosen, and Slate broke partially free, diving for the emergency controls while Rosa tried to bring the Glock to bear again. Another gunshot echoed in the confined space as the weapon discharged during their struggle, this bullet embedding itself in the elevator's ceiling.

In the chaos, Slate triggered the elevator, the door closing and the carriage now heading down to Palmer House's parking level, where armoured vehicles waited in the shadows.

Rosa hammered at the button, but Cortez grabbed her arm.

'Let her go,' Cortez said. 'We're alive, and now we have her confession.'

'You could have shot her!' Rosa cried out. 'You held a gun!'

'I held my officer's weapon,' Cortez admitted. 'But I won't shoot someone unless in self-defence.'

'And that *wasn't* self-defence? She's getting away!' Rosa said bitterly.

'She's panicking. People who panic make mistakes.' Cortez helped Rosa up, noting the younger woman's bruised ribs and shaking hands. 'She has no weapon, and her friends have disappeared. And remember, Harper's still out there—'

Before Cortez could continue, the distant sound of sirens reached them – multiple vehicles, approaching fast. Emergency response vehicles, but also something else.

Federal vehicles. FBI tactical teams. The sort of coordinated law enforcement response that suggested someone had called in serious backup.

'You see? Maybe she won't escape after all,' Cortez said with growing hope.

HARPER DROPPED FROM THE LIGHTING RIGGING JUST AS Colonel Crowe reached Mason Carrick's motionless form on the ballroom stage. Emergency medical personnel worked frantically around them while Chicago police tried to maintain order amongst hundreds of panicking guests.

Harper landed behind Crowe, noting the compact Sig Sauer the colonel held ready.

'Planning to finish the job, Oliver?'

Crowe spun at the use of his first name, weapon tracking towards Harper's centre of mass with military precision. Out of the corner of his eye, Harper noticed the approaching paramedics pause where they stood.

'Should have known you'd turn up,' Crowe said. 'Always did have a talent for complicating simple operations.'

'Simple?' Harper kept his hands visible while calculating distances. 'You orchestrated Syria, betrayed your own soldiers, then murdered my father when he threatened to expose you – sticking me there to either do it, or at least see it. That's not simple, that's systematic treachery.'

'Your father was collateral damage in a larger strategic operation,' Crowe replied calmly. 'Dominic got sentimental about a few dead SAS operatives, forgetting that intelligence work requires sacrifices.'

Mason Carrick's eyes fluttered open, surprising both Harper and Crowe.

'Oliver,' he said, surprisingly strong for a man with blood still staining his shirt. 'You wouldn't know sacrifice if it knocked on your door and came to dinner.'

Harper stared. Mason was alive. The shot that had looked fatal from thirty feet up had somehow missed vital organs, or Mason was tougher than anyone had expected.

Or he was wearing a vest and had prepared for this.

'You should be dead,' Crowe said, raising the Sig towards Mason's head.

'Disappointed?' Mason sat up. 'Sorry to complicate your evening, Oliver. But you were never as... forward thinking as I am.'

'Enough talking.' Crowe's finger tightened on the trigger.

'Oliver. Colonel Crowe,' Harper said quietly, 'you've got federal agents surrounding this building, witnesses recording everything, media coverage of tonight's events. Kill us here and you'll spend the rest of your life in prison.'

'Better than facing charges for treason and murder.'

The ballroom had emptied except for emergency personnel and casualties. Harper could see tactical teams moving through the space, identifying threats while paramedics worked on injured guests who'd likely gone over in the panic, or who had suffered heart attacks or worse during the shock.

'Syria was five years ago,' Harper continued, noting how Crowe's position exposed him to crossfire from multiple directions. 'My father's dead, the arms dealing's over, Slate's operation is blown. You could walk away from this, disappear, live quietly somewhere. Why make it worse?'

'Because walking away means admitting I destroyed good soldiers for profit,' Crowe said. 'Because living with that guilt is worse than dying here.'

Harper moved closer, his Hellcat trained on Crowe but not firing.

'Oliver, don't do this. Mason's not worth throwing your life away.'

Crowe kept the Sig pointed at Mason's head, but his eyes shifted to Harper with something like bitter amusement.

'Always the idealist, weren't you Harper? Always believing people could be better than they were.' Crowe's voice carried years of suppressed resentment. 'Do you know how exhausting it was, pretending to respect you? Pretending to care about your career, your development, your bloody moral compass?'

Harper felt the words hit like physical blows.

'Oliver—'

'*Colonel* Crowe to you, Harper. Just because I'm about to die doesn't mean we're suddenly mates.' Crowe's grip on the Sig remained steady. 'For years I had to watch you swagger around, thinking you were something special. The golden boy of the SRR, Dominic Kane's precious son, too pure to understand how the real world works.'

'I looked up to you,' Harper whispered.

'I know. That's what made it so bloody irritating.' Crowe glanced towards the ballroom entrances, where federal agents were moving into position. 'You want to know the truth? I volunteered you for the most dangerous missions, hoping someone would put a bullet in you. Save me the trouble of pretending to give a damn about your survival. And all you did was get better at not dying.'

Mason tried to move away, but Crowe pressed the barrel harder against his temple.

'Stay put. You and I have unfinished business.'

'The federal agents are here, Oliver,' Harper said, noting how the tactical teams were surrounding their position. 'It's over. Surrender, and maybe you can cut a deal.'

Crowe laughed bitterly.

'A deal? For treason, arms dealing, murder? I don't think so.' He looked directly at Harper. 'Besides, I'd rather die than spend the rest of my life in prison, knowing you were out here thinking you'd won.'

The sound of boots on the stage made Crowe's decision for him.

'Federal agents,' a voice called. 'Drop your weapon and step away from the hostage.'

Crowe smiled at Harper with genuine malice.

'I'll give your regards to your father when I see him in hell.'

He turned the Sig towards his own head and pulled the trigger before Harper could stop him.

Harper straightened slowly, looking down at the

twitching body of Colonel Oliver Crowe – the man who'd commanded his respect for years, who'd sent him on operations across three continents, who'd ultimately betrayed everything he'd believed in.

Around them, Palmer House was transforming from a crime scene to a federal investigation, with evidence teams documenting everything while paramedics worked on casualties. He rose, passing his guns to investigators as Mason Carrick submitted to questioning with corporate dignity, already requesting legal representation while providing detailed statements about Crowe's activities and Slate's operations, giving Harper a wink as he did so.

He was already positioning himself here as the whistleblower, the hero.

Harper looked around for Alfie Reeves, but the balcony was empty. His former comrade had vanished into Chicago's night, probably already planning his next operation against whoever remained on his list, hunting an off-books doctor for his gunshot wound.

Some ghosts, Harper reflected, *were harder to bury than others.*

Harper let out a long-held breath, thinking about Tomás Alvarez and forty-three sick children, and corporate executives who poisoned communities for profit. Justice was better than nothing, even if it came too late for some people.

'Sheriff Cortez?' he asked one of the FBI agents.

'Outside,' the agent, a young woman replied. 'She's given her statement, how you helped her take down Slate.'

'I did?'

'Yes, how she'd found links to Slate after closing a case in Prosperity, and asked you to assist?'

Harper smiled. Cortez wasn't taking credit – she was creating a new narrative to explain why Harper was around.

'I did,' he nodded.

OUTSIDE PALMER HOUSE, CHICAGO'S NIGHT AIR FELT CLEAN after hours in the hotel's contained chaos. Harper felt exhausted but alive, knowing the hunt was finally over.

Cortez appeared beside him, Rosa Alvarez close behind, both women looking battered but determined.

'Slate?' Harper asked.

'Escaped during the chaos, but we've got her confession recorded,' Cortez replied. 'Federal manhunt's already started. She won't get far. Meridian doesn't seem to be working for her any more, and Aegis sure as hell won't assist. She'll be on limited funds and favours.'

Rosa looked at Harper with something that might have been forgiveness.

'My brother would have wanted this,' she breathed. 'Justice, not revenge.'

Harper felt the weight of Tomás's death lift slightly. Not gone, never gone, but balanced now by the knowledge that his sacrifice had exposed the truth.

'Make him proud,' he said. 'Even though it's out, it's not over. There's a long road ahead, and a lot of people connected to the city will have to explain why blind eyes were turned. You think you can do that?'

'I know I can,' Rosa nodded. 'And Michael will help me.'

Harper nodded. With Doctor Santos by her side, there was a chance not only for justice, but also for healing for Rosa.

The hunt was over.

The reckoning had begun.

23

CLEAN UP

THE FEDERAL MANHUNT LASTED EXACTLY FOUR HOURS.

Harper heard about it while giving his statement, as well as his father's video message – the one taken from deposit box 47 – to one of the FBI agents who'd arrived before the end, although he'd already started thinking of her as "Clipboard" based on her obsessive note-taking. Through the Palmer House windows, Chicago's dawn skyline was painted in greys and pale yellows, emergency vehicles still clustered around the hotel.

'Veronica Slate,' Clipboard said, reading from her phone. 'Apprehended at O'Hare attempting to board a private jet to Switzerland.'

Harper wasn't surprised. Slate struck him as someone who'd always have an exit strategy. What surprised him was that she'd been caught at all – suggested panic rather than planning.

'She talking?'

'Lawyered up immediately. But with Sheriff Cortez's recorded confession evidence from Palmer House, Doctor

Kowalski's autopsy findings, Doctor Santos's notes, files and soil samples and the environmental documentation, we've got enough.'

A second agent – "Paperwork" in Harper's mental filing system – entered carrying a thick file. 'Carrick's legal team wants to discuss cooperation agreements,' he smiled. 'Full disclosure about Slate's operations, environmental crimes, political connections. Says he's willing to testify against anyone involved.'

Harper almost laughed. *Mason playing the reformed whistleblower, positioning himself as victim rather than enabler. Brilliant corporate damage control.*

'He wants immunity?' Clipboard asked.

'Partial. Claims everything else was Slate's operation using Aegis resources without his knowledge.'

Professional bullshit, but probably effective. Mason had decades of experience turning liability into opportunity.

'What's your assessment?' Clipboard asked Harper.

'Mine?'

'You grew up around him, right? Your father created Aegis with him?'

'Sure, but it wasn't that close a relationship.'

'You faced him in Prosperity then,' Paperwork said from the table. 'Give us what you think based on that.'

Harper touched his river stone.

'He'll tell you enough truth to avoid prison. But not enough to actually clean up the system.'

'You're satisfied with that outcome?'

Harper smiled – the sort that never reached his eyes.

'Justice is better than nothing. Even incomplete justice.'

It was a useful lie. The truth was Harper had no intention of accepting Mason's performance. His father's notebook contained pages of scribbled notes and names that when used correctly would expose systematic corruption far beyond Chicago. But using it required careful planning, not government bureaucracies with election cycles and budget constraints.

'We'll need you available for testimony,' Clipboard said. 'You staying at any of your "residences", Mister Harper?'

'I'm selling my residences,' Harper replied coldly.

'The one in Chicago?'

'I'm giving that one away,' Harper smiled. 'To a friend of the family.'

'So, where can we—'

'I'll be reachable through Sheriff Cortez.' Another lie. Harper would be gone within hours.

Clipboard sighed, placing down her pen.

'You're free to go. But stay in touch.'

Harper tipped an imaginary hat.

'Always,' he smiled.

HARPER FOUND A QUIET CORRIDOR AWAY FROM THE FEDERAL circus and pulled out his phone.

Time to protect his former regiment from the scandal Crowe's death could unleash.

The number he dialled belonged to Lieutenant Colonel Sarah Haynes, SRR personnel liaison, and one of the few people who'd understood Harper's reasons for leaving the service.

'Haynes.'

'Sarah, it's Harper.'

A pause.

'Christ, Liam. Heard you were in Chicago when things went sideways. You all right?'

'Fine. But we need to talk about Crowe.'

Another pause, longer this time.

'Secure line?'

'Secure enough. Federal investigators are going to ask questions about his military service, his connections to private security, his role in tonight's events.'

'Standard procedure for deceased suspects.'

'Except if they dig too deep, they'll find classified operations that have nothing to do with environmental crimes. Syria, weapons trafficking, staged deaths.' Harper checked once more to make sure he wasn't being observed. 'Things that could compromise ongoing missions and destroy careers of soldiers who served honourably under compromised leadership.'

Haynes was quiet for several moments. As personnel liaison, she understood the implications of having SRR operations exposed through civilian criminal investigations.

'What do you need?'

'Simple narrative. Crowe was manipulated by corporate interests, became complicit in environmental crimes, couldn't live with the guilt. Personal failing, not systemic military corruption.'

'The Syria operation?'

'Stays buried. Alfie Reeves officially remains dead—'

'Wait, Reeves isn't dead?'

Harper sighed, and for the next minute or two explained, as quickly as he could, what had happened in Chicago.

At the end, Haynes whistled down the phone.

'Shit, Liam. When you find trouble, you go in at a whole new level.'

'Wasn't intentional. Either way, I'd suggest his resurrection and corporate assassination work gets explained as PTSD breakdown of some other soldier and identity theft. No weapons trafficking charges, no staged death revelations, just someone stealing a name.'

'That's a lot of truth to bury, Liam.'

'Less truth than you think. Crowe's actual crimes were civilian – environmental poisoning, corporate murder, systematic corruption. Military secrets that don't relate to Chicago can stay classified where they belong.'

Haynes understood the calculation. Protecting legitimate operations while ensuring justice for crimes that actually affected civilian populations. Sometimes institutional survival required accepting incomplete disclosure.

'I'll coordinate with appropriate agencies. Limit exposure while maintaining investigation integrity.'

'Alfie's still out there. Escaped during the chaos.'

'We'll handle that through proper channels.'

'No, you won't. He's been dead to the world for five years, knows how to stay invisible. If he surfaces, treat him as armed and extremely dangerous. Don't try to take him alive.'

'Understood. And Liam? Don't go after Reeves, if he's out there. Leave that to us.'

'Of course,' Harper lied as he ended the call, knowing Haynes would coordinate with federal investigators to ensure military secrets stayed buried while civilian crimes were prosecuted. It wasn't perfect protection, but it would prevent wholesale destruction of his former regiment.

Alfie Reeves, however, was *his*.

OUTSIDE PALMER HOUSE, CHICAGO WAS CHAOS. THE FEDERAL investigation had transformed the hotel into a crime scene processing facility, with evidence teams documenting everything while paramedics treated casualties and media crews set up positions behind police barriers. It was the sort of organised chaos that followed corporate conspiracies when they finally collapsed under the weight of their own ambition.

Harper was walking away from it all when a familiar voice called his name.

'Little Liam Harper.'

Harper turned to see Mason Carrick emerging from a black Cadillac Escalade that had been waiting across the street, flanked by two men in expensive suits who moved like ex-military contractors.

Even cooperating with federal authorities, Mason maintained Aegis, it seemed.

'Uncle Mason,' Harper replied, noting the security positioning. 'Surprised to see you out of federal custody.'

'My lawyers are very good. And besides, I'm a victim, shot before I could give out the details of my sting operation.' Mason approached with his familiar calculating smile. 'I was hoping we could finish our conversation before you disappear again.'

'I thought we'd said everything that needed saying.'

'Did we?' Mason took a breath that looked genuinely painful. 'Your father was right about everything. The environmental crimes, the corporate murder, the systematic corruption. I let others manipulate our operations, convinced myself that accommodating them was necessary for survival.'

Harper studied Mason's expression, looking for tells. The

trouble with experienced operators was they'd learned to project whatever emotion served their objectives.

'What are you proposing?'

Mason moved closer, projecting paternal concern.

'There's still a place for you in what comes next, Liam. Clean operations, legitimate contracts, the sort of work your father believed in.'

Harper studied Mason's expression while noting escape routes. Even on bail, Mason was trying to secure Harper's cooperation through emotional manipulation and strategic offers.

'Still trying to recruit me?'

'Still trying to honour your father's memory. He wanted Aegis to be something better than what it became over time.'

'My father wanted a lot of things. Most of which you made impossible.'

Mason's expression shifted slightly, acknowledging the accusation while maintaining his concerned facade.

'Your father's death was a tragedy that—'

'Was a murder facilitated through operational negligence and corporate greed.' Harper's voice was ice cold. 'Don't insult my intelligence by pretending otherwise.'

Mason sighed, looking across the street.

'Then what do you want, Liam? Revenge? Justice? Or just the satisfaction of destroying everything your father built?'

Harper reached into his jeans pocket and touched his river stone, feeling its familiar weight while considering his response. Mason was offering him legitimate channels for pursuing his father's mission, official authority to expose corporate corruption, resources that could achieve justice through proper legal procedures.

Everything Harper had claimed to want, delivered through someone he absolutely couldn't trust.

'Full transparency? Complete access to operational files?'

'Everything. No corporate secrets, no hidden agendas. Just honest work protecting people while exposing criminals.'

'That's very generous, Uncle Mason,' Harper said finally, his voice carrying childhood warmth with an edge Mason probably missed. 'Full partnership, operational authority, complete transparency in honour of my father's memory.'

'Exactly.' Mason extended his hand with apparent relief. 'Your father would be proud.'

Harper shook Mason's hand.

'You know what, Mason? You're absolutely right. My father would be proud.' Harper's grip tightened slightly. 'He'd be proud that I can spot manipulative corporate bullshit from a thousand yards away. He'd be proud that I learned not to trust people who killed him for profit while pretending it was an accident.'

Mason's expression shifted as he tried to withdraw his hand, but Harper maintained his grip.

'Most of all, he'd be proud that when someone offers me exactly what I want in exchange for forgetting what they've done, I have the good sense to tell them to *go fuck themselves* with a smile.'

Harper released Mason's hand while maintaining his pleasant expression.

'Which is what I'm doing right now. With a smile.'

Mason's corporate mask slipped entirely.

'You're making a serious mistake.'

'Maybe. But it's my mistake to make.' Harper moved away now. 'Unlike my father, I don't trust people who smile while planning betrayals.'

Mason studied Harper's expression, recognising the stubborn determination that had characterised their relationship since Harper was twelve.

'The offer won't remain available indefinitely.'

'Good. Saves me the trouble of refusing it again.'

'This isn't over, Liam.'

'No,' Harper agreed without turning back. 'It's just beginning.'

As he walked away, he knew his hunt would continue exactly as Dominic Kane had intended – in the shadows, through unofficial channels, targeting people who thought federal cooperation could buy immunity from consequences.

But he also knew it'd be out in the open now. Mason Carrick had copies of the notebook pages – he'd know where Harper was going, and he'd prepare.

Good. Fighting's never fun when it's improvised.

HARPER FOUND CORTEZ AND ROSA ALVAREZ NEAR THE FEDERAL vehicles. Cortez's wounded shoulder was re-bandaged now, her posture suggesting the painkillers were working while she helped Rosa navigate victim support services and legal procedures that would ensure her brother's sacrifice led to meaningful prosecutions.

'How's the shoulder?' Harper asked, noting how Cortez favoured her left arm despite professional attempts to conceal the injury.

'Properly bandaged again, painkillers kicking in, full range of motion should return within a week.' Cortez studied Harper's expression with a perceptiveness that came from years of reading people who lied professionally. 'Saw you talking to Mason Carrick. Didn't go well, I'm guessing.'

'He offered me partnership in a reformed Aegis. Full transparency, operational authority, chance to honour my father's memory by cleaning up corporate corruption.'

'Generous offer. And you said?'

'I... refused. With a smile.'

Cortez laughed – the first genuinely amused sound Harper had heard from her since the Palmer House chaos began, rich and warm despite the circumstances that had brought them together. The sort of laughter that reminded Harper why he'd been attracted to her intelligence and strength rather than just her competence with firearms and tactical situations.

'I bet you said more than just "no",' she replied. 'How'd he take that?'

'About as well as you'd expect. Threatened me, warned me the offer wouldn't remain available indefinitely, suggested I was making a serious mistake by refusing his generous cooperation. The usual corporate intimidation disguised as a reasonable business discussion.'

'What happens to people like him?' Rosa asked, looking up from her paperwork with victim services. 'The ones who enable murder but never pull triggers themselves? The ones who profit from poisoning children while maintaining plausible deniability about operational details?'

Harper considered his response carefully while watching Chicago's financial district wake up to another day of normal business conducted by people who'd never face the consequences of their decisions. Corporate executives who viewed human suffering as acceptable costs for quarterly profit margins, politicians who sold regulatory protection to the highest bidders, lawyers who specialised in turning criminal conspiracies into civil settlements that preserved their clients' reputations.

'They adapt,' Harper said finally. 'Find new partners, different methods, better legal protection. They hire crisis communication specialists, donate to charitable foundations, sponsor veteran support programmes that provide excellent media coverage while their other operations continue poisoning communities.'

'But they also make mistakes,' Cortez added, understanding Harper's implication without requiring explicit explanation. 'Leave evidence, trust the wrong people, underestimate opponents who don't play by corporate rules.'

'And when they do?'

'Someone will be watching,' Harper promised, his voice carrying the sort of patient calmness that had sustained him through countless ops. 'Someone who remembers what they've done, who understands how their systems work, who's willing to operate outside official channels when conventional justice proves inadequate.'

It was both promise and threat – the sort of long-term vigilance that government agencies couldn't sustain through election cycles and budget constraints. Some battles required extended campaigns rather than single decisive victories, the patient accumulation of evidence combined with strategic timing to achieve justice that conventional prosecutions couldn't deliver.

'Rosa,' Harper continued, 'you've got federal protection, victim services, and medical support for Tomás's children. There's now emergency treatment for families affected by environmental contamination, ongoing monitoring to prevent future poisoning, comprehensive legal representation that doesn't depend on your ability to pay corporate-level legal fees. This is incredible work.'

Rosa nodded, understanding that the institutional support would provide a foundation for rebuilding her life while ensuring her brother's sacrifice led to meaningful change rather than just temporary prosecutions.

'But if you ever need anything else – anything official channels can't provide, any problems that require unofficial solutions – Sheriff Cortez knows how to find me.'

The subtext was clear enough. Harper was offering assistance for situations that couldn't be resolved through legal procedures or government agencies, the sort of problems that required someone willing to operate in shadows where corporate criminals thought they were safe from conventional justice. And, for Cortez, it was a subtle mention that he'd likely keep the AirTag she'd hidden on him, just in case.

'Thank you,' Rosa said simply, but her expression suggested she understood exactly what Harper was offering and why it might become necessary. 'For everything. For helping expose the truth, for making sure Tomás didn't die for nothing, for ensuring other families won't suffer what we've suffered.'

Harper felt the weight of Tomás's death shift again – not gone, *never* gone, but balanced now by the knowledge that his sacrifice had exposed systematic crimes that federal authorities couldn't ignore or bury through corporate legal manoeuvring. Environmental poisoning that would be cleaned up, medical treatment that would save children's lives, prosecutions that would deter other companies from similar crimes.

He remembered his line to the clipboard-wielding FBI agent minutes earlier.

Justice, even if incomplete.

'Lisa,' Harper said to Cortez, glancing towards Palmer House's service entrance where they could speak privately without federal agents documenting every word for potential use in future prosecutions. 'Walk with me?'

They moved away from the organised chaos of evidence processing and witness interviews, finding relative quiet amongst Palmer House's utilitarian infrastructure.

'You're leaving,' Cortez said. Not a question – statement of fact based on understanding Harper's patterns and the impossibility of his staying anywhere long enough for conventional relationships to develop.

'Within the hour. Need to be gone before Mason's people regroup and start tracking my movements again.'

'Where to?'

Harper considered his answer carefully; his father's notebook contained dozens of cryptic entries about Aegis operations.

'Wherever the trail leads. My father documented a lot of secrets before he died.'

'Dangerous secrets. The kind that gets people killed if they're not careful about how they pursue them.'

'The kind that require someone willing to operate outside official channels, someone who understands how corporate security companies actually work rather than how they're supposed to work.'

Cortez was quiet for several moments, weighing professional obligations against personal concerns that went beyond sheriff's department responsibilities. As a law enforcement officer, she understood the limitations of official channels when pursuing well-connected criminals who could afford teams of lawyers and crisis management specialists. As someone who'd worked with Harper in two separate investigations, she understood his methods achieved results that conventional procedures couldn't match.

'You could stay,' she said finally, her voice carrying genuine concern beneath professional assessment. 'Coordinate with federal authorities, work within official channels, build legitimate cases through proper procedures that would stand up in court.'

'Could. Won't.'

'Why not?'

Harper studied Cortez's expression, recognising genuine concern beneath her professional demeanour. She was offering him something he'd never had – partnership with legitimate law enforcement, someone who understood his methods while maintaining her integrity.

'Because official channels compromise when they should fight, negotiate when they should pursue, accept partial justice when complete justice is possible.'

'And you don't compromise.'

'Not any more.' It was both explanation and warning. Harper had learned that some enemies couldn't be defeated through conventional means. 'Lisa, what happened between us in Prosperity, what happened tonight – that was real. The attraction, the partnership, the way we work together.'

'But?'

'But I can't offer you what you deserve. Stability, honesty about where I'm going or when I'll be back, the sort of relationship that doesn't involve federal investigations and murder conspiracies.'

Cortez smiled.

'Did I ask for any of that?'

'No. But you should.'

'Maybe I like complicated. Maybe I like working with someone who gets results when conventional methods fail.' She stepped closer. 'Maybe I like you, Harper. Despite your complete inability to stay in one place for more than a week.'

Harper felt something shift in his chest – not the familiar weight of guilt and obligation, but something lighter. *Possibility*. Hope for connections that didn't require deception.

'What are you suggesting?'

'That when you're ready to stop running from whatever's chasing you, you know where to find me. And if you need backup for whatever impossible situation you stumble into next, you've got my number.'

It wasn't a promise of relationship or commitment – it was something better. Understanding without demands, support without conditions, a partnership that could survive Harper's lifestyle and dangerous work.

'Thank you.'

'For what?'

'For not trying to fix me. For understanding why I can't stay. For making it clear you'll be there when I need you.'

Cortez reached up and kissed him – brief, warm, carrying promise without pressure. When she stepped back, her expression was professionally neutral again, but her eyes held warmth that would sustain Harper through whatever came next.

'Be careful out there. The world's got enough ghosts without adding you to the collection.'

'I'll do my best,' Harper smiled.

'No, you won't. You'll do whatever's necessary, consequences be damned.' Cortez's smile was sardonic. 'Just try to survive it.'

THE BONNEVILLE WAS PARKED WHERE HE'D LEFT IT, HELMET locked to the seat, ready for whatever destination his father's notebook suggested next. Harper checked his phone – no messages from unknown numbers, no cryptic warnings from corporate operatives.

For the moment, he was ahead of his pursuers. That wouldn't last long, but it was enough.

Harper started the engine, feeling the familiar vibration that meant freedom, movement, escape from whatever complications he'd left behind. Chicago's skyline receded in his mirrors as he rode towards whatever impossible situation waited ahead.

But first, he had one more person to visit.

FRANK WAS WATERING PLANTS IN THE LOBBY WHEN HARPER walked through the revolving door, carrying a manila envelope that contained legal documents he'd never expected to sign. The doorman looked up from his gardening with the sort of surprised smile that suggested he'd been hoping Harper would return but hadn't quite believed it would happen.

'Mister Harper,' Frank said, setting down his watering can while straightening his uniform jacket. 'Didn't expect to see you again so soon. Thought you'd be long gone after all that business at Palmer House last night.'

'Had some paperwork to finish,' Harper replied, noting how Frank's expression suggested genuine pleasure at seeing him rather than the careful politeness most service workers maintained with wealthy tenants.

'Everything sorted out with the federal investigation?' Frank asked.

'More or less. Slate's in custody, environmental crimes are being prosecuted, children are getting medical treatment soon.'

'Your father would be proud,' Frank said simply.

Harper studied the older man's expression. Frank had known Dominic Kane as a person rather than just a tenant, had probably seen sides of his father that Harper had never understood.

'Frank,' Harper said, 'I've got something for you.'

He handed over the manila envelope, noting Frank's confusion as he examined legal documents that were clearly more complex than casual correspondence.

'What's this?'

'Deed transfer for the apartment. It's yours now. Once the insurance sorts out the repairs, that is.'

Frank stared at the paperwork for several long moments, apparently processing information that didn't quite make sense within his understanding of how wealthy people typically behaved towards service employees.

'I don't understand.'

'You've been taking care of my father's place for months, keeping it secure while I figured out what to do with his estate. You've been kind to me when you didn't have to be, helpful when it would have been easier to just do your job and nothing more.' Harper gestured around the lobby. 'The apartment's worth more than I'll ever need, and you've earned it.'

'Mister Harper, I can't accept—'

'You can, and you will. Property taxes are paid through a trust account, maintenance fees are covered, utilities are handled automatically. You don't owe me anything, you don't owe the estate anything. It's yours to do with as you want. Although I'd suggest selling it and retiring somewhere warm.'

Frank looked down at the legal documents again, probably trying to understand the implications of suddenly owning property worth millions in one of Chicago's most expensive neighbourhoods.

'Why?' he asked finally.

Harper considered his answer while thinking about his father's legacy, about the inheritance he'd never wanted and the responsibility that came with wealth he'd done nothing to earn. Most of Dominic Kane's estate would go to charitable causes, but some of it should go to people who'd actually earned his father's respect through years of loyal service.

'Because kindness should be rewarded. Because you've been more help to me than most of the people who were supposed to be my father's friends. Because I'll never use that apartment, even when it's fixed back up, and you've been taking care of it like it was your own, anyway.'

Frank was quiet for several moments, weighing the gift against whatever personal principles governed his relationship with wealthy tenants and their complicated family dynamics.

'Thank you,' he said finally. 'I don't know what to say.'

'Don't say anything.' Harper moved towards the exit, already thinking about the road ahead and whatever destination his father's notebook suggested next. 'And Frank? If anyone comes around asking questions about me, about where I went or when I might be back—'

'I never saw you today,' Frank finished, understanding that Harper's generosity came with the understanding that discretion was still necessary for everyone's safety.

Harper grinned widely.

'Exactly.'

Outside, Chicago's last-morning air carried the scent of approaching rain while traffic moved through streets that would soon forget Harper had ever been there. The city would continue its normal business while federal investigators processed evidence, prosecutors built cases, and victims received medical treatment that might save their lives.

Good people doing important work through official channels.

24

GHOSTS

TWO WEEKS AFTER PALMER HOUSE, HARPER FOUND ALFIE Reeves in an abandoned grain elevator outside Topeka, Kansas.

The trail had been methodical rather than lucky; off-books medical clinics, mercenary contacts from Alfie's corporate work – reverse engineered now Harper had an idea of where he'd been for five years – the sort of shadow network that existed beneath America's official economy. Harper had followed it across three states, tracking a ghost who'd become increasingly desperate as his options narrowed.

The grain elevator stood against the Kansas sky like a concrete monument to agricultural collapse, its silos empty for decades while prairie wind whistled through broken windows and rusted machinery. The sort of place where someone could disappear completely, either by choice or necessity.

Harper parked the Bonneville beside what had once been a loading dock, noting fresh tyre tracks in dust that suggested a recent arrival. No other vehicles visible, but that meant nothing. Alfie had learned to hide transportation the same way he'd learned to hide himself – professionally, thoroughly, with backup plans for every contingency.

The main building's entrance hung open, revealing darkness that could conceal anything from empty space to some kind of carefully prepared ambush. Harper approached carefully, his Hellcat ready but not drawn, listening for sounds that would indicate occupation or threat.

Inside, the elevator's industrial architecture created cathedral-like spaces where afternoon light filtered through windows while machinery stood like altar pieces to abandoned productivity. Concrete floors were littered with debris from years of weather damage and urban exploration, but Harper could see signs of recent habitation – cleared sleeping area, medical supplies, empty food containers.

'I was wondering when you'd show up,' Alfie's voice echoed from somewhere above, carrying down through the building's skeletal framework.

Harper looked up, seeing movement on what had been an observation platform overlooking the grain storage areas. Alfie was visible now, sitting with his back against a concrete wall, one arm cradled against his chest in a way that suggested ongoing problems with his gunshot wound.

'Alfie,' Harper called. 'You look like hell.'

'Feel worse than I look. Thanks for that.' Alfie's voice carried bitter amusement. 'Gunshot wounds don't heal properly when you can't risk proper medical attention.'

Harper could see the problem from ground level. Alfie's improvised medical treatment had probably prevented immediate death, but infection was visible even from distance – fever flush, laboured breathing, the sort of systematic breakdown that occurred when antibiotics weren't available in time and wound care was limited to whatever supplies could be stolen or purchased without documentation.

'Should have gone to hospital,' Harper said, beginning to climb the metal ladder that led to Alfie's position.

'Right. Walk into the emergency room with a gunshot wound, provide identification, wait for federal agents to arrive, or someone like you or Carrick to turn up and smother me with my pillow.' Alfie's laugh was harsh. 'Brilliant tactical thinking.'

Harper reached the platform level, getting his first close look at Alfie's condition. The infection was worse than he'd expected – Alfie had maybe a week or two left, possibly less if fever continued climbing.

'You could still surrender,' Harper said carefully. 'Federal authorities want testimony about Slate's operations, evidence about corporate murder conspiracies. You cooperate; they'll ensure medical treatment.'

'Cooperation.' Alfie's voice was dismissive. 'Like Crowe cooperated with Slate, like Mason cooperated with federal investigators. Everyone cooperating while the system protects itself.'

'It's better than dying alone in an abandoned building.'

'Is it?' Alfie studied Harper's expression. 'You think testifying against Slate will change anything? You think exposing corporate murder will prevent future corporate murders?'

Harper considered his response while noting details about Alfie's position, his available weapons, his physical condition. The fever was making him unpredictable, but military training was still clear in how he'd chosen a defensive position with multiple escape routes and clear fields of fire.

'Justice is better than nothing,' Harper said finally.

'Christ, you sound like a federal agent. All procedures and processes while criminals buy their way out of consequences.' Alfie shifted position, wincing as movement aggravated his infection.

'What about the recording?' Harper asked.

Alfie's expression shifted slightly.

'What recording?'

'The confession you've made while here. Probably a testimony about Slate's operations, evidence about corporate murders, details about systematic corruption.' Harper kept his voice neutral. 'The one you're planning to give me before you die.'

For several moments, Alfie was quiet, apparently weighing whether Harper was guessing or genuinely knew about documentation that hadn't been mentioned during their previous conversations.

'How did you—'

'Because I know you, Alfie. Because you've spent five years preparing for exactly this situation.' Harper gestured towards medical supplies and personal effects scattered around Alfie's position. 'Because you're too thorough to die without leaving testimony that could still damage the people who destroyed your life, a last middle finger after a botched op.'

Chuckling at this, Alfie reached into his jacket, producing a small digital recorder. He tossed it towards Harper, who caught it while noting how the motion caused Alfie visible pain.

'Three hours of testimony,' Alfie said. 'Names, dates, financial records, operational details. Everything I learned working for Meridian, everything Slate revealed during private conversations, everything Mason discussed when he thought I was just another expendable contractor.'

Harper examined the recorder, understanding its implications.

'This could destroy them,' Harper said.

'Could. Won't.' Alfie's voice carried the sort of cynical certainty that came from understanding how corporate legal systems actually functioned. 'They'll claim it's fabrication, demand chain of custody documentation, challenge admissibility based on recording methods. Their lawyers will turn it into years of appeals while they restructure operations and eliminate witnesses.'

'Why record it then?'

'Because someone should know the truth, even if justice is impossible.' Alfie's expression was resigned. 'Because maybe someday, someone with your resources and your willingness to operate outside official channels will use it properly. Maybe even you, having a listen, deciding to get revenge for your old buddy Alfie.'

'What do you want in return?'

'Nothing. Everything.' Alfie's voice carried exhaustion that went beyond physical illness. 'I want you to understand what you've done, what you've cost me, what your interference has destroyed.'

'My interference?'

'You ruined everything at Palmer House. Crowe was supposed to die, Mason was supposed to die, Slate was supposed to lose everything while I disappeared back into whatever existence ghosts maintain.' Alfie's voice was building intensity despite obvious physical weakness. 'Instead, Crowe killed himself and gets some kind of martyr status with the Government claiming he was some kind of hero, Mason negotiated immunity, Slate will probably serve reduced sentences, and I'm dying slowly from infection because you couldn't let me finish what needed finishing.'

'You were being set up,' Harper said. 'Slate's people were planning to eliminate you after the assassinations, blame everything on a lone gunman with military training and documented grievances. You would have died thinking you'd achieved revenge, but really you'd just been used as an expendable weapon.'

'Better than spending my last days hiding in abandoned buildings while the people who destroyed my life continue their operations.' Alfie's hand moved towards something Harper couldn't see clearly. 'Better than watching you walk away again while pretending you're helping.'

Harper recognised the shift in Alfie's posture, the subtle movement that suggested preparation for violence despite his weakened condition. Military training was still evident even through fever and pain.

'Alfie, this doesn't have to end badly. You can still—'

'What? Surrender to federal authorities who'll use my testimony to build cases that will be dismissed on technicalities? Accept medical treatment for cooperation that will be ignored when convenient?' Alfie's laugh was bitter. 'Or maybe just watch you ride away on your motorcycle while patting yourself on your back and telling yourself you tried to save me, ignoring the comrades who were killed in Syria because of me?'

Harper took a step backwards, maintaining distance while keeping his hands visible. Alfie was deteriorating rapidly, and fever was making him increasingly irrational about perceived slights and past betrayals.

'I'm not abandoning you.'

'Aren't you? Same way you abandoned me in Syria when I needed backup? Same way the unit abandoned me when Crowe decided my death was operationally convenient?' Alfie's voice was building towards something dangerous. 'Same way you abandoned me at Palmer House when you decided Crowe and Mason were more important than completing the mission?'

Harper felt cold understanding settle in his stomach. Alfie's version of events was completely divorced from reality – fever and psychological damage had transformed legitimate operational procedures into personal betrayals, turned professional decisions into abandonment fantasies.

'That's not what happened.'

'Isn't it?' Alfie was standing now, his movement revealing whatever he'd been reaching for – A Fairbairn-Sykes fighting knife, the sort of weapon that had been part of their favourite equipment during joint operations. Harper could see there was no reasoning with Alfie's deteriorated psychological state. The infection was affecting his judgement, the isolation had fed his paranoia, and years of believing he'd been betrayed had created delusions that couldn't be corrected through logical conversation.

'I'm sorry this happened to you,' Harper said simply. 'I'm sorry about Syria, about Crowe's decisions, about the way everything fell apart. But I can't fix the past, and I can't give you the revenge you think you deserve.'

'No. But you can stay here with me while we die. You can

face consequences for once instead of running away when situations become complicated.'

Harper recognised the threat beneath Alfie's words, the implication that he wasn't being offered a choice about departure timing or methods. Alfie had decided that if he was going to die alone, Harper would die with him.

'That's not happening, Alfie.'

'We'll see about that.'

Harper tucked the recorder into his jacket pocket while maintaining eye contact with Alfie, noting how his former comrade's grip on the tactical knife was affected by his injured arm but still professional enough to be dangerous.

'Don't test me, Alfie,' he said. 'I'm fighting every urge to put you down already, for what you did to Tomás—'

He was halfway to the ladder when Alfie attacked.

The knife angled upwards towards Harper's kidneys – a military technique designed for quick, silent killing. Harper twisted sideways, feeling the blade slice through his jacket while his training kicked in automatically.

They grappled at the platform's edge, both men fighting for control of the weapon while trying to maintain balance on concrete that was slick with industrial grime and recent rain. Alfie was weakened by infection but desperate enough to be genuinely dangerous, using pain and fever as motivation rather than hindrance.

Harper grabbed Alfie's knife hand and twisted, trying to control the weapon while avoiding the platform's edge where a fall would be fatal regardless of blade wounds. They rolled across concrete, both men applying techniques learned during the same training programmes, muscle memory overriding conscious thought while they fought for survival.

The knife changed hands twice during the struggle –

Harper controlled it briefly before Alfie recovered through sheer desperation, then both men grappled for the handle while trying to drive the point towards their opponent's vital areas.

Harper could feel Alfie's fever through their physical contact, the sort of heat that indicated systematic infection and rapidly approaching organ failure. His former comrade was dying already, probably had hours rather than days remaining even without knife wounds.

But that knowledge didn't make him less dangerous in close-quarters combat.

They rolled again, this time towards the centre of the platform where structural supports provided handholds and obstacles. Harper wasn't able to take a couple of seconds to pull a gun, and Alfie was too close now anyway, so instead he tried to slam Alfie's knife hand against the floor, hoping to jar the weapon loose, but Alfie twisted free and brought the blade around in a wide arc aimed at Harper's throat.

Harper caught the attacking arm and wrist, turning the blade tip away and redirecting momentum while slamming an elbow into Alfie's infected wound. The impact caused Alfie to scream in pain, loosening his grip just enough for Harper to attempt disarmament. Harper could feel Alfie's desperation through their physical contact, the sort of last effort that came from someone who had nothing left to lose and no future beyond the next few minutes. His former comrade was putting everything into this attack, spending his remaining strength on one last attempt to drag Harper down with him.

The knife moved between them as they struggled, sometimes pointing towards Harper's chest, sometimes towards

Alfie's, the blade's direction determined by whoever could apply more leverage.

They rolled again, this time with the knife trapped between their bodies, both men applying pressure while trying to control its direction.

The blade went in during the final roll.

Harper felt resistance give way, heard Alfie's sharp intake of breath, felt hot blood between them. For several seconds, neither man moved, both processing what had happened while trying to understand who had driven the knife home.

Alfie looked down at the tactical knife protruding from his chest, his expression more surprised than pained. Blood was spreading across his shirt, but his eyes remained focused on Harper's face.

'Well,' Alfie said quietly. 'That's that, then.'

Harper couldn't tell if he'd killed Alfie or if the blade had found its target through momentum and accident. The last moments of their struggle were blurred together, muscle memory and desperation creating chaos where individual actions became impossible to distinguish.

'Alfie—'

'Doesn't matter now.' Alfie's voice was already weakening as blood loss sped up his system's collapse. 'Question is whether you can live with not knowing.'

Harper supported Alfie's weight as his former comrade's strength failed, easing him down onto concrete while blood pooled beneath them. The knife wound was fatal – too deep, too close to vital organs, the sort of injury that would be lethal even with immediate medical attention.

'I'm sorry,' Harper said.

'For what? Killing me... or failing to save me?' Alfie's smile was bitter but not entirely without humour. 'Either way, probably an improvement... over dying slowly from infection.'

Harper held pressure against the wound while knowing it was pointless, muscle memory from battlefield first aid overriding logical understanding that Alfie was beyond help. His former comrade was bleeding out rapidly, had only minutes of life remaining.

Alfie's breathing was becoming laboured.

'Make them pay, Harper. All of them. The way the system never will.'

Harper felt Alfie's weight become heavier as consciousness faded, his former comrade's breathing growing shallow while blood loss completed what infection had started. Within minutes, Alfie Reeves was dead for the second time in five years.

But this time, it would be permanent.

Harper sat in the abandoned grain elevator for a long time after Alfie died, processing what had happened while trying to understand his own responsibility for the outcome. Eventually, Harper cleaned the scene as best he could without disturbing Alfie's body, gathered his equipment, and prepared to continue whatever journey his father's notebook suggested next.

He reached into his pocket and pulled out his river stone, rolling its smooth surface between his fingers while standing over Alfie's body. The familiar weight helped centre him, bringing him back to the present when memories threatened to overwhelm rational thought.

Some ghosts were harder to bury than others.

But this one at least was finally at rest.

The federal authorities would find Alfie eventually, probably through an anonymous tip that would lead them to the grain elevator and the evidence Harper would provide. But Harper would be long gone by then, riding towards whatever impossible situation waited ahead while carrying the weight of another ghost whose death might or might not have been his responsibility.

Slowly, Harper saluted Alfie Reeves, then turned and looked around at his surroundings, his eyes snagging on the open hopper — a wide, steel-lined pit in the floor that fed grain into the turning auger below, its dark mouth gaping like a promise. He remembered his vow earlier – the fight here was over, and now it was time to send Doyle's Hellcat to hell.

There was a rusted control box bolted to a nearby beam, its faded label half peeled away. Harper wiped grit from the flip switch with the back of his thumb, listened for a heartbeat, then pulled it. The auger coughed and shuddered to life, a low, hungry groan building into a metallic roar.

He then crossed the grit-strewn floor, pulling out the Hellcat, the weapon cold and heavy in his palm, and after wiping it down, held it above the churning throat for a long, steady breath. He'd gain a replacement, likely the Hellcat Pro Comp, one that didn't have history, or could link Harper to any killings Doyle may have performed with it.

Then, with almost a feeling of relief, he let go.

The gun struck the screw with a high, terrible ring; the machine screamed as steel met steel, sparks flaring like an obscene constellation. The Hellcat was chewed and spat, a torn, smoking scrap jammed in the conveyor, its barrel crumpled beyond hope, and the air stank of scorched metal and burnt grain. Only then did Harper turn, without a second look back, climb onto his Bonneville and ride off — away from Alfie Reeves, the abandoned grain elevator and Topeka, Kansas.

He had other places to go – he just didn't know where yet.

Want the next Liam Harper Thriller? CLICK HERE on digital, or turn the page...

Or consider joining the VIP Readers Club, and gain behind-the-scenes access and updates on new releases!

Liam Harper will return in his next thriller

CROSS ROADS

Order Now at Amazon:

mybook.to/LHcrossroads

Released 18th May, 2026

Gain up-to-the-moment information on the release by signing up to the Jack Gatland VIP Reader's Club!

Join at http://bit.ly/jackgatlandVIP

ABOUT THE AUTHOR

Jack Gatland is the pen name of *#1 New York Times Bestselling Author* Tony Lee, who has been writing in all media for thirty-five years, including comics, graphic novels, middle grade books, audio drama, TV and film for *DC Comics, Marvel, BBC, ITV, Random House, Penguin USA, Hachette* and a ton of other publishers and broadcasters.

These have included licences such as ***Doctor Who, Spider Man, X-Men, Star Trek, Battlestar Galactica, MacGyver,*** BBC's ***Doctors, Wallace and Gromit*** and ***Shrek***, as well as work created with musicians such as ***Ozzy Osbourne, Joe Satriani, Beartooth, Pantera, Megadeth, Iron Maiden*** and ***Bruce Dickinson.***

As Tony, he's toured the world talking to reluctant readers with his 'Change The Channel' school tours, and lectures on screenwriting, story craft and comic scripting for festivals and conferences such as *Raindance* in London and *Author Nation, The Global Publishing Summit* and *20Books* globally.

A Freeman of the City of London and an introvert West Londoner by heart, he lives with his wife Tracy and dog Darcy, just outside London.

Feel free to follow Jack / Tony on all his social media by clicking on the links below, to engage, discuss Declan and put the world to rights.

www.jackgatland.com
www.hoodemanmedia.com

Visit Jack and Tony's Reader's Group Page
(Mainly for fans to discuss his books):
https://www.facebook.com/groups/jackgatland

Subscribe to Jack's Readers List:
https://bit.ly/jackgatlandVIP

www.twitter.com/mrtonylee
ww.instagram.com/mrtonylee

Want more books by Jack Gatland? Turn the page...

Printed in Dunstable, United Kingdom

74279380R00229